Halo of Thorns

The Fall and Rise of a Lord of Darkness

Drew Bryenton

Halo of Thorns
Drew Bryenton

This edition Copyright © 2015 by Oxford eBooks Ltd.
Published under the sci-fi-cafe.com imprint.
www.oxford-ebooks.com
Story Copyright © 2014 by Drew Bryenton

ISBN 978-1-910779-00-2 (Paperback)
ISBN 978-1-910779-01-9 (ePUB)
ASIN B00HEUB8QE (Kindle)

Cover artwork by Jim Ellis

Book design and typesetting by
Oxford eBooks Ltd.
www.oxford-ebooks.com

sci-fi-cafe.com

One

A Shadow Falls

The Zengaji are brutish, violent, quick
to anger, inveterate grudge-bearers and
merciless executioners. They kill without
remorse, pity or the obstacle of morals.
In their favor, however, I must note that
they are at least excruciatingly polite."

Archivist-Doctor Nyvar Xeng, Supreme Redactor of
Saradrim

INSTRUMENTS OF DEATH.

Two razor fans – oiled, slippery and smoke-blackened. A brace of
wicked little knives, tucked snugly into his boot-tops and cuffs. Slicing
wires and hooks lay flat against his skin, wrapped up in sealskin
pouches beside darts, finger-needles and smoke globes. He carried
enough sharp artifice to inter an army.

And the swords, of course. Zengaji standard issue – uniform,
elegantly curved like the shadow of a reed in the wind.

Arnaud had paid them good money. But it was the stories which
had reeled the Zengaji in, down across the cracked-mirror plain of
the Desolation, into the crooked streets of the Old City. Stories laced
with nightmares, to be sure – but that was the hook. It had sunken
deep into the Clanfather's mind, sparking wisp-lights of glory behind
his eyes.

It had damned them all.

The Zengaji crouched in a dense wedge of shadow, down in the
lee of a shattered statue. The eyeless colossus was one of hundreds,
a triumphal avenue standing broken and gap-toothed down here in
the core of the Old City. The statues straggled halfway up the side of
a sunken pyramid, framing a doorway like an empty eye. It smoked,
soughing with a deep bellows-breath.

Twenty-seven of the Clan had breached the perimeter of the
Desolation, slitting the throats of the watchers in the dark. Twenty-
five had made it across the fused-glass plain without succumbing to
the traps and the creeping shadows. *One* now squinted through the
green-tinted bonelight at the target Arnaud had set them.

In retrospect, the fat old Ghuram had underpaid. There was every
possibility that none of the Amber Scorpion Clan would come out of

this contract alive…

The light of the bone torches made distance waver and stretch, like the shimmer over a water-hole in the deep desert. They were ribcages cupping globes of phosphor, held out in the hands of shattered Gods, and they provided just enough light for that last lone clansman to read the inscription on an obelisk of white jade.

That was the way into the final chamber. That was where, if Arnaud's dusty scrolls were correct, an empire's ransom of gold and jewels propped up the throne of the Unspoken One, the long-dead architect of the Desolation. Among the Ghuram he was called Grandfather Despair. To the Zengaji, however, he was just another foolish Northern legend; a paper demon with which to scare children. The Desolation was more than three hundred years old, after all.

It didn't occur to the Zengaji, as he flitted from shadow to shadow, to ask himself what power kept the green glow of the ossuary torches lit. Or what force levitated the octohedral megaliths between their pylons. It certainly never crossed his mind to question how and why creatures of sharp glassy shadow had slid out from the walls of the Old City to flense his Clansmen raw.

Zengaji *lived* to fight impossible monsters. Zengaji existed to hack apart demons. The fact that most demons were merely men with cruel tastes and some little sorcery made no difference.

This one was Zengaji through and through – 'a sword arm attached to some other useless flesh', as the scholar Nyvar Xeng once wrote. He took the crooked stairs two at a time, snarling behind his porcelain death-mask.

They came for him. They paid back his unstinting faith. They came to kill.

In the light of the witchfires the shadows of those marble Gods were ugly things, hunched and twisted out of true. When they peeled themselves from the flagstones their jagged edges were cold and sharp, and they came loose with a sound like breaking lyre-strings, snapping the bonds of sanity and reason.

The air was sharp with the ozone scent of sorcery, but behind his mask the Zengaji smiled. This was more like it!

Three of the creatures rushed him – eerie in their silence, their footfalls popping and squealing like broken glass. Obsidian finger-blades whickered through the air, slicing, clenching – too slow.

He was at one with the moment now, and good Zengaji steel met the shadows with a slither and clash, shattering glassy fingers, hacking into wrists and necks...

Up, and over the swipe of a scimitar hand. Down, spinning, shattering a pair of fragile ankles. Shards scored the black paint from his porcelain cheek. Block, and parry, and swing with the left, spinning in a poised pirouette, turning it into a roundhouse kick as he went. See the shadows stagger. See them reel, howling mouthlessly in astonishment.

Cracks ramified. Sparks guttered and skipped. Shadow-glass shattered and fell.

NO. MY CHILDREN! GONE!

The Zengaji felt the world shudder as the last of the shadow-things slivered to pieces. The ossuary lights flared for an instant, tapered up tall and thin. A grinding sound rumbled inside his head, outside of the world, as puzzle-pieces slid and locked...

Sorcery.

There was a triangle of darkness cast across the stairway by the stump of a shattered monument, and in that instant it fell away. Darkness that had been the absence of light became the absence of reality itself; a gulf as deep as the places between the stars. It was only open for an instant, but the Zengaji could feel it tugging at his soul, unraveling the edges. Feathering away little memories...

A dusty wind spun down into the chasm as he brought his blades up to guard, hissing.

His kind hated sorcery. It wasn't just that the Art was the preserve of fat old men, stick-thin ghouls and unhealthy minds. It was the antithesis of Zengaji honor.

That being said, this particular son of the Amber Scorpion Clan had a healthy respect for *power*. And the thing which came thrusting up into the world from that hollow darkness was a thing of power, pure and simple.

It was frost-rimed, and ancient, and steaming. It was carved from granite, a crooked ten-foot obelisk with more dimensions than should have been possible. Runes shoaled and ghosted above and below its polished surface, pricking tears from the Zengaji's eyes.

But it was the skeletons which placed it, named it, cataloged it in the endless tomes of the Clan's weapons scriptorium. Four of them, bound to the stone and to each other with a black iron chain through their eyesockets. The weaponsmaster had told them (with the relish of an academic sadist) that the binding was done while the subjects were still alive.

An Excoriator Minor. Artifact of the Angan Empire, lords before the Desolation. That it still existed was surprising. That it still functioned was vexing, in that it was probably a death sentence.

He was already airborne as the eyeless skulls began to howl, already sliding across the cracked marble as their one-note song clawed its way up the scale and into pain. Behind him the light upshifted green to white, then strobe-flash purple...

The Excoriator Minor loosed a beam of force the color of firelit jade, a solid rod of death slicing stone and shadow to ribbons. A dozen colossi fell, sheared neatly in half as the beam scythed across the chamber and flickered out into an emerald haze.

Stone hissed. Stone bubbled and dripped. Molten stone missed his face by inches, down tight behind a fallen statue. The Zengaji hardly dared to breathe as he leaned out around the statue's ornate crown.

It saw him.

The Excoriator moved slowly, levitating in a pall of dust as it rotated around its axis. It had all the time in the world. Indeed, if the damned thing was the toy of sorcerers, time was just a minor inconvenience to it. The spirits which powered the nekrological engine would certainly want to prolong his suffering. It would play counterpoint to their own.

But Zengaji were raised from birth to fight impossible odds. When he heard the hollow howl of the skulls again, the warrior came up out of cover screaming, blades flashing defiance.

Light crawled and twisted around the obelisk's crown. Light collapsed in on itself, and a beam of energy split the air, whipcrack fast. It zigzagged down the stairway, chewing up the marble, slicing deep. Dust roostertailed and billowed in the jade light. Stone shards scattered wide.

It was gone. The prey-thing had vanished, prolonging its life by a few more seconds...

Eight hollow eyes searched the darkness, chains pulled tight between them. Witchfire dripped from eight crucified hands.

Now!

Steel shattered them.

Rippled Zengaji steel hacked through bone, through mummified sinew and dry cartilage. Cold Zengaji blades bisected one hollow skull, spilling witchfire from within.

What had the weaponsmaster said?

"Never touch the runes. Never let them burn into your skin. Destroy the bones, and the imbalance will tear the thing apart. That is, if it

doesn't tear you *apart first...*"

He pushed back off the face of the obelisk, leaving the soles of his boots behind as two blackened stains. The thing was cold enough to burn. But it was listing, drunken in the air. Cracks ramified through the rune-etched stone as the light began to build again, accompanied by that grim inhuman howl.

The Zengaji looked at his swords as he landed, barefoot, framed in the incandescent eye of the Excoriator Minor. They were notched and pitted now – useless. Splintered against steel-hard bone and sorcery. It hardly mattered. Even a pair of the finest battle-blades wouldn't be able to stop the transfixing beam of the Angan war-engine.

He put them up anyway, spitting his contempt. Zengaji died with swords in their hands. Zengaji died *fighting*, or met their Gods in shame. Nyvar Xeng had some choice words to say about that, too.

Light coalesced and intertwined. Light upshifted with the sound of agony, up into registers beyond the human senses.

And in the strobe-flash instant before incineration, those notched and jagged swords swept low, scissoring something as thin as a dying whisper. They held it up in the path of the Excoriator's beam.

It was a fragment of glassy shadow – flesh of the things he'd so recently slain. Otherworldly flesh. Sorcerous, nacreous skin.

The Excoriator's killing light reflected from it in a storm of emerald fire. For an instant a meshwork of green played across the nekrological engine, across the pyramid and the stairway – across the whole sunken gallery. Then it flickered and died, ghosting away to nothing. The Zengaji let his mirror-shield fall.

His smile was tight and predatory behind his porcelain mask as the obelisk fell to pieces, sliced clean through across twenty-three distinct axes. Witchfire flared and spun out wide, silent as smoke.

"Anything else? Have you got any more for me, coward? Show yourself! Show your face before you die!"

Proud words, but they echoed hollow in the vast and empty chamber. There was no answer.

He picked his way through the broken remains of the Excoriator Minor, his eyes twitching left and right in the gloom. Step by careful step, up the face of the pyramid, until he could pick out the eyeless faces of individual Angan nobles and their conquered slaves in the stonework.

The door beckoned. The door sighed, smoking. Its lintel-piece was an eagle with the head of a wolf – more Northern madness.

The Zengaji crossed the threshold, his ruined swords clutched tight in his fists.

It was everything Arnaud had promised.

The inside of the pyramid was dressed in glossy green-black stone, a chamber which blurred away into shadows above and below. A narrow bridge curved out over the abyss – glass the color of smoke licking out toward a central dais.

The Zengaji understood.

Arnaud, fat old Ghuram spellweaver that he was, measured his wealth in carats. The Anganesse, masters of the known world three hundred years ago, measured theirs in *power*.

The dais levitated on a pillar of pale green witchfire; it was a cylinder of neatly cut stone, dressed tight without mortar or ornamentation. On it sat the throne.

From that high-backed seat, carved with the eagle-wolves of the old Angan Empire, a figure in beggar's robes considered him, long pale fingers steepled before a weary face.

Grandfather Despair. The Lamenter. Lord of Bones and Ashes.

The Zengaji stopped short of the bridge, inclining his head in a little genuflection.

"And a courteous greeting to you as well, Clanbrother Zuris O. Would it be trite to tell you that I've been expecting you?"

The man's voice was dry, cold – rasping with disuse. How long had he sat in this seething chamber, this power-focus? How long had he been alone?

"You know my name?"

"I remember all of their names, Clanbrother. Desra. Khani. Yeeran. All twenty-six of them. All nine hundred and thirty-seven who have ever come to my city to die."

Was there regret in his voice? Remorse? As a Zengaji, Zuris O was unfamiliar with the nuances of such emotions.

"It's the nine hundred and thirty-eighth who will kill you, then," he said. "Commend yourself to your Gods, nekromancer, if any will have you."

The man on the throne arched one eyebrow. Zuris was sure he'd been practicing the gesture for many long centuries.

"Very nice. Did your poor Clanfather teach you that little speech? I'm almost flattered. But tell me, Zengaji... why kill me at all?" He chuckled. Sick. Mirthless. *"And what makes you think you can actually do it?"*

If anyone else had asked that of Zuris O they would already have been trying to claw their intestines back into their belly. But the sardonic little smile on the Lamenter's face was enough to hold him back. After all, the fact that this man – this creature – even *lived* was legend enough. His powers were whispered of in tones of dread by every credulous fool in the North.

Perhaps they weren't quite as foolish as the Zengaji had assumed. He screwed up his courage.

"You'll die because we promised your death to a paying client. You'll die because the Clan demands your blood."

"You *are* the clan now, Zuris O. Walk away. One last chance."

There was pity behind his words. Tired, cynical pity. But it was the dismissive little wave of one slim-fingered hand which did it. He'd come this far. He'd seen them die. He'd felt the warmth of their blood as it spattered his skin.

He let the swords take over.

Darkness rose up to meet him like a wave. The Lamenter, Grandfather Despair – he moved like a puppet, pinned to the air, two slim black blades flying up out of the darkness and into his hands.

Darkness coiled. Darkness hissed and looped and struck. Cobra-quick, vital.

For once in his life the Zengaji had met his match. His ruined swords struck sparks from the Lamenter's blades as they spun and skirled and chimed, gnashing steel, grinding edge on edge.

Here, close to the nekromancer's face, Zuris could see that he was ageless – his skin was like pale wax, smooth and cold, and his eyes were sunken deep in bruise-purple sockets. That little smile danced upon his lips as he pressed in, quicksilver-smooth, predatory, his blades blurred to liquid in the dark.

The Zengaji held him. Barely.

He broke away sweating, heart pounding, feeling the ache in his forearms bone-deep from impacts like hammer blows. He measured his stance, bringing his blades up again.

He knew it was no use.

But...

"But Zengaji always die with a sword in their hands, don't they? I've read Nyvar Xeng on the subject. Fascinating man. A complete prick of course, but still..."

The Lamenter left his swords hanging in the air and rolled the kinks out of his neck, clasping his hands inside his sackcloth sleeves.

"You're the first, you know. I do like a little exercise, but you're the first who's made it this far. So I think I owe you something. Yes."

"You owe me nothing but your..."

"Oh, my *death*, I suspect. I've had quite enough of it, thank you kindly. Observe."

His fingers twitched. Runes etched hot across the air. Oily tin / lightning / snow – the smell of sorcery.

And the darkness rolled back, grumbling like far-off thunder. It peeled apart in veils, revealing two glowing figures nailed to the walls of the pyramid, hanging from their bleeding hands.

One was pale, fey, dark haired and silver-eyed, robed in seamless white. His tears, where they dripped and ran across his cheeks, were thick and black as oil. An alabaster youth crucified, beautiful in his suffering.

The other was just as grotesquely perfect, but older, aquiline and stern, half-masked in steel and armored for war. A mane of tawny hair straggled across his face as he hung in his torment, empty red eyes blazing.

They were haloed. They were divine. They twisted up reality around them like crumpled paper.

"Commend yourself to the Gods, Zuris O. To these two, anyway."

The Zengaji staggered, dropping his blades. Waves of nauseating force tore through him, blurring the image of the Lamenter as he drew closer.

"The young one gives me the power, Zengaji. Enough to keep people out. Enough to keep those who would worship HIM away."

He leveled one finger at the old God, the war-God... the one the Northerners prayed to before battle.

"Peace, Zuris. Peace for three hundred years. I bought it. I earned it. But I'm tired."

Tectonic grinding now, realities sheared and skewed, darkness boiling with laughter. The eyes of the captive Gods transfixed him, pleading...

"You're young. You're strong. You got this far. And all they need is a focus, Zengaji. All *I* need is release."

Those hands were working now, tearing the mask from his face, letting the darkness in.

"I'll gladly die when we're done. I'll *welcome* death. But first...."

He felt the power intersect. He felt the axes of it meet, neatly quartering his soul.

The Lamenter chuckled, patting his cheek. "First, you'll *replace* me."

Two

Chosen of the Dead

"We fear the unknown more than anything else. And who amongst us dares to truly know himself?"

Emperor Khanagar Trasse
- Twenty-fifth Thearch of Anganesse

WAS I ALWAYS a monster?

Oh yes - that's the word they use in their pious little histories – men like Nyvar Xeng and his self-congratulatory ilk. I'm a *monster*. A scourge. A demon. Some have even waxed poetic and called me 'a deathless tyrant from beyond the seventeen hells'.

Fools, all of them.

That kind of one-eyed clarity comes at the cost of perspective, and they forget that the monster was once a child, afraid of monsters himself. The Zengaji at least has never really had such fears – those savages teach the Way of the Killing Strike from birth. Have no illusions about him, for he *will* replace me. After what the Gods have done to us, they deserve to share their torment with a hired killer.

But back to the point in hand.

Of course I wasn't always called Grandfather Despair, or the Lamenter, or Soul-flayer. Lord of Ashes is my favorite, perhaps because it comes from my own people. It proves that they've utterly forgotten where I came from.

No, I had a name once, and a family to remind me of it daily. I had the usual run of little hopes, common to a child of the Khytein Moer – sword-saga conceits of treasure, fame, and blood. I had a lot more than a city choked with death, that I can assure you. In fact, the hut full of idols my father had stolen from the tribes he'd conquered frightened me. Especially the death Gods. *Especially* the ones with all the human teeth...

Anganesse took most of it before I became what I am today. I gave away the rest to avenge that theft, mostly because I was proud and foolish.

As to the legends, what can I say?

Yes, I command the dead. Yes, I consort with the Aemortal. And yes, all the worst parts you've heard are true... the more gruesome tracts you edit out when telling your children about my exploits. Is that enough to make me a monster?

19

Perhaps it is.

But I like to think that my motives were much the same as yours would have been.

How many of you have had that dream – the one in which your most treasured enemy is tied down to a chair, bloodstained shackles creaking and straining? And there you are, leaning into the pool of rushlight. There's the hot and intimate weight of the knife in your hand...

How many of you are lying to yourselves right now?

That's the difference, you see. *I* never lied.

I thought I was telling this tale for the sake of poor Zuris O, before he takes his place on the throne. On closer inspection I thought I'd caught myself craving absolution, or worse yet, *forgiveness*. Most vexing.

I take great pride in the cultivation of my mind, and I had thought that such irrelevancies were weeded out centuries ago. Now that I'm awake again my Cerebrex has been quickened, and I've spent many hours scanning the neural topiary of that vast nekrological organ. There is no weakness. As any ghoul will tell you, human brains are easy to work with. Encysting them in crystal and animating them with the *vitae mortis* makes them even more pliable to one's will.

No, I believe I have decided to recount my story for a much more selfish reason; one that even a maestro such as myself can't edit out of the neural architecture of the Cerebrex. Without *spite*, what mind would be a mind?

It's for spite that I want you to know the truth.

Men like the insufferable Nyvar Xeng have already got me pinned down to a page with their trite little analyses. History wants to footnote me, classify me as evil, and carry on. But I fear that I'm just too difficult. I want those simple moralists shown up for the fools they are. I want them ridiculed for far longer than I'm feared.

So yes, I *am* a monster. But only in the truest sense. I'm a dangerous beast with no clear taxonomy, a thing from off the edges of the map. But I can sketch out the path. I can shade in the detail.

I can show you how you get from wherever *you* are to where I am today.

Come. Indulge me.

Who knows - you might enjoy the journey a little more than you should.

"It were the music which unmanned us, though. Even more 'n the sight o' them savages comin' at us through the bloody snow - the music, it fair put nails clean through me. O' course, the screams soon drowned out the worst of it..."

Guild-Sejant Huw Gamaris
- Survivor of the Khytein Annexation

I WAS THIRTEEN years old when I realized that I wasn't a warrior.

There on that windblown hillside, with the icy rain in my teeth and the stench of shit and rawhide choking in my throat, hard up between the steaming furs of Ulkar on my left and Colm on my right. That's where I grew up and stopped believing in the sagas.

The shield strapped to my arm was heavy, waxed bronzewood dragging me down to the ankle-deep mire. The leaf-bladed *kuris* in my other hand was just as bad – yet another way the old songs had lied to me. Sword-slaughter heroism was hard work, cold and tedious. The other army hadn't even shown up yet.

"Here, whelpling! Take a belt of this, and keep that shield up. We're not hanging our arses out into arrow-fire like the Touched!"

Ulkar thrust a rough gourd toward me in the press of bodies, letting a cloud of alcoholic fumes roll over me from his toothless mouth. I fumbled it between shield and *kuris*, slopping a mouthful of liquor down my tunic. Well, at least it would keep the rust away... the trickle which burned its way down my throat was as hot and raw as anger.

"Over here, Kuhal, dammit! That's the last drink we'll see before this business is done!"

Colm was younger than Ulkar, but he was a head taller – linchpin of the shield wall. Aside from the naked, tattooed madmen we called the Touched, he was the one the Vhaur were most afraid of. Their warbards would have burned little effigies of him last night, praying to the Gods that his courage would wither up to nothing.

"Last one before you feast in the hells, perhaps," muttered Ulkar. "I heard they bought the Angan's help. Jerrold Sinder's men."

If this had been the longhall, Colm would have been at the old man's throat for talk like that. Luck meant a lot to the Khytein Moer. But that bleak hillside was another world. It was Colm's place, and instead he just laughed, a bitter bark behind his raven-winged helmet.

"Let them come, you fat old grandmother! Let them break themselves against our shields. I'm ready to die whenever you are."

Not really the kind of talk I needed to hear, then. Not when the sound of the drums was starting up behind our lines, and the low thrum of the draken-horns warned of enemies on the horizon.

I stood up on my tip-toes, peering out between a gap in the rounded shield-tops, and I fancied I saw them through the rain – a jagged black mass, heaving and spiked against the clouds. The Khytein Vhaur, our enemies. Icy tendrils of water ran down my back as I squinted into the haze, picking out flashes of color – banners and flags snapping taut in the gale. Their warbards were at the fore, striding among the capering Touched with Lyrecasters held at their hips. A skirling song preceded them, sliced up by the wind.

Ulkar's elbow knocked the breath from my chest.

"Remember, boy – don't try any of that sword-song bollocks. Cut low, hack the bone, bring them down. The longspears behind us will keep them back, so long as we don't shit ourselves and run."

My father had told me all this a million times. But of course, he was the whole reason I was here in the shield-wall in the first place, not back in the ranks with the other whelps, manhandling a ten-foot ash spear.

"And whatever you do, don't drop that damned shield! Not until they sound the call to slaughter."

"*Sardach altu mahuran, Khytein'i Moer sulan!*"

The drums pounded once, shaking my teeth in their sockets. Tiny beads of rain shivered on the edges of *kuris* swords and broad-bladed spears. Then they took up a slow and dolorous beat – a dirge for the coming foe. Our warbard, Aerik, was out there in the open, tuning his lyrecaster with his back to the enemy. Not a care in the world. You could almost believe that he was sitting by a sun-dappled pool, cradling the long slim instrument's horns as he prepared for a wedding feast.

But we all felt the power as he spooled it in, gathering and weaving impossible forces around himself and his lyrecaster's strings. Its twin necks glittered in the rain as droplets of water evaporated without touching them. And it was by that power that all three thousand men of the Khytein Moer heard his voice, as calm and sure as if he were right beside each one of us.

A few half-hearted Vhaur arrows slucked home into the mud around Aerik as he stood, running his fingers across the fretboards. He paid no heed to them – it would be a lucky archer who could aim at that distance, in this rain.

"Well, friends. Well. It seems that the Gods have seen fit to answer our prayers. The Vhaur fools must be hungry for the feast of Anghul!"

That prompted a ripple of nervous laughter. Men facing battle didn't really want to think about the corpse-God's kitchen, where cowards cooked and ate their fallen friends over and over again...

"But perhaps we can spare them such a meal, eh? Perhaps we can send them to the other place instead!"

This time the warbard backed up his words with a jangling riff on the lyrecaster, filling the air with slippery lightning. The laughter was louder as the bard's power stole into three thousand drink-addled minds.

"I think that these fools are tired of living! I think they're tired of this good land, sick of women and sunlight and song. Shall we show them mercy? If I were an arse-born loon like those thugs behind me, I'd pray for death as well."

His fingers blurred across the strings as the tempo of the drums picked up. And the lyrecaster began to sob and howl, weaving, tweaking, slipping its needles into men's minds...

Behind six thousand glazed eyes, the spiked black shadows of the Vhaur became weak and laughable things. Swords and spears clattered against bronzewood shields in the rain as the battle-line took up the chant, winging it across the valley to the foot-slogging Vhaurish warband.

"Sardach altu mahuran! Khytein'u ad Moer sulan!"

That was the call to unleash the Touched.

Aerik's thralls at the drums pounded louder now, sweating as the rain skipped and blurred on the tattooed skins of their drumheads. The music was tugging at the souls of all of us – longspears and shield-wall sword-heroes alike. But for the Touched, the vessels of the divine madness... well, for them the skirl of the lyrecaster was like the voice of the Gods. Swift knives cut loose their leather bindings, and callused hands shoved them forward between the ranks, sending them staggering and sprawling in the mud.

Off to our left, in the gap between our longhall's shield-wall and the axemen of the Horned Boar, I saw Gharn one-ear pitched headlong into the thick black slurry, still drooling blue from the warbards' potions. His teeth were purple-black with the residue of hellcap mushrooms and bonebark, and his lips were pulled back in an awful, painful smile. I'd seen wolves gone mad with hunger in the deep winter. I'd seen them twisting on the end of hunting spears in the snow. That was the look on Gharn One-ear's face as his eyes flickered, pinhole-black and crazed.

The lyrecaster whined and thrummed, hot over the pattering rain. The drums thudded and heaved.

And the music picked up the Touched, dragging them to their feet on invisible strings. Out along the front of the battle-line they began to spin and dance, sending their blades looping out wide on lengths of iron chain.

"Watch 'em, Kuhal! Watch what they do now!"

Ulkar nodded at the Touched as the rain sluiced their bodies clean, revealing summer-lightning scrawls of blue tattoos. It was the skins of the Touched that made the warbards' drums.

"Best part of the battle, this. Best part... well, bar the looting!" He ran the back of one hand over his greasy beard, squinting into the gray distance. "Sometimes one of them mad buggers is all it takes. I've seen shield-walls break and run when the Touched come staggering at 'em!"

"Shut it!" snapped Colm, reaching over in front of me to grab a handful of Ulkar's hauberk. "The Gods won't be mocked, you old fool. Do you want to curse us all?"

Ulkar jerked away, grunting. Arrows hissed by overhead, black-fletched scrawls against the gray. They sprouted like weeds from the churned-up mire of the hillside.

"I mean no jest by it, Colm," he said, and there was a soft, wire-thin menace in his voice. "The boy should watch what the bards can do. Makes a change from all the pious nonsense they usually spout."

As I've said, anywhere else, any other time... but this was the field of war. Three ranks of longspears were crowding in behind us, eager spectators watching the veteran and the hero face off over my head. The nosepiece of my oversized helmet was down around my chin, and a cold trickle of rain slipped between my hauberk and my skin as I tipped it back.

Colm knew that it was his duty to keep the shield-wall together. If he gave in to the fire behind his eyes and knocked Ulkar down there'd be a weak spot in the Khytein line... and worse, he'd answer to my father after the battle. Not that old Hurik Scalp-Taker had any love for his thirty-seventh son... no, it would be a matter of pride and ownership. I belonged to the chieftain's household until my eighteenth birth-night, as valuable as a good pair of boots or a sturdy mule.

"Just remember this bloody courage of yours when the Vhaur have a sword in your guts, Ulkar," he grunted. "And if you..."

But Colm never got to finish.

At that moment the belly of the clouds flashed violent green, lit up by a pillar of fire from across the valley. A whirling storm of mist blew out in a spiral – rain turned to steam by the sorcerous blast. And with it came the voice of our enemy.

"Aerik! Aerik the Dickless! Aerik the woman-handed pox-ridden son of an arse-born whore! Answer me, you dung-eater! Answer me and die!"

The silence which rolled across the valley behind those words was deafening. Even though both hillsides bristled with fighting men the sound of the rain pattering on leather and steel was as clear as carillon bells.

I think that every eye was on our warbard at that moment, and he knew it. He turned slowly, nonchalant as you please, ignoring the rain and the eldritch glow behind him. Tiny threads of lightning played across the v-shaped necks of his lyrecaster, underlighting his face until all the youth and beauty drained away. That was when I recalled the little legends about the man... whispered hints that he'd been alive to drag my father the Scalptaker into the world when his birth went wrong; that he'd seen the age of the Anganesse before they worshiped their martyred God.

None of us really saw the face he turned on the Vhaurish warband, but we longspears out on the flank caught a glimpse. There was enough cold hatred there to give even Colm nightmares.

"Of course I bow to your expertise in matters of the pox, Gernish. But *dickless?* Your daughters will all tell you otherwise."

We could all see the master warbard of the Vhaur by the nacreous glow of his lyrecaster – a single-necked thing with human skulls surmounting its tuning pegs.

"Gernish Maudrin," muttered Ulkar, nudging me in the ribs hard enough to bruise. "They say he keeps a sharpened spoon around his neck to pluck the eyeballs from..."

"Oh, and the Vhaur say that *you* sneak into their hovels at night to rape their livestock! That doesn't make it true!"

The old warrior glared at Colm, his frown almost lost in a thicket of unruly hair.

"Watch him, boy. This is where the fun starts..."

There was little chance of me taking my eyes off Gernish Maudrin, sharpened spoon or no. He was a fascinating picture of ugliness brought to its very apogee – hunch-backed, milky-eyed and scraggle-bearded, his false teeth almost slipping from his mouth with each oath and imprecation. Hands like dried-out roots twisted the skulls on his lyrecaster as green fire dripped from its strings, pooling around his feet.

"Brave words from a dead man, Aerik. You knew this day would come."

"Then let's give you a funeral to remember, you old bastard. Whenever you're ready!"

Gernish Maudrin laughed. And the dying started.

Both bards let fly at once, their fingers blurring across the strings as two hundred-span arches of fire leaped out across the valley. Beneath the flat silver glow of their collision the Touched screamed, scrabbling and lurching forward under a rain of nacreous sparks.

Every man rocked back on his heels from the blast, spearman and axeman and archer alike. This was the wild stuff, the feral song, and in its gristly heart there was no place for strategy. Aerik's hands wrung sobs and moans from his lyrecaster like the sounds of passion and dying, while in the stony stream-bed below the Touched came together with the sound of cleavers chopping meat.

Chains looped and whirled. Blades hacked and rose in bloody arcs, all in silence beneath the hell-choir of the song.

Then my father was there, galloping across the front of the Khytein Moer on his bronze-armored destrier. Coup poles streaming with feathers and fingerbones on chains flew out behind him, slick with witchfire. In that moment I was perhaps even proud to be his son... not that his eyes rested on me for a moment. Against the magic of Aerik and Gernish Maudrin, this was his own.

"*March*, damn you! March while the wild song holds them! Gut these fatherless dogs and give them to Anghul!"

So, perhaps not the most eloquent of speeches. But it got the unruly bulk of the Khytein Moer moving, shaking itself out of torpor like an irritable beast. Behind the Scalptaker came his idol-bearers – servants on horseback carrying long poles, hung with the dead Gods of defeated enemies. I had always hated the damned things, all carved grimaces and nailed-on strips of flesh, but the sight of them inspired my fellow saga-heroes. Ulkar grabbed me roughly by the shoulder.

"Shields up! Slice low, hack the bone, and remember I have your left, Kuhal. Colm and I, we'll get you through this."

All the belligerence had gone out of the old brawler's voice as we began to slog our way down the hillside. Colm grunted on my right, tugging the nosepiece of his helmet down.

"Just get *yourself* through it, you shaggy old fool. I'll not dig a grave that wide!"

Momentum began to build behind the horde. Ahead of us the rain sliced the silhouette of the Vhaur into a blur, all spikes and angles. They were moving too, a glacier of metal and creaking leather and rancid flesh. Between us the Touched still raved and gibbered, hacking, slicing - some faceless now, some maimed, but all limned about by the glow of the wild song. Above our heads the twin arcs of fire poured into a low-hanging star, a writhing knot of force.

And still the crescendo built.

"Second rank! Spears down!" screamed Colm, his breath hot against my neck. "Third and fourth, ready on my mark!"

We were almost running now, the press of men behind us forcing us down the slippery incline. Through the eye-slit of my helmet I caught a mad flicker of violence – Gharn One-ear with a cleaver in each hand, ravening over the headless wreck of a Vhaur in the stream-bed. The water ran crimson, churned to mud and gore.

The ground shook as the heavy cavalry swept past us on the flank, banners flying above a storm of churned-up sod. Each rune and glyph sizzled with unnatural fire, the tips of their *yari* trailing sparks. The spear-shafts of the second rank came down, and a thicket of steel bristled over our shoulders, dripping in the rain. Now my gut clenched, the sword-handle slippery in my hands. Now Ulkar was bellowing over the sound of Aerik's warsong, his eyes wide and bloodshot.

Impact.

The Vhaurish shield-wall stood ankle-deep in the bloody stream, and we struck them in a curling wave, steel raping in through gaps in their line. Men screamed like slaughtered animals, trampled down bleeding, bones shattered against shield-rims and sheared through with blades.

The sagas had all been lies. Battle smelled of shit and terror, and I saw it all through the slit of my oversized helmet. We heaved and hacked, cursed and prayed and died. But Colm held the center. And despite the leaden ache in my arms I kept my shield up, even under the onslaught of Vhaurish blades which fell as steadily as the rain.

"Butcher them! Wings of the hawk, men, and send them down to the damned!"

All those hours of drill seemed foolish as a black-toothed Vhaur axeman tried to hack his way through my shield. I squeezed my eyes shut and heaved with all my might, screaming. But the hours spent on the drill-yard looked far less foolish as the third and fourth ranks fanned out to our sides, spears whirling and glittering. They struck at the same time as Ulkar, who brought his *kuris* around in a flat blur to take off the top of my assailant's head. His black-toothed lower jaw twitched and flopped uselessly as his body fell away, pulped under the crush of iron-shod boots.

The wings of the hawk is an old battle-tactic of the Khytein Moer. The songs speak of it in terms of glory, of flashing steel and righteous fury. The reality was hideous. Vhaur bellowed like stuck pigs in the mud, sobbing for their mothers. Ash spear-shafts dripped red as they burst through leather and skin. We of the first rank surged forward, herding them with our shields, chopping low to shatter ankles and shins. Spears rose and fell as the jaws closed, macerating flesh...

Then -

Light bloomed in silence, unfolding from above.

The next thing I remember I was spitting mud from my mouth... or at least what I hoped was mud. There were indescribable pieces smoking all around me, and my shield was gone, shattered to matchwood.

Ulkar scrambled over to me, his beard half burned away. He was shouting something, his alcoholic breath choking in my nostrils. But the only sound in my ears was a shimmering echo, like the aftermath of thunder. I brought one of my hands up in front of my face, and I saw the edges of it lit up with green-blue fire.

Somehow Ulkar managed to manhandle me to my feet. Of all the longspears, we were the last men standing... or at least the last who still had legs. I will never forget seeing Colm lying there in the stony stream-bed, a satisfied little smile on his lips. His pale blue eyes looked up into the rain from under a sheet of bloody water, and there was nothing left of him from the waist down.

"Come on! *Run*, you arse-born fool! Up the hill! The bards have lost control..."

I could hear again. Not that it was any comfort. All around me in the unnatural darkness I heard screams and prayers, the panic of dying horses and the moans of wounded men. The drums had stopped their pounding, and the silence left behind the warbards' song was almost choking.

"What happened?" I asked, slipping and foundering on the treacherous incline. Ulkar just grunted and redoubled his efforts, almost tearing my arm from its socket.

"Something broke the wild song. Something's coming..."

I pulled away from him, turning, as I felt it resonate up through my bones. And I watched as Ulkar's 'something' came.

Across the valley the Vhaur were in full flight, all thoughts of honor driven before a storm of panic. Where Gernish Maudrin had stood there was a crater bitten out of the hillside, still smoking. But the sight of that ragged horde in rout was nothing compared to the immense form which came sailing down the valley under a cloud of steam, evaporating the rain around it.

It was as long as three plowed fields, an arrowhead of stone turned on its edge and planed flat across the top. A small castle tower had been erected on that smooth gray surface, and sickly light boiled up out of its crown, painting the belly of the clouds. Down the length of the great vessel stood thick tubes of copper and glass, each one the girth of an oak, and from these arcane engines streamers of lighting whipped and writhed, earthing themselves against great metal masts at the bow and stern of the Keel.

For that was what it was – one of the war keels of Anganesse, the dark fleet of Provincial Governor Jerold Sinder.

The sheer size of the thing inspired dread. The fact that it *moved*, floating through the air like a ship through calm water... that was enough to knock me speechless on my arse in the mud.

I hardly even heard the rolling thunderclap sound of the Keel's guns firing in battery, shredding the fleeing Vhaur with chain-shot. I certainly couldn't hear Ulkar's curses as he dragged me bodily from the battlefield by one arm, dead weight. But I did hear the voice of the great stoneship's captain, amplified by Angan nekrology. It was as calm and cultured as Ulkar's was coarse and brutal; a voice of glass and satin which seemed to whisper right beside me.

"Have no fear, men of the Khytein Moer. We are here to bring you

peace."
     And that, dear friends, was the moment at which I passed out cold. No warrior at all, you see.

"Some people don't like cats. Uppity things, they say - no respect, not like a dog. Some people say that cats are vermin. But cats... well, cats say that some vermin consider themselves to be people."

The collected teachings of Old Mother Aeveris

AT THE TIME it suited my Lord Father to blame the Angan nekrologists for the disaster. It certainly put them on the back foot when it came to the tedious business of negotiation, a job which the Scalptaker normally left to Aerik, or at a pinch Colm. As both of those worthies were gone – in one case, half-missing, in the other, vanished – the task devolved to my father himself, which put him in an even more murderous mood than usual.

Of course, with the benefit of hindsight I now know that it was *me* who broke the wild song. No intentionally, of course – even the most callow youth knows not to interrupt a duel between Powers. It was just that along with the rest of the changes which puberty wrought on my body came the awakening of something *other* in me... something I had tried to deny for several furtive and shameful years.

That? No!

You mean like the Thousand Swordsmen of Faeros, in that old myth? Oh, if *only* it had been that simple! While the other boys of the tribe made their fumbling advances to the womenfolk, and hid certain indiscretions under their sleeping furs, I was busy fearing for my immortal soul.

Allow me to sketch you a picture of young Kuhal da'Hurik Moer.

Start with feet three sizes too big, legs too long for their leather breeches, a body with more wiry muscle than I had any right to, and a pair of hands inherited directly from my father – shovel-sized things with all the delicacy of Ulkar's singing voice. I was petrified of the acne advancing across my hollow cheeks, devastated that the Gods had given me such a thin and unlovely nose, and mortified above all else at the mane of straight black hair which I was forced to tame with rawhide bindings and kilt-pins. At the front, just over my left eye, it sported a single hank of fire-red, which I assiduously dyed with charcoal and fat so as not to stand out from my horde of older brothers.

This was the image which confronted me in a mirror of beaten bronze each morning. But it was something else entirely which had me worried. It had begun with the cat.

My fourteen mothers (for Khytein custom never allowed the real one to step forward from amongst the Scalptaker's wives) kept an army of semi-feral cats around the longhouse, sometimes up to forty at a time. Not only were they evil, anvil-headed bags of spite and vengeance, they were also, when the mood took them, graceful, useful, and occasionally personable creatures. In my later life I have found that many pretenders to my throne keep cats to accentuate their own air of deadly grace. I have always just kept them because, pound for pound, no other domestic animal is more vicious.

And because, when I was nine years old, I brought one back from the dead.

It was high summer, and the Northern Hills were roasting gently under a merciless sun. Three of my brothers had decided that the most enjoyable way to pass the heat of noonday would be to find their youngest sibling and throw him down the well... a location that at least would be cool at this time of day, but also, it must be noted, full of slime, frogs and newts.

The chase which developed sent me scrambling under the longhouses of our village, through choking dust and piles of firewood stored up for next winter. It was tight and claustrophobic down there, and I knew that my brothers would soon give up the hunt, but one of them - I believe his name was Rordan – was made of sterner stuff. He had me by the ankle, deep under the black-painted hut where my father kept his collection of idols, when my scrabbling fingers encountered something soft and furry and cold.

The poor thing could have been dead for a week, for all I knew – in fact, I had no idea what the little sack of bones was at all. I picked it up and rolled onto my back, hurling it full into Rordan's snarling face...

But there was blood on my hands, skinned knuckles weeping from my scrabble through the woodpiles. And when I touched the sad, dead little thing I felt it kick in my grasp.

Well, if anything, that only made me throw it harder. My scream was likely even louder than Rordan's... especially seeing as his face was smothered by a hissing, spitting but unmistakably *dead* black cat. All the while I could feel it, twisting on the end of an invisible thread which pierced my mind. My frustration wove sinews around those lifeless bones, and my sheer cornered panic drove its wicked little claws into my brother's skin, drawing more blood.

The smell of it assailed me. It was intoxicating - what I imagined the Touched must feel when they took their draughts of Hellcap and Bonebark for the solstice dance. Images flickered through my brain like a storm of windblown leaves; black and white pictures seen through the eyes of a cat. They were overlayered with rich strata of colored smells, resonant veils of sound, hard, needle-like thoughts...

For an instant my breath stopped. My heart may have done as well. I remember looking up through a knothole and into the candle-lit space above me, where the war-Gods of a hundred tribes leered back. One, in particular seemed to grin with knowing certainty – a broken Angan statue in a half-mask of metal, beaten to resemble the upper jaw of a skull. Its ebony eyes were pupiled with discs of silver, and they held my panicked gaze for a long instant before I came back into myself.

Rordan's screams were receding into the distance by the time I collapsed backwards, propping myself up on my elbows. The cat prowled a few tight circles and settled down, paws tucked underneath and two tiny yellow lights flickering deep in its skull. I knew with grim certainty that it could wait much, much longer than I could.

The little creature made no effort to resist as I picked it up by the scruff, scrambling out from under the longhouse into the light. Indeed, by the time I'd blinked the dust from my eyes and recognized the circle of upside-down faces staring down at me, it gave all the impression of being a mere bag of bones again.

"'Th...that's it! That's the thing! He brought it back to life, uncle!"

Rordan didn't look quite so tough with his face smeared with snot and blood. A spreading stain ran down the leg of his woolen breeches, puddling on the dry earth.

"He's a warlock! A thrall of Anghul! The bards should kill him now!"

"And since which season have the bards been compelled by the will of a twelve-year-old piss-pants?"

They knew that voice. It froze them like sparrows on a winter ridgepole.

Aerik parted the little crowd with his usual quiet authority, making the people step aside without knowing why.

"Perhaps I've missed a vital message from the Gods? A new edict scryed out in a smelly little puddle?"

That brought a ripple of strained laughter from the crowd. As I've said, the Khytein take matters of luck and superstition very seriously indeed. There were grown men there – sword-swinging warriors of the shield-wall – who would gladly have bludgeoned in my head just to be sure that no black magic tainted the village. Aerik had very craftily aligned them with a snot-faced child, and quite probably saved my life.

"The boy says that *this* one brought that dead animal to life. Says it attacked him and tried to eat his soul!"

Aerik raised one eyebrow at the speaker, a bellicose old drunk named Tharn. He hunkered down in front of me, plucking the dead cat from my fingers.

"Is it true, then? Have you satiated the Corpse-God with the blood of ninety-nine virgins? Have you drunken from the chalice of skulls, and gained power over the dead?"

I could only shake my head mutely as he inspected the cat and handed it back.

"How about the path through the Forest of the Impaled? Did you nip down there this morning and claim the great axe of Sulun Man-Flayer? Is it hidden in your pocket right now?"

There was more laughter from behind him, and over the warbard's shoulder I could see Tharn cursing and spitting.

"I suppose at the same time you didn't meet the tiny little men of Gar-Gateem, and partake of their spider-venom wine? How about the two-headed troll who lives behind the moon? Any word about his crippling gout?"

None of the others could see it, but Aerik winked at me before he turned back to the crowd, suddenly all stern authority again.

"If any of you superstitious fools want to accuse the Scalptaker's son of witchcraft, you can do it in person. I'm sure he'd be glad to hear your opinion of his family's honor. Tharn? No? Anyone else?" He shook his head, while the people around the edges of the little crowd began to slink away in ones and twos, pretending that they were never there. "The heat must have curdled that slop between your ears! When there's black magic to be dealt with, *I'll* be the one to tell *you!* Now go! Back to work! Or perhaps you believe that the harvest will be taken care of by elves and goblins?"

Tharn was the last to leave, finally sagging and breaking beneath the Warbard's stare. Then it was just me and Rordan, alone in the bristling presence of the most feared man in the tribe. Believe me, at that moment our father didn't even come close!

Aerik may have been old - in the same way that winter or darkness is old – but he was quick. He had Rordan's ear pinched between two fingers faster than the strike of a serpent.

"One day, Rordan da'Hurik Moer, you will be a great warrior. You will take the steel, and wear the crest of the Horned Boar, and you will reap many hands and scalps in battle. But that day is not today. If you so want to *hunt*, then forget your little brother, and get you to the forest!" My brother twisted like a hooked fish in that relentless grip, and I 'll confess that his discomfort gave me no small pleasure. "Three fat rabbits before nightfall, child. Or I'll turn your eyeballs into red-hot stones!"

That pitch and tone were ones I'd learn well in the coming years. They call it the Cold Voice, the one that slides into your head like a paper-thin blade. It certainly got to Rordan, because as soon as Aerik let go of his ear he was off and running.

"Could you really do that?" I asked, hugging the dead cat to my chest. Aerik certainly looked like he could as he loomed above me. I remember the smell of his robes, the starched blue linen reeking of cloves and aniseed. "I mean... can anyone?"

The Warbard arched one silver eyebrow as he hunkered down to face me.

"Not the kind of question I'd expect from someone who was almost killed for witchery. I thought a *monster* like you would know all about the dark arts." I squirmed under his gaze, trying desperately to become invisible. "But no, Kuhal. No one can, thank goodness. It's just that most sorcery – that which doesn't come from the Gods – is done inside people's heads."

"*Eyeballs* are inside your head! Couldn't you just..."

The Warbard sighed, resting his hand on my shoulder. That was the only way you could tell his true age, because it was as light as the fall of a feather.

"Well, there's no doubt in my mind, child. You aren't any more a necromancer than that dead cat in your hands. Which, by the way, smells *terrible*. I'd advise you to bury it as soon as you can."

I looked down at the poor little thing, all bones and ragged fur. Had it ever really come to life? Or was it all just...

That's when I caught the flash in Aerik's eyes, and I realized. Most sorcery *is* done inside people's heads. Most people do it to themselves.

"I'm glad, you know," he said, standing with a pop and click of stiff joints. "The Calling of Anghul is a hard path. It only comes from a great imbalance between life and death, the kind we haven't seen for a thousand years. Anyone with that calling would be wise to keep it a secret, I think. A time would come for them, and I'd be waiting."

I think I knew what he meant, even at nine years old. But I asked him anyway.

"To teach hi... I mean to teach *them*, Sir? To teach them the way?"

"Oh, I suppose so. If that's what it took. But it's more likely that I'd have to kill them. To stop them going bad, you see? And if I thought that there was such a person here, among the Khytein Moer... well, I'd have to watch them very closely. I wouldn't want to miss that time, if it ever came."

With that he turned and left, raising two fingers pressed together over his shoulder in the gesture for farewell. They say it came from warriors of different clans meeting in the no-mans-land of the Stormwood – that it meant 'I'll turn my back on you and trust you... but only because there are archers of my clan in the trees'. The two fingers were the ones an archer would use to draw his longbow.

Looking back it seems quite apt. There was never a sign for 'I won't blast the flesh from your bones with sorcery unless I think you're possessed by the spirit of an evil God'.

As for nine-year-old Kuhal – well, I buried that little dead cat under a cairn of smooth river stones, down among the roots of a willow tree. And when the small crawling things of the forest had picked its bones clean I went back there, tossed the stones in the river, and collected the cat's earthly remains in a rabbit-skin pouch. I didn't know if the spirit of a cat would mind being carried around in rabbit fur, but then again, I don't really know why I did any of it in the first place. All I knew was that those clean white bones tingled in my hands when I picked them up, and a tiny star winked inside the empty skull, masquerading as a trick of the light.

Aerik had been right.

It turned out he *was* watching me. All the way through those awkward in-between years he was there, a long gray shadow with his clay pipe smoking and his lyrecaster swinging from his hip, raising that one eyebrow whenever I caught his stare.

I grew. My bones ached. I chased girls, and forgot about magic, to the best extent that I could. But I carried the cat's bones in their skin pouch until it was worn smooth as velvet.

And that night, the night after the battle, the night when my Father (the world's worst statesman, by all accounts) was trading hooked words with the Anganesse... well, that night I was glad of my silly, half-formed little superstition.

We all have the same Gods. The same
Pantheon, fed by the beliefs of a hundred
different tribes, prayed to in a score of
tongues. We give them different names,
but in the end they are all facets of
the same bright, clear jewel. And like
a jewel, what they do best is take our
own reflection and send it back, subtly
distorted..."

Song Harmensis
- Philosopher-King of Faeros on the shallow sea.
(Before the Angan Conquest)

IT WAS PEACE.

That much was evident by the sheer amount that the Moer
warriors drank – or rather, the amount they quaffed violently, soaking
the servants who stood meeky behind them. The Anganesse may
have been masters of the whole damned continent, but they huddled
together in abject shock as bones, cups, hunks of bread and one or two
knives arced and spun between the trestle tables of the Scalptaker's
feasting hall, all accompanied by the skirl and thump of an ale-sodden
six-piece band.

Now, I'd said before that my father was the world's worst statesman,
and that may have been a touch on the uncharitable side. What he was
was blunt, forthright and unswervingly honest, which confused ten
hells out the the Angan contingent... they were the kind of men who
thought around corners for a living.

To be honest, I was ignoring the negotiations, as I'd have to lean
with my elbows in my half-brother Serwyn's roast duck to hear half
of what was being said. I was only at the high table because of the
dramatically thinned ranks of the Khytein Moer, anyway... and most
of the conversation seemed to be deliberate, sidling evasion on the
part of the Anganesse and off-color anecdotes from the Scalptaker.

But I caught the gist of it. Half-garbled whispers circulated around
the table, hissed by servants and muttered by drunken, nodding
warriors. The Thearch, far away beyond the horizon in Urexes, had

finally finished his long campaign against the Floating Kingdoms of the shallow sea. And now he needed resources – wool, timber, coal, gold, iron and meat and grain. Half the world, it appeared, didn't just subjugate itself, and the garrisons of the Angan army were stretched thin. That was where we came in.

Even the dullest child knows that Khytein - or what *was* Khytein, back in those long-summer days – sits like a rind atop the globe, between the Grinding Ice and the mountains of the Hiledoran. It's a hard country, chopped up by the tendrils of the Stormwood where they push into a million hanging valleys and empty, glacier-carved fjords. But we were rich in simple things; the kind of things an empire needs at the bottom if it wants to churn out great marble buildings and philosophical diatribes at the top. All Khytein needed to become the storehouse of the Thearch was a strong leader – a warlord brute ugly and unwashed enough to bend the local tribes under his whip.

Governor Sinder had put his money on Hurik da'Thirgrim Moer, who certainly fit both of those descriptions. Today - despite the magical cataclysm which we all blamed on the Angans' floating Keel - Sinder and my father had narrowed the competition down from four to three. The ragged red flap of skin and hair nailed to the ridgepole of the feasting hall was none other than the scalp of Ardral Sunderspear, and despite what we'd said about them earlier in the day (when they'd been trying their damnedest to hack our hearts out), there were many clansmen of the Khytein Vhaur dotted around the tables, sellswords with more pragmatism than pride. Barely one in three was engaged in knife-throwing, bellowing insults, or flat-out brawling at any given time.

Because of all that noise I may have missed most of the negotiations. But I surely heard the end.

My father hammered his great gold drinking-horn down on the table, hauling himself to his feet. By then he must have gone through a whole cask of black ale, but if any man could stomach such excess, it was the Scalptaker. His shadow was huge and hulking across the shield-hung walls as he drew himself up to his full height, firelight glittering from the armored rings woven into his beard.

"*Peace. Victory. Plenty.* These things the Anganesse have promised. But weak little men are often known by their hollow words. So I have extracted proof from our *honored allies*" - a term he probed with his tongue like an ulcer - "Proof that their Thearch won't play us false."

Even the band had wound down now, their banshee-pipes

deflating with a flatulent hiss. Three hundred shaggy great warriors of the wild north fingered their axes and *kuris* blades under the tables.

"The war Keel *Triumphant Interdictor* will be ours! Jerrold Sinder has pledged his greatest stoneship to the horde of the Khytein Moer, in return for a single little concession. So that the eunuch-priests of Urexes can try to tempt us with their martyred God, I will send them my three youngest sons. They'll likely come back as castrati* in white dresses like these fools beside me, but what of it? I've always *enjoyed* making more sons!"

Well, I can tell you honestly that I was the only one not laughing at Hurik the Scalptaker's mimed pelvic thrustings. The rest of them were seduced utterly by the thought of unleashing a war Keel of Anganesse on the other tribes of Khytein, an act which compared to spanking a petulant child with a mace. Never mind that it took a crew of trained nekrologist-priests to keep the damned thing airborne... Sinder would keep his corpse-white hands firmly around the reins of his toy.

"Come, bring them up here! Sangar, Lutis, and little Kuhal. Raise a horn of ale for my sons, who've finally proven themselves useful!"

I was utterly speechless as they manhandled me to the front, where a hatchet-faced old Angan priest was waiting. The only reason he didn't check our teeth like a horse-trader was because my father was right there, and he mistakenly believed that such disrespect might earn him a place on the trophy-wall.

"Capital! Such, hmm, *strong* young boys! They will be given the finest education, of course."

I tried to protest, I think. But the the all-enfolding stench of Hurik's furs smothered me, along with a first-of-its-kind paternal bear hug.

"Do us proud, lads! When you return to the Khytein we may not listen to your fool religion, but we will honor you for your sacrifice." He stepped back, looking pointedly at our trousers.

"Actually, hmm, My Lord Hurik, the priests of Esau aren't eunuchs at all. In fact..."

The Scalptaker snorted, clapping the white-robed Angan across the shoulders so hard that he winced with pain.

"You could have fooled me! If the lot of you were rolled together, you might have enough muscle between you to make one Khytein woman!"

"Quite," said the priest, in tones of clipped restraint. "But *we* are the ones who have the keels, Scalptaker. We are the ones who chose *you*, and not the Vhaur or the Roege. Now, if you'll excuse us, we must retire to our quarters. Your sons are no doubt eager to receive the benediction and get some well-earned sleep."

"But..." Hurik gestured with his horn of ale, taking in the roasting spits, the untapped barrels, and the giggling, moaning piles of furs and bodies in the shadowed corners of the hall. I suppose he thought that this was a finely honed argument.

"I'm *sorry*, Lord Hurik. But we must go. Now that your sons are to be united with the brethren of Esau, they must observe the same religious rituals as the Thearch himself. And that means prayer, sleep, and the avoidance of strong drink."

The Scalptaker looked more horrified at this than at the threat of castration. He knocked back his own horn of ale in one gulp, as if he was worried the Angan God would turn it to water.

"I'll send for you in the morning, then. We can finish this treaty with writing, like you southerners do. Then I'll take possession of my Keel!"

They all bowed, then – a gaggle of shaven heads bobbing up and down like peaches in a water-barrel. Our fate was sealed.

"Come, novices! Our God is eager to welcome you!"

I should have tried to run. I think my mouth was still gaping open in horror. Perhaps this was the punishment I got for disdaining the life of a warrior. Or perhaps... but I put that thought aside as an escort of hard-faced Angan soldiers marshaled the three of us outside. The band had already started up again by the time we pushed through the hanging curtain of finger-bones which covered the doorway.

The pouch was still there – the worn-down rabbitskin pouch full of tiny bones. It was warm to the touch, hanging at my belt right next to my hunting knife. As I closed my fingers around it it lurched like a beating heart.

As soon as we left the torchlight behind our escort stepped aside, and the Angan priest loomed over us. He was as tall and thin as Aerik, but utterly hairless – even his eyebrows were only a filigree tattooed into his skin. A smattering of liverspots speckled his scalp, but his eyes were like ice-blue stars, distant and merciless.

"I'm not sure if you understand the complexities of our faith, children," he said. "But I'm sure that you savages know the word 'hostages'. That's what you are now. Don't think that my friends here will hesitate to run you through if you try to escape."

Sangar, the fifteen-year-old saga-hero, tried to lunge forward at the old man, but a pair of crossed spear-shafts blocked his path. The

Priest smiled.

"Martyrdom is a great part of our creed, boy. But not so soon. The Thearch has much use for missionaries to bring His Word to the faithless." A single wrinkled fingertip rested on Sangar's forehead, rocking him back on his heels. "Most of them come back to us in pieces."

Lutis was crying, great silent, racking sobs which would have disgusted our father. But unlike his grief or Sangar's rage my mind was utterly clear. Clear and empty as the vault of a summer sky. In that crystal emptiness there were voices, faraway whispers drawing closer...

The pouch at my belt twisted, mewling.

"Take them to the Keel. Make sure they don't escape... not that it should be much of a problem. This one's weeping like a girl, this one's intent on getting a sword through his guts, and as for the littlest... I think his mind's gone wandering." The Angan guards laughed, jabbering to each other in their Southern language as they herded us away. "By the time they see this hovel-pit again they'll be disgusted by it. That's how the Empire wins!"

And perhaps he was right. The village of the Khytein Moer didn't even have a name, and in the autumn it was a mire of sucking mud and half-rotten wood, a bite taken out of the great forest seemingly at random. The Keel which loomed over it was bigger than any ten of our longhouses stacked end to end, a sheared splinter of mountain stone skinned over with licks of lightning. The closer we were marched to it the higher it loomed, blocking out the moonlight, and for a second I wondered how in all hells we were going to climb aboard. But a wicker basket on a long chain hung down from one of the many trapdoors on its underside, and I could see the ruddy glow of a clay pipe up in the darkness where a crewman was watching us.

"Oh, it seems a waste to trade you three for *this*," said the Priest as we were herded into the basket. It began to sway and shudder alarmingly as hidden machines reeled in its chain, lifting us up out of the mud. "But don't worry. Lord Sinder isn't half the fool your fat old father is. Do you really think a pack of stinking barbarians could even get this thing off the ground?"

His chuckle was greasy and self-satisfied, accompanied by a mocking little smile.

Then the darkness enclosed us, and something split that smile bloody.

It all happened blindingly fast.

The Priest reeled back, blood and broken teeth flying from his mouth, squealing like an animal. Then the first of the guards went down, a *kuris* bursting from between his lips like a long silver tongue. It wrenched loose sideways, taking off the top of his head.

Sangar tried to break free from the guard holding him, but he was far too slow. True to his Priest's word, the Angan took him low with his broad-bladed spear, levering him up and over the edge of the basket. Lutis actually managed to get one hand free, and some of Hurik's pride was regained as he drove his fist squarely into his captor's groin. But he was one against six – I was held tight by a pair of strong arms, and I could only watch as they opened his throat.

Someone in the darkness cursed, and I heard a voice hiss my name.

"Kuhal! *Drop*, now!"

It was the Cold Voice, and it went right to my knees, turning them to jelly. I slipped from my captor's grasp and hit the floor of the basket just as something humming rippled through the air above me, accompanied by a murmur like those far-off voices in my head. A second later a patter of warm liquid fell down around me. I looked at the back of my hand, and saw that it was blood... crimson-bright, but not my own.

"If you value your sanity, don't look," said the voice. It was above me in the dark of the hold, accompanied by the deep red glow of that weed-pipe. "Just climb out of the basket and follow me."

Gods help me, but I looked. And it was just as terrible as I'd been warned; the other guards were dead, diced to ribbons by a thin gold wire that had cut a handspan deep into their flesh. The ends of it still quivered, humming up at the edges of hearing.

The voice sighed. "I thought I told you not to..."

"Oh, go ahead and look, boy! Go ahead and see what will become of all your foolish tribe!"

That got me out of the basket fast. I felt cold stone against my back as I squinted up into a pale green glow.

It was the priest, and his hairless scalp was lit up with runes. A nine-pointed star hung above his skin like a skullcap of light, picked out with eye-watering curls of script which seemed to twine and slither grotesquely. In his hands was a long, curved dagger. And it's tip rested against the throat of Aerik, Warbard of the Khytein Moer. He was still smoking his long clay pipe.

"Don't listen to him, son," said another voice behind me. My eyes twitched right, and I caught sight of a pair of hairy-backed hands, wiping the blood from a long silver *kuris* blade. "He knows he's a dead man. He just wants to screw one more little boy before we end him."

"Me? Dead? You savages are stupider than you look! This Keel brought a full company of soldiers, and by now..."

For the second time that day, light bloomed in silence all around me. But this time it came up through the trapdoor cut into the Keel's belly, charring the wicker basket I had just stepped out of. A puff of sparks swirled in on a hot, dry wind, filling the hold with the smell of burnt hay.

"By now they're all helping their drunken 'allies' fend off the Roege and Vhaur who're attacking the village. Sinder isn't going to be a happy man, Ulan Veth."

This time the exchange was even faster. The Priest barked out a command word, filling his cupped hand with fire. It flew toward the shadow-man with the leaf-bladed *kuris*, and he caught it on the flat of the sword, melting it in a splash of molten steel. Aerik twisted away from him at the moment he loosed the spell, the pipe still clenched between his teeth. He plucked a long white hair from his head as he fetched up against the wall, muttering under his breath as his fingers wove it into a loop...

All this in what seemed to be a heartbeat. Then Ulan Veth had me by the throat, his knife pressed up against my jugular. I was enveloped by the stench of sandalwood, incense ground into the fabric of his robes... that, and the mortuary smell of death.

"*Hold!* Hold or he dies, barbarians! You know what I can do with the soul of an innocent..."

I heard a noise behind me – the clatter and ring of a broken *kuris*-hilt on stone. Aerik spun his loop of silvery hair between his fingers, taking a long draw on his pipe as he circled in close.

"So what? We'll just make your death more painful if you hurt him, Veth. In the end he's just another of the Scalptaker's pups... and I've already told this one that his time would come."

"How sweet of you," snarled the Angan priest. "Did you predict your own death as well, you old charlatan?"

There was a chuckle from behind him, from out of the shadows.

"No, Ulan Veth. We only scryed *your* funeral."

Aerik looked me right in the eye then, spinning his hair-thin thread around his little finger. It had turned to gold, just like the wire which had cut down the Angan guardsmen.

"Kuhal," he said... "Remember what happened to your brother."

Then all hells tore open at once.

A huge, hairy fist looped in out of the dark, connecting with Ulan Veth's ribs with a sound like shattered kindling. I saw the knife pull back, the tip dripping green witchfire, and I knew that the Priest meant to drive it into my heart. Then Aerik's singing wire was there, humming through the air to coil itself around Veth's wrist. His other hand spat a rod of force, hurling his assailant back into the dark. But he felt the feather-light touch of the wire, and he turned to look at Aerik with eyes full of terror.

"Oh, Esau save me..."

"Not tonight," said the Warbard, and he pinched his fingers tight.

I spun away as Ulan Veth's hand came off at the wrist, still clutching its sacrificial knife. His howl of pain and rage seemed to blur reality around us as he collapsed to his knees, the runes carved into his skin flickering and dying.

But there was no blood. The Angan Preist's flesh seemed to be as dry as paper, fibrous and mummified beneath his skin, and it seethed with flickers of lightning. As he turned to look at Aerik his face cracked into a madman's smile.

"Burn," suggested Ulan Veth.

And he turned that flaming stump on the shadows.

A sheet of sizzling green fire raved from his shattered arm, catching the shadow-man in midair. His bristling black pelt caught instantly, and he howled, crashing to the floor in a smoldering heap.

Ulan Veth was laughing now, but I couldn't hear him. My world had turned to glass – an abstraction in which time itself flowed like honey, thick and slow. I watched the Angan priest bring his arm around, the claws of his other hand digging in just below the stump. I could see him aging with every sliver of a second, the witchfire spilling out of him until his skin was pinched tight around his bones. Ten more degrees of arc and that raving fire would consume me utterly. Fifteen more and Aerik would melt like a candle in a blacksmith's forge...

But I had all the time in the world. The pouch at my belt convulsed like a dying heart, and something in my mind snapped, cracks ramifying out across the darkness.

Aerik hadn't meant Sangar or Lutis.

He was talking about *Rordan*, and the cat...

I had plenty of time to reach into the mind of that little dead cat. Tendrils of my will picked out its bones, binding one to another, locking and sliding them into place like the pieces of a puzzle. The thing which wriggled out through the drawstring neck of the pouch was a perfect little machine of bone, its eyes glittering with yellow fire. It clawed its way up inside my cloak and to my shoulder before Ulan Veth had time to see it.

Sei. Your name is Sei, and you are my vengeful hand...

I pointed my finger. I felt the command, there on the tip of my mind. And my little bone familiar went skittering down my arm, leaping at the Angan's face.

Time came swinging back, like a pendulum on its arc. I saw the light in Ulan Veth's eyes go out as tiny claws ripped through his skin – skin drawn pale and tight over his skull by the cost of his sorcery. Each claw left a glowing green scar behind it, and the Angan screamed, scrabbling at his face with both his hands.

It was a reflex action. It must have been burned into the primate parts of his brain, the same as it is in us all. But the sad fact of the matter was that Ulan Veth had only one hand – and one flickering torch of witchfire.

That was the first time I'd ever seen a man's head explode – although it wouldn't be the last. I felt, with painful clarity, each tiny bone of my cat familiar flying off in different directions – a mental pain like pulling teeth. But the ecstasy which came after it... the euphoric strength which scrabbled up my spine... that was another thing entirely. I have tried every drug, tincture, potion and herb which this world offers up to the jaded libertine. And nothing, my friends, *nothing*, compares to the *vitae mortis* of a sorcerer's dying scream. Eventually, I would learn to prolong them.

Back then, if I recall, I just stood there with my mouth open, staring at the smoking stump of Ulan Veth's neck. His body toppled over in a sad little heap, trailing a pillar of sickly white smoke.

Part of me was sickened by what I'd done. But even then, it was only a *tiny* part. The rest of me wanted so desperately for Aerik to be proud of my power... more than I'd ever wanted the approval of Hurik the Scalptaker.

I turned to him, a lunatic smile plastered across my face... but he was gone.

For a second I didn't even recognize the withered old body which lay curled up against the wall. Its hair was yellowed and peeling off in chunks, its skin a funereal shade of gray, tight-stretched over a skull all painful angles. A pair of eyes like milky quartz pebbles stared out from bruise-purple hollows, and... and...

Some sorcery is done in people's minds. That's the glamor which makes an old, old man seem more powerful than a hard-bitten veteran of the shield-wall. But some is paid for in other ways. Beneath the power he'd wound around himself tight as a shroud, this was the true face of Aerik Stormsong, Warbard of the Khytein Moer. Where a shard of rune-etched skull-bone had sliced open his neck he was just as dry and empty as Ulan Veth had been.

I felt a hand on my shoulder, tugging me away from that sad little dead thing. I heard a gruff voice, one that will forever be entwined in my mind with the smell of burning grease and fur.

"Come on! You can't follow him where he's gone! All we can do now is help the living!"

I wanted to rage against that brittle old corpse, but strong hands held me back. I bit down on my own lip, hard enough to draw blood, as a cape of smoldering pelts wrapped me tight.

"No! He can't die now! He told me he'd be *waiting*. He told me he'd teach me the way!"

The shadow-man picked me up under one arm, as effortlessly as a sack of rags. He strode over to the trapdoor in the floor, wrapping his free hand around a swinging length of chain.

"Kuhal, I've always found that people are most inconsiderate about when they choose to die. And as for your training... well, there's no time like the present. After all, there's a battle going on down there!"

I twisted my neck up and sideways as far as it could go, catching sight of a tangle of black beard, braided with tiny bird skulls. The man's teeth were mismatched, a set of fangs torn from the jaws of a dozen predatory animals, and around his neck...

I remembered, with sickening clarity, what Ulkar had told me just this morning. There was the little spoon, sharp around the edges.

"Oh, I won't bite," said my captor, testing our combined weight against the chain. "At least, I won't bite *you*."

Then he stepped off into space, his cape flying out behind him like a pair of ragged wings. I tried to stifle a scream, without much success.

Because I wasn't only falling out of the sky toward a fire-lit charnel yard of mud and heaving bodies. I was also the captive of the warlock, Gernish Maudrin.

The Mageblight -

Much has been written of this affliction, and much more told as superstitious fables, ignorant mutterings and peasant folk-tales. It is not known why the exercise of power inevitably mortifies the user; only that contact with the Divine begins to turn mortal flesh to something other - ageless, cold and crystalline, filled with latent energy. Some say that communing with the fragments of the shattered Maker calls like to like, and turns the Adept into living glass. Others say that the Blight is in fact a defense against levels of sorcerous force which would tear mere human flesh asunder. One thing is clear, however - the more power a practitioner uses, the more they succumb to the blight.

Ulsari Mareth, Chaplain
-Surgeon of the Anganesse Ninth Legion

AT THE TIME I was no theologian. In fact, the sum of my religious training was that there were Gods, they were usually angry, and that everything about me, my powers, and the feelings I got when I spied on girls in the bath-house was wrong.

I had no idea why the pain of a dying Angan priest tasted like honey and cinnamon. I didn't even know why both Ulan Veth and poor old Aerik were so withered and dry inside, just like I am now.

Years later, a southerner called Solland told me about the Angans and Esau – how he wasn't their true God at all. I still remember the vividness of his simple story... the dust, the hard, flat light, the dry wood of the crucifixion tree soaking up innocent blood...

He wasn't meant to come into this world. Solland's people, the nomads to the south of the Shallow Sea, had worshiped the young God for seven hundred years before the Angans came. A pastoral deity, with a shepherd's crook and a lantern carved into his hands; he hadn't exactly hardened his people for war.

Old Anganesse – and this is in the days of the Republic, mind, when they were supposed to be led by wisdom – they followed a sterner God, a spirit of the forge and the battlefield. That faith gave them discipline enough to conquer all the lands around the shallow sea, and fly the banner of the eagle-wolf over Solland's country too.

They were cruel masters. Engineers, civilizers, thinkers - all true. But it takes *slavery* to carve monuments like the Colossus of Faeros, knee-deep in the ocean. Esau's people sweated under the lash of their new masters, digging irrigation canals and re-directing rivers. And, against all the strictures which have bound the Gods since the dawn of belief, he got it into his haloed little head to do something about it.

You and I both know what happened next – they nailed him to a tree for his trouble. That's why the Anganesse always wore those little 'X' shaped trinkets around their necks. Who would have thought that a religion could prosper with a torture device as its symbol?

Apparently what followed was two hundred years of some of the bloodiest civil war which the continent of Sarem has ever seen. It appears that half of the Republic was proud of killing a God, and the other half was filled with hand-wringing remorse. That second half started a rebellion, which would have been utterly crushed by the Legions if it hadn't been led by a strange young man called Ulriq Trasse. He was the soldier who thrust his spear into Esau's side while the young God writhed on the killing frame. And he was also the first nekrologist.

That was the power which Ulan Veth had been wielding, when he scourged Aerik and Maudrin with witchfire. That was why the war keels of Anganesse carried great ossuary batteries; glass and copper tubes filled with the bones of men.

It was the other end of the balance, or so Gernish Maudrin would tell me, which made me what I was. All that death, ground out long and slow by the millstones of nekrological psience... it had to have its opposite. Gruesome as it seemed, my new-found affinity for the dead was a natural as summer is to winter.

Not that he told me *then*, when we were falling out of the sky and into a storm of mud and flame. On that night, I had to work on instinct alone. I had to *improvise*.

Oh, he said it was his plan all along – a kind of baptism by fire. I secretly think that he was just as scared as I was, and had all the forward-planning skills of a dewfly. Whichever it was, though, I can't curse the ragged old warbard *too* vehemently.

After all, if it wasn't for his half-arsed rescue attempt, I'd likely be singing the praises of a crucified God right now, as old and twisted as Ulan Veth. Not that I claim to be anything less than either of those things...

And if he hadn't thrown me into the middle of a pitched battle, with black mud in my mouth and the screams of the dying ringing in my head, I might never have met *her.*

They say that love is blind. Which explains neatly why you feel in your heart an emotion which is generated about two feet lower down...

Zenephar Kells, Brothel
-Master of the Western Prefectures

It wasn't an easy landing. Despite his power, Gernish Maudrin had been weakened by his battle with the Angan priest, and we hit the churned-up mud in the shadow of the war Keel hard, carving out a shallow crater. Runnels of black water oozed back in as I struggled to stand, creeping into my boots and under my clothes.

The Longhalls were burning. That was my first impression – flames curling up from the mossy thatch behind a wall of heat. Against this hellfire backdrop of blazing timber and straw moved shadows out of nightmare – spiked, heaving things with insect-legged silhouettes. As my vision cleared I realized that they were little knots of fighting men, swords and spears and axes rising and falling in a manic dance.

"Come on, you little bastard!" huffed Maudrin, hauling me to my feet. "We've both got work to do! You have to bring me Aerik's lyrecaster, and I have to find your father."

"*What?* Don't you have one of your own?"

"A father? No. I was sired on a leprous dog by the spirit of the harvest moon! I mean the '*caster*, boy! By Anghul, you're not the sharpest arrow in the quiver, are you?"

Indeed, Gernish Maudrin had his own instrument unshipped from behind his back now – a flat, carved blade in the shape of a canoe paddle, with a long neck and four human skulls as tuning pegs. It was six feet long if it was an inch, and I caught myself wondering how he'd concealed it...

"Don't ask questions, whelp. Just *go*. Or do you really want someone like Ulan Veth to get his hands on Aerik's magic?"

As he spoke, the bard plucked a bone pick from between his teeth, aiming the neck of the lyrecaster at a gaggle of Angan soldiers. They were busy hacking an old woman to pieces, and in their sport they probably never even heard the creaking, jangling sound of Gernish tightening his strings.

But they heard his whistle.

51

"Hey, you scrotum-faced pox-mongers! Over here, if you think you can do more with a real man than suck him!"

That caught their attention. Four slit-eyed helms tilted up, while four grins shone in the firelight.

"That's one of them! One of their witch-priests! Get him, lads!"

The next instant saw them blown apart.

Maudrin fired off a quick flurry of notes, way down deep in the bass register. I felt them rattling my bones, even from behind him... but the Angans caught the sorcerous blast head-on, and it must have done something terrible to their insides. Gernish nodded to himself, pick between his teeth, and he adjusted one of his tuning skulls by a fraction of a turn.

"Are you still here?" he asked, as four men slumped boneless to their knees behind him, blood and worse bubbling from every orifice. "Stay out of sight, find me that 'caster, and if you're cornered... just do that thing again." He wiggled his fingers at me in a pantomime of magical power, then turned away.

"Any more of you want some? Come on, you pig-raping dung-eaters!"

I realized, a little belatedly, that this was Gernish Maudrin's idea of a diversion.

I took to my heels and ran, staggering through the shadows and the mud. It was only as I came up against a low stone wall that I realized I had a shadow of my own... a tiny thing skittering along in my wake. Sei scrambled up to the top of the wall as I peeked out over it, rubbing his smooth little skull up against my cheek. Obviously there were no hard feelings there about being blown to pieces... each tiny bone was back in place, wired together by a skein of faint green fire. I was utterly certain that nobody else could see it.

"Well, It's good to see you too," I whispered, ducking down behind the dubious cover of the wall. "Any idea how we get through that lot?"

Of course Sei couldn't answer. No vocal chords – and after all, he was only a cat. But the problem that faced us both was very real.

From where I cowered (and believe me, that's what I was doing), I could see the whole beaten-earth hardpan which pride would have me call the village square. Usually it was equal parts market, parade ground, fighting pit, brothel and livestock pen, but now... now it was Anghul's hell split open.

Black-painted Vhaur and fierce Roege warriors were swarming up over the central pallisade and into the square, falling on the defenders like wild animals. It didn't help that some of the Vhaur had changed sides and fought for the Khytein Moer, or that some of the Khytein Moer had decided that an alliance with the Anganesse was a bad idea. Spirited political debate was in full swing, as were a horrorworks of axes, pikes, flails, *kuris* and maces, churning the hard-packed clay to a crimson slurry.

Predictably, Aerik's deerhide lodge was on the other side of the square.

I cast about for a way forward – there was no way in all the hells that I was going to plunge into that screaming, heaving cauldron of flesh and metal. But it was Sei who found it for me, clambering up and over my head to the low-hanging eaves of an as-yet-unburned longhouse. I followed along, pulling myself up by one of the ornamental spears which followed the ridgeline of the building. The little skeletal cat trotted ahead of me as I tried to keep my balance, dragging the spear free from the thatch as I went. The dried-out trophy head mounted halfway down its shaft just wouldn't come loose...

I was glad of that the next instant, because some myopic Angan archer mistook it for my own. An arrow as long as my arm thocked home into the mummified old relic, right through one sewn-shut eyesocket. A whispering flight of bolts followed, and I clung to the thatch, ducking for cover.

But I'd chosen the wrong spot to go prone. Khytein architecture isn't one of the most enduring schools of engineering, and this longhouse was probably not burning only because of the damp rot in its timbers. I went through the thatch, spear in hand, and landed on my arse among a gaggle of old women.

It could have been an embarrassing moment (at least fifteen of these people could claim to be my grandmother), but instead it was one of abject terror. There was a rune-etched skull hanging in the hovel's doorway – the pale, sneering face of an Angan priest.

He was wearing the same long white vestments as Ulan Veth. These robes, however, were spattered with equal measures of blood and manure, tiny chips of bone glistening wetly in the torchlight. He called out to a pack of soldiers behind him, and the look in his eyes was murder.

"Kill them all, men! An eye for an eye, says Lord Sinder – we are to make an *example* of these oath-breaking vermin."

Red-faced, sweating soldiers crowded the low doorway around him, and I caught a glimpse of his black-gummed smile. That was when I felt the eyes on me... not just the hard, black-pebble eyes of the

Southerners behind their helms, but the expectant eyes of thirty-two grandmothers.

I looked down at the spear in my hand. The arrow-shot head winked back at me, grinning.

Here they were, defenseless old women being threatened by outlander thugs. And here *I* was, a strong young son of the Scalptaker, a bloody saga-song hero with his battle-spear in hand.

The Angans didn't give me time to protest.

"Gut the boy first," growled the Priest, folding his stick-thin arms across his chest. "Then crucify the rest."

Hairy hands reached out for me. Swords voiced their oily scabbard-rasp in the gloom.

And Sei fell on the first soldier's back like a storm of fish-hooks, twisting his sword-swing before it could flense me to the spine. I took my chance, thrusting the heavy ornamental spear forward, and I was just as surprised as him when its rusty point slid straight through his eye. He reeled backward, pulling the thing from my fingers, dying on his feet as blood spumed from the wound.

"Savage little whelp! He's got Davic! I'll have your balls for that, runt!"

I felt a sickle-shaped Angan blade whisper past my cheek, close enough to pare the peach-fuzz of hair from my skin. But, as that same glassy detachment from up in the Keel's belly washed over me, I realized that I wasn't afraid. Huffing, stubble-faced men grunted and heaved at me, their blades moving slow as dust motes in summer air. All I had to do was not be where they were, and then...

I clearly felt Davic's head hit the dirty rushes on the floor. I felt the little spark in him go out, even as Sei sunk his teeth into the fleshy beak of the Angan priest's nose, eliciting a sound like a pig in a mangle.

And I slipped my mind into his body like a slippery wet glove, feeling the weight and heft of it under its thick leather armor.

Davic's sickle-sword came up smooth, carving another man's calf muscle clean from the bone. It kept going, driven by all my terror, his muscles far more powerful in death than they were in life. Eventually I'd learn that a living mind can only demand so much of its flesh. But if one is prepared to use that flesh to destruction...

Steel hissed through belly, crotch, spine. Steel spun wide, flying from Davic's dead white fingers, to stand quivering in the ridgepole of the building.

And suddenly it was over. I collapsed to the floor, retching, as three Angan soldiers wept and howled in agony. I think they might have lived, despite their injuries. Even the priest might have survived, as Sei curled himself up on my shoulder, trying to lick the blood from his claws with an invisible tongue.

Hands lifted me up, warm and callused from decades of back-breaking woman's work.

"Go on, son. Get back out there. They need you."

My mouth felt as if it was stuffed with graveyard earth, and I couldn't protest as one of the old women pressed a salvaged sickle-sword into my hand.

"Anyway, you *don't* want to see what happens next," said another. I caught a glimpse of a heavy iron skillet raised up against the torchlight. Shadows shuffled in from all around, surrounding the wounded Anganesse.

I had heard, once, about a far southern tribe, beyond the Shallow Sea. They said that it was better to die fighting them than to be given to their women. My brothers drew some predictably ribald conclusions, but let me tell you... after I backed out of that doorway, away from the thuds and crunches and hideous wet screams... I knew exactly what they meant.

I emerged just in time to be run down by a cavalry charge, led by my own father.

Hurik looked every inch the barbarian lord against the backdrop of blazing longhouses – a shaggy black shadow, his armor inlaid with bronze scrollwork and runic seals. A cape of sewn-together scalps fluttered dry and gruesome in the furnace-breath wind, and his spear clattered with fingerbones as he dropped it down, driving its broad blade through the bodies of an Angan soldier and the Roege warrior he was grappling with.

Statecraft, as I've said, was never his strong point.

Behind him came every Moer noble who was still sober enough to stay astride a saddle; an avalanche of stinking horseflesh and leather and metal. They were indiscriminate, crashing up against the foe like a wave curling in on the shore, and once again the sagas proved to be lies. There was no honor in this butchery – this welter of drunks in armor cleaving their way through a press of wailing meat. Half the dead were our own tribesmen, hacked limb from body from head by axes dripping gore. Battle cries were bellowed and slurred over the screams of the dying, and I crawled through the mud behind a watering trough, trying to drown them out. It was no use.

"Run them down! Rip them ragged! I'll have my bloody Keel, or drive you all to the Hells before me!"

That was my father, roaring as he unshipped his axe from its deerhide scabbard. But the Angans' war-cry was much, much more savage than his.

Sei must have smelled the bonepowder smoke, even over the stench of excrement and death. It came down the invisible wire between us, just in time for me to upend the bronzewood trough and scramble underneath. Then the Guns of the *Triumphant Interdictor* spoke, and the nobility of the Khytein Moer ceased to be.

The bonepowder of the Angan Nekrologists was one of the greatest reasons they ruled an empire. I never saw the tongues of green fire stab out from the war Keel's sides, or the clouds of black smoke which followed. But I heard the chainshot come hissing down from above, and I felt its impact. Every part of me felt it, like a axe-handle to the soul.

Horses screamed, their bones shattered like kindling. Men roared and howled like beasts. And sharpened armspans of iron chain spun in hot, pruning warriors off at the neck, the waist, the knees – shearing their mounts in two as six-pound balls of metal whirled through the dark. The carnage was absolute.

I knew this with utter certainty, because the dead were all around me. Even though I was huddled under a wooden trough, sobbing and gasping in the mud, I could see the webwork of pale green fire in my head, the twisting skein of soul-stuff woven between them and the bloody earth. Filaments wrapped tight around their comrades, their homes, their fallen axes and spears – and as I watched they began to wither and curl up, tugging free and snapping with tiny brittle sounds.

The more fanciful among you would no doubt hope for moaning spectres, grinning skulls drifting up like smoke... but the real world is seldom so melodramatic. Within a handful of heartbeats all that was left was the scrawled outline of each dead thing's bones, a constellation of witchlights prickling behind my eyes. They disappeared when I opened them, replaced by two pairs of black-gloved hands.

"He's under this one. Probably scared half to death, the poor little bastard!"

"Just put your back into it, Conn. *You* would probably just have stood out here with your mouth open!"

They'd found me! Who or what *they* were scarcely mattered at this point – the Anganesse would spit me on a spear, the Roege were known cannibals, and my own people would hardly recognize me. I wore a solid crust of mud, blood and excrement from head to toe, and from what I'd seen the surviving Moer were deep in the blood-rage.

As if to emphasize my point one of the pairs of hands slipped away, just as an ululating war-cry rang out over the square. There followed a sound like a finger being run along a greased bowstring, and the cry gurgled away to nothing. I fancied I heard the sound of heavy meat slapping into the mud.

"Makara, come on! I can't lift this thing on my own!"

"Can you lift it with an axe in your spine? That's what he was going to give you!"

"No time to argue! Just *heave*, damn you!"

There was nothing I could do as the heavy bronzewood trough rolled away. Sei hissed and spat, but he cowered back from the two shadows scrawled against the firelight... and for good reason.

The larger of the pair was armed with a bowblade almost as tall as he was, the slim steel knives which followed its curve dripping with fresh blood. But it was the other one which had Sei arching his clean-picked spine.

She was dark-haired and slim, a pale wraith of a girl with a thick band of black charcoal painted across her face, obscuring both jade-green eyes. Raven feathers and malachite beads hung from the thin braids at her temples, and her armor was a sheath of black leather, plated with scales of bronze. All this I took in, with the wide-eyed stare of one of the Touched.

What Sei had seen was the lyrecaster in her hands.

"So, you must be Aerik's apprentice. Maudrin told me you looked like a drowned lamb."

Embarrassment had me choking on my own tongue as Conn – the bowman – dragged me to my feet. A half-hearted patter of arrows whispered past us, and he turned for a second, drawing and firing with nonchalant ease. An Angan fell from the Keel above, plunging down like a rag doll into the burning feasting hall.

"You *are* Kuhal, aren't you? The one with the... the, well, you know..." He made the same little gesture which Gernish Maudrin himself had done, waving his fingers in the air.

"Oh, this is him, Conn," said the girl, her lips twitching into a sardonic little half-smile. "How many other Moer have a pet like that one?"

She pointed the neck of her lyrecaster at Sei, who was once again perched on my shoulder. He hissed at her, but there was no vehemence to it... I suppose he was smart enough to know that she wasn't really the enemy.

We had plenty more of *those* to worry about.

"Then let's move, Moer. We're best to get this over and done before those Southerners can regroup."

"*Finally*, he says something I can agree with."

Makara's smile was no less wry or captivating as she slung the 'caster over he shoulder, inviting me into her little joke. Then we were off again, pelting across the square under the desultory bow-fire of the Angan soldiers. I didn't want to look down at the nameless pieces we were stepping in.

"In here! Come on, Moer, you're supposed to know where he kept the damned thing!"

She pushed me in through the hide curtains of Aerik's lodge, while Conn spun in the doorway, carefully sending three black arrows to their marks in Angan hearts and eyesockets.

"But I... I've never been in here before! No one has! He's... he was..."

"Hurry it up, Makara! I can see them massing beyond the pallisade!"

"Maudrin said you were his apprentice! And you're supposed to be a nekromancer! Of all the stupid, foolish, suicidally dumb wretches to get lumbered with..."

"Hey! I can't help it if your master couldn't get his facts right! I thought he hated Aerik, anyway! You heard the two of them this morning!"

If anything, the churning rage in my stomach was made all the more violent because of the other emotions she brought bubbling to the surface. Makara was instantly the most infuriating person I'd ever met... which I should have known was a bad sign.

"Listen, you little mud-rat! They were *supposed* to be enemies. It was *traditional*. But when your people get attacked by homicidal ghouls like Jerrold Sinder, you put tradition aside! Now, close your eyes!"

From outside came the thrum and whack of Conn's bowstring again. Even I could hear the bark of Anganesse voices over the flames now.

"What's taking so long? I've only got so many arrows, you two!"

She's not much older than me, really, I thought, as one of Makara's cool white hands pressed up against my forehead. I closed my eyes, feeling something twist under her palm…

And the green fire was there - tendril webs of it, ramifying out like frozen lightning. Traceries of cold brilliance flickered in the dark, and the corpse-fires of the dead tapered up like candle flames. All those lines converged here, on this little round yurt with its carved wooden cupboards and chests…

I opened the other eye – the hidden one. Or perhaps Makara did it for me.

It was like staring up at the sky on a moonless night. Pinpricks of power traced every finger-touch Aerik had made, branding his soul into the fabric of this place. I almost sobbed with grief as I felt his spirit move through me, but then he was gone.

In his place I saw the shadow of his lyrecaster, picked out with shimmering lights.

"Good. I knew you could do it." When I opened my eyes, Makara's face was only inches from my own. Her nose wrinkled with distaste, and she smiled that sardonic little smile again. "You just needed the proper motivation. And a bath. Although that will have to wait."

Certain images flickered through my mind. I don't have to go into detail, surely.

But before I could embarrass myself further Conn came back through the doorway, his face sheened with sweat. His long black hair, which had been bound up in a trio of copper coils, now hung loose, and a gash across his temple dripped bright blood.

"If…if you're quite finished… I think we're going to need Master Gernish for this one."

"Nonsense!" said Makara, pulling Aerik's lyrecaster from its hiding place behind a lacquered Kalmaji clothes-chest. "With this thing, I can take a score of those Southern goat-rapists! I'll…"

Conn grabbed her by the back of the neck and thrust her head outside the lodge.

"How about a hundred?" he asked.

The young warbard ducked back into our company, much chastened.

"I'll admit that *could* prove to be a problem. But you forget, Conn, we've got a nekromancer with us. An honest-to-the-Gods *black magician.*"

The pair of them slowly turned to look at me. I blinked a crust of mud from my eyes, looking nearly as foolish as I felt. How could I tell them that I had no idea what I was doing?

"I'm going to talk to him anyway. This is just a little outside the scope of our training."

Makara unrolled a twist of wire from somewhere on her person and stretched it into a tight triangle between three of her fingers. At once it started buzzing, setting up strange harmonics in the air. For some reason it made my back teeth hurt, and brought the taste of oily metal to my tongue.

"Are you three fools in trouble already? You need a wet-nurse, not a warbard!"

The voice came from that tiny twist of wire, and despite being as high and sawing as a mosquito's whine, it was definitely Gernish Maudrin. All doubts were erased when he began cursing, using expletives even my father had been too prudish to utter.

"There! Done! That should get them off your backs for a while... just don't die for another minute or two!"

Oh, how easy it all sounded.

That is, until the hide walls of the lodge were torn away left and right, ripped in two by a sorcerous wind.

"That's him! That's the one... the boy-child! He killed Ulan Veth! He must be taken alive!"

The three of us were utterly surrounded, naked under the blades of a hundred veteran soldiers. In the center of the village square, white robes red to the waist with gore, stood another of Esau's preisthood, trembling with barely contained fury. A coil of thick gray smoke was still rising from around his hands, and the runic skullcap carved into his scalp sizzled with fire.

I was getting heartily sick of the Anganesse clergy. But what could I do? All around us massed a legion of the Thearch's troops... the butchers who'd all but depopulated our village. They were Ulan Veth's little surprise for the poor dead Scalptaker - a garrison of 'advisors' to hold his people to ransom. Events had moved just a little faster than the Southmen had anticipated.

"Accursed one! Seed of darkness! Esau's fire casts you out! The seventy-seven nether hells embrace you as... uuuuuurrrgh!"

Conn had done us all the favor of shooting the priest through the throat, making him twist up on himself like a scrap of parchment. He collapsed to his knees, bubbling blood, his hands still trying to form a conjuration of power.

And;

*"To hell with taking him alive! Kill the lot of them!"*bellowed the

scar-faced old Angan captain. He stepped over the gurgling wreck of his master, drawing a serrated gladius from its sheath.

A hundred callused hands brandished their swords. Two hundred eyes blazed hatred from behind their helms. And above us, the *Triumphant Interdictor* exploded.

The air-shock was like a slap from the Sky-God's hand, and I felt the earth itself heave beneath me. Gernish Maudrin had silenced the guns of the war Keel once and for all, ripping the guts of it raw. Even as I tumbled through the air, clutching Sei to my chest, I saw the ghost-lights of its ossuaries go out, letting gravity take hold.

Wood splintered against my back. Pain came with it; a brace of knives slammed home all down my spine. The cracking sound I heard then must have been my collarbone, my ribs, my arm... though at the time even those flare-bright shards of agony seemed far away.

Above my little home village the shadow of the *Triumphant Interdictor* spun like a sycamore seed, falling slow and lazy for all its bulk. Chunks of rune-etched stone bounded across the square, rolling, crushing, leaving a slurry of red behind them. Little bodies spun black against the fireglow, trailing gossamer threads of witchlight...

Then the Keel came down.

It buried its knife-blade prow in the ruins of the feasting hall, like a tombstone for Hurik the Scalptaker's dreams of domination. Fractures in the stone split it lengthways, one half heeling over drunkenly to dam the river, the other driven yards deep into the earth. Whole crenelated towers sheared loose, raining down amid the thrashing boughs of the Stormwood. The moon shone like a leering eye through the great central void of the stoneship – that well of emerald flame drilled clear through the thing's heart.

Then that, too, came loose, and the bound energies which heaved a slice of mountain into the sky tore free, punching spires of raving energy out from the central well. One tapering spike sliced clear across the valley, obliterating the peak of hookback mountain. The other feathered away against the stars, dragging the clouds along with it in a ragged spiral.

I believe that I was laughing at this point.

What was left of Sinder's pride and joy toppled to the earth as my head rolled to one side, just in time to see Makara stagger to her feet. The impact of all that remaining metal and stone drove her back to her knees, but Aerik's lyrecaster was still in her hands.

The Angan Captain had seen it. I was more than a little surprised that he was still alive, but then again, a man like that must have been a veteran of some of the bloodiest annexations the Thearch had ever orchestrated. He had his gladius at Makara's throat in an instant.

"Drop it or I kill her, warlock," he growled, looking out into the smoke. I couldn't move my head – my mind was tethered to a husk of lifeless meat. But I knew who the soldier was talking to by the curling lines of force which pulled at the corners of my eyes, tentacles of brightness caressing the surface of reality.

Gernish Maudrin brushed the smoke aside like a curtain, his artful grotesquerie burned away. This man stood as tall as Aerik, but he was built like a Stormwood bear, all greasy black furs and bronze armor. His lyrecaster sighed, breathing in his hands.

"Try me, Angan. I can get myself another apprentice, but you can't get yourself another soul."

I saw the Captain grit his teeth. I saw his eyes narrow and his knuckles whiten around the handle of the blade. And as its razor edge pricked blood from Makara's throat, something cracked inside my mind.

The flames tapering up from a thousand butchered bodies suddenly flared, cold and bright as stars.

NOT. ONE. MORE.

I heard that voice. Later, they told me that it came from out of my own throat, but at the time I'd never have believed it. It sounded like a storm-wind ripping trees up by their roots, and it slammed my head back against the ground with concussive force.

Makara told me afterward that the dead rose then, as soon as I blacked out. By all accounts it must have been hideous – broken bodies ripped and burned and shattered, bone grinding slick on gristle as they dragged themselves from the charnel mud. I'm almost glad I never saw it. If I did, I may never have been able to do it again.

But they rose. And they killed. Only one Southman made it out of that village alive, and him with his flesh cut to ribbons.

Even Gernish Maudrin looked at me differently after that, and he always kept the campfire between us at night during the months of hard-scrabble fear which followed. I could see reflections in his eyes of the things Makara and Conn told me about – the grinning, half-faced dead, the screams as Jerrold Sinder's men met a hard, hard death at their hands... and worse.

Other survivors of what they called the Oathbreaker's Night said it was my father Hurik who brought his men back from the Otherworld, to avenge the Angan's treachery. They took a certain perverse delight in describing the spilling guts and glistening bones, but to me it was just a dark, dark dream.

Unfortunately, it was one which I am yet to wake from.

And it was one which the whole world would come to share.

Three

The City of Tombs

"The Savage doesn't understand reasoned argument. He has no respect for semantics or pretty words. What the Savage understands is the politics of a boot across his neck, and the more times he feels it, the more acquainted with civilization he becomes."

Brother Governor Jerold Sinder
- Pontifex of Anganesse

So BEGAN THE wolf times. The hard times, when my people were hunted and harvested and driven out before Southern swords.

It began with that one tiny village, a place I now know was just a speck on the face of the world. But the Thearch and his armies were waiting for the merest excuse. They came down on the Khytein hammer and claw, burning and raping their way deep into the Stormwood before the tribes could muster any resistance.

Even when they did, there was nothing but a kind of doomed nobility to their defiance. A shield wall, even one emboldened by the wild song of the warbards, couldn't stand against the steel and discipline of ten thousand marching Southmen. They razed the forest before them, and dragged hooks on chains beneath their terrible keels to rip trees from the ground. They dammed rivers and drowned villages, tore up crops and butchered families, and all along the path of their advance sprung up thickets of the crucified – defiant Khytein nailed up in imitation of the southern God.

All this I learned later, from ragged bands of survivors fleeing through the misty expanse of the Stormwood. North, always north, up to the knife-blade peaks and deep fjords of the Grinding Ice. I suppose many of us thought that the Anganesse wouldn't follow us there. We were wrong.

For months Gernish Maudrin, Makara and I lived like outcasts. My broken bones healed wrong and warped in the cold of that long season, and ever since I've walked with a limp. Makara had it almost as bad, though her wounds were of the mind.

As for Conn – all Gernish would say was that he was needed elsewhere. It took me a week to pry loose whether he'd lived or died.

But there was little time for feeling sorry for individuals that autumn, as the wind from the north turned to ice and razors. Sympathy and trust were the first casualties of what the Angans called the Cultural Annexation, and those who harbored such soft emotions were the second.

Because Sinder's men weren't killing us. No - that would be too trite, and far too easy. There was a method to their slow advance, grinding northward week by week, rounding up whole townships and clans and marching them off to the south.

Those few refugees we met under the dripping canopy of the Stormwood told us what they'd seen there – great log palisades thrown up around makeshift garrison towns, masons and neckrologist-priests forging weapons while their Khytein captives slaved for them. The fires never went out in the furnaces there, and from the highest hills we could see their smoke on the horizon, boiling up to stain the clouds.

They called it 'processing', and it was meant to civilize us. But those other refugees had a haunted look to them, and they assured us that nobody ever came out of the camps. That was the news that changed our direction.

I heard Makara and Gernish arguing about it that night, when they thought that I was asleep in my furs. About how "the fulcrum couldn't fall into their hands," and "this is all because of what *he* can do."

That was another thing. We'd spent months together, but I knew Makara less then than I did in those few instants when we were right on the edge of death. In the daylight she was somber, meticulous and cold... hardly speaking a word to me except to relay the old warbard's orders. But sometimes, when the embers of the fire were dying and the cold bit bone-deep, she would roll over in her sleeping furs and cling to me like a drowning child. Sometimes she spoke, and sometimes she wept quietly. But I was too much of a coward to ever see if she was actually awake. I kept my back turned away and burned with shame.

It was if this whole cruel war was somehow *my* fault.

It took me a few weeks to realize that it actually was.

Jerrold Sinder didn't need slaves, or land, or glory. He wanted me strung up on some nekrologist's rack, with all my secrets pinned down tight like specimens. He wanted to be able to control the dead.

If dying inch by inch hadn't been involved, I would gladly have given the power to him. When the wind blew from the north, and another meal of frozen stale bread made my teeth ache, I would have given the bastard anything. Hells, I didn't even know what I'd done myself! The only evidence of it was in the depths of Makara's eyes... a kind of awed revulsion, detached from the clumsy Moer child who passed his fourteenth birthday huddled up against a treestump in the snow.

Then came the night of the Argument. Gernish Maudrin won it by snapping something about there "not being a Khytein to save if we didn't use him now"...

And that was that. The next morning we set off for the southeast, up into the foothills of the Hiledoran. We weren't running anymore.

We were preparing for war.

"Defeat cuts deeper than blades. That much is true. But it's after defeat that your supposed friends cut you the deepest."

General Ephris
- The Exile of Ravenstrand

From the rocky saddle of the pass it looked like a vast and spreading stain. The settlement straggled halfway up the valley, mud-brown and grey with low-hanging smoke – a wretched place, stinking of defeat.

Even the sentinels who stood watch were starving – hollow eyed and hollow cheeked, they tracked us with arrows which trembled against their bowstrings. Makara snorted in derision.

"Conn *can't* be here. He'd never let it get so bad!"

Gernish Maudrin only huffed, his breath glittering in the frosty air. All three of us were wrapped up against the cold, with deep and shadowy hoods concealing our true identities. Months of living wild in the Stormwood had added to our disguise – we were just as wretched as the sentinels we'd passed, and almost as weak.

"This isn't an army. It's an open grave! If Sinder finds this place..."

The warbard's hand lashed out too fast to follow, grabbing his apprentice by the forearm. There was a look of utter weariness in his eyes.

"*Don't say it.* Words leave echoes, and even if they didn't... these people already know. Hearing it is just salting the wound."

Makara twisted away, but there were tears in her eyes. She knew that Conn was here, and that made it so much worse.

We trudged between rows of makeshift hovels, through the smoke of peat fires smoldering under empty pots. Glazed eyes followed us, sliding off us like rain... we were just as ragged as the poorest dispossessed, and Gernish had slipped effortlessly back into his charade of hunch-backed infirmity.

It wasn't a long walk down the gullet of the valley, but the things we saw along the way were enough to turn my stomach – empty as it was. The dead were piled like cordwood by the sides of the muddy path, waiting for their place in mass graves. The eyes of the men and women who turned the wet black earth were as empty as those of the corpses they buried. And between the canted rows of tents and sod-roofed huts we saw the dying – plague victims wrapped in furs and canvas, put out in the snow by fearful relatives.

Makara pulled her hood forward to hide the tears running freely down her face. But I was sickened by more than just the sheer hopelessness of the refugee city. I was sickened by my own reaction to those frozen stacks of cadavers... the way a part of me felt a little less hungry and a little less tired as we passed them by. I could see the tapered green witchfires pulled out taut from each grinning corpse, and they bent in around me like a cage.

"I... I can't be here, Master," I stammered, clutching at Gernish Maudrin's furs. I'd taken the oath of binding that first night in the Stormwood, making me his apprentice. "The dead..."

The warbard nodded, the bird skulls in his beard clattering together.

"I know. I've read about the Dark Sight, and what it means. Just keep your eyes closed, and hold onto my arm. We're nearly there."

I went one better and tied a scrap of rag across my face, masquerading as a blinded victim of the plague. But it made no difference to the glassy green flames which boiled behind my eyes, and the rest of our trek through the camp had the quality of a waking nightmare. Believe me – nightmares are a specialty of mine.

When the cloth was torn from my face I was looking at Conn.

It had been barely six months since Oathbreaker's Night, but war had changed him. The young warrior I'd met amid the fire and ruin of my father's village had been just as tall, dark-haired and thin as the man who stood before me now, but there were lines etched into his face which aged him beyond his years. His hair had been cropped back to a stubble, but for a top-knot held together with copper rings, and his eyes were shadow-haunted, sunken things... nearly as dark as Gernish Maudrin's.

"Khual Moer. Gods be merciful, but I never thought I'd see you again." His smile was a small and fragile one, hinting at the hells he'd gone through since last we'd met. "And I see you've brought trouble along with you. How did you manage to survive with this wild savage eating all your supplies?"

He was talking past me, to Makara, and a glint of mischief lit up his face for just an instant.

In that moment I was sure that the young warbard was going to split Conn's lip, but instead she threw her arms around his neck and hugged him half to death. Gernish and I both looked equally uncomfortable, and as for Conn...

"Makara! I'm trying to keep a little of my dignity! After all, this *is* an execution!"

And so it was.

Behind Conn, across a hard-packed square of earth and reeds, stood a long scaffold bar, looped over with nooses. Three men stood on a trestle two feet out of the mud, masked in sack-cloth and painted with crude funerary sigils. A ragged crowd watched from around the edges of the square... eager to see, but scared to come too close.

"A bad business, Conn. We need every able body we can get."

"Maybe so, Gernish. But these ones are doing more for Jerrold Sinder than for their own. We have to set an example."

Makara slowly slipped from Conn's embrace, horrified. The Khytein were never a people for the rope or the stake. Our criminals were exiled, or slain clean by their War-chief in single combat. This was an Angan rite, and it was worse, in a way, than the open graves we'd passed to get here.

"Who judged them?' asked Gernish Maudrin, his cold hard voice paring ribbons from the air. "You? Or was it the word of the mob?"

Conn took a step backward, his smile cracking around the edges.

"It was the *Council*. The leaders of the Four Tribes. They agreed to..."

He was stopped by the triple-crack of breaking bone. Behind him three men danced on air, their support kicked away by a pair of masked warriors. Each one wore a ragged cloth hood and a pair of deer antlers bound with thorns – the mark of Anghul.

Makara tried to rush forward, but Conn stopped her, holding her back.

"They were traitors!" he hissed, gripping her wrists tight to keep her hands from his throat. "A rapist, a thief, and one of Sinder's spies. If we hadn't done this clean the mob would have skinned them slowly!"

Behind him the weak kicking and writhing of the hanged men ran down. The wretch on the left dripped blood and piss from his blackened toes. The one in the center had slipped the executioner a coin or two, and an antler-headed man swung from his legs, choking him quickly.

I believe I screamed at that point. You would have too. It was as if the Gods had cracked open the top of my head, pouring in blind white light.

I could see thick skeins of witchfire twisting up from the dying, thrashing bloody from their mouths. They were searching for release, but the runes daubed across their bare chests chained them down. There was only one lightning-rod for that outpouring energy, and it was *me*.

"No!" I pleaded. "Go back! I can't help you! I can't..."

But the dead were far beyond reasoning.

Above the sound of their souls tearing loose I heard the crowd begin to mutter and growl. Gernish Maudrin stepped over me, throwing back his hood, and the muttering turned to gasps and prayers.

"The dark man! He helped Hurik raise the dead! The warlock!"

Something told me that the warbard's legend had gotten away from him. Something else told me that this could put us all on the scaffold next to those poor doomed bastards...

But that part of my mind was tiny, melting like a snowflake in a candle flame. The rest was reaching out for all that sweet dark suffering, and I was powerless to stop it.

The first dead man was mine by the time the crowd began to surge forward. The second was wrapped around my will as Conn put his first arrow through a gaunt gray refugee's head. By the time I had the third man's bones wrapped in invisible wires, Gernish Maudrin had his lyrecaster unshipped, loosing a jangling hum of pure fear.

It was the hunger which did it - months of grubbing for frozen roots and choking down rotten meat. It resonated with the hanged men, blurring into their desperate desire for more life, for one last breath...

I heard ropes snap. I heard screams. I caught a glimpse of a horror walking, masked in sack-cloth, it's head lolling bonelessly to one side, and then...

An axe split it lengthways.

The threads cut, red-hot, with the sound of lyrecaster strings. I broke free of the death-trance just in time to see a huge and familiar shape kick the head from a ghoul's broken neck, and then Ulkar was upon us.

He bulled Gernish out of the way, knocking him from his feet, and in that moment I remembered his superstitious hatred. But it was Conn who he was after, closing one huge hairy fist around his neck.

"I told you you shouldn't have brought him here! Tharn Hektus was *right* when he called the child a witch!"

Conn threw him off, scowling.

"Power is power, *councilman*. We don't have the luxury of choosing our allies in this fight."

Gernish Maudrin helped me up as he clambered to his feet... slow, I noticed, and with the unsteadiness of great age. Sorcerous power is rooted in belief, and the illusion of strength is the same to a warbard as the real thing. Ulkar had done more than knock the wind from Maudrin's belly – he'd *diminished* him, stolen a sliver of his soul.

Now he clawed it back.

"Tharn Hektus was *right*. He might have been the most wretched drunk in all the four nations, but he knew power when he felt it. Young Kuhal *is* a warlock, and he raised the dead on Oathbreaker's Night."

Shocked faces. Blank eyes. He had the crowd now, winding their tension tight like one of his 'caster strings.

"But tell me, councilman... do you think he has any love for Anganesse? The people who killed his family and let them burn? *Do you want to see the wrath of a warlock unleashed on those Southern mother-rapers?*"

Ulkar wouldn't look at me. That hurt more than the dead-fish stares of the refugee crowd, I'll admit. The man who'd stood with me in the shield wall, in a memory which was already warm and dim with reminiscence...

I was nothing but a dangerous weapon now, to all of them. Like a *kuris* honed too sharp that can nick your thumb to the bone.

"I speak for the nations when I say we don't *want* that kind of power. We can beat the bloody Southmen with *this!*" he hefted his five-span war-axe in one hand, spitting into the dirt. "This way is clean. This is the way of our ancestors."

"And how's it been working out so far? Look at us, Ulkar, and tell me we don't need all the help we can muster."

Runners had gone out through the shanty. Now they returned, bringing the leaders of the other clans with them – along with an even larger crowd. An argument between the Khytein's warlord and the legendary baby-eating monster Gernish Maudrin was much better sport than a mere hanging.

"Listen to me! *He's* the one the Thearch wants! I've talked to the survivors, Maudrin. I know the questions Sinder's men put to our people, under their irons and sorcery. This could all end, if you..."

"If we *what?*" asked Conn, pushing the head of Ulkar's great-axe down out of his face. "Has our great war-chief lost his will to fight? Are the Moer selling their children to the Thearch now, cowering in their beds?"

That cut deep. I certainly didn't want to be typified as a *child* when Makara was standing right there next to me. Or at least she *had* been, up until a second ago...

She was staring at the horizon – at the scrub pines and boulders which stood in silhouette above the pass. Her lyrecaster was in her hands. In the moment of hush while the whole camp waited for Ulkar to swing his axe I could hear its strings humming.

Gernish Maudrin had heard it too.

He looked Ulkar in they eye, as hurt and as *old* as I have ever seen a man. The warlord's last words came loose like rotten teeth, spat into the silence.

"He's not one of the Moer. Not after his father... and my brothers... *desecrated*..."

"Gods preserve us, you fat old fool. *What have you done?*"

The Draken-horns came first, great twelve-foot copper pipes droning their flat cry between the hills. Then came the first explosions, high up on the pass, as clods of earth flew and trees shattered. From down here we could all see the sentinels picked up and thrown end over end, tiny stickmen burning.

"Death used to mean an end to suffering. Now it means *nothing*," said Ulkar, turning away. He still wouldn't look me in the eye. "*You* have done this, Kuhal, scorn to your father's name! I've only done what was needful to lay this horror to rest..."

"Traitor," hissed Conn, his bowblade sweeping up in a silver blur. At this range the arrow he held trembling against its string would spit Ulkar's head and the three men behind him. "You've killed us all!"

There was neither restraint or remorse in the young warrior's heart. He fired in a single smooth motion, lips pulled back from his teeth in a snarl. But the arrow stopped an inch from the back of Ulkar's head, spinning slowly in midair. Beneath the rising screams and cries of the refugee camp I heard the shimmering harmonic of sorcery... an injunction finger-tapped out on the fretboard of Makara's lyrecaster.

"The Anganesse have his family, Conn. He's a fool, not a monster."

Gernish Maudrin plucked the arrow from the air.

"Although you *did* hang the messenger who helped you broker your treason. That's hardly a noble death."

Ulkar's shoulders slumped, and he held up his weight on the thick bronzewood haft of his axe. Sixty-two winters cut deep into the lines on his face.

"Sinder told me he only wanted the boy. He said they'd send Zengaji – quick, in and out. Not this!"

"Are you really surprised that he lied to you? Or are you more of a fool than I give you credit for?"

"I just wanted to make it *end*. This is no war for my kind, Gernish Maudrin. The council only chose me because I was the last Moer nobleman left."

A shadow fell across us as he spoke. Not one shadow, but two, I saw, as I squinted up into the pewter snow-light. They intersected like blades right above us, one cruising high and slow, the other sliding in fast, like a knife into belly-flesh. Bursts and cracks of green fire issued from the inverted towers which hung below them, while stubby triangular sails creaked and strained above, adjusting their trim in the air.

These were the *Triumphant Interdictor*'s sister-ships – knife-shaped monoliths lumbering through the sky under the power of countless ossuary batteries. The fire they spat was linked chainshot, and it tore into the hovels and tents of the refugee city like a storm of scythes, mowing down hundreds of people.

"Kill him and be done with it! We have to get out of here!"

Conn spun his bowblade down until its razor-edge lay against Ulkar's throat. The old warlord seemed to accept it, willing Conn to strike with his eyes.

"No. We can't escape this place without breaking their line. And we need good men for that." Gernish Maudrin held out his hand, pulling Ulkar to his feet. "If you want glory and the Long Sleep, this is the time, Moer. But if you live to see me again, I'll watch you dance on the end of a rope."

Conn was speechless with fury. But I saw the wisdom in what the old warbard had done. Ulkar wouldn't see the sun set on this battlefield. And for all his foolishness, he'd at least take a few hundred Southmen with him.

The war-keels hung heavy above us, squatting on the sky. We were the last people left in the square, alone but for the dead. Off in the distance the draken-horns howled, heralding carnage.

"That's not good. That's not good at all," muttered Gernish, as a ratcheting, steel-grinding sound issued from above. I found myself looking up -and up, and up – into the barrel of a wolf's-head cannon, its snarling iron jaws dripping witchfire. Around the edges of its firing port I could see Angan nekrologists turning wheels and swinging censers, loading a glass shell filled with bonepowder into the breech.

"Go! *Run!* Don't lose sight of the boy, and keep him alive! I'll meet you at the southern pass!"

Makara grabbed me by the arm as we scattered, Gernish Maudrin leaping one way, Ulkar another...

And then the square simply ceased to exist.

The Angan gunners turned it upside down in a spray of steaming mud, gouging out a crater deeper than I was tall. Chunks of gallows and crude huts and bodies whickered past my head as Makara threw me down, sliding into cover behind me.

Something was struggling and kicking underneath me, and I knew exactly what it was. I pulled the drawstring on my pouch and Sei came tumbling out, still managing to look indignant despite having smooth bone instead of a face. Makara reached out and scratched between where his ears would have been.

"If there's enough flux in the ether to get this little fellow up and about, Gernish is going to need all the help he can get. Come on!"

We plunged into a river of frightened people, whole families carrying everything they owned on their backs or pushing rickety handcarts through the mud. Some fled to the north, others to the south, and yet more were simply curled up crying as the crowd broke around them. It was easy enough to spot Conn, though, because he was standing alone atop the tallest building in the encampment, firing off black-fletched arrows in a steady, unerring stream.

Not up at the keels, though they had drifted further out over the empty ground between the camp and the safety of the hills. No, it seemed that Jerrold Sinder wasn't leaving this slaughter to the skill of his nekrologists.

We saw it as we clambered up a pile of baled straw and joined him.

Behind a ragged line of upturned wagons and thorn-bush barricades, the Angan legions were forming up. Those broadsides which had ripped the northern pass open had been more than just a brutal warning shot – they had cleared the way for eight phalanxes of spearmen, each a hundred strong. The cold gray light glinted from crescent-moon shields and long spears, while black horse-hair plumes flickered and snapped in the wind.

Every now and then one of the Anganesse would flick his shield up to the height of his slit-faced helm, catching one of Conn's arrows. These were veterans, then... not so easily pinned to the dirt by a lucky shot.

"Faceless Ones," said Conn, by way of greeting. He let loose another arrow as he turned and dropped below the parapet, wincing as one of the Angan warriors deflected it with the edge of his shield. "They wear black masks under their helms to scare the enemy. Jerrold wants you to believe he *grows* the bastards in some alchemical kitchen."

"It works for me," I replied. "Who's to say he doesn't?"

Now the Faceless Ones snapped into perfect ranks, and the bark of their centurions was audible over the pandemonium below us. A patter of short, broad-headed bolts rattled the timbers around us, slung by small crossbows built into the Angan's shields.

"They don't even have to be faceless – a spear through the guts seems scary enough!"

Conn looked at me sideways, and I could tell he thought I was full of saga-stories. By which I mean, of course, *lies.*

But Makara shut him down.

"I saw you in the shield-wall, Kuhal. But that's no way to fight these Angans... not even your famous Wings of the Hawk can smash through so much heavy armor."

"Then how *do* we fight them? There's no way I can..."

Well, they both knew how that sentence ended. My little performance at the hanging was proof enough that my 'gift' was uncontrollably wild.

"We won't have to, Gods willing," said Conn, peeking up over the parapet. A few more stubby bolts thwacked home, bracketing his silhouette. "Ulkar may be an idiot, but he can rally a shield wall, even against these monsters."

And here they came.

These weren't the proud Khytein warriors the saga-songs praised. They were weak and sick, the most of them, but they'd rather have left their own eyes behind than their bronzewood shields and their *kuris* swords. Against eight hundred of Sinder's Faceless we had mustered almost three thousand fighting men – tattooed Roege, Vhaur in their ragged furs, Sorm with their finger-bone necklaces clattering... even a pitiful few Moer, tall spears flashing as they formed up. Ulkar was at the head of the Moer formation, and the cold sunlight slithered across the blade of his axe. Out on the other flank, I saw a row of men kneeling in the mud, naked but for chains and blue spirals of ink. With an iron chalice in one hand and a knife in the other, Gernish Maudrin was blessing the Touched.

We were supposed to be running. But there was no chance of

that. From up here all three of us could still feel the ground tremor as three thousand Khytein bellowed their warcries, and the human-skin drums began to beat out their dirge. Conn would never turn his back on a battlefield. Makara would never turn hers on her Master. And I had nowhere to go without them.

Now the Facless Ones had other things to worry about, and it was possible to peer over the parapet, watching the Angan force prepare to face our charge. Their shields spun and interlocked, forming a curved wall in front of each phalanx – a wall through which broad-bladed spears bristled. Khytein arrows stood quivering from the white-lacquered timber of that armored shell, not one finding its mark.

Above us, the keels hung silent. I caught myself wondering why they didn't just raze the encampment, churn it all to mud and bones with their terrible wolf-faced cannons. Then I realized that Jerrold Sinder had no use for me dead. It's a strange kind of egotism when you're actually right... but for terrifying reasons. I could almost imagine the torture irons bubbling in my eyesockets as Gernish ran his fingers down the lyrecaster strings, calling the wild song.

Witchfire answered him. Glowing spheres and jags of energy coruscated around Khytein blades. The Touched began to babble and twitch, swinging their chains in furious arcs, staggering forward...

And the Faceless Ones broke.

At least, that's what I thought at the time. In that instant the wild song was in me, and we were invincible, we proud northern heroes. Our tide of sound and fury would roll over the Anganesse like inexorable death. And the eight great phalanxes *had* split open, shields sliding and locking like serpent scales.

But it wasn't fear that did it. Jerrold Sinder knew us, and he knew how we fought. He knew a glorious old wardog like Ulkar would never deviate from the sagas.

The darkness beneath those shields was lit up with cold fire. Copper and glass winked back at the Khytein as they charged, desperate for a weakness to punch through...

They were swivel-guns, brought down from the keels. Sinder knew that we had to have our rituals, our slow and measured dance before the slaughter. Ulkar's observance of the rites had given the Southmen all the time they needed to mount and arm their bonepowder murder-engines, and now they spoke.

Eight cracks rang out, as grim as the sound of snapping necks. A great cloud of smoke blew back across the Angan line, while in front of it, across the churned mud of no-mans-land...

The Touched were torn from existence. Those guns fired a barrage of hot iron shards, brazier-heated black metal inscribed with runes. All of the wild song's magic wasn't enough to stop them shredding out in an eightfold fan, shattering chains and splintering bones.

Despair rolled in with the echoes. The preternatural strength of the Touched was our spearhead, the tip of our blade. Without them, the Angans thought we'd crumble, sick with superstitious dread.

They hadn't figured on Gernish Maudrin.

Back then I knew little of the ways of sorcery – of how it's a *balance*, a flow that raves through every particle of the sorcerer's body, threatening to turn him inside out. Now I stand in awe of the way Gernish picked out the harmonics in the wild song, bending strings and notes until they flowed seamlessly into a high-pitched storm. Clashing echoes blurred the sky as he drew in the music, aiming it down the skull-studded neck of his 'caster.

I watched his arm come round in a single windmill arc, fingers blurring across the strings. I watched all four skulls shatter in an explosion of witchfire and bone. And then something cracked inside each of those Faceless phalanxes... the glass ammunition of the murder-guns.

"Get down!" shouted Makara, jamming my head below the parapet. I saw Conn's eyes widen just before he, too, gave in to reasonable caution and buried his face in the thatch.

In the Dark Sight I saw it all anyway. Those long, lanternlike cartridges were the size of a fat man's thigh, and each one was filled with the powdered bones of the dead. When the rune-etched brass hammers of the guns cracked them open, the bound souls within burst free with cataclysmic force, spitting red-hot iron. Now they were freed by the wail of Gernish Maudrin's lyrecaster, and they punched out in twisting streams, tentacles of corpse-fire spearing through bodies as though they weren't even there.

They didn't leave wounds behind them. But those poor unfortunate Anganesse who felt their touch had their souls stripped out from inside them. To me, it sounded like raw meat being ripped from the bone – but everyone else just heard the screams. That, and Ulkar's warcry.

Ardach na'thelem ur malachnai! Asral ghul sulan, Anganii?

Or, to put it in the common tongue -

"Mercy is burned and buried! Which one of you Angan corpse-

rapists dies first?"

Three thousand gaunt northern savages pelted across the gore-soaked mud, trampling the bones of the Touched. Gernish Maudrin threw down his ruined 'caster and went with them, drawing a pair of oversized *kuris* from beneath his furs.

Even I was up on my feet and howling as metal met lacquered wood and flesh with a sound like the cleaver of Anghul. Spears twisted and gored, lifting men off their feet, impaled. Axes shattered shields and plowed on through collarbones and ribs. Above it all rang the echoes of Makara's lyrecaster, setting up a blurring resonance in every shard of metal within earshot.

Conn stood back to back with her, shielding her from the one or two Angan crossbow bolts which flew stray. His bow hummed in concert with the lyre-strings, a deep bass thrum driving arrows through unprotected flesh a quarter-mile distant.

The Faceless Ones wavered, falling back in disarray. A shield wall can't hold without discipline, and those scaled phalanxes had split wide open. For a second I convinced myself that we were going to prevail, and that euphoria was enough to push the Dark Sight back.

But the Faceless Ones weren't stinking savages. They had the arrogance of an empire behind them, and the Thearch at their backs. A charge like that should have broken their will, but the Faceless were far more terrified of their masters than they were of a horde of Khytein refugees. They cut their losses with cold disdain, pulling back to allow the mob some killing space. As our ragged vanguard tore their comrades bone from sinew they reformed their ranks, shields spinning and locking with a series of sharp little clicks.

The Khytein advance was in utter disarray when they swept back. Easy victory had hung in front of the desperate refugees like a lure, and now they were blood-drunk, raving and scattered before an advancing wall of spears. Ulkar was bellowing and swinging his axe around his head in reaping arcs, but it was too late to rally. The jaws of Sinder's trap closed in, winking with watered-steel fangs.

Then the dying started in earnest.

"Now we run," said Conn, his voice leaden. "Ulkar's done for. There's nothing between us and those Faceless but butcher's work."

"What about Maudrin? He's still down there!"

"Makara... I don't think he's..."

Then came a sound like breaking stone.

"It's already too late," I said, smiling. "Sinder knows where I am.

All those warriors are dead where they stand..."

"He's slipping!" shouted Makara, wrapping her hands around my head. She pulled them back as if she'd been burned. "Conn, we have to get out of here!"

"Not while I can buy you some time!" he grated, putting another arrow through an Angan eye-slit. "GO! Unless you can make those corpses walk, Kuhal!"

Four rods of darkness slipped loose from Sinder's Keel. I could feel the weight of them pressing down on the world, like fingers pushed slowly into my brain.

"Those are *Excoriators*, Conn! When they start channeling power the imbalance is going to be *bad!*"

"Worse than this?" he asked, sending a black-feathered shaft home through a Faceless One's chest. "I find that hard to believe, Makara!"

"In the age of the Rholian Secession, Thearch Somar the Pious used the power of the Excoriators to sever a mountain. He then caused it to be cast upon the citadel of Ghen, crushing twenty thousand men within."

The voice came out of my mouth, but it wasn't my own. It was dry as coffin-dust, and it spoke with a kind of amused detachment, as though the horrors it recounted were unbearably droll.

"When the Ghuram thaumaturge Niyal Nine-fingers tried to bend one of us to his will, he and ten of his acolytes were turned to pillars of smoking ammonia."

"Can they do that? Really? And is he *right?*"

"Unfortunately so. The only one who can defeat those things is Maudrin, and even then only with a demon's luck..."

I clenched my fists as I fell to my knees, the voices of the Excoriators echoing in my mind.

"You might have some small chance to command us, child. In a few more decades. If you could lens the focus through your own soul, perhaps..."

"Oh, don't give him false hope, Degree Nine-Seven Spinwise. He's only going to be with us a few more minutes."

"Shame. Shame. Sinder never lets us play with our food."

They came down as rods of jade fire, spearing deep into the bloodied earth. Eyeless skulls grinned as they heaved themselves upright, drinking in the screams of their prey.

I saw Ulkar raging, charging at the nearest Excoriator with his axe held high... and then came a lightning-flash of green, the world drained away to monochrome as it bent around a bolt of searing power. The poor old fool was stripped away to black bones in mid-swing, his axe spattering the warriors behind him as a spray of molten steel. Power clawed and raved, ripping, burning...

The Nekrologist's engines were indiscriminate. With every lick of green fire a dozen Khytein fell... and as many of the Faceless with them.

Makara was right about the feedback.

I could feel it in the roots of my teeth, a throbbing ache which pulsed to the same rhythm as the Khytein's man-skin drums. The dead were out there, breaking the umbilical bonds to their broken flesh, rising in a cloud like smoke above the battlefield. Just minutes ago the choking horror of the hanged men had driven me into myself. But this time there was a terrible clarity to the Dark Sight as it wrapped itself around me. In that glassy, slow world the Excoriators blazed like torches, flaying the souls from a dozen men at a time. They warped and lensed reality itself, dragging whorls and bubbles in their wake. But it was the dead who called to me. Angan and Khytein alike, shades like constellations of burning motes...

They were of one voice. And it was screaming out for vengeance.

Chroniclers of history like Nyvar Xeng would say that something in me snapped at that moment. That *this* was the tipping point, the instant when a poor confused child was overwhelmed by darkness. Some of their sympathy is real enough, I suppose... but most of it is born of fear.

And all of those wise old fools are wrong. I heard that hell-chorus, and I *embraced* it. I'd lost so much, and been pushed so far that winter... I'd seen every certainty of my childhood broken like matchwood. More than that, I was sick of being treated like a delicate little artifact, an oddity for sorcerers to bicker over. Even my so-called friends were only bodyguards... it was all too obvious that Makara's concern for me came from Gernish Maudrin's command - and nothing else.

So I shattered the glass. I let them in. I told them to *rise*.

I felt a skein of living threads writhe out from my mind, coursing down my arms and rippling through the air. They were invisible to the screaming, cursing warriors down in the killing ground, intent on the urgency of meat and metal. But I cast my will out over them like a fisherman casting his net upon the waters, letting the hungry tips of those threads burrow into butchered flesh, licking and caressing nerves and muscles, binding up bones...

I stood, power-drunk on the edge of the parapet. A trickle of blood leaked from my nose as I brought my hands up, smiling.

And they walked.

Bone and sinew sheared bloody, marrow kissing the winter air, sightless eyes burst and dripping... they heaved themselves up with arrows punched through their chests, with sword-wounds cleaving them near in two. Some were headless, fumbling with hands like claws. Some were split in half, just skin and slithering organs below the waist. But they heard me. My howl of outrage shook the Excoriators themselves to their cores, snuffing out their fires like candlewicks.

Now the screams from the battleground took on a new urgency. Hands scrabbled and gouged, teeth bit down on hot flesh... and by the Gods, I felt it all.

Feedback blew me backward from the parapet, reeling. There was blood weeping from my nose, my ears, from around my eyes – blood metallic and warm on my tongue. The sensation blurred into the ecstasy of a hundred cannibal ghouls, while their pain scalded me, hot wire and claws under my skin.

But it was *laughter* which bubbled up from inside of me. Pure, blind hysteria.

I saw Makara, far away and fading. I saw Conn put an arrow to his bowstring and aim it right between my eyes. Down through a tunnel of black heat and blood I saw Gernish Maudrin fall to his knees, a single golden lyrecaster string wrapped so tight around his fists that it left gashes down to the bone.

As he pulled it taut the Excoriators exploded.

That took me down harder than any arrow could. Sorcery sits behind the world, like the canvas behind a painting, and when those abominations died they didn't just warp and twist the weave of it – they tore right through.

There are *things* on the other side.

There aren't words for them. Even I don't know whether they are many or one... a melange of memories and anguish churning in the utter cold out there.

But they are always hungry. I felt the threads which linked me to the dead pull taut and snap one by one, souls fraying and ripping as they plunged into the rift. Each one felt like a needle of ice driven through my skull.

I barely had the presence of mind to clutch Sei to my chest as I fell, digging my fingers in tight to stop his little soul from being ripped away...

The world can't take such punishment. The Gods, as Aerik would have said, are jealous of their flawed creation. The rifts were already changing as I hit the ground, filling up with the orange glow of sunset. Some force had bent them around to a place less dangerous than the outer dark, and now there were four mirror-shard slivers of ocean hanging above the battlefield. Salt water poured from them in foaming torrents, lapping at the edges of the shantytown.

"How fortuitous. These Khytein rats will be drowned instead of incinerated. Far less distasteful!"

I opened my eyes to see a pair of white leather boots, brushed by the hem of a long white robe. Little thread-of-gold runes glittered along its edge.

"This is the one who's caused us so much trouble. I don't expect he'll prove much sport for the inquisitors, but still... we *must* know what makes him tick. Take the others to the holding cells."

A face blurred into my field of vision – upside down and indistinct. A man's face, but sharp and pale as that of a porcelain doll, with little lines of black makeup curling from the corners of his eyes. His lips were a tight thin gash, pulled taut into a smile.

"Kuhal da'Hurik Moer. I see it pleases you to play with people like toys, child. In *that*, at least, we have something in common. So sad we won't really get the chance to know each other..."

Sei arched his back and hissed as one of the man's thin white hands reached out toward me, his fingers winking with black onyx rings. I tried to move, but once again I was helpless, just like on Oathbreaker's Night. There was nothing I could do as Faceless soldiers took Conn and Makara, wooden clubs rising and falling in a haze of blood. A single drop fell on my captor's face, and it left a crimson tear-track as he leaned in closer to me, filling the air with the scent of rosewater.

She held out her hand to me before the final blow fell. And there was a pleading in her huge, dark eyes which had nothing to do with the hell unleashed all around us. It was a hell far more personal.

"Oh, what I'll do with your power! Even the Thearch himself won't be able to stop me! I'll..."

He never got to finish.

At that moment a shield came whickering in at head-height, a blur of lacquered wood connecting with a Faceless soldier's teeth with a sound like an axe biting into a stump. I noted with glazed detachment that the top of his head was held on by nothing but a twist of muscle as he fell. Then a black figure landed among the Angan warriors, sliding across the roof of the building with a *kuris* in either hand. Sheer momentum drove their edges through bellies and throats as he came to a halt, down on one knee.

Across his back was the twin necked lyrecaster of Aerik Stormsong.

"Jerrold Sinder, as I live and breathe. I would never have figured you for a child-molester."

The man in white hissed as he recoiled from me, his hands a blur. They came back out of the wide sleeves of his robe holding a long-handled knife, its short serrated blade only half the length of its hilt.

"As you live and breathe, Gernish Maudrin? You'll be doing neither for very much longer, I assure you."

Maudrin only grunted, saving his breath. Because he wasn't looking nearly as wild and powerful as he used to... slaying the Excoriators had cost him dearly. His pair of *kuris* swords hung heavy in his bloodied hands, and his brow was already beaded with sweat.

But he was as much of a glorious old fool as Ulkar himself. And while he still stood...

"Kill him!" spat Sinder, ordering his men forward. For the six who Gernish had killed their were a dozen more waiting.

Blades sang and chimed. Chained witchfire sparked through scale-armor and flesh, lighting up the Faceless from within. And Jerrold Sinder brought the handle of his knife up to his lips, smiling that tight little smile.

A note rang out above Gernish Maudrin's curses and the Angans' screams. I felt the dark, slippery power of it as it licked down my spine, little hooks blurring through the air...

But even louder came the crack of breaking bone.

Gernish Maudrin fell to one knee as his femur shattered, impacted like brittle glass. It wasn't enough to stop him. The old warbard heaved himself up with a sheer effort of will, butchering through another warrior's chest with a mighty sword-stroke.

Another note rang out, this one high and piercing. Bones shattered in Maudrin's left hand, twisting it up into a ball of blood and pain. A leaf-bladed *kuris* clattered to the ground, but he still forced himself onward, his dark eyes fixated on Sinder's face.

"You're not getting away this time, you corpse-worm! I'm going to..."

Another note. Another tinder-wood crack. Another spasm of pain creasing up Gernish Maudrin's face.

He was crawling now, his legs shattered and useless. Blood dripped from his mouth as he used his sword to drag himself over to me, all grim determination.

"You might as well say goodbye to him, old man. When you're dead, young Kuhal here is going to help me with my research. It's *sad* how so few of my assistants survive."

But 'goodbye' wasn't the word on the warbard's lips. Neither was it a final pithy curse. Instead, Gernish Maudrin heaved himself up on one elbow and rasped...

"Hold on tight."

I didn't have time to think. I just wrapped my hands in the coarse black bearskin of his cloak as he rolled over, injuries forgotten, and swung Aerik's lyrecaster out from his hip.

"But... you can't! He was your *enemy!*"

Gernish laughed, bubbling blood as Jerrold Sinder brought his knife up to guard.

"That was more of a *traditional* thing, Anganesse. *This* is what it means to be a true enemy of Gernish da'Ethbrok Maudrin!"

How his broken fingers formed the chord, I'll never know. Likely it was simple, bloody-minded will. But when his single flashing *kuris* sheared across the strings, the result was cataclysmic.

Sorcery is a balance. Gernish and I flew backwards as if we'd been fired from the bucket of a trebuchet, plucked from the roof of the building by an almighty blast of noise. The sunken valley scudded by below my heels as I hung on grimly to the warbard's furs, looking back to where we'd stood.

The blastwave flattened Sinder and his men. Conn and Makara too; Gernish Maudrin's suicidal plan hadn't spared them any thought. Timbers and bodies flew up and out in a tumbling cloud, pattering into the cold salt water.

And then...

Then we were through the rift, under the light of a setting sun, and the ocean came up to meet us. It seemed an inopportune time to complain that I'd never learned to swim...

"The Free Reavers of Faeros accomplish only three things with noteworthy skill. Sailing a ship, making love to a woman, and driving steel through a foeman's chest. Unfortunately, they oft strive to accomplish all three feats while stinking drunk, and more likely at the same time."

Archivist-Doctor Nyvar Xeng,
- Supreme Redactor of Saradrim

MOST CHILDREN IN this latter age learn about the world from scrolls and tutors – I hear that in Ghuram they have entire academies dedicated to educating the young, and turning them into useful merchants. The Kalif of that land knows where his taxes come from, and no mistake!

But I learned two very important geographic truths by being thrown through a rift in the sky, clinging to the stinking furs of Gernish Maudrin.

The first was that it can be twilight in one place while the sun shines in another. The second was that in the winter seas of the north there exist islands of floating ice.

It was the people of one such crystal-blue ice-spire who saved us... men from a tribe splintered off from the Khytein race back in dark antiquity. I remember little of our time with them, because an unnatural illness had taken me under, wracking me with fevers and chills. All I recall is their warbard – a hard-faced woman wrapped in sealskin and furs, with eyes like tiny buttons of jet. Her name meant 'Sings-to-the-Gods', and she spoke with Gernish Maudrin at my bedside in a strange language of whistles and clicks, all the while flicking sly glances in my direction which she didn't think I noticed. After all, I was trussed up like a mummified Faeroan king in scented bandages, seal fat, herbs and white bearskin.

We didn't share any words in common. Even the servants who tended me couldn't understand the simplest phrases in Khytein'an. But I knew as soon as I saw Sings-to-theGods' face one morning that Gernish Maudrin had died. For one, she carried his heavy black cloak over one arm... the one he'd never taken off in living memory. But it was the pity in her eyes which gave the truth away. She laid the bearskin across my feet and left without a word.

I grieved, down in my delirium. I saw the two faces of the Vhaurish warbard in my dreams, one stern and cold, one milky- eyed and cackling mad. Between them they must have driven the poison from my blood, because I lived.

Two weeks later I was able to leave my quarters. I was weak as a winterborn colt and twice as thin, but the nervous smiles and incomprehensible whistles of the ice-folk were welcome, accompanied as they were by steaming bowls of creamy seafood chowder. Wriggling things with tentacles and antennae slipped down into my belly without ever being identified or categorized, and even when I found out where the cream came from I still held out my carved seal-skull bowl for more.

The answer to *that* mystery came when I was well enough to stagger outside.

Because our ice-island was on the move.

The people of the utter north are nomads, and they follow the shoals of cold-water fish in an endless circle around the pole. The sealife there is bountiful – redfins, razortooth bass, flying swordbills and silverheads - all preyed upon by seals, dolphins, and the giant, hump-backed predators we southerners call *leviathenes*. Of course, the name for them among my hosts was an unpronounceable keening and clicking... one which translated as 'sacred givers of milk'.

From the broad back of the island I could see their braided tethers pulled tight against a hundred black iron rings. Each ring was set on a long, barbed shaft sunk deep into the ice, and knotted tight with salt-caked leather. These were no ordinary bonds – the leathery twists of braid were as thick as Ulkar's thumbs, and they were fashioned from some supple, rubbery hide I'd never seen anywhere else.

At least, until I looked to the other end of the tethers...

I heard a pair of the northmen laughing to each other behind my back as they took in my reaction, but I was too overcome to care. Ahead of me the dark swells of the ocean heaved with broad leathery backs, flukes churning and sliding through the salt foam. The leviathenes were each the size of a longhouse, dappled gray and black above and creamy white below. Their sledgehammer heads bulled through the waves as their flukes worked tirelessly, driven by the motion of their flat, paddle-like tails.

"They're not fish, you know. They're more like a seal or a dolphin.

These people say they were the first beasts, before time was set in motion, and that *we* come from *them*."

The sight of a hundred leviathenes straining at their traces almost numbed me to the shock of hearing a Khytein voice. But not quite. My hand was on the little knife tucked into my belt as I turned to find a tall, powerfully-built man standing behind me, squinting down at the churning sea with a pair of bright purple eyes.

"My apologies, Kuhal. It's just the sight of all those monsters in one place... well, it makes an old sailor a touch uneasy. Breathtaking though, isn't it? They raise them from pups on the ice, train them, tether them by hand..."

"And just who *are* you? Are you going to tell me that Jerrold Sinder sent you?"

The man laughed at that, revealing a mouthful of gold teeth.

"In a way I suppose he did. It's what he's done which set my feet upon the path. But if Governor Sinder ever presumed to give me *orders*, he'd be wearing his own arse for a hat."

Well, I'd seen what suffering the corpse-white Angan lord could wreak. But the stranger's bravado made me smile, for the first time in many long weeks.

"I don't suppose you have name, do you? It's just that slicing the arse off an Angan nekrologist would make a worthy saga-song..."

My visitor doffed his broad-brimmed hat and bowed, in parody of an Anganesse courtier.

"Elion Morekh, a Free Faeroan and lately lord commander of the Sea Reavers. Most assuredly at your service... for a fee!"

That turned my smile into a laugh.

"My Lord Admiral, you're definitely talking to the wrong Khytein refugee. All I own is a great stinking bearskin and the clothes I'm standing up in."

Elion Morekh's face became hard and serious so suddenly it was as if a shadow had flickered across the sun.

"I never said that the fee would be *gold*, Kuhal da'Hurik Moer. Tell me – did you have any love for the Night Walker? The one you called Gernish Maudrin?"

I nodded dumbly, but the tiny tears at the corners of my eyes betrayed me.

"And does it sit now like an anchor in your chest? Would you forge that cold dead weight into an edge?"

For some reason, the Faeroan's words cut right through me.

Perhaps it was the first time I'd really accepted the old Warbard's death… and what it meant. Gernish Maudrin had died to protect me, and to bring me here…

Elion Morekh's hand fell on my shoulder as I turned away, watching the leviathenes churning and straining at their traces.

"Do you offer me *revenge*, then? Is that why you're here? Do you know what I am?"

"Gernish told us. Aerik Stormsong told us. There are more abroad in the world who hate the Thearch than you know, son. They told me to sail north more than a year ago, and I charted my course without question."

A year ago! Before Oathbreaker's Night – before the battle, and Makara, and the terrible power seething like molten metal in my bones…

I heard Ulan Veth's voice in my head. *"Did you predict your own death as well, you old charlatan?"*

The look on my face as I turned back was all the agreement Elion Morekh needed. Gold flashed in the sun as he grinned.

"Revenge is not a gift among my people, Kuhal. I offer you nothing for free. You'll pay your passage back to Khytein with Jerrold Sinder's suffering."

I spit on my palm like the savage I was, and after a second of indecision the Faeroan did likewise, clasping my hand tight in his great callused paw.

"Then the first thing I'll need to do is go and collect my friends," I said. "Consider it an *investment*."

From Stormwood deeps and midnight heath
The Wildkin come with sharpened teeth
To rip and rend the flesh of men
At dark of moon they walk again
Claws of thorn and skin of oak
Choking darkness, once awoke
The Wildkin hunt 'till break of day
Then gnaw the bones of tender prey

A traditional Khytein children's rhyme, explaining perhaps some of the more interesting neuroses of this savage race...

WE CAME ASHORE on a hissing wash of spray, our little longboat carving through the dark water like a dagger through silk. Elion Morekh's pirates (for there is no other word for such men – stubbled, salt-caked, bawdy killers that they were) handled their oars with the skill of long experience, and after we disembarked they dragged the black-hulled boat high up on the strand, covering it with dunegrass and seaweed.

Their stealth was more out of habit than necessity – we had landed at the head of a long, forked fjord, leaving Elion's ship anchored beneath a sheer wall of dripping stone. Tiny bats circled the masts of the *Shadow of Blades*, dipping and weaving amongst the rigging from their nests in the hollow cliffside.

I stole a look back at the man o' war as Elion lit a small lantern and swung it overhead. A spark of red light answered us from the decks of the lean, outriggered vessel – confirmation that we were safely back on the Great Dry. I would have kissed the ground at my feet if a dozen pirates hadn't been watching me.

Despite the fearsome competency of the Faeroan crew, and the scimitar lines of the *Shadow of Blades* I had spent the last week hung over the rail, spattering my rations down the side as a film of vomit.

"It'll pass, Khytein," said the Admiral, slapping me a shade too heartily across the back. "We're back in your land now, and my poor Reavers are as fond of forests as you are of the sea."

He smiled as he said it, but I saw the furtive looks and muttered prayers of the Faeroan sailors as they peered into the dark of the

Stormwood. These men were used to horizons blurred into the edge of the sky, not the choking old growth of the northern woods.

"We've cut as close as we can to the northernmost Anganesse outpost... here, one fjord to the west." Elion used a stick of driftwood to draw in the black sand, cutting a precise little 'x' and sketching in the twisting gullet of the fjord. "Bring that lantern, Arn! Here... we know this bloody place too well, don't we lads? We've been living off plundered rations that the Angans meant for their soldiers..."

"And we're still not dead from them!" put in an anonymous wit at the back of the pirate band. Elion Morekh chuckled, flicking his driftwood stylus across the sand to hash out a range of low hills between us and the Angan port.

"They have one of their accursed 'Processing Camps' here, just upriver from the sea. Our best way in is to waylay one of the barges which carries supplies in to them - and bodies out."

I couldn't help but think of Makara then. It must have shown on my face, but only Elion caught it. The other Reavers made the sign of the Triad, or spat, or muttered angry curses under their breaths.

"Was it the same in your nation? Did they try to..."

"To what? To *civilize* us? Oh yes. But things were different for us. They sunk our floating islands, and chained us to the land. They killed our priests, and our teachers, and as for the might of Faeros, the Free Captains, well..."

A man kneeling in the sand leaned forward into the light - a tall Faeroan with a crescent-moon scar across his cheek. One of his eyes was a milky white moonstone cabochon.

"We was to send our own ships down, they said. That, or pay the forfeit." He brought his hand into the pool of lantern light, and I saw that it was not a hand at all, but a gleaming metal hook. Hours of careful sharpening and etching had turned it into a beautiful, razored weapon. "One hand, one foot, and one eye I paid. They called it the Thearch's Due."

"Here they just work the men to death and rape the women," said Elion Morekh. "Sinder must build 'civilization' from the foundations up." More angry muttering followed, and I heard the sound of blades whispering out of scabbards in the dark. "So what say you, lads? Do we have the cure for the Thearch's spreading plague?"

"Faeroan Steel! And Angan blood!" came the reply, spoken with vehement hatred. Elion Morekh held his lantern high and looked to me, with a mis-matched constellation of glittering pirate eyes behind him.

"Then lead on, Kuhal Moer. We have an infection to expunge, and none will expect an attack by the Free Reavers *overland!*"

I smiled, happy to indulge in his little piece of theatre. These men needed to hate the enemy more than they feared the twisted gnarl of the Stormwood.

I set off before anyone had time to voice their trepidation, and not one of them would dare be seen as a coward. Elion Morekh caught up to me with his long stride, tucking his wide-brimmed hat under one arm and clutching his lantern tight. Crazed shadows lurched and spun as he ducked under branches and loops of thorn.

"Are you sure you really know where we're going? I'm no Khytein, but I *am* a navigator..."

"All we need to do is head uphill to the west. Then we march until we strike the river, wait for a barge, and..."

"And?"

"And put out that damned lantern! There are those in the Stormwood who get *hungry* when they see a light like that..."

"I'm sure they'll reconsider robbing us when they see our numbers!"

"I never said that all of them were human!"

That made him blow out the lantern wick with more than a little haste, and we crept on through the darkness – though creeping should ideally be undertaken with far less stumbling and cursing. It wasn't long before clouds slid across the face of the moon, and a half-hearted rain turned our march into a sodden ordeal.

Up steep ravines and through gullies choked with rotting pine needles we went, slithering and crawling along the beds of icy streams when the path grew impossible to follow. And just as I had given up hope in my own skills as a forester (having been roughly as skilled at this fine old Khytein profession as I was at being a saga-song hero), I scrambled over the top of a ridge and saw a light on the horizon.

Off over a tar-black expanse of dripping treetops I could see the grey rush of the river, and on its banks stood a jumble of hard-edged darker shadows – buildings raised up by the Angan invaders. From behind the low walls and spiked pallisades of the camp came the glow of sullen banked-up fires, reddening the belly of the clouds. Two tall metal chimneystacks reared up beyond the fireglow, secured by guywires and still sighing a thick and heavy smoke.

"En evil place," growled Elion Morek, pulling me down into

the mud. His proud Faeroan garb as filthy, covered with moss and rotten leaves, but he carefully put on his wide-brimmed hat before he motioned his men forward. "They chained together ruined hulks in Faeros to make their prisons. When we sank them, those who still retained their wits gave thanks for a good clean drowning."

The thought of all those pale hands in chains groping against rotten wood sent a chill down my spine. It was even worse than the tricking raindrops which preceded it.

"We had better hope for all our sakes that there are still people alive in there. We need allies to help take the walls…"

"And Angan scum to torture afterward," finished Morekh, a grim look in his eyes.

"I don't think the guards here will know much of Sinder's will. Questioning them won't do us much good."

"Who said anything about *questioning* them?" chuckled the hook-handed reaver who'd paid the Thearch's Due. "All I want's is some raw fresh meat to…"

The first arrow went clean through the leather boss of his hook, pinning him to the trunk of a scrub pine. The second plucked the hat from Elion Morekh's head.

"Ware! Foes! All hands to battle stations!"

In the dripping dark the slither and rasp of steel rang out, as Morekh's free reavers unshipped their blades. Behind me, the hook-handed would-be torturer was grunting and cursing, trying to work himself loose.

Then there came a hissing sound from among the knot of wild-eyed seafarers, followed by a flurry of sparks whipped downhill by the wind. I barely had time to shut my eyes before a thunderous report went up, and through my fingers I caught a flash of dazzling red light. For an instant the image of my knucklebones was burnt across my vision, and then came the screams.

I stumbled to the ground as Elion Morekh spun past me, a saber in each hand. Above the hilltop a low-hanging star burned bloody red – one of the alchemical flares which the men of Faeros used to warn of shipwrecks. By it's light I could see who was doing the screaming… or more accurately, *what*.

My people have a wealth of nice little bedtime stories about the Stormwood and its denizens. It's safe to say that nine out of ten of them are just designed to scare the piss out of unruly children, of which the average Khytein village has a constant excess. But some of the others…

well, some of the others were whispered about by the warriors of the shield-wall only after a night of strong drink and reminiscence, when the fires burned low and men muttered about gnawed bones and bloodied scraps of skin nailed to the trees.

The creatures which ringed us about were entirely black, glistening oily in the red light of the flare as it swung overhead. Their eyes were startlingly white, and their limbs bristled with jagged growths, spikes and crooked twigs still bearing thorns. Each one was armed with a short bow of horn, blackened by charcoal. Each one had an arrow nocked, and that thicket of obsidian points surrounded Elion's men like a wall of teeth.

Some hissed. Some spat. Some gave vent to terrible keening screams, like nothing human.

"What hell is this we've stumbled into, Khytein? I thought you said you knew this forest!"

"I also said there were things watching, Captain! This is the Stormwood, not some whorehouse pleasure-garden!"

"*Khytein*? Which son of the North stands amongst you?"

The voice came from overhead, high up in the trees. An odd number of piratical eyes scanned the pine boughs in a panic, until a chuckle of oily laughter followed.

"You do realize that if you run, you're all dead," said the voice, this time from a completely different direction. "My little lads have poisoned teeth, you know..."

"Made from the Greybark, and the Bard's Bane, and the Winter's Shade?" I asked. I'd worked out who these creatures were as soon as I heard a human voice. I pulled myself to my feet as I slopped a double handful of mud and pine needles from the front of my tunic. "This is no time for games, whoever you are. Your villages have burned while you've been out here playing Feral. *Khytein'u ad Moer sulan!*"

There was no rustle in the branches, but two light footfalls accompanied a shadow which unfolded in front of the ring of savages. It was taller again by half, slim and black and spiked like its thralls, and it was self-assuredly their master. In its hand it carried the unmistakable double-curved shape of a bowblade, it's edges rubbed with charcoal ash.

"We know it too well, Kuhal da'Hurik Moer. That's why we were going to quietly butcher a few of those Anganesse and satiate the shades of our fathers. But then you and your friends had to come staggering into our lines and *ruin everything!*"

The dark figure stepped forward and reached up to its cheek, unhooking a hidden clasp. I saw its face fall away, a wooden mask carved in the grimace of a demon... and I beheld Conn, his eyes ringed around with circles of ash, and a crown of leaves and thorns woven into his hair.

"You're lucky I can swim, Warlock. Gernish Maudrin seemed to want you alive more than the rest of us. Where is the old bear, anyway?"

The look in my eyes must have said it all. Conn's smile turned into a bitter, bloodless line as he fastened the mask back across his face.

"I hope he has found his peace, then, for all he and Aerik have set in motion. And you – you might still help us. It looks like we'll be needing your friends' assistance after all."

"You *know* this creature? Gernish said you were a caller of the dead, but this?"

Elion Morekh was not a man easily put in fear. But there was no way for him to know that these spiked and oily demons were in fact just the Feral Children of the Khytein – orphans and the rape-get of warriors who lived wild in the Stormwood. Conn had found them, and made them his army of vengeance.

"*Creature?* At least I don't go to battle looking like a perfumed man-whore!"

"At least I don't wear twigs and rags, hellspawn! And on that account, you also owe me one new hat!"

I'm certain they would have argued nose-to nose and snarling all night if it hadn't been for the horns down in the valley. Their low and mournful bellow rang out from the processing camp as fires were kindled along its walls, and voices shouted warning in the Angan tongue.

"I think they've seen your pretty fireworks, Elion," I said, looking up at the slowly falling flare-star. "So much for the element of surprise."

The feral children and the pirates dropped prone as the gates of the camp creaked open, rough-hewn logs carving ruts in the mud. White-armored Southmen with hounds on leather traces cursed as they stormed through the breach, brands burning and long tridents winking in the firelight.

"Slavehunters. They think this is some kind of escape."

"I know them. Bastards love nothing more than to decorate those pig-stickers with little children's corpses."

Well, there was at least one thing Conn and Elion could agree on.

They gave each other a grim and knowing look over the top of my head, and nodded.

"So we fuck them then?"

"With steel, Captain. And hard."

Just then a second echoing blast reverberated from the hills, coming from around a bend in the river. I turned to see the black bulk of a barge nosing between the mossy boulders down in the ravine, flaming braziers lighting up the cross-wheel banners of the Thearch at its bow. At that moment the flare above us guttered and died, and I noticed a rind of pearl-grey light above the eastern hills. Dawn would be upon us soon.

"Do you really think we should do this *now*?" I asked. "At the risk of sounding like a coward, we'll be out in the open when the sun rises, and they outnumber us twenty to one. Not counting the men on those barges..."

Conn's eyes were slits of white at the bottom of two pits of shadow. His fingers dug into the meat of my shoulder like claws... what little of it there was left after months of frantic flight.

"They have Makara, Kuhal. We weren't here without reason. I...I thought you knew."

Despair, in the Dark Sight, is just as plain as the gray pallor of death on the face of the plague-struck. It twisted in him like thorns around his heart, a love turned to suffering. And damn me, I *envied* him. Because that kind of pain, and the reckless hate it had given him, can never grow without love before it. To my eldritch eyes he was already half the demon he played at being.

"With steel, then. But not like glorious, saga-drunk fools. Elion? Do you think your reavers can take a pack of Angan river- scum? " My voice was pitched low, sawing at the minds of the listeners in imitation of poor dead Aerik. Despite alone made it work.

"Does a eunuch have to piss sitting down? We'll gut them like fish before they can cry for their mothers."

"Conn? Can these wildkin of yours draw the Angans away from the camp and into the forest? Can you make sure they don't come back?"

"I'll make them part of a horror tale, Kuhal. There's darkness in the Stormwood, even in the light of day."

"Then listen to me closely. Because as soon as the sun crests those mountains, I'm going to walk into that camp and get Makara. If you haven't done your jobs, not one of us is going to live past breakfast."

There must have been something in the Cold Voice I used which made them believe me. Hells, there must have been something in there that helped me convince *myself*. That, and the stories of Oathbreaker's Night were enough to make a band of hardened warriors listen to a man-child not yet old enough to own a razor.

"You're just going to walk in the front gate? What are you going to do after that?"

I smiled, and I felt the pinprick of claws up my back as Sei slithered loose from his pouch to smile with me. Elion Morekh told me afterward that the chill little sparks in the dead cat's eyes were reflected tenfold in my own.

"I'm going to ask them very, *very* nicely to die. Any questions?"

There were none.

And that, dear friend, is how I came to find myself slogging knee deep through a mire of churned mud and shit, between the gates of the Angan Thearch's northernmost outpost. I'd watched Conn and his wild children melt back into the Stormwood's shadows and thorns, and heard their hunting horns luring the southmen on into the green-dappled gloom. I'd seen Elion Morekh and his men go swarming down the darkened cliffs ahead of the morning light, happy to have a ship to fight for, even if it was only a flat-bottomed river barge.

There were none left on the bowman's walk to challenge me. Slipping between the gates I took stock of the dismal little hell between those four rough-hewn walls... a sucking flat welter of clay and manure with long, low barracks-houses raised up out of it on stilts. The stench of sulphur, dysentery and hot metal hung like a fog about the camp. Smoke came trickling slow and heavy from a pair of great iron chimneys which topped the only stone building, slung out along a rickety pier by the riverside.

Then I saw the slaves.

My countrymen weren't in chains – that would have been far too costly in precious iron. Instead they were gathered together in a great gaping pit, ringed around by Angan soldiers too lazy, high-ranking or cowardly to go chasing Conn through the Stormwood. About two hundred in all – sharing flatbread and salt beef as they leaned on their long spears. These were not the Faceless... not by a long way. But they were a force sufficient to keep ten times their number of dirty, emaciated Khytein captives from scaling the slippery walls of the hole. During the night a sailcloth cover had been pulled over the great square pit, but now it was drawn back on wrist-thick ropes, all the better for the slaves to receive their morning lesson. I ducked down and crawled beneath a row of hovels, drawing closer. Now I could see what the Angans were staring at – and what their captives were being taught.

It wasn't easy for me to concentrate on the grossly fat Angan priest who trod the boards before the pit. His backdrop was a row of rotting bodies strung up on a long gallows tree, and behind him yawned an open grave. Little sparks crawled up my spine, and Sei arched his back, kneading my shoulder with his claws. I caught a moment's fevered vision of a white-laquered shield-wall pushing forward, of bodies twisting and tumbling down into a pit lined with sharpened stakes...

Those had been the unrepentant. The rest had foresaken their Gods to save themselves, and were branded with the wheel-and-cross of the Thearch.

"Your kinsmen doom themselves. You know now the power of Esau, the light of Anganesse. Has he not crushed your demon-Gods beneath the might of his will?"

The fat priest was red in the face. Thugs with rawhide whips paced the lip of the pit beside him, their eyes slitted.

"And we know why they come, don't we? We have prayed that the witch would break. We have prayed that Esau in his mercy would show her the light of his truth. But she is still defiant. And now these pitiful northerners who come to save you all will learn their folly." His florid face was split by a grin like a dripping wound. Hard black eyes glittered in the rising sun. "There are no Khytein here. Just obedient sons and daughters of the Thearch. And together *we will burn the heretic!*"

A sack-cloth curtain fell away. Runes daubed on it had clouded the Dark Sight. Behind it was Makara, bloodied, unconscious - and crucified.

The guards cheered first. The whips licked out, raining down suffering on those in the pit. Their adulation was a chorus of groans and screams.

You may have noted that I was a bit out of my depth here. Why I did what I did that day I can only guess at, now that I've turned the memory over in my mind for centuries. It's like a stone worn smooth by running water, and it has none of its original sharp-edged urgency. To call it love would be a saga-song lie, and all too trite. To call it infatuation would be closer, although it was not just with Makara – a girl who I barely knew.

I was in love with an image of myself that was worthy of her attention. I was infatuated with a future Kuhal da'Hurik Moer who could make her forget Conn and Gernish Maudrin. I'd played at being that person for a while – all the way from Oathbreaker's night to this prison-hovel up on he line of the tundra.

So, damn me, I stood up. An impressive five foot eleven in mud-stained sealskin and leather, a hank of red hair standing out against the black like an exclamation point, and a dead cat hissing and spitting on my shoulder.

"You'll grovel in shit and beg her for mercy," I said, the Cold Voice catching in my throat. Anger boiled through me as the piglike Angan shrieked and pointed.

"Guards! It's him! The witch child! *He must be taken!*"

"Do it *now*, fat man, and I'll only take your tongue and your fingers. You others drop your weapons and I'll let you live."

They couldn't see the witchfire rising in wisps and threads from the open grave behind them. All they saw was a ragged boy, unarmed, facing down two hundred hardened murderers.

"He'll let us *live!* Oh, merciful Esau! And when we've got him bent over a barrel that's not all he'll give us!"

The ringleader was a bandy-legged spearman with one eye and a mouthful of blackened teeth. He made them laugh – and that's the last thing he ever did.

Rage helped me find a dead man's memory, torn bloody from the massacre at the refugee camp. A hanged man, his neck broken, tottering forward until Ulkar's war-axe sheared him in two.

I slammed it into the leering Angan's mind like a stake hammered into soft earth. He felt each tendon sever, every inch of his flesh unspliced by the axe's razor edge. Ulkar – a drunk old bastard, but a fiend with a whetstone.

The Angan dropped to his knees, pallid gray. He dropped to his face in the mud, blood leaking from his open mouth.

The priest squealed like the swine he resembled. Fingers were scrabbling at the damp clay of the pit wall. Whips popped and cracked. Swords were unsheathed. Fingers of bone and rotten meat scrabbled at the walls of the open grave...

"Guards! Seize him!"

That shriek galvanized them. But before they could clear the gap between us, the low stone building by the pier flickered with fire.

I heard guywires snap, and saw the foot-thick metal ring which had held them down smash the gallows to matchwood. A sheared hawser sliced through a dozen Angan soliders, biting them off at the waist. The smell of bonepowder filled the air, pungent and sickly sweet, and then came the crack of an explosion. Blocks of granite the size of wagons went skyward, tumbling slowly end over end against a backdrop of fire.

They came down at the same time as the chimneys.

One of the great iron stacks crushed the pallisade wall, toppling guard towers as it fell. Chunks of stone gouged craters out of the mud as they smashed the barracks to kindling – one fell into the pit with my countrymen, pulverizing a score of them in a heartbeat.

The throb of death-energies behind reality numbed me. The hairs on the back of my arms were standing straight up, green sparks on every tip.

The second chimney came down sideways, and it rolled. Hawsers thrashed and threshed. Splinters of wood pierced eyes and guts like arrows. Some unlucky few were driven under – flattened by its bulk. It came to rest straddling the pit, framing the Angan priest down its long black barrel.

I didn't move an inch. I didn't even twitch. I hear that in the legends it was because I was unafraid of the carnage all around me. In truth, it was because Makara had woken up.

Black iron nails were hammered through her wrists and ankles. I felt the outline of that pain, and it was enough to feed the fires in my chest and in my belly – the growing storm-surge of the damned. Makara raised her head and smiled through split and broken lips. Her eyes were all but swollen shut, but they still flashed fire from behind a straggle of bloodied hair.

"Make them *suffer*, son of Anghul. Avenge us."

I thought for an instant that she meant our people. But there was something else there, behind the flesh and blood which made up the young Warbard. Something heavy pressed up against the weave of the world through her – something utterly wrong.

She sensed that I saw it, and the veils wrapped tight around her mind again. Then she fed me all the pain they'd given her, and I passed it on.

"Raiders! Rebels! Light the beacons!"

For all his bulk the Angan priest moved quickly, scuttling away from Makara as she fixed him with a ghoulish grin. This one was much younger than Ulan Veth, and his zeal burned much more brightly. I could see the slippery gray filaments of his sorcery writhing out from his pores, slithering down his arms and into his cupped hands.

"Your people will perish, witch! But I'll see you burn for me first!"

A globe of pale green flame filled his hands, and I could smell burning hair and incense. Makara spat in his face.

And what I had hoped for all along unfolded inside my mind. A black gate cracked open inside me, just as it had done on Oathbreaker's night. This time I knew how it would feel. I brought it on, forcing the crack wide, and the darkness over the threshold reached out hands to welcome me.

The Sight was everything. I saw the dead in all their contortions and dismemberments – the crushed, the burned, the ones cut down by Elion Morekh and his murderous crew. It was their cannonade of bonepowder guns which had begun the slaughter. I caught glimpses of hell in the Stormwood – of a man kicking and choking a foot off the ground, a waxed cord lashed tight around his throat. Conn's bowblade opened his throat and tension did the rest, ripping his head from his body with a pop of separating vertebrae.

I saw the Angan priest reach out his hand toward Makara. Liquid gray power bled into the world through him, from a source of grief and agony too powerful to contemplate.

But at his back... ahh, yes. The Slaughterborn.

Tendrils of witchfire plunged down into the open grave behind Makara, a rain of incandescent threads streaming from my hands. There were no individual voices in that pit of misery and loss. There was just a bellow of wrath, cut through with weeping.

I tweaked it. I *used* it. I made promises and caressed rain-slick bones with my mind. Blackened muscle and tendon meshed.

Before the Angan could spit flame from his hands a shapeless limb reared up behind him, twenty feet long and composed of interlocking corpses. It twisted, serpentine, sloughing off grey-green ribbons of dead skin, and its shadow pinned him.

"Oh Esau's cock, *what the hell is...*"

At the end of that lumpen thing was a splay-fingered claw – each digit was an arm or a leg. The palm was all mouths and teeth, babbling and gnashing as they came down hard. Boards creaked as the rest of the Slaughterborn knitted itself together, heaving itself up from the grave in a rain of necrotic filth.

From under its hand came muffled screams, and the sound of a hundred mouths chewing and ripping. A head unfolded from its shoulders – nothing but lidless eyes and doughy white flesh.

"*We hear you. Let us die.*"

Its voice was a hurricane wind, driving nails before it. It peeled the surface off my mind, but I held.

"*What do you want from us?* **Let us die!**"

I looked around me, and noticed that the battlefield had gone quiet. Angan soliders stared slack-jawed at the Slaughterborn towering over Makara on her crucifixion frame. Khytein who had escaped their prison pit fell to their knees. Ossuary batteries spilled burning bones. I forced myself to concentrate, and I saw the names of the dead... little sparks trapped in my fist.

"Slay the southmen. Level this place. Then you will be released."

Time came back, and sound with it. The tread of the Slaughterborn shook the muddy ground, and it picked up a baulk of framing timber like a club, battering a begging soldier to pulp.

Its bellow freed men from their stupor.

They scattered, Khytein slaves and terrified Angans both. Scything swings of that nail-studded log sent men skyward, up and over the pallisade... but I had my own agenda. I pelted down the hollow length of the fallen chimney and up the side of the execution platform, Sei skittering along before me. By the time I reached Makara he was already worrying at one of the crucifixion nails with his little teeth, growling to himself in frustration.

"Why in all hells can't we ever meet in better circumstances?" she said. "I suppose Conn has something to do with this foolishness as well?"

It was meant to sound like bravery. But she only just managed to stammer out the words, and she could barely keep her head up.

"Him, and an entire crew of Faeroan reavers. You didn't think we were going to leave you at the mercy of these bastards, did you?"

I unsheathed my dagger and began to pry at the nails, but it was obvious that this wasn't going to work.

"Firstly," she said "These Anganesse have no mercy. And secondly..."

I felt a pulse of power crackle through her bones, outlining the skeleton beneath her flesh for an instant. The wooden torture-frame began to creak and groan, and as I watched the nails unscrewed from out of Makara's wrists and ankles, clattering to the boards one by one.

I barely caught her as she fell, and I was shocked by how little she weighed. Almost like the dried-out husk of Aerik Stormsong in his death...

Sei nuzzled his polished skull up against her cheek. Behind her, the bloodied frame had sprouted shoots and tiny leaves.

"There! That's him! The little whoreson is trying to save his witch! Kill him!"

I smelled them before I turned. Sweat, shit, blood and rancid meat – beer and murder on their breath. The smartest of the Angan garrison had slipped around past where the Slaughterborn raged, tearing buildings to scrap, and now they huddled behind their leader, a shaven-headed Sejant with a long spear and a scar curling his lip into a humorless grin.

"Butcher him, and his beast goes back to the worms! Come on lads - we can take him!"

They came on in a rush, spearheads flashing in the watery sunlight, yellowed teeth gritted... and all I had was a dagger to oppose them. That and the Dark Sight was just enough.

I could see the bones of the Sejant under his slick-slithering muscles... the knot of an old wound healed wrong in his leg. So I planted my boot on the fracture point, feeling the razored edge of his spearblade slice a line across my cheek. Another spear tore through my jerkin, tugging at the leather and spinning me sideways, but the damage was done. Bone splintered, and my dagger flew underhand, predicting the Angan's fall. Years of having martial discipline beaten into me by the Scalptaker's men turned the edge just right, and it opened his throat even as he howled in anguish.

One was not nearly enough.

The third spear went in through my thigh and pinned me to the ground. I threw the blood-slick blade, but its pommel caromed off a rusted helm, white enamel cracked and peeling. Hard eyes flashed in the winter sun as the rest of those blades poised above me...

And the crack and boom of a bonepowder cannon swept them away. A hail of ruined armor, hot iron, bone fragments and gore painted the boards crimson, leaving nothing but smoking, meat-filled boots in front of me.

"Do you think, child, that you could tell your beast the difference between an Angan pigfucker and a noble son of Faeros? It's nearly finished with the slavetakers, and I have the horrible feeling that it *doesn't want to stop.*"

It was Elion, of course, and beside him stood the giant of his crew, a hulking brawler called Soap. The name was more than a little ironic, as Soap was not only the largest man I'd ever seen, but also the filthiest.

To give you some idea of his size, he was carrying an Angan cannon under one arm, holding its muzzle up with a length of chain.

"It's not an honorable way to fight, y'lordship," he rumbled, displaying a grin of scrimshandered ivory teeth. "But it gets the job done."

I stifled a scream as Elion pulled the spear from out of my flesh. It had pierced through to the other side, clean. Rough hands pressed a plug of moss and herbs into the wound.

"Time is of the essence, young Kuhal. It's already coming this way..."

And indeed it was. The Anganesse were broken or scattered, cowering in the mud or scrabbling their way up and over the ruined pallisade. Lesser clerics and nekrological menials were with them – rats flushed from their nests as the Slaughterborn wallowed and weltered through entire buildings, its thousands of mouths babbling and screaming.

"Have your names. Be free. Seek your peace."

The words blurred through the pain in my mind, and I saw Makara's eyelids flicker open as she heard them too.

In the Dark Sight the Slaughterborn blazed incandescent. A thousand twisting filaments of fire whipped out from its skin, threads and sparks streaking into the sky. It stopped in mid stride, the gnawed corpse of a black-robed nekrologist in one claw, a club streaked with blood and pulped organs in the other.

And then it fell apart. Momentum brought a tide of slick bones and rancid meat sluthering across the square to slop down into the slave-pit, carrying pieces of twisted-up armor and scraps of cloth with it

"He's coming," said Makara. "Sinder. He's been talking to me, all the time I was on the cross. He was *waiting*."

I could only stand with the help of Elion Morekh, but I'd felt the Slaughterborn unravel. I was sick with aftershock and pain.

"We were supposed to just let you die, then? Let that fat fucking priest have his way with you? Was *that* the plan?"

She smiled, and my anger ratcheted up another notch.

"Yes... that *was* the plan. You could see what that pious slug wanted, and it wasn't to save my soul. But he would have doomed them all. You know that this place is *for*, Kuhal? Do you?"

It wasn't really a question. Makara clawed herself to her feet, swaying, pushing away from Soap as he tried to help her. "They were making powder here. And ossuaries, too. That's why they needed so many Khytein to 'help' them. That's why they killed the ones who wouldn't accept the Thearch's brand.

I caught her memory of it, like a sheen of oil on the churning waters of her mind. Haggard slaves marching into that low stone building, masked in rags because of the poisonous smoke. And fewer coming out each day...

"*Raw materials*, Kuhal. The faithful are shriven of their sins in death. They serve. *Only the righteous may face blessed Esau without first being cleansed in the furnace of his light.*"

Flesh to ashes. Sacred bones bound with the seething energy of trapped souls...

"I could have broken them. I would have snapped that greasy bastard's neck between my thighs and used his power to shatter the ossuaries. I'd have turned this whole place into a crater of glass. But you..."

I slapped her. Hard, a backhand driven by despite and self-disgust. She didn't flinch – instead she returned the blow with a punch that rattled my teeth. I looked up, one hand to my split lip.

"I'm a bastard, and a son of bastards, and saga-fucked since birth. Me, and Elion here, and Conn, all thinking with the contents of our breeches, apparently. But you know what? I'm *good* at it. Being the predictable bloody warlock seems to be my calling in this shit-stained life!"

She laughed, cuffing a trickle of blood from her lips with the back of one hand. The crucifixion wounds at her wrists were already puckered closed into star-shaped scars.

"If you and my foolish brother want to do things the hard way, then you can. My life hasn't been my own since Gernish Maudrin..." But she stopped, fixing me with a sly and venomous smile. "Just sound your war-horns, kill the stragglers, and get me to the barge. Sinder's coming, and we're going to need an army."

Her brother? Shit! How could I...

Conn's spiked shadow filled the ruined gateway. He held a severed head in each hand. They were gagged with thorns.

From behind him came the sound of human-skin drums.

Then the ache, and the fear, and the smell of rotting flesh came up behind me and dropped me into the moment again. Far away, through the writhing clouds of the Dark Sight, I could feel the great stone bulk of an Angan war-Keel coming about, pale white hands crooked like claws against the rail.

"I know where I can get an army," I said. "but you're not going to like them very much..."

"It is man who raises the Gods' temples
and wields their sacrificial knives,
however - man, who is at heart a creature
of hierarchies, politics and scheming.
So it is that the tribes and nations of
the world each take their patron Gods,
granting primacy to the deity which holds
sway over their hearts. Sorcery is what
we call that love and fear reciprocated.
Power is what we call that love and fear
well managed."

Uros Kalthisides,
- High Priest of the Horned Eye in Ythe

WE FLED SOUTH, and every damned soul on board knew where we were going. I couldn't hide what I was anymore, and a strange reckless doom had taken hold of me, a kind of gleeful acceptance of my predestination.

I was marked – *outcast, warlock, witch-boy*. Get of a dead chieftain and unmistakably beholden to the shunned God in our crude little pantheon. In ordinary times they would have taken me out into the forest and dashed my brains out with the thighbone of an elk, carved with runes. The warbards would have taken certain parts of my anatomy as totems and fetishes to placate Anghul, the Antlered One... the faceless entity who sat across the campfire of the sun from our own feral God Ceirmakh. Our deity was a warrior youth - the wolf-child who was slaughtered each graves-eve in the dead of winter, and reborn to save our souls from freezing solid to our shadows.

Nonsense, of course. Except that I could raise the dead. Nonsense, until you could see the bloodied end of an elk's femur coming toward your face in a flat, unstoppable arc...

These weren't normal times.

Which meant that to the survivors I was a portent – powers walked the world, evidenced in my scrawny frame and old, old eyes. The fact that their starvation, enslavement, rape and harrowing were part of a war between invisible Gods somehow made it bearable. I wasn't yet monster enough to tell them otherwise.

Conn was even more of a talisman to the lost. They called him
the Wild King, winter's thane – a scrap of superstition which went
back almost as far as the dead place we were sailing toward.

Winter's king was crowned with thorns and wildflowers for a year,
back in the days when our ancestors raised stone circles and spiral
barrows. He played the part of Ceirmakh on graves-eve... including
the part when the man dressed as Anghul disembowelled him with a
ritual hook.

His wildkin were just children under their warpaint. But they were
children who had killed three times their number of Angan invaders,
and their eyes were as hard as frozen iron.

Elion Morekh was once again king of a creaking wooden hell,
though this time it wasn't caked in salt and fishguts. As the only
men who could navigate the great flat-bottomed barge, the Faeroans
unashamedly took charge of the Khytein survivors, and even
persuaded Makara and Conn's feral children to help them.

We were three hundred, give or take, and if we could have
forgotten where we were going or who was behind us, it would have
been almost a respite from the war.

As it was, they looked to me for leadership.

They would have been better to follow Makara, even though the
news of Gernish Maudrin's death had thrown her into a mood of grim
despair. In those days crushed up together on the barge she seemed
to almost disappear, becoming thin and transparent in the sun and
invisible in the shadows. Some nights I was sure I heard her crying
softly to herself, and I couldn't sleep, clenching my fists at my sides as
I raged at my own inability to help in even the most normal, human
fashion.

They looked to me for leadership, just because some accident of
creation had put a fracture in my soul.

And so I led them toward the last of my kind who had lived among
the Khytein... the reason they were tribal warriors, and not city-
builders and conquerors like the Anganesse or the legions of old Ythe.

Soon the hills on either side of the river smoothed flat, blurring
into a wide land of reeds and steppe grass. The Stormwood straggled
along on the left bank for a few more ragged miles, and then it, too,
descended into thorny tatters, giving way to to wide fields under a
gray sky. Black swallows looped and dipped among the broken teeth
of standing stones, and silence clamped down hard on the world,

muffling the creak and groan of the great barge's progress.

People started talking in whispers. Some of them shot me looks of betrayal and fear, as though it was a surprise where this river led. Did they think I was going to lead them somewhere else?

On the third day we reached the first of the barrows – a wall of earth bisected by the river and clothed in gray-green grass. Two black obelisks stood atop the rampart like a gateway, the left-hand sentinel stone heeled over crooked. In the Dark Sight they boiled with shadow flames... a fact which I assiduously kept to myself.

"Do you think he can help us?"

The last thing I had expected at that moment was her voice. Makara was next to me at the rail, and a little of the old steel and anger was back in her eyes. She'd become painfully thin, but she was arraigned for war in black leather armor and scale, her lyrecaster slung across her back on a loop of chain.

"I don't know. But I can feel his soultaken under the earth. They're only barely asleep now. And at the centre of the labyrinth... he's awake, and watching us."

"Then perhaps you'll have your army. Or perhaps we'll find out just why Sothara the Deathless was driven into this necropolis nine hundred years ago. You're the one who's going to have to convince him."

"Into the dungeons, alone, with torch and longsword like a hero?" I laughed. "And I suppose you're going to tell me you're not at all curious enough to follow me down?"

I caught the faintest outline of a smile before she turned away, looking back along the length of the barge. It was a floating shantytown of the wretched and the dispossessed.

"I'd rather face what's left of the old bastard than wait for Jerrold Sinder to catch up with us, Kuhal. And considering what Gernish Maudrin told me about your *importance*... I'm sure he'd have wanted me to go first."

I stared down into the churning water as she turned away, but stiffened as I felt her hand on my shoulder. I couldn't turn around.

"Do you ever wish, Kuhal, that we were born in some different time? Where you could just be you, instead of what you are?"

I heard the catch in her voice. I could feel my cheeks burning red.

"And what would *you* be?" I managed, hunching my shoulders against my own trepidation.

"I'd like to just be *me*. Instead of what..."

She must have realized she had said too much. Her hand darted away, as if my skin was hot iron.

I took a long second, screwing up my courage, and I turned, ready to wrap her in my arms, to share at least a little of our common humanity before power consumed us.

But she was gone.

I slumped back against the rail, my heart beating loud in my throat. Fool! Had I actually thought that we could...

Her hands on my shoulders froze me solid. Her forehead, rested lightly against the back of my neck was more frightening than any blade.

"Can we just try it, then? One night alone – and after that you'll be the warlock, and I'll be the witch, and the world will tremble before us."

I felt her breath warm in my ear, and I reached over my shoulder to take her hand.

"Will it mean anything, then?"

"Tomorrow the people we are now will be dead and gone, Kuhal Moer. Now, are you coming with me, or not?"

And the river carried us both on into the darkness.

"There is no such thing as forbidden knowledge. Knowledge finds its level like water, and like water pent up behind a dam, knowledge concealed and denied breaks out under pressure..."

Sothara da'Urgon Roege
- The Antler-Crowned King

THREE WAR KEELS of Anganesse came drifting in low over the fens and marshes, pushing down the reeds with the cold wind they drove before them. Swallows flitted from beneath their shadows, feeling in their bones the vast and unnatural power of the things – mountains with castles upon their backs, heaved into the sky by the art of pious murder. Green lightning crawled across the chains and stays which kept them aloft, and a dim glow underlit the wells of ossuary bones drilled through their hearts.

The architecture of the Labyrinth bought us time.

It lay under a skin of grass and turf after nine centuries of neglect, but this had once been a power-focus, the first and only city raised by my people. They'd done it against their will, of course – slaves to the Herald of Anghul, the enemy of Ceirmakh... a cheerful fellow called Sothara da'Urgon Roege, the Bone Collector.

Under the sod lay avenues and plazas, the broken sockets of standing stones like missing teeth, barrows filled with the dead in coiling serpent spirals... a necropolis which had grown up around the step-sided pyramid of the Black Tyrant himself.

Thanks to this hump-backed mound the keels could come no further. In the Dark Sight I could see a pale vortex spiraling in toward the apex of the pyramid, tugging and tweaking at the clouds. They'd forced Sothara into a slice of time folded in on itself, and the world gnawed at the anomaly so created with the tenacity of waves grinding a rocky shore to sand. If Sinder was fool enough to bring his keels closer the vortex would crack his ossuray batteries and shear stone and glass like paper.

"They'll have to cross the river once they've disembarked. Soft ground, and no good for horses. Of course, if we actually had an army to throw against them, we could split them in half as they crossed and chop them down piecemeal."

Conn stood with me on the lower slopes of the pyramid, his black hair tied into an elaborate topknot and held in place with slim daggers. He'd taken to wearing a crown of blackened thorns and holly, more at the behest of his feral children than for any religious certainty. Winter's Thane was nothing until he was sacrificed, after all.

"Eight thousand infantry. Eight hundred of them the Faceless, the rest spear levies from the south. Six hundred lancers, Ghurami horse-archers out on the left flank, and who knows how many crossbowmen." Elion Morekh peered through an ornate tube of brass and walrus ivory , frowning. "The Ghuram don't look like the usual mercenaries, either. They have a covered palanquin among them, which suggests somebody with power is overseeing his investment."

"Like you're overseeing yours?" I asked. Here, close to the rift which imprisoned the Tyrant, I had a constant feeling that someone was breathing over my shoulder. Elion chuckled.

"I'm beginning to think that I've made a very costly gamble here, young Kuhal. Sinder has all that..." he gestured expansively at the snapping white banners and neat rows of tents across the oxbow of the river - "While we have about seventy warriors, and a handful of women, children and cripples. You begin to see how my cards are nailed to the table, hmm?"

Behind us, in a hollow in the face of the pyramid, Makara was weaving melodies with her lyrecaster. The wind sliced them up and spun them past us, little sharp fragments of song picking and prying at the locks Sothara had set on his own prison.

"We'll have our army. Even *I* can feel those things twisting in their graves," said Conn. "Those barrows are full of dead warriors – eighty years worth of them, from every tribe the Tyrant held under his sway. Kuhal will raise them all."

Well, that was the plan.

But Kuhal da'Hurik Moer was more than a little apprehensive about one or two of its finer points. To iterate – while my power seemed to thrive under the most dangerous of conditions, this was brinksmanship of a higher order. Sinder had brought with him a force sufficient to grind us into oblivion, never mind that Esau's gifts wouldn't help him here. And secondly – the part I truly feared, and which I hadn't so much as whispered, even to Gernish Maudrin in the Stormwood – the power took more from me than it gave. *Little memories, splintered off from the rock of my soul and replaced with the rage of dead men...*

Was that what happened to Sothara? It seemed I'd be in the unenviable position of being able to ask him face to face.

Chords meshed and reverberated through ancient rock. Water gushed in cold stone cisterns underground. And with a sigh like a death-rattle the great doors of the pyramid heaved themselves open, inch by inch. Makara soon stood framed against a mouth of darkness, the head of a stair which spiraled crookedly down into the earth.

I had woken up alone, that morning. And her promise was true – today she was all business, as if the person I'd held last night was indeed dead and buried.

"Are you ready for some hero's work, then?" she asked. "It's you and me, Kuhal – let these other master tacticians see to our defenses."

"If this fails, there'll *be* no defenses, girl," said Elion. "But if there's treasure down there..."

"We'll be sure to bring you a nice crown or a scepter. Just don't blame me if it's cursed."

"There's no treasure. Not in *this* tomb. He's not concerned with things as cheap as gold and jewels." My voice must have sounded as grim and hollow as the black pyramid itself. "There's something else, though. Something he's reaching out for, even across the rift..."

Conn and Makara shared a concerned flicker of a glance with Elion Morekh, then looked back at me.

"Is his mind up to this? I'm all for raising a legion of ravening Khytein ghouls, don't get me wrong, it's just that..."

"If we die, and Sinder dies with us, I'll still be happy. We don't have any choice."

"Aerik believed in him. Maudrin too. And it looks as though our beloved Provincial Governor isn't taking any chances..."

I pushed past them all, and had already reached the first landing by the time that Makara came running after me.

I wasn't a *thing.* I wasn't a weapon of last resort. Or so I told myself, secure in the knowledge that part of me knew I was lying.

"Hey! Slow down! You could break your neck on these stairs, Kuhal!"

I was in no mood for reasoning. I didn't want to point out that with Sei skittering along ahead of me on light little claws I could easily pick my way through the choking darkness.

"And apparently if Jerrold Sinder broke *his* neck at the same time then your brother would be more than happy. I never asked for this, you know!"

Makara didn't slap me. She wasn't that kind of girl. This was an iron-hard sucker punch which lifted me off my feet, sending me sprawling down to the next landing. I slid to a stop at the foot of an eyeless stone sphinx, feeling for broken teeth, and she was standing over me before Sei could get between us.

"You think *I* asked for this? You think I *asked* to be married to Gernish Maudrin when I was thirteen? This is life and death, Kuhal da'Hurik Moer, and death is easy. *Life is hard!*"

She kicked me in the ribs and kept walking. Sei tugged at my sleeve.

"So, we're even for back at the..."

"Not even remotely!" came a receding voice from down the stairwell. "But if it's any consolation, I think I've broken my hand..."

Something roared in the deeps. Dust sifted down as the whole tottering staircase shook. I heard Makara curse as a vast section of marble and statuary sheared away, tumbling into the abyss, and then she was back on the landing with me, a sword in her hands.

"Tell me you didn't hear that! I thought it was just a legend!"

"A legend about what? Why didn't you tell *me?*"

The roar came again, and this time it was accompanied by a lightning-flash vision behind my eyes – immense hands of wood and bone and wire scrabbling and gouging at the staircase below us. I caught the merest glimpse of a head carved from pale milky stone, four impassive faces staring from its four sides as it spun, suspended above a hollow chest. Makara knotted one hand in the front of my tunic.

"We never told you because we wanted you to come down here of your own free will. Now – jump!"

I had little choice. She dragged me over the edge with her, and as soon as my boots cleared the landing an impact from below shattered the pillar of stone it was built upon. We seemed to fall forever, but it was no more than a few frantic heartbeats. Then impact shock drove daggers into the soles of my feet, and I rolled down a dozen steps, dazed.

"Married to him? Married? But then..."

"Sothara wasn't put in here by his enemies. His kingdom was overthrown by a great conclave of Warbards, who gave a greater part of their power to one chosen to be Winter's Thane. For a very, very short span Ciermakh walked the earth, and the Tyrant knew he could never face him. The flaw in the plan was time, of course. Gods can't manifest here – not without doing the same kind of thing Gernish did to those Excoriators. The world won't take it."

"So?"

"So Sothara conjured himself a wrinkle in time and wrapped it around himself. He only expected to hold it for a week or two – as long as the warbards could stabilize their makeshift God. But that's what they counted on. Aerik..."

"The *same Aerik?* Or was my head injured more badly than I thought back there?"

"The same Aerik," Makara said, dragging me down another three turns of the crooked stair. "He put a tiny disharmony in the spell. Now if Sothara lets go, all that time will hit him at once. His heart will turn to dust."

Another roar. Another world-shaking impact – though this time I actually saw the titanic fist which pulverized the staircase just behind us. It was a thing of jointed wood, metal and bones... whole skeletons woven between cables and spars.

"For nine hundred years? *And what in all the hells is that thing?*"

"A guardian. Sothara knew that his armies, living and dead, could never defeat a God. Half of his sworn Khytein would follow the Wolf Child and turn on their master. So he came down here, and left the city to tear itself apart. He was sure his enemies wouldn't have time to fight their way past... *that!*"

This time it wasn't just a vision – I saw it with Sei's eyes first, and then with my own. A head torn from some unspeakably ancient statue, its four marble faces cracked and worn smooth by time, rotating slowly as beams of cold blue light stabbed out from its empty eyesockets. Parts of its arms were the same pale stone, crusted with moss and lichen, wired down to iron-hard old oak and human bone... a graveyard full of it. The sound it made in my head was like the babble and howl of the Slaughterborn, but different – far away and despairing.

Still, it had fists, this thing. Knots of carven stone the size of carthorses which it swung with a sound like Elion's ship tacking against the wind. Wood and wire creaked as it brought one great wrecking ball around, shattering another pillar.

It saw us. It *bellowed*, blasting dust from the chasm walls.

"*Move*, damn you!" shouted Makara, her voice coming in through a storm of echoes. Sei was already running, a turn below us on the spiral, and the stairs behind him were falling away behind his skeletal paws. I ran.

"You didn't really... I mean, if he was *nine hundred years*... and you..."

An arm all scrimshawed femurs and oak pulverized the stone at my heels. The eyes of that smooth, impassive face came up out of the deeps right behind me, and I saw something through them – a face within the light, little more than a skull stretched tight with leathery skin.

Makara spun back, lashing out at the thing's other arm as it came down in front of us, pinning us on a short stretch of stairway. Her knife suck fast in the ancient wood of the guardian, and it wouldn't pull free. Now I could see into the hollow chest of the thing, where a single human body was hooked and nailed up at its heart. This one was clad in scraps of rusted mail and leather; its face all but gone, but still turning, blind, to plead with me.

"Let us die. Send us down. Please... we can't..."

Makara screamed as the guardian drew its fist back, ready to crush us utterly. But all I saw was the pattern of the thing – an intricate tracery of fire like a sketch of all the constellations. Where the Slaughterborn had been chaos this was excruciating order, lines of witchfire stretched tight between the guttering stars of human souls. There wasn't a knife-blade's width to force my mind between them.

The fist reached its zenith. Makara's hands closed around my arm. And Sei jumped.

At once a shiver ran through the cruel geometry of the Guardian. Lines bent and flickered as the little cat wormed his way between ribs of wood and metal, down to where a gold-capped nail pierced the thing's heart.

I hammered against it with my will, but it was like punching stone – all I earned myself was pain. The thing's fist shivered, taut at the top of its arc.

Now Sei's little teeth were working the nail loose. Now wires snapped and the flare-lights of souls burned brightly, straining...

This time I imagined the blade of a spear. I just let everything else fall away into darkness, and imagined a sliver of razor-edged metal, slippery and pointed...

I thrust my mind into the pattern behind that thought, and I slashed deep into the Guardian's heart. Nails flew like stoneshot, clattering against the walls of the shaft. Sei sunk his needle teeth into a dead and dessicated arm, feeling paper-thin skin peel back from the bones beneath.

"Damn the Bone Collector! Kill him in my name! Send him to his Antlered God by the right of Akhal da'Maron Roege, greatest of his generals..."

Those empty eyes under their iron half-helm flared blue for a second, transfixing me. And then I had control of one of the Guardian's great stone fists – the arm which Sei had freed from Sothara's spell.

Makara almost slipped from the tottering platform as I swung it wide, taking a chunk out of the chasm wall. Then it came back in an unstoppable arc, fracturing the side of the thing's head. One ancient statue face crumbled, the light in its eyes extinguished. From inside the cage of bone and wood Akhal Roege screamed, and smoke began to billow from his mummified flesh.

"Yes! Destroy my prison! Destroy..."

The huge wrecking ball fist came back again with a sound like the wind through the Stormwood, and this time the Guardian's head exploded. Sei ran up the thing's other arm as shards of stone blew wide, wire unraveling and melting as the corpse at its heart burst into flame.

"Now would be a good time to jump," I said, wrapping my arm around Makara's shoulders. Half stumbling, I leaped aboard the collapsing form of Sothara's Guardian – a headless wreck already slowly toppling into the abyss.

Behind it we fell for what seemed like an eternity. The ruined hulk smashed through bridges and stairways of stone, clearing our path down and down into the cold darkness, limbs torn off in splinters, internal gears and mechanisms sloughed away until we spun and tumbled amid a cloud of bones and debris. In a haze of blurred, spinning images I saw Sei pelting down the wall as fast as he could run, faster than our free-fall, defying gravity. Far, far above, the platform where we'd made our stand detonated into molten rock and flinders... Sothara was vengeful, but far too slow.

Now I could see a silvery reflection below us – the flames of the Guardian's wreck reflected from water. I twisted in the air until I could see Makara's face – she had her lyrecaster in her hands, and she wore an expression of fierce concentration.

"Water! We're going to be alright! Just hold your breath!"

"Stupid! At this kind of speed that water will feel like stone! I'm going to have to break the surface tension myself!"

I remembered the feeling of hitting the northern ocean, half-wrapped in Gernish Maudrin's furs. Even that had felt like a slap with the flat of a battleaxe. Perhaps Makara was right...

Then we were out of time. The burning hulk of the Guardian splashed down in a hiss of oily smoke, and Makara's hands ran up the neck of the lyrecaster, producing a tooth-rattling scream. I saw the water below us belly out into a shivering dish a sliver of a second before we hit, tiny beads of spray dancing on its surface...

Then the world went ice-black and upside down.

When I awoke it was with Makara's face looming over me. Her lips were only inches from my own, and her breath smelled of honey and wood smoke. I coughed up a mouthful of water and rolled over, gasping for breath.

There was a taste on my lips, like warm iron. They were the only part of me which wasn't utterly cold.

The realization slapped me across the back of the head just like my dear departed father had done so many times, and once again it was because I was inexcusably dull. Even if was just to force life back into my feeble little body, the girl had *kissed me*. Bright blood beaded at the corner of her mouth, and her eyes seemed huge and shimmering in the gloom. Perhaps there was hope for us. Perhaps last night...

There was a moment, I was sure of it. But it slipped past me as I fumbled for the right words.

"You should have told me you couldn't swim," she said.

"I can't swim in armor and boots, if that's what you mean," I managed, slithering across the stone to a half-broken pillar.

"Huh! Some thanks, necromancer. I hope you can handle Sothara better than you handle a little water."

Whatever had been there was gone. In the privacy of my own head I gave myself a stern kicking.

Sei rubbed up against my leg, nudging me to my feet. Makara was already striding off into the half-darkness, into the mouth of a tunnel framed by many-limbed demon statues.

"Wait! I didn't mean..." I cursed, trying to wring the water out of my tunic as I staggered after her. Typical!

I caught up with her half way down an eerily lit ceremonial hall – a rib-vaulted expanse glowing pale blue-green. Bowls of pale witchfire shimmered in the hands of skeletal carvings.

"It's not that I'm ungrateful, or anything, it's just that..."

She laid a finger across my lips, head cocked to one side.

"Can you hear him? The breathing? He's still alive, and he sees us."

Oh, he did indeed. My indignation withered up like eunuch's balls as I heard a low, oily chuckle, and felt stone grinding on stone.

Predictable. So very villainous. Those carvings weren't carvings at all, but Sothara the Bone Collector's sanctum praetorians.

Cold burning eyes flickered to life all around us, and broad-bladed spears were torn loose from their mountings with the sound of rust giving way. The collective sigh of a thousand dead men stepping down from their pedestals was like a mournful wind.

"So. Now, in your need, you seek me out, child of the Khytein Moer. I can feel the defilement of your land through the roots and stones, all the way up to the light. And you think I will help you? You, of all the accursed races of men?"

I think Makara heard him too, but what she caught was the edge of a whisper. I heard the sound of granite tombs crashing shut deep underground.

"I think we should go with them," said the warbard. Spear points hemmed us in.

"You *think?* I suppose we have a choice, then?"

The dead crowded around us, the blades of their spears pointing the way.

I could feel them, of course, pushing up against the membrane of the Dark Sight, but there was no urgency or rage in these ancient things. I could taste – and it really *was* a taste, right in the back of my throat – the sadness and emptiness of the Bone Collector's slaves, but the centuries had ground their personalities down to echoes. His will bound them up tight – that, and the calciferous tendrils which coiled around their bones like the webs of underground fungi.

We were led down a great vaulted tunnel which looked like something *grown*, not hewn from stone. Makara was as silent as I was – awed, perhaps, by the mighty craft of our ancestors. There's a lot you can achieve with slavery, and even more if your slaves keep working after they drop dead. Sothara had delighted in images of death, and the walls were a carven litany of bloodshed, burial and undead servitude.

Eventually we were ushered into a huge high chamber, its sloping walls meeting at an apex hazed by smoke. Torches burned there with the green flicker of witchlight, and I noticed that each one was a human femur, burning without blackening the bone. The scene which they illuminated was as bizarre as it was horrific.

Just a few paces in from the great arched doorway a shimmer

in the air traced the edge of Sothara's prison of time. I knew this because of the bodies, held up against the air and strewn across the ground. Outside the wavering haze they were bones, picked clean and smooth. Inside, they were horribly fresh, still charred by the massive discharge of magic. Those who had been picked up by the blastwave of the Warbards' spell were sliced in two by nine centuries of stasis – those parts of them within the boundary still fresh and bloody, those without nothing but bones and dust. It made for some truly interesting cross-sections; ones which a scholarly Ghuram physician would have found invaluable.

At the heart of the distortion stood Sothara's answer to the curse. The tyrant was still enthroned, seated on a huge bone chair and wrapped in a cloak of shadows. A circlet of steel holly was wrapped around his head outside his cowl, and a pair of antlers branched out from it in praise of Anghul. But there were numberless images of the Bone Collector, because he had encysted himself in crystal. A great multi-faceted gem as clear as water had grown up around him, and at its point a thick rope of mycelial filaments scrawled away toward the apex of the pyramid. There was a point at which the coiled and clotted strands passed through the wall of time, and here they seemed to be knotted in and around themselves in an eye-watering torment of geometry.

All of the Sotharas - one in each facet of the gem – turned to look at us. They all moved slightly differently, and when they spoke the voice echoing out of that bottomless cowl was like a chorus of pained whispers.

"So, at last you come. I can smell the stink of them on you, boy... the ones who sent you to kill me."

Makara's bravery was as hard and brittle as volcanic glass in the Dark Sight, but the Bone Collector seemed to smoke with blackness, great swirling clouds of it billowing from his shoulders like a cape as he hunched forward. Deep in the cowl were two smouldering yellow-green eyes, and they drilled into my skull without mercy. I tried to stare them down, but I knew that the lies I'd prepared wouldn't fool this ageless thing.

"I wasn't sent to kill you. I come asking aid for what remains of your people. I..."

It took a while for me to work out that the hacking, coughing sound coming from within the cowl was laughter.

"Help? *You?* I can see your rabble through soil and stone, child, and I can see what comes to crush them. Even if I was set free from this prison I'd never aid the whelp of Aerik Stormsong and Gernish Maudrin. Where are they? Have they come to gloat over their past victories before they die?"

Lies wouldn't work. Not in the furnace heat of that stare. But half-truths might just fool a creature who was quite clearly mad.

"I *watched* them die, Sothara," I said, trying to sound grim. "Stormsong burned before my eyes, and Maudrin was drowned for me. That's what you smell on me, old witch... the echo of their doom."

A finger like a withered branch beckoned me. A long, rusted blade had been bound to it with copper wire.

"Closer. Fear not, child, the barrier will hold."

I could sense great power as I stepped up to the the barrier. It came up through the soles of my feet, like the sensation you feel just before a lightning strike. I placed my hands flat on the hot, slippery membrane of Aerik's old spell, and it felt like living flesh.

Then agony earthed itself through me – a blade hammered through my skull. I heard Makara stifle a scream as my back arched, my hands bound tight to the wall of sorcery and burning, burning...

"You think you can lie to me? To one who was ancient with subtlety when you were nothing but potential semen? I can feel what you are, boy, but you scorn the God who we both know you should bow to. You scorn them all."

Another withering blast of pain racked me, and I believe I cried out. A red blur filled my vision - and in the red, slithering tendrils of black...

I looked up.

Something dark and old and violent moved deep in my brain – perhaps, I thought at the time, it was the pride of all my dead ancestors, finally sick of my poor attempts at saga-heroism.

"And what are you going to do, little one? Even your death wouldn't entertain me for a moment!"

Maybe. But not so long ago the girl standing far too close to me had kissed me. Certain glands and clusters of hot brain tissue thumped and seethed, demanding an act of idiot bravery.

I spat against the barrier, making it sizzle and hiss. And I inhaled power, raw and furious, deep into my bones.

"Our people die, so our Gods must already be dead," I whispered. *"Now it's your turn."*

Makara told me later that it was like the sunrise. A green and tainted light, but blinding, erupting from my body as a snarl of lashing tendrils, devouring magik as dawn does the darkness.

The praetorian dead exploded. Fragments of incandescent bone scythed through the air, but I was untouchable, and Makara had already scrambled for cover as the witchfire raved and burned. Now it was eating into the dome of null time, stoking the furnaces inside me until I could actually *sense* Sothara, his soul squatting on reality like a fat black spider.

He was immeasurably ancient, and fractured somehow, so that his laughter was an unhinged chorus in my head. But the Warbards' prison-spell was melting like fat in the cookfire before my onslaught, and now I was able to focus all that throbbing power into a drill, a spike that would rip through his essence and destroy him...

I thrust my arm forward, screaming, into the crystal around Sothara's throne. A hundred leering facets threw his face back at me.

This time the agony drove me clear across the hall. More than just the ancient tiles and carvings broke when I struck, and I suppose if there hadn't been so much raw power binding up my bones I would have been dashed to jelly.

There came the tiny, musical sound of crystal cracking.

"I suppose I should thank you for your impetuousness, boy," chuckled Sothara. *"Nine hundred painstaking years I've been weaving my snare, and you've almost set me free with an instant's stupidity."*

I groaned. There wasn't much else I could do.

"Not quite free, Lord Sothara. But maybe free enough to make a bargain."

It was Makara, of course, and her Lyrecaster was held high across her chest, her fingers coaxing a sad, quiet song from its strings.

On his throne, the cowled and steel-clawed necromancer shifted slightly. The facets of his crystal prison shivered.

"What kind of bargain? And why should I trust you, girl? The stink of those filthy shamen is all over you!"

Makara laughed. The strings of her lyrecaster thrummed and sobbed along with the sound of it.

"I know how you wove the crystal warding, Bone Collector. Your counterspell to the Null Focus of my masters. Each instant is a thousand instants, is it not? And for each choice we make, a thousand new worlds are born."

She came stalking forward, drawing darkness behind her like a cloak. The lyrecaster's whine and thrum was hypnotic... but I could see tiny cracks skittering across Sothara's warding, now. Where they met and forked green light came bleeding through.

"The will of *one* Lord Sothara in one sliver of time would never be enough. But ten? A hundred? A thousand? There might be just enough overspill between the worlds for you to work some slow enchantment. There might be enough for you to watch the world outside your tomb slowly forget you. But..."

"*But what, little witch? It scarcely matters now. This is the world in which an untrained child tried to strike me down. My other selves lent me power, and I will return it.*"

"Leaving them trapped. And out there, the world has turned. New masks are worn by the old Gods. Anghul has been... reduced."

"*Is that why your sickly little death-boy scorns him?*"

She shrugged.

"Perhaps. But think on this. If he's such a fool, can you really be sure Aerik and Gernish Maudrin and the rest are really dead?"

"*I can see what's at my gates, girl. If they wouldn't stand and fight against* that..."

"But *that* is not their most ancient enemy. Those Anganesse across the river were seen as nothing but a test for the poor young wretch you've already beaten."

Oh, I liked that. But I could see the little smile twitching the corners of Makara's lips from where I had managed to crawl to my knees. A nightmare ten centuries old, and she was playing with him like an angler who has hooked a pike.

"*Him? He has some power, but it is crude. With a few decades of beatings and lessons, perhaps...*"

"Or with the Pale Armour. With the Incantus Instrumentorum."

The crystal prison around Sothara swirled with milky light. When it cleared, I could almost pick out a face in the shadow of his cowl.

"*No. There's nothing you can offer me now which would make me part with them..*"

"Not even this?" asked Makara, pressing one hand to the crystal . "Can you feel the resonance, Bone Collector? You know the song of this soul, don't you? You know that for the elder Warbards death is not death, just as life is not life. Just as it is for you."

Now there was definitely a face floating behind Sothara's glowing eyes. But the look on it was one of raw hatred.

"*Maudrin! Stormsong! They still live! I...*"

"If you rise again now, weakened, they will not be merciful. Death *will* be death. But that would mean the end of all Khytein. The Angan wolves would pick the bones of the north clean."

There was a long silence. It played out like thin wire, and finally it snapped.

"Tell me."

The lyrecaster song rose up, gentle and pervasive as Makara stepped back from the throne.

"I am the daughter of Issan Roege and the Stormsong, tenth wife of Gernish Maudrin the nightwalker, sister to the chosen of Ceirmakh who is Wild King. I will stand as hostage to you, if Kuhal Moer may wear the Pale Armour and wield the Incantus Instrumentorum for a night and a day."

"And afterwards? How do I know he will given them back?"

"My life would be forfeit. Imagine the joy, Lord Sothara, of wringing the life from Aerik's daughter and the nightwalker's soul-sworn..."

"Or I could kill you where you stand. Both of you. The boy's soul alone would grant me enough power to face the shades of your accursed Warbards."

"Would it? *Really?* Make you choice, Sothara. I don't have your kind of patience."

This time the pause was even longer. I could see the agony of choice in the Bone Collector's eyes... hells, I could feel it in the way the whole world grew tight as a tattooed drumhead while he clenched his fists.

That... and something else. Just as I'd felt another presence behind Makara's back in the filth and blood of the processing camp, now I caught the very edges of a mind working through her, calming the very real fear which slithered over the top of her thoughts. *Something alive which should have been dead...*

The crystal shattered along a thousand faceted lines, and Sothara was rising from his throne even as the shards spun away, winking in the light of his burning eyes. Little traceries of liquid fire dripped and sizzled along his claws, along the wire which bit down to the bones of his fingers.

Makara's lyrecaster moved at the same time, levitating between her hands as its strings blurred into a rainbow of translucent glass – colours woven in and out and around each other in impossible ways. Gernish Maudrin was there with her, a thing of shadows and light which was more edges than solid shapes, and his fingers worked in perfect harmony with hers, caressing and hammering at the strings.

I opened my mouth to scream, but all that came out was a thick, thorny rope of power, dragged up from deep inside me. *Unpleasant* was not even close to the word to describe it.

Then I saw the flying fragments of crystal stop, hanging motionless in the air. They spun around to that Sothara was faced by a hundred distorting mirrors, two hundred burning eyes.

They were his own, but not his own.

The same was true for the hands that reached out of them on impossibly long shadow arms – hands with knives for fingers, spitting and popping with witchfire. They carved into the dry, mummified flesh of the Bone Collector with a sound like branding irons on leather, shredding and tearing.

His scream went from a bellow to a high-pitched shriek as he was undone.

Fistfuls of soul-stuff stretched and tore. Sothara's face was ripped away in three directions at once. He was reaching into a pair of crystal shards with his own hands, frantic, flailing...

And then he was gone. Utterly torn apart.

The crystal shards fell to the floor and smashed with a sound like icicles snapping in the cold of winter.

In the darkness which followed, I heard Gernish Maudrin's whisper.

"Some of him chose right, and some chose wrong, but all of them *chose*. None of them could stand to see only one walk free."

"And the Incantus? The Armour?"

"You know you were watching his eyes when you spoke those names. He might as well have drawn us a map, the old fool. Now, pick him up. We have much to do."

I felt hands close around me – callused fingertips and smooth palms. I heard stone grinding on stone, and saw a pale green light, hashed by a spinning filigree of vines and flowers. I felt cold bone against my skin, and felt straps tighten, sealing me inside...

Then I heard the voice of the Incantus Instrumentorum, and I felt black earth in my mouth, cold roots twisted through my ribs, a rusted sword in my hand...

A thousand upon a thousand times over.

I was legion.

"Worship a God and he will give you power -so say the credulous. Tune your soul to resonate with the divine, and you will feel the flow and fire of sorcery. Let a nation raise up their chosen God, and they will be changed by his dreaming. But despise a God - slaughter his followers, crush his temples, defile his holy places, and you will know him just as well. Hate is as intimate as love. Doom is just destiny's shadow. Therefore, strive in all things to disbelieve."

Yissus Ul
- Antipriest of the Murathic Zengaji

MY MIND CAME into the emptiness of the Instrumentorum like ink billowing into clear water. It was a cold place, and dark, but wherever I looked lights began to flicker, spiderweb chains of them linking in great constellations.

I was inside the ball of spinning gold webwork, with that clenched in turn within a net of ornate black iron. But I was also *outside*, struggling to my feet inside a heavy suit of armor. It was sickeningly warm against my skin, smooth and milky in the light of the Incantus, but it was filled to bursting with power.

Slowly the drunken sensation ebbed away, and I was able to see the intricate patterns inside the Instrumentorum layered over Sothara's throne chamber. I held a hand up to my face.

"They are rising," I croaked, looking down at a tangle of bone-white roots, all meshed and thorny. My fingers were under that calcified crust somewhere, clenching in visceral heat. "Is... is there another way out of here?"

Makara was alone, on her knees where the power had left her. I brought the Incantus hovering around with a gesture, lighting up her face as she pushed a tangle of hair out of her eyes.

"Sothara was a fool, but not that much of a fool. He had his own rat-hole to escape from, but as to where – that's *his* Cerebrex you're holding, Kuhal. You tell me."

Indeed, now that I could see the Incantus Instrumentorum clearly, I could make out what it was made of. It was a ball of grey-pink brain tissue, an arm's-length across, flickering in stasis. Already my mind was twisting along the webwork inside it, growing, pulsing... and the feeling was almost indescribable.

Liken it to anger, perhaps. The rising madness, the righteousness – but it *went on growing*, until the part of me which was Kuhal Moer trembled beneath a thunderhead of my greater self, all afire with power.

I'd never worshiped Anghul. I had little time for the Gods. But his shadow was cast before the light inside me, all thorn-hung antlers and long black claws...

"This way," I said, with utter certainty. Sothara's thoughts had burned their own trails into the stuff of the Incantus, and it was all too easy to read what was left of his mind. "I must be up there when they awaken. They have slept for so long. They *hunger*."

Makara nodded, slinging her lyrecaster over her shoulder. And we ran.

Out through a door behind the throne – a slab of rock a handspan thick which I slapped aside effortlessly. The pale armor was not all twisted bone – there were tendons and muscles of witchfire slicked over it like a mirage, and they possessed all the strength of the men who had been ritually slain to build it. I saw them die under Sothara's iron blades as I took the spiral stairs three at a time – *swift Zengaji and hulking Khytein, fat-bellied Ghuram eunuch swordsmen, black-skinned Akuulites and Ras-kamur hashishin, their flesh boiled off in black cauldrons and fed to ghouls, their bones woven and softened by magic, building a tangled cuirass, a helm of skeletal faces...*

Building the nightmare form which clenched me in its embrace, and which erupted from the sunlit turf in a spray of soil.

The Anganesse were across the river. But the necropolis funneled them into a wide plaza between two long, hump-backed mounds of earth, and Sinder was nothing if not cautious. I could see him in the middle ranks of the white-clad Angan army, leading his Faceless Ones of foot. Out to the left flank came the Angan lancers, their horses barded in silver and white. Pennants cracked in the warm breeze, bearing the mark of Esau.

But on the right came the Ghuram irregulars – horse archers with curved scimitars swinging from their saddles and repeating crossbows in their hands. They had taken the high ground of the western burial mound, and their horses picked their way between the stumps of standing stones as they advanced. Behind them came the swaying palanquin I'd seen before my descent.

The middle of the Angan army was made up of conscript soldiers – men of a dozen races who fell under the White Empire's sway. They were not clad as grandly as the Faceless, and I was willing to bet that they were the same type of scum as the men we'd slaughtered in the processing camp.

Below us, on the slope of the overgrown pyramid, Elion and Conn had drawn up two ragged lines of defenders. Young Feral archers were stringing their short bows behind a skirmish line of Faeroan pirates and refugees in stolen scraps of armor – not even enough men to form a shield wall.

As Makara scrambled muddy from the tunnel of earth the first of them turned and saw me. I must have been quite a vision – near twice the height of the scrawny orphan who had descended into the black pyramid, now bulked out in a full suit of bone-white plate. My face was hidden inside a helm of skeletal faces which seemed to twist and scream in agony. Balanced on one palm I held the Incantus Instrumentorum, the great Cerebrex of the Bone Collector, and in the other I carried his sword, the black iron slab called Cryptfeeder. No wonder they shouted as they did.

"*He has come! The Antler-Crowned King has arisen! He walks again!*"

Makara gently placed her hand on my arm, looking up into the eyes of that nightmare helm.

"Let them believe what they must, Kuhal. See – the Anganesse believe it too."

"But what do I do? I can hear his whispers, Makara, but none of it makes any sense. I can feel the ones under the earth, but I don't have the words to call them!"

She was right, though. The front rank of the Angan army had stopped, pointing. Banners dipped and tangled as the white-clad soldiers piled up behind their terrified comrades.

"It's not about words, Kuhal. Let them feel the way through to freedom. Be the edge and the threshold. *Command* them."

I was young, and stupid, and I was still more than a little intoxicated from that accidental kiss. So I tried.

Only the pale armor kept me upright as ten thousand voices rose up in a storm. Lines of green fire speared out from the Incantus as it spun, piercing the mounds and barrows of the necropolis, and as they burrowed down I could feel them weaving into my mind, sending tendrils of my will into the cold earth.

The legion of the black serpent. The legion of the blood eagle. The legion of the white spider. The legion of the broken sun. More – hundreds more. Each one was a rune burning inside my eyes, hung on the spiderweb of the Incantus.

"Uuurhbnehfff..." I burbled, forgetting for a moment how to breathe, stand, think or use my tongue.

They had been interred in wells of unmortared stone, wrapped in their war-cloaks and armed with *kuris* swords of bronze and great wooden shields. Ritual embalming and runes of preservation had dried them out to husks of leather and bone behind their corroded helms, and many of their weapons were little more than broken stumps.

But they came.

I heard Sothara's voice come echoing up out of the Instrumentorum as the screams began. The Ghuram horsemen wheeled and reared as spears erupted from the earth below them, piercing the bellies of their mounts and throwing archers from their saddles. Those who fell never regained their feet – skeletal hands dragged them down into the dirt, peeling away skin and flesh with hard, insistent claws.

"Go on. Let it sink into you. Every one who dies brings us closer together..."

It was Sothara – or what was left of him. My mind was spread so thin that I couldn't pin him down inside the immensity of the Cerebrex, but it seemed he was just as artful as Gernish Maudrin. He'd made plans for immortality, and they hinged on possession. *My* possession.

The earth was heaving and boiling now as his old legions wormed their way up into the cold daylight. The Ghuram had fallen back around the palanquin of their master, and a frantic bodyguard of surviving horse archers and bald-headed eunuch swordsmen was hacking at the wights who assailed them.

Down in the throat of valley, between the burial mounds, Angan horns rung out, marshaling the panicked throng into ranks. I could see Jerrold Sinder among them, calm amid the cursing, and he was talking to a knot of white-robed priests. As I watched he levered open a great silver-bound tome, dripping with silk bookmarks. Fingers pointed, and heads bobbed up and down in unison.

The spell which had held Sothara was gone.

And that meant it was possible to force open the densely layered bands of magic over the necropolis. It meant they could finish this with the keels.

"Do you have any choice? Use my minions and crush these Southern insects, Kuhal. Soon you won't even remember that name, but you will remember the power..."

I gritted my teeth behind the great helm of bone and willed my army forward. It was true. I could feel the old necromancer's memories leaching into my mind from the Instrumentorum – memories of the stormwood in winter, grey on grey, of a witch with sharpened black teeth in a cloak of autumn leaves, of a rune-carved bone club swinging in to fracture my... *his*... tiny skull. Memories of how these dead men had fought, back when they still had eyes and warmth and breath.

They were slow and purposeful, but that just made them all the more terrible. A shield wall of the dead formed up as I willed it into being, hundreds of warriors spanning the valley from edge to edge. *Kuris* blades hammered against rotten wood in challenge as the dead shuffled forward, grinning their merciless smiles. I could see through their eyes in a kind of fever-dream haze – the front ranks of the Angan army praying and white-knuckled, leveling a forest of spears at the bellowed order of a their sejants.

I was a spark, flitting back and forth along the pale strands of witchfire, goading and bullying the dead into motion. The Incantus thrummed with power, casting my mind wide. And all the while I could feel Sothara gaining ground.

Now the dead were shambling. Now the dead were running. They went pelting over the grass, silent, smiling, leathery lips pulled back from yellowed teeth.

The great clumsy shield wall crashed home with a sound of grinding steel and screams. Spears punched clean through desiccated flesh, but the wights kept coming. My legions pushed forward, hacking with mechanical purpose, and the feeling was like clenching a fist, a slow, crushing sensation driving the Anganesse back. Blades did their butcher-work, unsplicing flesh, and the ground was dewed with crimson. Here and there a wild blow from the southmen would shatter a skull or shear through a brittle spine, and a spark of witchfire would wink out. But spears were useless against the dead. And the dying pain of so many souls blurred my thoughts like Ulkar's rotgut liquor, giving me the strength to push back against Sothara's will.

"You really think you can stop me? There's just nothing to you, child – fifteen winters and fear, that's the sum of you. That, and some sad infatuation..."

I saw black arrows hissing across the sky, plucking Angan warriors from their feet. I saw Elion Morekh leading his men forward in a skirmish line, high across the face of the barrows. Then I saw Makara, fallen at my feet, and I realized just how far I'd gone into the Instrumentorum.

She was kneeling, holding her hands up above her as if the arch of the sky was falling. A twisting haze swirled over us both, and as I watched that curved dome of force was struck again and again, hammer-blows raining down from out of nowhere. It was not my sorcery, or that of the Bone Collector – it was the geomancy of the necropolis itself which was being attacked, the old wardings nailed down with standing stones and trilithons.

Out on the barrow's crest, where the Ghuram were desperately holding back the dead, lightning danced across the shattered stones. Something was pulling them from the earth like rotten teeth.

It was Sinder.

Forcing myself to move was hard. The pale armor was heavy, or else I had been horribly weakened by wielding the Incantus. Either way, it seemed to take an age for me to tear my feet from the ground. I was suffocatingly aware that inside that shell of spiked bone I was just a gangly, beaten child... but so long as I had Sothara's power to draw on, I could do something about Makara's pain.

It wasn't even really a choice. A mental hell-broth of saga songs, hormones, feverish imaginings and idiot pride got me moving, my will fraying at the edges as I went. Sothara was laughing.

"So it's a warrior, is it? A shield-breaking hero, all bronze and steel? Burn yourself out, boy. I'll take what's left of you."

Images blurred as I brought my hulking form up to a run, the flat weight of Cryptfeeder held out to one side, the Incantus Instrumentorum clenched in the opposite fist. Little worms of purple fire licked across the fingers of bone where they touched the iron filigree.

I saw Elion Morekh spin out of the path of a charging Angan lancer, his scimitars flowing like liquid to cut the rider down. His men - pirates, refugees and Khytein warriors – were poised on the flank of the northern barrow, ready to strike down into the belly of the Angan army. But they were so few...

I watched the grinding press of the dead down in the valley's throat, seeing through their eyes. It was carnage, raw and bloody, men scrabbling over the fallen to flee, only to come up against the shields and blades of the ranks behind them, driven relentlessly forward. Those few wights who pushed through the press, though... they were hacked down by the Faceless, shattered by half-moon axes which never tired.

I saw myself in the eyes of the dead, and I must admit, I felt a little like the fool Sothara had described. Heroism is a disease... never forget that. It's usually fatal. My enemies learned this fact, one at a time, or sometimes together in a single swooping rush of black metal and bone.

Stupid, stupid, stupid, stupid!

My face was hot and numb from Makara's kiss of life, and my head was being torn apart. But to the foe I was a huge pale shape, scattering the living and the dead before me. The press of bodies slowed my wild plunge.

The great flat slab of Cryptfeeder seemed to move with terrible, inevitable slowness, but when it connected it went through whole ranks of Angan bodies like a reaping wind, lopping off the tops of shields, the shafts of spears and all manner of screaming flesh. A backhand with the flat of the blade picked up a wide-eyed Angan sejant and flung him almost as far back as the impassive Faceless, his ribs staved in like matchwood.

We children of the Khytein were raised on stories of sword-swinging heroism - lies designed to twist little minds into shield-wall glory-fodder. But in the embrace of the pale armor I was all those legends and more, the strength of a hundred men wrapped around the bones which entrapped me.

I even knew to bring the Incantus around in front of me when a wedge of axe-wielding Faceless came hacking their way through the fray, the sigil of Esau burning sickly white on their helms. It was Sothara's voice which slithered out from between my teeth, but the effect blew apart my horror. The sphere of gold and iron spat a solid rod of shimmering heat, plowing a furrow through the bloody mire of battle. Everything in its path turned to ashes in an eyeblink, spiraling away on the wind.

"Fall back, you fools! Leave him to me!"

Sinder's voice was quiet, but it carried.

I think everyone on that battlefield heard him as though he was whispering right into their ear. And because he was a monster, and commanded more fear than the thing I had become, a circle of warriors expanded away from him like ripples on the surface of a pond, leaving us facing each other across a span of muddied turf.

"You know she can't stop the spells from unraveling, don't you?" he asked, infuriatingly calm. "And I suppose you know she doesn't really *want* to try so hard to hold them... or do you? How much did that old fool trust you with?"

I couldn't even answer. At this point neither I nor the Bone Collector actually owned my teeth and tongue. But something native to both of us brought the bulk of Cryptfeeder up and around, ready to obliterate the pale sorcerer.

"Fuck your mother," we both slurred in badly accented Angan.

He laughed.

"So you're a *hero*? Child, there's not enough of you left to be *that* foolish. Sothara trapped you even more easily than I have, and now it's going to take *surgery* to cut him out..."

He drew his blades, then – two long thin bone-handled swords cut down the middle. Where the blood-groove of a Faceless One's gladius would have been there was a birfurcating incision, making each sword into a two-tined spike. They slithered together in his hands and began to hum, just on the edge of hearing.

"Luckily, I'm going to enjoy it very, very much. And for the record – I gutted my mother with a carving knife on the day of my ascension to the priesthood. She was a withered old bitch, but she surely could *scream!*"

Before I could even remember the first of Ulkar's lessons he was on me. The tip of one sword sheared through the bone armor of my chest as Sinder spun up and around, rising until his feet touched down on the immense flat slab of Cyptfeeder. This put his hands at waist height, and in line with my skull-encrusted helm – just the right position to follow through with a backhand swipe, diagonally across my face. I flailed at him with the Incantus, roaring in surprise and outrage, but he was already gone – up and over my shoulder, scoring a groove down the wire-bound triple-spine of the pale armor's backpiece.

I spun with Cryptfeeder held out at right angles to my body, a gray blur which should have cloven the Angan sorcerer in half. But instead he flicked his wrist up with insouciant disdain, and caught all that tonnage of black iron on the crossbrace of his sword, his back still turned.

There was so much *weight* to him. For all that he was ancient, and by the lore of such things should have been as paper-thin as old Aerik Stormsong, Jerrold Sinder may as well have been a bony talon of rock, upthrust from the planet's core. Sparks burst and scattered on the wind as his face twitched into a smile, and I saw his blade begin to blur with noise, a harmonic which made my bones ache from within.

"Anghul's balls! What in the name of all hells is this thing, child? You never said he was..."

But Sothara never got to finish. He and I had been undone in the same instant, and only dumb momentum had kept us on our feet. Sinder looked back over his shoulder at the bloodied bone hulk which cradled a desperate Kuhal Moer inside its chest, and he whispered a Word across his blade. Sibilants curled out like wicked hooks as the hum sliced it up, amplified it, *sent* it...

The armor cracked. The helm fell away in two pieces, the cuirass crumbled and split, and my legs went out from under me as bones nine hundred years old felt antiquity catch up with them, hard. The spirits bound to the pale armor flickered across my sight, moaning as they were torn to pieces.

"Good. It's far more fitting for you to be on your knees, savage. Down there, at least, you can begin to realize how *stupid* you have been. Did you think you'd stop civilization with some stolen power and a dead God's bitch?"

Sinder's hand was cold and pale, and his skin was like smooth, slippery marble. He grabbed me by the throat, hauling me up to look him in the eyes. But something dragged me down – the immense left arm of the pale armor, still woven tight around my own flesh and blood, and still with its claws laced into the outer mantle of the Incantus Instrumentorum.

"You – both of you – could never be challenge to Anganesse, or even to the most humble of her servants. You were an *inconvenience* – which to me is far, far worse."

Even the inky tendril's of Sothara's will shrunk back into my skull under the penetrating gaze of Jerrold Sinder. What looked out from his porcelain-doll face was an intellect chilly with the frost of centuries. He was like Anganesse itself; callously self-assured, morally unassailable - and utterly without mercy. But unlike the nation which had spawned him he had no redeeming veneer of civilization. Not at that moment, anyway. Not when he raised his sword to hack off my arm, reckoning it easier to simply maim me for life than to ask me to drop the Incantus.

The magikal feedback in the air had built up to a steady sub-surface hum, like swarms of distant insects heard through summer heat. But my terror – after all, it isn't every day that an implacable sword-wielding madman limbers up to hack your arm off – must have pushed that background field of slippery energy to overload. Three things happened in swift succession.

Firstly, I lost control of my bodily functions, and hot piss spattered the bloody grass. Secondly, Jerrold Sinder snapped his head up and around, his nostrils flaring as if he'd scented blood. And thirdly, one of the great trilithons atop the southward barrow detonated, sending granite shrapnel tearing through the Ghuram host.

Most of my undead soldiers were fallen, now – cut off from the will which had driven them up from the earth, and from the organizing power of the Incantus. Those who remained were kept going only by the mad, pathetic and frankly insane spirits which clung to their bones like smoke, gibbering and raving over nine-hundred-year-old atrocities.

The blast finished off the last of the Ghuram, and my few tottering wights with them. But the hooded figures carrying the palanquin calmly set their burden down, and proceeded to fold back the cowls from their faces.

Sinder drew in a sharp breath, like an afficionado anticipating the first notes in an operatic fugue. His fingers around my throat twisted, making me look up the slope of the barrow to its crown.

"Now we will see, child. The wards are failing. My keels are coming. And the Silence can begin his work."

The things beneath the cowls weren't human. Not in my first sight – where they were grey-skinned and oily, with nothing left of their faces above the nose. In place of eyes or hair – or even the dome of a skull – these things had smooth bowls of white bone, in which purple flames flickered and boiled. Their lips were pinned shut with long, jeweled skewers, but the noise they made had nothing to do with human speech. Each of the things had been *altered* – its throat cut open and pierced with bundles of bone-white reeds, so that when they gave voice it was to an insectile drone.

In the Dark Sight they were even worse. I could begin to describe the meshings of weird angles, the bleeding razorcuts of light, the liquid edges and the toothed eyes, but... well, this vellum would burn in your hands. Suffice to say that I bucked in Sinder's grasp like a hooked mackerel, but he was too strong. Between his fingers and the dead weight of the pale armor, I was stretched out as if on the rack.

I let go of the Sight, and my last few wights collapsed into piles of bones. Because even the Excoriators had been nothing compared to the psychic foulness of the thing *within* the palanquin – a thing which now made its presence known. If I had looked at it with my psionik eyes open, my brain would have boiled like soup.

The ragged curtains billowed, and then flashed into flame. The piping of the palanquin-bearers became a skirling shriek, and I think that every living creature on the battlefield fell silent as something huge and lumpen stirred, opening its eyes.

Now, I have seen horrors. I was raised in a nation of offal and bone and blood-slick iron, and I had already witnessed death in all his grim and bloated guises. I had communed with the Slaughterborn, and the mind of Sothara the Bone Collector (who was still with me, coiled up tight as a fist in the Incantus).

But the force which emanated from the thing Sinder called the Silence was enough to make me choke back vomit. It was wrath, and disgust, and loathing – but not against the world, as it was with the Angan sorcerer. It was self-hatred, and impotent rage, and all that festers inside, turned outward.

The thing revealed within the palanquin squatted atop its timbers like an oiled toad. Vast and doughy rolls of flesh cascaded away from a pustule of a head, shaven smooth and ornately tattooed with purple runes. Thousands of piercings through nameless flaps, bulges and protrusions supported a web of silver chains which bound up the creature, and its arms were withered, atrophied sticks, endlessly twitching and flopping without purpose.

But there was intelligence in its eyes – tiny, burning chips of onyx set in deep, shadowy sockets. And from each corner of the thing's mouth a pair of long, livid scars curved back almost to its ears.

"Consider it both an education and a privilege to watch him work, Kuhal," purred Sinder, as the lips of the Silence parted, all the way along those purple-pink scars. The creature's belly was convulsing, his gorge pumping as something forced its way up from inside of him. "Surely even you savages have heard of the Nine Now Nameless? Well, this is one of them. The Black Shepherd, Sister Pain, the Devouring Wind, the Shining One, That Which Walks, the Hanged Man, the Burning Dark and the Eyeless are busy elsewhere, but my Lords could spare this one. Watch and learn!"

Sinder had recited the names of the Nine (which I *had* heard of, in the campfire stories of traveling pedlars) like a holy litany, but there was nothing sacred about what was happening up on the barrow. The Silence had its jaw stretched open to a grotesque size, and the head of something pale and phosphorescent was questing blindly up out of it. As I watched, a coil of the thing's body was vomited up, and it began to heave itself from out of the Silence's throat in dripping sections.

It was a serpent of pale, foul light – light which did not truly illuminate, but which cast everything it fell upon in a kind of jaundiced, sickly glow. Its skin was like the slick bulge of a grub or a maggot, covered and constricted by a tight, ragged sheath of translucent film. In fact, the whole great beast (for now it was all out, looping in the air like smoke) looked particularly unwholesome, rotting and covered in sores. Its face was like the three-week-dead skull of a crocodile, missing its lower jaw entirely, and its eyes were milky white orbs weeping pus.

"His throat was altered and his tongue cut out when he became a *Ghanpuri* of the Hooded Serpent in Ghuram" said Sinder, as if teaching a class on the perversions of sorcery. "But the Lady of the Venoms is a dead goddess now, and the Silence is the last link she has to this world. What you see there is a *Mha'ugaar*, a void wyrm – the shadow of her unuttered sacred words."

It moved with a speed and suddenness I would hardly have imagined. It rippled and snapped like a silken banner as it skimmed down the side of the barrow, plowing into and *through* the terrified ranks of my Khytein refugees.

They had been forced back up the side of Sothara's pyramid, the high ground their only advantage as Angan regulars pressed them hard with spear and sword. But the Mha'ugaar broke them.

It didn't leave a mark in the mortal realm, but any warrior it so much as touched turned suddenly pale and cold, breathing his last as a vapor of ice crystals. I dared not look at the thing with the Dark Sight; even with mundane eyes I could see the tatters and wisps of soul-stuff sucked down into the Wyrm's maw.

"It's... it's horrible! Make it stop!" I stammered, as the vile thing came around for another pass. It slammed sideways into a group of Conn's Wildkin archers, freezing them in mid-draw. Bowstaves and bones snapped from the utter cold of it, and it let out a rasping gurgle of satisfaction.

"It *can't* stop. It must feed now that it's free. Really, child – this is all for your edification. Don't be so foolish as to scorn the work of your friend the Silence. Soon you will know him like a brother!"

The smile on Sinder's face wasn't mocking – it was the horribly genuine, waxy grin of a zealot. And now his steely fingers turned my head to look at Makara.

"No," I whispered, clenching my eyes shut tight. She was only just staggering to her feet, pushing her hair back from her face with one muddy hand...

"Yesssss," hissed my captor, and there was savage joy in his voice. "Make this moment part of yourself, boy. Hate is power! Hate is *transcendence*!"

Hooks made of Sinder's will pried my eyelids open, and I saw.

Conn was there, right in the path of the onrushing Wyrm, his halo of thorns blazing with blue, wintry light. Even from this distance I could see that his eyes were wrong – the flat gray of frozen nail-heads, and his bowblade spun in his hands as he whirled aside, raking its wicked edge into the serpent's flank.

It lashed him with a flick of his tail, but he was too fast, ducking under it to come back to his feet smiling. Thick, slow gelatine oozed from a long gash in the Wyrm's belly, and it moaned, low and angry. Then it struck again.

This time it looped in from above, trying to spear down and simply engulf the wild man who opposed it. But there was a tiny shred of Ciermakh's power here, left over from when the wolf-boy walked the earth nine centuries ago, and like called to like. Conn was so fast he was less than a blur, and this time his bowblade unspliced a rope of greyish muscle behind the thing's skull. Conn followed through by drawing and firing an arrow right into its left eye.

The Mha'ugaar reared back, howling, and I couldn't help but grin. Sinder noticed, and his grip tightened, all but choking me.

"Keep watching," he grated. "You'll find that a little hope just makes this all the more painful..."

Behind Conn, Makara had unshipped a small leather pack from her back. She drew forth two shining shards of something reflective and glassy, then used the edge of one to cut the back of her arm open in a shallow gash.

Conn took his assault to the Mha'ugaar, his bowblade whirling and slicing as it reared up, his feet sidestepping and almost *dancing* as it lashed out with its tail. A dozen criss-crossed wounds hashed its belly now, and it had learned to fear him. It circled warily in the air, coiling in on itself, the stub on an arrow still protruding from one dripping eye socket.

He was laughing as he leaped in to finish the thing, drawing a long curved dagger from his belt with his right hand, while the bowblade blurred in his left. Up, and he vaulted off a sickly coil of the serpent, rising up over its head. Wings of shadow snuffed out its corpse-light, and the two blades met deep in its throat, eliciting a gurgling shriek.

Then the second and third Mha'ugaar slammed into Conn, still pinned to the air in mid-strike. They quartered his soul just as his blades had done to the spine of their brother, merging and flowing through each other as they tore his essence from his living bones. A rime of frost glittered on the wild boy's skin as he fell. I believe the last look in his eyes was one of utter, horrified surprise.

He shattered when he struck the ground.

"You see?" sneered Jerrold Sinder. "Hope is just prolonging the inevitable. You'll..."

One thing I've learned over the years – and a fact which Ulkar had always been pleased to teach me over and over again on the training field – was that an overconfident enemy is, in a way, the larval state of a dead fool. One can become the other with just a little tilt in the right direction. While the pale-skinned sorcerer had me by the throat, he had utterly discounted the fact that I still had a hand free. And, as a savage barbarian bastard, my person was liberally salted with small, individually named blades designed for every task from skinning a bear to cleaning the filth from under my fingernails. I chose the *tsangu*, a ritual dagger for committing suicide by self-evisceration. No Khytein Moer had actually performed the ritual of the Last Walk in living memory, but the little hooked dagger was a kind of crude reminder that a man's lord could demand it of him. It was also five inches of sharpened iron which missed the Angan's eye by a hair's whisper.

He twitched out of the way just in time for the *tsangu* to carve open his perfect cheek. A spatter of alarmingly thick, crimson blood welled out of Sinder like sap, and he blinked, once – utterly without pain.

But his coven felt it. Like the drummers who attended our Khytein warbards, the robed priests who were weaving power behind a living wall of the Faceless were bound to their master. Feedback sliced ribbons from their faces in a ramifying shockwave of shared agony, and the spell faltered.

"You irritating little..." snarled Sinder, letting go of my throat to slap the knife from my hand. But the rest of his words were drowned out by a sound like slabs of metal being torn in half. Something hammered on the other side of the sky, and I rolled aside, struggling to tear my arm from the last inert chunk of the pale armor, still holding the Incantus. It felt as if spikes of bone had burrowed clean through my hand and wrist – which was more than likely the case. I saw Sinder's shadow fall across the sphere of iron and gold, and so I anticipated the blow which axed me to the dirt. It didn't hurt any less.

The Angan had quite lost his composure. Above him a gyre of bent lightning was ripping the sky apart, clouds shredded into skeins of ink and marble. But his eyes were worse. He drew back a foot to stave in my ribs, then thought better of it. He hunched over me instead, and there was honest to Gods *foam* at the corners of his mouth.

"Well, we *could* have taken the warding apart piece by piece, and some of us might have lived," he said. "But you had to know better, didn't you? Between you and that mindless whore of Maudrin's..."

Makara's voice came from right behind Sinder's shoulder, and for the first time I saw actual fear on his face. Not to do things by halves, he changed it into the panic-snarl of a mongrel dog.

"Oh, so very *cultured*," purred the young warbard, her words as rich and deep as the finger-thick bass strings of a lyrecaster. "And as for 'mindless whore'... we'll talk about that pleasantry later. Right now, we invoke the Rite of the Crucible. Do you agree to Trial?"

Her voice was different. Gernish Maudrin's inflection wrapped around Makara's words like wire around silk.

Now, I'd never heard of the Rite of the Crucible. You haven't either, because in these latter times there are only a poor few Powers of the Third Tier left. If they want to see who is the strongest, they shuffle papers and dispatch armies and generally perform a kind of geriatric coitus with siege-works and delegations of lawyers. Long ago – well before Gernish Maudrin spoke with the voice of my would-be lover in the middle of a necropolis battlefield – the Powers of the Second Tier (a tight pantheon of unbelievably aged sorcerers, the meat-puppets of old Gods, and certain syphilitic demigods) had decreed that a framework for one-on-one magikal combat was needed to prevent whole swathes of Sarem from becoming hexed wastelands.

As I said, at the time, I knew nothing of the Rite. But I knew about the circle Ulkar used to draw in the dust with his boot when one of his recruits needed taking down a notch or three. I knew the smile he got on his face when some saga-addled lordling crossed the line into a world of multiple fractures and face-altering education.

Sinder wore that smile now.

"Done, done, and three times done," said the Angan. "By Esau, my power, and my living heart I invoke..."

"Good," interrupted Makara, and there was the hint of both a girlish laugh and Maudrin's oily chuckle in her voice. "We challenge the Silence."

Even when we go down into stone and sand and glass, our law will stand. When the Rite is called, only one may survive. Two will Witness, and one will triumph, and neither hand nor stroke of power will fall upon the Watchers, or those blind to the light of the Unmanifest. Those who break the hallow will suffer to burn, and their husks will be cast into the Outer Dark, powerless, forfeit, world unto ending...

The Principia Lex of the Last Conventicle, translated from its pillars of black jade by sub-redactor Vhulia Tling of Saradrim

THERE WAS A reason behind the madness of challenging one of the Nine. Realization dawned very, very slowly in me just exactly where Gernish Maudrin was hiding, as I detected his own particular brand of cunning in the trap. It was one of those acutely embarrassing revelations which comes far too late, and along with it came another – my mind had gone wrong.

The tumult of battle (and my own clumsy stab at heroism) had pushed the sensation back, but it was there, and it was growing. A bitter taste trickled down the back of my throat, and the world – which, you'll admit, was already quite a surreal vision of horror at this point – was wavering and twisting like a heat mirage.

But this one horrible little thought bubbled its way to the surface, even as Jerrold Sinder laughed above me.

Makara was far more powerful than I had realized. She was pregnant with Gernish Maudrin's child, and through some sorcery *the little unborn thing contained the old warbard's soul.* That tiny knot of flesh and will inside her would neither grow or be born, however – it was simply a sanctuary until he could arrange his own resurrection.

Sinder had no idea. He thought that the whole challenge was just a far less subtle snare – one which prevented him, momentarily, from grinding my skull into the dirt.

"I suppose I don't even have to guess who you call as witness? I will stand second for my lovely Silence, of course. And when you are destroyed, these few pitiful scraps of an army will be taken. Processing will help them atone for their hubris."

Indeed, Elion Morekh and the remains of his crew – wretched landlocked pirates and refugees all – were hemmed in by spears now. A valiant last stand sounds wonderful when it's set to music and poetry, but much worse when you can see the bloody steel in front of you.

"Very well, corpseworm. We begin!"

This time the voice was nine parts Maudrin to one tiny echo of Makara. Her hands were bleeding as she snapped the two pieces of mirror together, face to face. The backs of them were black – a deeper black than any object had a right to be, and she stretched the square thus formed out between her fingers, changing its shape *here* and *here...*

The Silence looked like an insensible slough of meat and fat, but the thing's mind must have been sharp enough. Its pet Wyrms boiled up from above the shattered remains of Conn, arrowing through the air toward Makara, and at the same time it loosed a terrible shriek through the pipes in its throat, leading a chorus of its Mutilated bearers. A pillar of lightning which streamed from the tip of a nearby obelisk suddenly bent at right angles, hammered across the valley by their will.

But Makara's hands had done their work. Now she placed the black mirror in the air before her, and plunged her arms through it up to the elbow...

Giant grasping fingers erupted from the shadow of a broken monolith – a shadow the exact shape of Makara's mirror spell. They snapped shut on one of the Mha'ugaar even as the lightning came crashing down on the young warbard, only to shatter into crazed shards of light a handspan from her head. If I hadn't felt any love for her before, I would have at that moment, because she didn't even blink. Instead she caught the lashing tail of the Mha'ugaar with her other hand, and with a twist she tore it apart.

Plasmic foulness spattered down like rain, burning the grass with cold. But that crackle and grind of vertebrae and ribs was too much for the sorcerous beast to withstand, and it died before the husk of it hit the ground, evaporating into dirty mist.

Makara pulled her hands back from the black mirror even as

the Silence countered her technique, chopping the air with one of his stunted arms and severing the top of the monolith as if with an invisible blade. The shadow, now a different shape from Makara's focus, reverted from a yawning chasm to a simple trick of light and shade... but the battle was joined. The mirror changed shape again, and another great clawed talon erupted from the side of a fallen statue, palm flat to the onrushing charge of the remaining Wyrm. The Silence was already heaving and pumping as he struggled to vomit up an even larger serpent-beast, this one swelling his gorge like that of a bullfrog.

Makara's giant shadow-hand slapped the remaining Mha'ugaar down hard, and friend and foe alike winced as they heard its bones shatter. Twitching, pulped, the thing tried to rear up again, but now the young warbard's hand was a fist, and it drove the rotting apparition's skull down into the mud, sending the wyrm back to the outer dark.

The Silence cut his losses. One of his twisted limbs hacked at the air again, and Makara pulled her hand back just in time as stone and shadow exploded. Or *almost* in time – a spray of bright blood flew from her knuckles as the mirror shard collapsed in her hands.

And now a greater void wyrm – the mother of those cold and ugly things – was lumbering up into the air, its phosphorescent eyes burning with foulness. This one was not just bigger than its spawn – it was more grossly deformed, and a sheaf of wriggling black tentacles lashed from its throat. Its lower jaw was split in two, lolling open as its immense carcass coiled around an obelisk, and the tip of its tail was a rattle of spiked bone big enough to crush a longhouse flat.

Sinder laughed above me, a look of childlike wonder on his face. But I was busy. Not just watching the battle, but calling out to Sei, who I hadn't seen since my mad charge into the Angan ranks. Perhaps my little familiar would be able to set me free...

The hammer of bone came down on Makara as she tried desperately to work her shadow-mirror, and she only just managed to duck and roll out of its path. Shards of stone flew in splinters, and only the sheer will of both the young warbard and Gernish Maudrin himself kept her bloody fingers clenched around the glass. The Mha'ugaar bellowed in frustration, lashing the air with dark, glistening tendrils, but these were much easier work for a child of the Khytein. Makara's free hand swung a slim *kuris* in a blur of silver, chopping through them even as the bitter cold of the wyrm warped and shattered the blade.

The beast squealed in agony, rearing up, the stumps of legs along its pale flanks churning the air as it rose.

And Makara brought her lyrecaster around on its chains – the great twin-horned instrument of Aerik Stormsong, its strings sizzling with blue fire in the dark. The shard of mirror was her pick as wild harmonics blurred through the air, the notes of an intricate song which should not have been able to be played with a mere ten fingers and two hands.

The Mha'ugaar loomed over her like a wave, seething with venom. But just as it began to fall Makara ran her mirror-glass the length of the lyre's strings and thew it into the air. The halo of sparks around the instrument was sucked into that little shard of darkness, and I swear the echoes of the song followed it – the memory of those notes torn from my mind as well.

A simple little tune, wrapped around a core of such complexity and weight that it was almost...

Well, *alive* was the only word. It began unfolding the black glass even before it reached the zenith of its arc.

Facet after facet slid out of nowhere and clicked into place, quick as raindrops merging together into a trickle, then into a flood. Arms, legs, fingers, a head rising up from a wide chest of glittering crystal, and inside them all a swirling maelstrom of blue fire and darkness. The thing's eyes opened just in time for those immense hands to catch the Mha'ugaar, and its feet were driven a a full tenspan deep into the earth as it landed, taking up the weight.

I laughed, unhinged. Sinder was slack-jawed and gaping. Angan soldiers and Khytein alike threw down their weapons and screamed.

It was Aerik Stormsong, as tall as Sothara's black pyramid and made of hollow glass. He gritted his teeth as the great Mha'ugaar tried to slither through his fingers, but it had nowhere to go. Huge as it was, it was a matched by the sheer size of the old bard's avatar, and he was utterly relentless.

The Silence howled as Aerik took the wyrm's tail in both hands and swung it in a blur, hammering its body into a row of standing stones. Trilithons burst, steaming with cold. Foul ichor spattered as Aerik brought the thing back a second time, a screeching, writhing mass of pulped flesh and jagged bone. This time he lined it up on an avenue of obelisks, radiating away from the black pyramid, and when he brought it down the unyielding stone pierced the wyrm in ten places.

Arcs of lightning flew from the Silence, and from the hollow skulls of his attendant slaves, washing over the Stormsong like rain. But they couldn't touch him now. I understood, there on the ground beneath Sinder's boot, how Aerik had cheated death. He had become the wild song itself, and used his lyrecaster just as Gernish Maudrin had used the flesh of his unborn child.

A huge hand of glass and shadow reached out for the Silence, poised to pluck him from his palanquin.

Jerrold Sinder recovered from his shock admirably. He'd been expecting to see his enemy crushed, a defiant little girl torn apart by the horror of one of the Nine. Instead he'd seen his pet monster bloodied and humiliated, and his victory almost turned to defeat in a span of heartbeats. Like any civilized thug, he appealed to the law.

"Broken! The Rite of the Crucible is void! I call upon the Powers of the Second Tier to witness justice in their name!"

He took in a breath, and every one of his priests and acolytes choked to death on their own screams. The chanting which had been meticulously unweaving the wards was severed, cut off as Sinder simply ripped the life-essence from his thralls.

Then he aimed his bifurcated sword at the giant avatar of Aerik Stormsong and spoke a Word.

The hand which reached out to the Silence shattered, raining down wicked shards of glass. The Mutilated seemed not to feel the glittering blades slicing into them, but the Silence surely did – his reedy bellow of pain was like a physical blow. Sinder spoke again, and this time I actually saw the ripple of unspeakable force which tore out from his sword. It blew a hole the size of an oxcart through Aerik's chest.

I had no idea at the time what the two elder bards had risked. But Sinder knew that they had made their souls forfeit by helping Makara in her duel, and he punished them with fury.

"First the foolish old man," he grated, panting as he hurled another bolt of force against the tottering hulk of the Stormsong. Discordant notes rang out as Aerik collapsed to his knees, a glittering sleet of broken glass cascading from him as he disintegrated.

"Then that foul bastard of Maudrin's...."

This time it was a twitch of his clawlike hand, fingers twisting into a knotted fist. Makara screamed as something ruptured deep inside, and I knew that her unborn child had been torn apart. She fell to her knees in the mud, writhing in pain, and Elion Morekh ran to cradle her head in his hands. Sinder was done with her, however.

He sent a final blast of energy ravening across the valley, and the last thing I saw of Aerik Stormsong was the frozen grimace of defiance on his face. An instant later it was blown to pieces.

"Now," gasped the Angan sorcerer, plunging his sword into the earth and leaning on it heavily. "Where were we? Ah, yes..." he ran the back of his hand across his lips, and his arm came away smeared with thick bright blood. "Break the whelp, take his power, and set this crooked world to rights. Starting with the righteous punishment of these rebellious slaves!"

A dark triangular shadow fell across us both as he screwed up the remainder of his power, and the riven sky turned to stone. The keels were here, and under their guns the last of the free Khytein would fall...

Then I felt the Incantus thump beneath my fingers like a heart. It was the same sensation I'd felt years earlier when I touched the dried-up husk of Sei, down under the longhouse of the Horned Boar in summer, and I strained to turn my head and see what was happening.

It *was* the little dead cat, but this time he was more than just polished bones. The fraying wards around Sothara's necropolis had saturated the air with the hot-metal scent of magik, and the thing which came darting through the stunned, half-mad ranks of the Anganesse was a shimmering blur of green light – the ghost of a cat pulling a fluttering skein of something along in its wake.

Sinder snarled, and loosed the bolt he'd been preparing for me at the nimble apparition, missing by the flick of a tail. Now Sei was past the last stumbling guardsmen, through the ring of dead acolytes, and he leaped lightly atop the Incantus, his spirit form sinking into the mesh of iron and gold even as his bones collapsed outside it. The twisted ribbons of light he carried in his teeth went with him, curling in knotting into the Instrumentorum in eye-watering patterns.

Time stopped.

In the frozen instant which followed my mind fell into the pattern of the Incantus. The filigree of spinning metal becoming a fall of dead leaves, and the darkness blurred into a clearing in the Stormwood. It was a place of ritual – there was the smooth and bloody stone carved with runes, and held down with his head in the bowl of it was Sothara.

Gernish Maudrin held his left arm, and bore down on his neck. Aerik Stormsong held his right, and his fingers were coiled in the old necromancer's hair.

"No time for explanations. They'd break your mind in any case," said Aerik, as if I hadn't just witnessed a titanic shade of him smashed to splinters with magik. "You are in the Incantus, and it's one with your mind. All this is happening in the time between Sei reaching you and dear old Jerrold hacking off your arm to stop us."

"I would have chosen something other than a cat," grunted Maudrin, his dark eyes twinkling. "But he did well. And I suppose it would have been hard for a raven to carry both of our souls..."

"All you need to know is this," said the Stormsong, pulling Sothara's head up from the stone. His eyes were glazed and his skin was beaded with sweat – here he was more wretch than monster. "We drugged you. Makara drugged you, with that kiss you're so moonstruck over. So that if this old fool tried to take your mind he'd run up against a whole lot of messy chemical emotions. Glands and such. Not his forte after nine hundred years undead."

"What you have to do is this. *Survive.* What we're going to do now will critically destabilize the Incantus..."

"He means it's going to blow up..."

"But you should be able to hold onto some of his knowledge. Technical things. How to raise the dead with a little more.... finesse, for example."

"Now – take the club. And make sure you swing it hard enough."

It was in my hands. A carved elk femur with a great chunk of obsidian lashed to one end. The runes sliced into the bone seemed to writhe and glow as I stepped forward, bringing it back over my head. Sothara's eyes were as wide and deep as drowning pools, and I screamed, hammering that chunk of black rock down toward his skull -

(   )

I was still screaming as I opened my eyes, and it became a bellow of rage as I brought the Incantus Instrumentorum up and around to block the swing of Sinder's blade. The force of it knocked the Angan sorcerer back, and I'd pulled myself to my feet by the time he recovered. The second blow of the great metal sphere collided with his sword in a storm of sparks, and the third, and the fourth. I drove him to his knees.

I was panting, my breath furnace-hot, and my muscles ached from swinging the weight of all that bone armor and runic iron. But my mind was my own again. All that was left of the Bone Collector was a skeletal web of memories, cold and inert.

I raised the Incantus over my head. It was spinning faster now, flames licking up from inside, and the iron was glowing red. One last blow, and I knew that it would detonate, sending both Sinder and I to the hells.

"Do it," he rasped, pushing himself up to one knee. "Strike me down! Martyr me, and there will be a hundred more to follow. Do you really think your ignorant bards are the only ones who can cheat death?"

Above us I heard the slide and grind of metal. Bonepowder guns – whole batteries of them – aimed down from under the keels, ready to tear my friends apart.

"Go on. Give them a reason to fire! Kill me, and your friends die too. Your pitiful nation ends in blood, Kuhal – one way or the other."

He was smiling. An infuriating half-smirk, so smug, so secure in his own power...

I looked up. Above us the two great war keels hung like thunderheads of stone, drifting slowly as hundreds of gunners primed their great flame-spitting weapons. I watched circles of carven runes the size of houses slide past, glowing green against the grey. My gaze was sucked in, over the lip of the great ossuary well drilled through the stoneship, a maw a hundred spans across fretted with lightning.

Through it I could see the second Keel, and for an instant I matched the same blazing runes carved into its belly. I looked down at Sinder.

"No," he said, catching on far too late. "Not here! There's too much..."

But I never heard the end of his plea. I had already swung my arm back as far is it would go, and with a great heave I flung the Incantus Intrumentorum *up* – right into the seething eye of the ossuary well.

The bone armor unraveled as I threw, disintegrating in a comet-tail of burning pieces. But the spinning ball of incandescence kept rising, clear through the first Keel and up into the core of the second, where they were aligned.

Sinder was right. Here, in this place, with the wards broken and raw magik arcing and flaring... this was a place where sorcery could wake horrors and wonders.

The detonation of a necromancer's soul was like a spark in a distillery.

The explosion tore the highest Keel to pieces, fracturing it along its axis with a sound like the crack of a dead God's bones. Castle turrets spewed green fire before their individual stones were peeled away, consumed in a growing sphere of energy. Molten rock rained down, and evaporated before it hit the ground.

Huge severed chunks of the stoneship bounced and rolled among the Anganesse army, pulverizing whole ranks at a blow. As I watched, the arrowhead prow of the Keel harrowed the flat top of Sothara's pyramid, scattering sod and grass and the black marble beneath. I saw Elion Morekh and his hulking crewman Soap scoop up Makara and duck into an exposed tunnel mouth, just before an entire great shard of granite sheared off the ledge where they had stood.

Then the power broke, and for the second time in my life I felt the soul-deep chill of the outer dark.

Sinder and I – and the few hundred Angan warriors under the shadow of the lower Keel – were spared the worst of it. But those on the upper decks of the remaining stoneship must have been roasted alive, blown to ashes a second later as unchained powers raved and seethed. Through the empty eye of the ossuary well I saw the sky itself crack, and watched, horrified as vast things, half gelatinous, all eyes and twitching appendages... well, suffice to say they were locked in spasms of either murder or lust, or *both*.

I felt their hunger for a second, and then reality lurched, tottering. This time it wasn't a cold ocean which filled the cracks. It was the black, star-scattered night sky, and it rushed toward me...

No.

It was the Keel, falling.

Sinder saw the runes flicker and fail, and he swayed to his feet, clenching one hand around my throat.

"You stupid, complicating little fool," he rasped, as a mountain fell from the sky around us. We were centred in the eye of the well, and as the stoneship hit the ground we were cupped in its void. The flat bottom of the Keel shook the earth as it struck, crushing an army to pulp, but somehow Jerrold Sinder kept his feet, holding me up out of the mud.

"I would have killed them clean, boy. Clean and once and forever. But now I have to make all this loss worth my while. Now I have to make them *suffer*."

Around us the ossuary batteries winked with lambent fire, painting Sinder's face as a death-mask. We were down at the bottom of a well of bones, entombed in the dead hulk of the Keel.

The last thing I saw was the smile on his face as he brought his fist back, and – all veneer of civilized grace burned away – brought it forward to hammer me down into the mud.

Four

Song of Ending

Do not spite the knife which cuts you
as you sharpen it. We shape our tools to
our own nature, and like a eunuch slave
raised for war, a knife which hungers for
blood is a proud reflection of its master.

Akhazi proverb, from the thirteenth kingdom era

WE SAILED FOR the gap in the Hiledoran known as the Bloody Gates, heading for the highlands of the Angan vassal state of Ontokh. Up above, the crew of the war Keel *Valor Eternal* kept watch for draken amid the ragged clouds, while its nekrologist-priests whipped the arcane engines of the stoneship into a rumbling fury. Sinder was running for home, and by the time I'd recovered from my wounds I found out why.

I had expected chains.

Well, when you're the captive of a deathless monster like the dear Provincial Governor, and he's promised you suffering in generous amounts, wouldn't you expect the same? But I awoke on cool satin sheets, in a room high in the Keel's tower. I awoke, in fact, because a hand was pressing a cold cloth to my forehead, and because, behind the pervasive smell of hot bones and oiled copper, I could detect freshly baked bread and ripe berries.

Veteran of several hangovers, even at my tender age, I faked delirium. Through slitted eyes I watched a white-clad slave woman (a Ghuram, branded with the wheel-and-cross upon one golden cheek) step away from the bed, hurrying to the side of a similarly clad Ontokhi.

"Come on! The chorus will be starting again soon. Let's get out of this place!"

"Have you changed his pillows? The housemaster told us to treat him as an honored guest, and I'll not take another whipping for the sake of a few screams. Well?"

"I don't see why they didn't leave this one chained up like the rest of them. If the Akhazi weren't marching then the Maggot wouldn't have to hurry so..."

"And which of the guards are you sleeping with to spout such nonsense? Have a care how you name our pale Lord, Silde – he has ears everywhere."

Silde – the Ghuram – laughed, but it was a bitter thing.

"The Maggot hasn't got time for the likes of us, Olena. And if you must know, it was that young Sejant of the gunnery decks, Garmond." She giggled. "He told me that the acolytes were playing at dice, and one of the navigators said..."

"Pillows! Now! If you want to miss out on Lord Sinder's sweet music, you had better hurry!"

If found out what Olena meant only a handful of heartbeats after they closed the door. That was when the screaming started.

Brass tubes like sprays of calla lilies depended from the high ceiling of the chamber, and cries of anguish, sobs and moans began to echo from them one by one as I lay on the bed below. They cried out in the language of my birth, so I knew they were Khytein... though one or two spat curses in the pithy Faeroan tongue.

Realization gripped me as I listened. These were my friends, my allies... captives like me. And the torturers of Anganesse, down in the heart-strata of the Keel – they weren't asking them any questions. This little show was *orchestrated*. Who knows how many had suffered while I slept? Had it been days, or weeks or...

I leaped from the bed, naked, wrapping one of the red satin sheets around my shoulders as the doors of the room creaked open. Still the hideous shrieks, groans, wet, cracking noises and horrible laughter rang out, blurring into one terrible voice. My legs were weak, but I stood to face the apparition framed between the marble pillars with as much dignity as I could muster.

It was Jerrold Sinder, and he had come in all his courtly Angan finery – loose trousers sewn with tiny seed pearls, a wide sash belt, and a knee-length robe embroidered with golden thread on white. His long pale hair was bound up in a circlet of silver wires and black feathers, and from this confection of metal depended a train of long black ribbons. Each finger was sheathed in segmented silver armor, the nails smooth teardrops of ivory. But all of this was overshadowed by the symmetrical folds and edges of his outer cape, a thing of flat, angular panes of some translucent fabric which shimmered in rainbow colours. It was as if the servants who flitted about the outer edges of the thing had wrapped Sinder inside the reflection of diamonds, hammered out into geometric jags and turrets which moved with him.

There were a lot of servants. At least two of them were midgets, whose task it was to place hexagonal silver tiles down in front of the Provincial Governor so his bare feet never touched the floor. They scurried to retrieve the rune-etched plates from behind him as he approached. Bodyguards in the black masks and tall helms of the Faceless fanned out to either side of the door, and behind Sinder thronged a collection of scribes, fops, blades, heralds, acolytes and attendants who conducted a very polite, near-silent vicious brawl for the pleasure of standing nearest to their Lord.

"Ahhh! Our honoured guest awakes," purred Sinder, tilting his head to one side in a way which made me think of predatory birds. "Leave us. We have much to discuss."

If the chorus of screams and begging had any discernible effect on the gaggle of courtiers, none was graceless enough to show it. Their faces were a gallery of porcelain masks as they moved to comply – makeup tracked with sweat lines and glittering with crushed jewels.

The immense, ethereal outer cape folded down with a series of audible cracks, until it was nothing more than a slim white rod, which was wrapped in silk and removed. The midgets, minstrels, guards and other sundry human jewelry melted away, leaving me alone with Jerrold Sinder, a single Faceless One robed all in black – and the Ghuram slave, Silde. The masked warrior held both of her wrists in one hand.

"Please! My Lord, I beg you! I..."

Sinder slapped her, casually, without even really looking. It was still almost enough to break her neck His eyes were on me, watching my reaction.

"*Shut up*. Your disrespect has earned this – now, be edified in silence."

I pulled the sheet closely around my shoulders and took a step forward, but the Faceless was too fast. A long saber was in his hand before I could blink, its tip aimed at my throat.

"No, Khytein, you don't want to do that. He's so very keen to gut you, after what you did to his brothers. Just watch."

One of Sinder's segmented armor-rings clicked as a tiny blade sprouted from under its ivory nail. Now Silde struggled in vain, bloodying her wrists against he Faceless One's steel gauntlets. But her captor was implacable. With a slow, almost loving caress of his razor-edged finger he stripped the linen shift from her body. Her sobs merged into the background chorus of screams from the calla-lily pipes above.

Sinder didn't turn back to me, but he raised his hand up over his shoulder so I could see it clearly.

"And should not disrespect be punished, even more strictly than any other transgression? Because it is from disrespect that all other rebellions and follies flow, is it not?"

Claw blades sprung forth with four tiny, oily little clicks. The tip of the sabre pricked blood from my chest as I snarled.

"No! Stop this!"

The pale sorcerer turned, his eyes all leering mock-innocence.

"Oh? Do you want her, then? I had promised you every luxury as my guest, but I hadn't thought you man enough to desire such..."

"No!"

"Then you *don't* want her? Take a good look..."

Silde had turned her face away, hanging limply from the Faceless One's grip.

"I said *no*, you bastard! You..."

"Good," snapped Sinder, suddenly cold. He grabbed Silde by the neck and lifted her effortlessly into the air. "Neither do I."

And with a contemptuous gesture he threw the Ghuram slave-girl out through the window. We were more than a mile above the jagged rocks of the Hiledoran, and the whole Keel seemed to shudder as she fell, lurching in the air.

"A clumsy lesson, but a good one. I've come to offer you far more mercy than you deserve, child, but I would have you know that such qualities are in desperately short supply. Sit."

Something bumped up against the back of my legs, and I collapsed gracelessly into a carved bluewood chair. Sinder's servants were utterly silent, moving on deformed feet tightly bound in velvet. They placed a table between us, laden with the bread and fruit I had smelled earlier.

"You have been given this chance by politics, boy. One of my cherished brothers, the Pontifex of Estaron, has forbidden any but the Faithful from setting foot on the lands where Esau walked. To this end, he has, in his wisdom, ordered the crucifixion of a trading caravan who were - so they said - quite ignorant of the new law."

"Akhazi," I whispered, still clutching the sheet tight around my shoulders. I was still half bile and anger, but I caught my own reflection in a polished brass plate, and I saw just how emaciated I'd become. Reaching across to throttle the pale Angan lord would only see me fly like Silde had done.

Sinder nodded, once, and very slowly.

"Akhazi. Yes. The Children of the Naked Sun are quite displeased, and they march north to punish us in the name of the Coldblood.

For the last three hundred years the men of the utter south have been content to watch us conquer other pale-skinned northern heretics. Now they have become indignant, and demand that we cede the entire province of Ghuram to them as recompense for our 'crimes'. It cannot happen."

"It would shame the Thearch," I hazarded, possessed by the need to seem worldly wise in the ways of politics. Luckily, politics is nothing but the drunken clan feuding of my people written on a grand scale. "He would lose face before his warriors."

"Put like a savage, but true enough," said Sinder. "We can beat the Akhazi, but the war would end us both. Still, there are those among the Hierocracy who cry out for blood. I, for one, urge a peaceful solution."

I laughed, against my better judgment, and Sinder raised one perfect eyebrow.

"I'll make no secret of it – I wanted you destroyed. I wished to wring the power from your corpse. But time has swept us both away. If you want to live – and if you want to see your friends released – you will listen to my generous offer."

Another scream split the air, trailing off into mad, babbling prayers. Sinder smiled.

"You can think about it as long as you like, Kuhal – just remember what your time costs those below. Now – consider this. I am willing to name anyone you choose as provincial governor in the north. Khytein will become a vassal state like Ontokh and Rasuul, and I will rule there in name only. In truth, I'll be very busy in my new role. Because *you* will submit to the rite of soul-binding, and become one of the Nine. The Silence will not survive the wounds inflicted on his mind, and we have need of a new Nameless One. One who can raise an army of the dead to rout the Akhazi."

He sipped tea from a bone-white cup decorated with a pattern of stars. He sounded for all the world as if he were offering me a new horse, rather than utter slavery.

"The binding is painless, permanent, and irreversible. And the person who brings the Thearch not just victory, but a new and thoroughly deniable monster, is sure to be elevated to the rank of Archpraetorian. This would suit my plans admirably."

He put down his cup with a prim little click.

"And *that's* your most generous offer? Would you like me to whore for your armies as well?"

"The alternative is *death*, of course. Though at this stage of the game, I truly would regret killing you. There's simply not enough time to learn your secrets, and it would be mere torture and execution for its own sake." He sighed. "Try to see reason, child! Your nation is lost, your friends are dying by inches, and I could crush your mind with power right now. Hollow bravado has no place here."

I thought of Silde, of the look in her eyes as Sinder picked her up with a single hand. Of the shock which ran through the Keel as she fell...

"You couldn't. You can't," I whispered. "Use power here, and this whole damn rock will smash to pieces when it falls."

The look Sinder gave me should have burned my face from my blackened skull. In fact, if I hadn't been absolutely correct, it *would* have.

"Very well. But it is still well within my power to have your friends and countrymen suffer, Kuhal. You will hear every instant of agony, and know that you can..."

He was interrupted by a blast of brazen horns, ringing out from the flat deck of the Keel below. Once, twice, the deep-bellied note echoed off the peaks, and then it was followed by shouts of alarm.

"Draken! A ravening of them, off to starboard! All hands to the ballistae!"

Cursing, the Angan sorcerer rushed to the window, careless of his finery. A chill wind sent his ribbons and feathers streaming as he spun away, and I took his place in a heartbeat, eager to see those creatures which we Khytein had considered only a legend.

"Don't think about jumping, child," warned Sinder as he turned in the doorway. "A grand gesture won't save your friends, or your nation. And when I'm done with these beasts, you will perhaps have had time to consider my offer."

I had no time for his words. There, out on the curling edge of the storm, rode a whole ravening of serpentine horrors, scales flashing in the pale sunlight. They flew with their great membranous wings spread wide and their lithe, clawed limbs tucked in tight to their bodies, tails lashing as they used them to swim through the air currents. I was reminded of the insect-hunting bats which haunted the Stormwood, but these were on a far grander scale – each one was a long as a feasting hall, from the vanes at the tip of their tails to their scaly snouts.

And they were *fast*!

There are fools – men like the good doctor Nyvar Xeng and his kind – who will tell you that the draken of the Hiledoran must have been myths, or at least creatures spawned and sustained by old magik. That they could never fly. But I have seen the iron-hard bones pressed under stone of flying beasts even bigger, from the dawn ages of the world. And more than this, I have seen a ravening of draken on the wing, speeding to the attack, like swallows the size of warships.

The *Valor Eternal* had very little rigging – what few masts and stays it had were for the small trim-sails which kept it level as it rode the air. So the first of the draken was able to skim the flat deck of the Keel at head height, braving a gauntlet of ballista bolts and bowshot. It jinked and swerved as nimbly as a hunting hawk, rolling with its wings half-folded before its great yellow eyes fixed on some likely prey.

Hands uncomfortably similar to my own – though scaly, huge, and tipped with wicked claws – lashed out in a blur, and an armored sejant of the Faceless was plucked from his feet, still trying to wind back his crossbow. The creature didn't pause – its arrow-fast swoop became a plunge down over the side of the Keel as it flared its wings, and that long neck twisted, jaws snapping...

I just managed to glimpse a shower of bright blood, hanging like mist in the air, before the draken's tail slashed through it and it was gone.

Now came more of the great beasts, shrugging aside a hail of arrows and dodging the larger bolts of the Keel's siege bows. As they plucked men from the deck or threw them screaming over the side I noticed that there were figures crouched low on their backs, hanging tight between the massive muscles which powered their wings.

They were half-naked despite the cold – tattooed in orange and red, their hair bound into great shaggy ropes with cord and wire, and they shared the lean, emaciated look of their airborne chargers. They stood tall in their leather stirrups as they came roaring past, answering the Angan arrow-storm with their own small recurved bows, picking off targets one at a time. Where their bolts struck flesh men screamed and flailed madly, because some alchemy caused them to burn as bright as tiny suns.

Now came the crack and boom of the bonepowder murder-guns, and a dark-winged draken was plucked from the sky, its wings crumpling and folding back as it fell. Gears ground and rumbled as more of the guns were turned skyward, but the drakenriders were quick to see their peril, and dark shapes descended from out of the sun to rip and ravage the gun crews, tearing the weapons from their mounts. Glass shells of consecrated bone shattered, sending green veils of fire licking over the stone of the Keel, almost as high as my eyrie window.

One of the riders must have noticed the flames, because he suddenly let loose a piercing whistle, pointing with his bowstave. His mount was crouched on the deck, hemmed in by armored spearmen, but with a twitch of his heels it leaped skyward, knocking a score of men sprawling in the downdraft. As the creature struggled to gain altitude a ballista crew cranked back the windlass on their great bow, aiming for the draken's exposed belly.

Nyvar Xeng has also stated – vehemently, and with the self-righteous tone which inspires otherwise calm sages to thoughts of murder – that the draken of the Hiledoran could never have breathed fire. In this, I will grudgingly admit that he is correct. What those terrible, graceful bastards do is *far* more dangerous.

As I watched, ready to scream a warning, the rising draken calmly turned its head and spat a mist of pale white venom at the ballista crew. It settled like gentle rain, and for an instant I thought that the beast was just hissing its rage, like one of my mothers' half-feral cats.

Then the ballista platform exploded.

Searing flame erased the crew from existence, melting steel and vaporizing flesh. The thunderclap of the draken's wings drove a blinding white wave of fire across the deck, and though it lost its furious heat within a heartbeat or two it was still enough to char and blister a dozen wailing southmen. Those wearing metal armor fared the worst, as they writhed and howled, roasting alive in their mail.

I had barely registered the gleeful horror of all this when the light was eclipsed, and a sound like acres of wet sailcloth in a gale filled the high tower. There were screams from above, and a Faceless One plummeted past my window, arms windmilling wildly. Another followed, this time with an arrow through his temple and white flames boiling from his open mouth.

The stones shook. Grinding, crunching sounds came closer...

And the immense head of a draken came in through the window frame, borne on a long slender neck as wide around as my waist. Its yellow-amber eye fixed me with an inquisitive stare as it calmly took a bite out of the table, swallowing bread, berries, roast quails and a piece of bluewood in one gulp. I hardly noticed the figure which slid off its back.

"Don't be afraid of him. He's a spoiled little princess, really," said a voice behind me. I spun around with an utter lack of grace, then scrambled to bunch the red satin sheet around my waist, because the voice belonged to a tiny, slim woman armed with a recurved bow. She was wearing a deerskin halter, long felt trousers and very little else. Questions about cold and altitude were driven from my mind as she smiled, scratching at the draken's snout. It thrummed with a deep, belly-full purr.

"And you. Fly on them, then, do you? With the. And..."

The door burst open, and the bow was up and drawn before I could finish stammering my greeting. But all that came through it was a corpse – another Faceless of Sinder's personal guard, his guts flying out behind him. A man in felt breeches followed a second later... barefoot, he was no taller than the woman who had preceded him. Both were pale-skinned and almost painfully thin, with dark hair and unsettling indigo eyes, and both were marked upon the neck, cheeks and forehead with runes in orange and red.

"Is this the one?" he asked, sheathing a curved sword at his belt. His accent was strange, but the language was almost the same as that of the tribes, and there was no doubt he was talking about me.

"This is him. The salt-men said he was like this. Though they never mentioned that he wore a dress."

The man grinned broadly, displaying an expanse of artificial gold teeth. He reached out and clasped my hand.

"Death-boy. Son of the Moer. I am Imkhantu, and this is Jenan. We have been sent to *rescue* you." He spoke like an adult explaining the rules of a game to a dim-witted child.

"Hey! I don't need rescuing! And I'm not stupid, you know!"

Jenan shrugged.

"Well, you *did* get yourself captured..."

"There was a battle! And sorcery! I didn't want to be captured, but..."

"Ahhh," said Imkhantu. "You're a *coward*, then. You lacked the spirit to fight to the death."

"We *all* got captured. Elion, Makara – hundreds of us. At least I was unconscious when – "

Then both of them were laughing, and I felt my face burning red with embarrassment. I stalked away, throwing open a large cupboard and burrowing into a pile of linen with my hands. There had to be some trousers around here somewhere!

"Elion Morekh fought on land? And he *lost*?"

"And he's a prisoner, here? This we must see, sister! This we must chronicle for the people!"

I turned with a pair of breeches in my hand, brandishing them like a weapon.

"By all the hells we will! I'm not leaving without my friends! Although any good strategist would warn you that there are *two hundred* fighting men aboard this Keel. They might take offense to your plan."

"Two hundred you say?" asked Jenan. "Well, we are two warriors of the Skyborn. We wouldn't want to make it difficult for them and call a third."

Imkhantu laughed again, and didn't stop until I'd struggled into a pair of what looked like Jerrold Sinder's own loose satin trousers, all embroidered with gold. Then he let out another of those ear-splitting whistles, and the tower lurched, two great draken launching themselves back into the fray.

"Our souls will continue to vex the southmen," said Jenan, grabbing me by the arm. "Now, we go to find that braggart Morekh."

The Keel was in chaos. Half the crew had been slaughtered by sorcery above Sothara's tomb, and the upper decks had been razed all the way back to the stone in places. Perhaps Sinder's men had been ready for a lone draken, a mad old sire driven by territorial angst and hormones. But this was annihilation with wings, and the three of us pelted through corridors filled with screams.

Garrison halls and armories had become makeshift surgeries and morgues. Slaves huddled together as grim shadows scythed through the smoke. And everywhere the hungry hot flames, gnawing at the granite bones of the stoneship...

Now we came to the spiral stair down into the belly of the Keel, and the cool air was a relief. None of us had any idea where the prisoners were being held, but the traditional lore of dungeons suggested that the deeper, darker and more awful our surroundings, the better chance we had of finding them.

This meant fighting our way through the Keel's second watch, roused from their beds by the oaths, profanities and boots of Sinder's sejants. Imkhantu and Jenan came down on them like the draken they called their 'souls', dragging me along behind them.

Life is a learning process.

I learned that day that the Skyborn were descended from the disciples of Yissus U'l, a heretic cast out from the conclave of Murat.

Not that I needed tomes or scrolls to tell me, because at the time I was simply dead weight behind the speed and fury of their blades. The pair were Zengaji, just like our friend Zuris O, and they were of a sect deemed too extreme even by the Antipriests of that bloodthirsty people.

Many, many Angan soldiers learned the same lesson, in the short time it took to clear the guardroom corridor. It would have been more effective for Jerrold Sinder to march his men into a storm of sickles and glass than for them to try to stop Imkhantu and his sister. Even now, all I remember of that wild few seconds is a rain of hissing arterial spray, limbs flying severed, heads rolling on dirty straw, and the blur of swords under torchlight.

Then the door was locked and barred behind us, and another spiral stair led down into deeper darkness. Curses and screams were drowned out by the sound of axes biting into wood at our back.

"Tell me something," I panted, ducking to one side as a spearhead came bursting through the door timbers "If your people fight like that, why don't you just march on Anganesse and rule all of Sarem?"

Jenan grinned, her teeth pointed and white amid a mask of blood.

"There are only forty-four Skyborn Murathi with souls. The rest are *kal'hentu* – the peaceful ones – religious scholars, farmers, wardens of the eyries. Even forty-four would be no use against four million."

"Although they would fear us in our deaths!" said Imkhantu. "Rule is tedious, Khytein. Life is for enjoying good food, wine, enemies and women, not for counting gold."

Forty-four of them. Which meant that someone had mobilized these people's *entire nation* just for me.

Jenan chuckled at that jibe about enjoying good women, and pushed her brother ahead of us down the stairs. This was the deepest level of the Keel, and I could hear the weak groans and muffled sobbing of prisoners in the red glow ahead. Firelight painted crooked shadows across the stone – bars and bones, chains and hooks surrounding a great circular pit. Around its edges were stacked row upon row of cages, some large enough to accommodate whole families, others so small that bone-breaking contortions would be necessary to fit even a child inside. Anger burned deep in my chest as I saw that this was precisely what they had been used for.

I have never seen the appeal of torture. As a self-confessed evil overlord, one would assume that it would be second nature to me, but when you have at your disposal things like the Cerebrex, and the subtle tools of lapis and gold which can unsplice human minds, you don't need the crudity of the rack and the hammer. It's not that I'm squeamish about pain – the Gods know that even back then I'd seen more than enough of it. It's the *torturers themselves* who I find uniquely repulsive. To a man they are bland, boring, prosaic, banal and rational. The fact that they do what they do without the merest chuckle of madness; that it's just another job, and one in out of the weather – *that* is what makes me hate them. And while I do not, as a rule, torture, I am a fucking *connoisseur* of executions.

At the time it was pure anger which propelled me across the reeking chamber, even before the two Skyborn Zengaji could move. The miasma of death swirled in choking clouds there, but I knew that to use sorcery in the bowels of a Keel was to die. So instead I ran at one of the hooded Angan painmasters screaming, grabbing a red-hot poker from a brazier as I came. The pale, doughy man looked up from his work as I leaped, and the sizzling iron caught him clean in the eye, punching through to boil his brains.

There was no helping the... thing... he'd been tending to. The Dark Sight revealed a soul held by mere threads of witchfire, and a face peeled open with cruel hooks. I ended its pain with a gesture, and felt the Keel tremble. About then, I realized what I'd done.

"He's killed Scorm! Where in the hells did that bastard come from!"

"Grab him! Back to the cages!"

"What are you waiting for? He's just a child!"

It was then that I noticed that the Skyborn hadn't followed me. And that Jerrold Sinder was most generous in his support of the agonizing arts – there were ten more torturers in the flame-lit chasm, with the kind of implements in their hands that only men of their profession have want or need for.

No sorcery. And all I had in my hands was a rusted pair of pliers...

"Leave one of them for me, I pray you," said a voice behind the firelight. "A lack of proper vengeance gives me the most *awful* indigestion. The fat one with the bonesaw would be a favourite."

Though it was scarcely more than a croak, I recognized that voice. It was Elion Morekh, sometime admiral of the Faeroan Free Reavers, and no amount of torture, starvation or imprisonment would cure him of his bravado. Though the figure who limped into view was far from the glorious old pirate I remembered. Could it have been so long?

Instead of a cutlass Elion carried a long-hafted bardiche, crusted with blood. He held it in his left, because his right hand was a ball of dirty bandages, and his wild grin shone from a face all sunken eyes and scraggly beard.

"You're welcome to him," I said, uncertain. Other shadows moved behind the Faeroan captain; some crawling, some staggering, but all – even the most broken, even the smallest – with more than just reflected firelight in their eyes. "But I don't know if I can handle the others by myself."

"I wasn't talking to *you*, Khytein," he said. And then the Southman behind me- the one who had been silently reaching around my throat with a carving knife – gurgled and collapsed.

It was impossible to see it all. What I caught was a flicker of hook-bladed throwing stars, a hiss of flying arrows, and the shock of souls torn from flesh. One of the Angan excruciators took an arrow in his gaping mouth, and flames jetted from his blackened eyesockets as he toppled backwards, venting a howl like a burst furnace.

Elion bowed low, eliciting a wince of pain.

"Thank you, noble Skyborn. I will repay you with gold, ale, songs, silk and the arts of lovemaking as is appropriate. But for now..."

"I'll take all of them but the last," laughed Imkhantu, vaulting down from atop the wall of cages. "Though in your current state, a night with my sweet sister would surely kill you."

Elion shrugged, smiling.

"If I am fated to die..."

"He means I'd stab you first, and him second," said Jenan, detaching herself from the shadows. The last remaining torturer dropped his bonesaw with an audible clatter. "What about this one?"

The Faeroan's smile turned cruel.

"No time for the straps and chains. Nail him to the table."

The torturer began to blubber and plead, wringing his meaty hands together. It didn't much help his case that they were crusted with dried blood.

But my eyes were on the silent, sullen crowd of survivors behind him. Some were Khytein, others members of Morekh's crew, and yet others were from the far-flung provinces of Anganesse – Rasuuli, Ontokhi, Ghuram, Ythean, all in varied states of wretchedness. The little terror which had been picking away at my mind ever since I awoke finally worked its way to the top of my thoughts.

"Where's Makara?"

"You like pain? You like to see the insides of a man's flesh? Well, prepare for an education!"

"Where's Makara?"

I found Soap, the huge cannon-weilding Faeroan sailor, there in the back of the crowd. He was missing a foot, and propped himself up on a balk of timber. When I met his eyes he looked away.

"Where is she!"

This time I lost control, and the shout had a little sorcery behind it. Pain oozed and dripped from the very stones in the pit, and I used it to screw my words deep into the minds of all there.

Imkhantu snarled. Jenan nocked an arrow to her bow. Several of the poor wretched prisoners moaned and collapsed.

"I'm sorry," I said. "But... I have to know. Did she die in the necropolis? Did Sinder..."

The rest of my words were drowned out by the grind and slam of huge metal doors high above us. Light spilled down into the torture pit, and with it came the unmistakable brimstone and iron stench of the Angans' bonepowder guns. A ring of wolf muzzles in brass snarled down on us – a score of the vile weapons, each crewed by censer-swinging acolytes and leather-suited engineers.

"Did I kill her?" came a sardonic purr of a voice, drifting down like silk. "No. I would never be so profligate with talent such as hers. But as to any other... indiscretions... which I may have perpetrated – I really do think that imagining the possibilities will torment young Kuhal Moer far more comprehensively than any amount of hot iron and knives."

It was the Provincial Governor himself, of course, and he came picking his way down a spiral stair cut into the dungeon wall, all immaculate pearls, satin and silver. His long white hair was unbound, and it hung down over one of his ember-red eyes like a veil, masking his cruel smile.

Elion Morekh didn't take his eyes off Sinder for a moment as he slit his prisoner's throat. The long folding razor in his hand had appeared from nowhere, and in that moment of near hysteria I wondered exactly where the old pirate had hidden it.

"So you've come here to die. You'll forgive me for taking my time, I'm sure... your hospitality has left me a little cold."

"Shit and corpse-grease. I could have blown the whole festering stew of you to pieces without even showing my face. You..."

"You would have condemned yourself if you did, groundcrawler," said Jenan, three arrows tight against her bowstring at once. "Fourty-four Draken pretty much guarantee it."

"Not while we fly higher than your lumbering reptiles can, little one. And I'd remind you that thanks to the accuracy of my gunners, it's now only *forty-two*."

"And when the air inside your Wardings goes stale? The Archaeon has..."

"I'm well aware of what your precious fucking *Archaeon* wants," spat Sinder, stopping on a ledge of stone ten spans above the pit. "And I've told him that the decision is not mine to make. The decision belongs to Kuhal, son of the Scalptaker, and he is already considering my *very. Generous. Offer.*"

He bit the words off like mouthfuls of prey-flesh, his composure cracked and slipping. All eyes in the chamber were suddenly on me.

"No," I said. "He wants me to replace the Silence. And he's already killed Makara. I..."

"So you'd rather be the captive of the Zengaji pariahs and their great rotting Wyrm? The damned thing is as likely to eat you as to help you, child!"

"I think what we have here," said Elion Morekh, "is what you Anganesse call an *impasse*. In Faeroan, the phrase translates roughly as 'having successfully begun to rape an octopus,' which I think is far more poetic."

"I would wager," said Sinder, very carefully, "That there's no word for such a thing in Khytein, is there? I mean... not only because the common octopus is unknown in those lands."

If he was trying for a laugh, he was playing to the wrong crowd. But he did turn his head away and lift two fingers pressed together over his shoulder – the sign Aerik Stormsong had made back in the ancient past, when I was just a confused little boy dragging a dead cat in a bag.

"We'd fight for it," I said, out on the brittle ice with Sinder. I could hear the sound of tendons, jaws and knuckles tightening all around me, like the sound of the rising sap in spring. "Ceirmakh would decide, in a trial by combat."

"Then if you'll permit me a little barbarism? I propose that you and I settle this matter, to save the precious lives of your Faeroan and Skyborn friends... not to mention a few hundred Angan soldiers."

There was a rush forward of volunteers to stand as my champion, and any one of them would have seemed a better option than a scrawny teenaged orphan without even a sword to his name. Sinder held up a hand to stop them.

"Hold, and hear me out. We fight until one yields, no blood, no killing. If Kuhal wins, you will all go free – or at least, I will give you all to the care of the Draken and their Archaeon. I'll also tell Kuhal exactly where to find his dear, lost little Makara." He chuckled. "And if I win, the lich-child becomes one of the Nine. You all die. Excepting, of course, one of you two Zengaji puppets, who can crawl back to the Archaeon and tell him he is honour-bound to let this Keel pass."

Instant chaos. Furious uproar. Sinder smiled as his foes shouted and pointed and swore and cursed.

"And if we refuse?"

"Then we do this the old fashioned way. Steel and meat and fire. But I promise you two things. First, that no matter who wins the battle, every one of you will die under my guns. And second – I will take what I know about Makara to my very unlikely grave, should *any* of you goatfuckers prove skilled enough to *furnish me with the need for one.*"

"Do you take us for fools? There's no way that..."

"I'll do it," I said, stepping forward. Grim calculations blurred behind my eyes. No sorcery here – he would face me as evenly as a twisted creature like Sinder ever could. And I *knew* things, now. Sothara the Bone Collector had spent decades in spiritual communion with the most cunning, brawling, vicious warriors he could capture and flay, and his memories were mine. True, Sinder was ancient and slippery in his own way – but he was overconfident, too. Really, I had no choice. *Kill the monster. Rescue the damsel. Glory and songs and immortality.*

I met Sinder's eyes, and there was a glitter of respect behind his practiced sneer.

"Someone give the whelp a sword," he said. And then he began the duel in exactly the way he intended to go on.

By cheating.

Heroism, like altruism, is a form of cerebral pox which compels its victims to sacrifice perfectly healthy lives for abstract scraps of nonsense like 'honor' and 'valor'. The cure, sadly, is usually terminal to the patient, as is more than often delivered by an adversary possessing those infinitely more sane traits grouped together under the slur of 'villainy'.

'On the Principles of Unnatural Philosophy'
Perceptor Third Grade Orpith Glote, Saradrim
Academiat

HERE IS WHAT I was thinking when I caught Elion Morekh's blood-crusted cleaver out of the air -

Sinder is old, and wily, and probably trained in the courtly arts of swordplay - which don't rely all that heavily on brute strength. But he has no sorcery, here. The merest cantrip will allow the Keel to remember that it's half a mountain, and it will fall.

I'm no warrior, but at age fifteen I am already bigger than him, and where I come from being 'no warrior' still means having practiced with spear, mace, sword, club, bow, knife and sling more regularly than most Angan conscripts who fancy themselves battle-striding heroes.

And what went through my foe's mind as he sprung from above the torchlight, all hideous smile and flying hair?

From this height, I'll have all of one hundred and five heartbeats to kill the bastard before we hit the ground.

Sinder never landed. He wove and unleashed a rubric of levitation as he leaped, surrounding himself with a sparkling nimbus of light. And the world went into gut-wrenching free-fall as the great grinding engines of the Keel failed.

I twisted sideways as I flew upward toward Sinder, who was measuring the angle of his blade to slice me clean in half. So much for 'no blood'... but a crippled and deformed thrall of the Nine would be far more interesting, after all.

His twin-tined sword missed me by a whisper, and I drew in power for a spell of my own, feeling the knowledge flow into me from out of the darkness in my head. It was as if the whole Incantus burned green and ghostly in the depths of my memory, and as I crafted the spell I knew why.

"Three months! I was unconscious for *three months?* What were you trying to do to me?"

It was a blast woven from pure pain, leeched from the walls and racks and cages below me. Ten thousand gibbering screams tore through the air in a contrail of green fire, catching Sinder on the arm and spinning him through the air like a rag doll.

"I tried to peel your mind open with sorcery, of course," he snarled. "But you had gone too deep. You were fighting your own little war in there."

He pushed himself off the smooth stone and flew at me as I searched the ghost incantus for a flight spell of my own. There – Sothara had compiled whole tomes of them. Here and now, only the most crude would serve.

"I defeated Sothara. I took his knowledge."

This time I met Sinder's sword with my own, and the impact threw me backwards in a spray of sparks.

"Am I supposed to be impressed? Are you going to flatter yourself by saying that *I'm next?*"

Hundreds must have died in the torture pit, but I needed only a handful of souls. I unbound them from the instruments of their deaths, promising release, respite, revenge...

"No. There's only one thing I need to know from you. And it doesn't require you to have all of your limbs attached."

A blurred spiral of ghosts arrested my fall just before I slammed into the metal roof of the pit, and I felt the runes lining up in my mind for a second sorcerous blast. This one was a bone-breaker, and it sizzled through the air to be parried away by Sinder's blade, making the tines shriek with resonance.

The Keel was spinning now in its death-plunge, and I flew through one of the open gun ports into a great vaulted hall filled with carnage. Sinder followed, and we traded blows and spells amid flying bodies and censer smoke, while the huge brass barrels of bonepowder cannons hammered from wall to wall to floor to ceiling, wrecking and crushing all in their way.

Death made it easy. I ripped souls away from corpses one by one, bound them with dark runes and hurled them at my foe. He, on the other hand, was fueled by the faith of the slain, the souls given up to Esau in the last moments of mortality. I quickly learned to dodge the crackling shafts of energy which Sinder launched from his fingers, after one of them grazed my cheek and melted the stone behind me.

But he learned to fear my blade. When the rolling, spinning madness of our free-fall brought us together our weapons blurred and chimed and rebounded, raining sparks. And while Sinder used his power to defy gravity, there was precious little left over to lend him speed or strength.

We fell through an arched doorway all carved with winged wolves and saints, and into the biggest room I had ever seen, still fighting. I hurled my foe away with a blast of death-agony and hung there, the world cartwheeling around me as I tried to make sense of it all.

Here were the acolytes, each at his stone pulpit, ranged in a half-circle around a raised altar. Icons of Esau stared down in mute pain from the walls. The steersmen were chanting frantically, all out of harmony, but they were immune to the churning hell of our fall, each one shielded by a glowing ward beneath his feet.

There were the immense, village-sized millstones which produced that eternal grinding noise – the engines of the Keel which kept it airborne. And between them...

The green light of the ossuary well was crazed and flickering, more caged lightning than furnace glow. Through a gap no wider than my outstretched arms I could see ranks of copper-capped glass pods, each stuffed with the bones of the dead. The green fire within was the soul-stuff of the enslaved, and the great runic prayer-wheels here in the heart of the Keel should have been the whip to their backs.

But Sinder was desperate now, and the sorcery he wielded had brought the wheels to a standstill. Now he drew in a deep breath, just as he had done back on the necropolis battlefield, and the acolytes at their lecterns screamed and died. Vile power swelled up his frame until he squatted on the air like a toad, full to bursting.

And he shrieked as he came at me, sword burning black, eyes rolled back to pearlescent whites, his free hand dripping with threads of liquid mercury.

I didn't try to parry his blow. I didn't even try to evade the hissing spears of silver fire which leaped from Sinder's fingertips, twisting into a lance of boiling metal.

Instead I imagined the shield-wall, the fortress of muscle and wood and steel which had been honed to a fine art by my people. I brought the image back of that rain-swept hillside – *the mud, the burn of Ulkar's foul rotgut, the blood swirling in the rocky stream...*

And the dead obeyed. The swirling helix of souls which had borne me up expanded into a sphere; interlocking, spinning, power leaved tight as draken scales against Sinder's assault.

Despite all of this, the impact still pushed my eyeballs back into the tender meat of my brain. My bones jumped in their sockets as the tip of Sinder's lance struck home, splitting open into sharp steel petals. It met the crackling meniscus of my shield with a sound like a drill biting stone, and it threw me back toward the millstones, arms flailing.

Sinder folded in his wings of feathers and ribbons and dove after me, his eyes narrowed. In his other hand he was building up a second sorcerous blast, ready to crack my defenses open.

"That little trick won't save you twice," he snarled, opening his fingers wide to accommodate a seething ball of energy. We fell between the millstones and out into the well of the Keel as he spoke, and suddenly there was nothing below us but ice – the high slopes of the Hiledoran.

"I... I'm n-not the one who needs saving," I panted, as row after row of glass and copper ossuraries spiraled past me. The Keel was spinning around the axis of its central void, leaving Sinder and I as the still point at its centre. "It's them. THEY need saving from YOU."

He realized what I meant an instant too late, and let loose an inhuman shriek of rage, crazing the glass across a swathe of those bone-stuffed coffins.

Then the colour bled out of the world, and time stood still.

I welcomed the Dark Sight, and let the chorus of weeping, cursing, howling madness all around me in. I was a *necromancer*. And Sinder had brought me to an open grave, the fool.

Imagine a sphere, a globe as wide as the horizons, all built from bones. Hang raw flayed skin and meat across this grisly firmament, then give it a thousand voices, a galaxy of mad and staring eyes, a patchwork of tormented faces. Feel the fraying and blurring together of memories which makes such a tortured composite thing *one*. Comprehend with horror that it *lives*. And then imagine you stand at its very centre, with its words slicing through you like mountain-sized knives.

That was the heart of the war Keel *Valor Eternal*, laid bare in the

Dark Sight. Although language, constructed as it is by sane minds and human tongues, can only do so much to convey the staggering, drooling madness of it - the feeling of tottering on the edge of gulfs of mindless infinity.

YOU CAN *HEAR* US?

YOU CAN FEEL OUR SUFFERING?

YOU CAN... GIVE US FREEDOM?

The voice was a storm tearing through me. It took all of my will to keep from being ripped soul from flesh.

"Is that what you want? An end? Like the slaughterborn?"

There was silence, and a ripple heaved through the walls of flesh. A rumble of voices built like far-off thunder.

NO! WE WANT MORE! MORE!

I forced my way up through the after-echoes. I pulled my mind back together, thread by thread.

"A wise man once told me that vengeance doesn't come for free! Is that what you want? *Revenge?*"

The response was less a word than it was a gale of razors. Oh, I knew what they desired now.

"Then... we can make a bargain," I gasped. And I told them how.

The Keel stopped falling.

A fist of raving green light stabbed out from the top and bottom of the well, melting the icefield below us and blasting the clouds away above. I heard the screech of Draken, following us down with Skyborn Zengaji on their backs. The ground was so close that I could feel the warm breath of steam which billowed from the snow.

I opened my eyes.

The light had gone out of the ossuaries – all ten thousand of them were now nothing but inert coffin-sized tubes of bones. They had sprouted pale tendrils of green lightning, stretching out like fingers to a swirl of ghostly shapes. The wraiths of the dead, still bound to their scrimshawed and gilded remains, but freed through me to have their revenge.

They held Sinder in a viselike grip, emaciated fingers pulling his finery taut in all directions. Some of them smoked and frayed where they touched his ancient flesh, but that pain seemed only a minor inconvenience to things which had suffered for decades. Their faces were scrawls hashed across an eye-studded mist, bitter and distorted.

The look on the Provincial governor's face was infuriatingly calm by comparison.

"They can't kill me, you know. They can't even hurt me. Part of the psience which binds them to the Keel prevents it."

"*They* may not be able to kill you. But how about a two-hundred span drop?"

The icefield below was melted back to stone – a jagged mass of wind-cracked boulders. Sinder squinted down at it, calculating.

"Perhaps. Perhaps not. Are you willing to bet your life on it?"

I smiled with what I hoped was grim humour.

"We can always fly a little higher before they let you go."

This actually made him laugh.

"Oh, I have certainly underestimated you, Kuhal. Even if part of you is Sothara, and part a story-sotted virgin fool. It's such a shame that you won't join me instead of throwing your life away."

Now, I'm quite a reasonable man, despite what all the maimed, burned, mad and accursed will tell you. But I'd really wanted Sinder to start begging for his life a long time since. I hit him – hard – a blow to the side of the head which would have laid most men out cold. A little frission of approval ran through the assembled wraiths.

"Where's Makara?" I grated. He chuckled, he shoulders heaving. He lifted his head, and a tiny drop of slow crimson blood trickled from the corner of his mouth.

"Did you actually think I'd tell you? You really must be just as stupid as your dim-witted father, boy."

This time I *really* hit him.

It was an utterly dishonorable blow with a jolt of sorcery behind it, and I swear I felt his sternum touch his spine as my knuckles hit home. Ribs cracked like rotten twigs, and a savage part of me savoured the look of sudden pain on Sinder's face.

At the same moment, the wraiths let go.

The Provincial Governor flew backwards, between the rows of ossuary batteries, and into the gap between the great runic millstones. The spirits of the enslaved poured in after him, a driving wind made up of gibbering voices, hands and eyes. And though he scrabbled against the smooth stone he could find no purchase. They had him trapped.

Those immense wheels usually amplified the chants of the Keel's acolyte-engineers, grinding against the soul-energies of the dead to keep it aloft. In their open position they provided the only safe passage into and out of the well, for those times when the ossuaries needed changing, or if they malfunctioned. They had snapped open on huge coiled springs as soon as the Keel began to fall, and the crew had tried numerous sorcerous injunctions, rubrics and curses to re-ignite the well.

Now the crew were dead, and I could feel the insubstantial fingers of the wraiths worrying at the millstones' mechanism. I held out my hand to my enemy.

"Sinder! Come on, damn you! I won't let you die until you tell me where she is!"

Now the wheels were turning – still suspended two armspans apart, but rumbling up to speed, their rune-carved edges flickering with fire. I stretched out as far as I could, levitating just inside the ring of ossuaries, scrabbling for his hand. Sinder pushed and slipped on the smooth granite, his beautiful face a mask of terror.

"No! Don't let them... Don't let them... I promise you, Khytein, I'll..."

But it was too late.

The millstones released with a snap of shearing metal, and they came together like jaws. At the last instant I managed to lunge for Sinder's hand, and I pulled one shoulder, one arm and his head clear of the grinding stone as it snapped shut.

The batteries began to glow with fitful fire. In another few heartbeats the well would be filled with cataclysmic power, and I'd be just as dead as...

He opened his eyes.

Damn him, but the miserable, tenacious old bastard actually stopped the wheels. They choked on his ancient flesh just long enough for him to speak – though how he did so without lungs or breath I'll never know.

"She... she belongs to Urzen now. The soulsmith, in Korisal. I... I tell you so you'll let me go. Please, Kuhal. Don't try to raise me..."

He could only hold the wheels so long. With a sickening crunch they cut loose, grinding the better part of Jerrold Sinder's body to grist.

His face changed as he died. The years held back by sorcery sliced into him like knives, and he let out a rattling sigh, choking off into a thin cloud of dust.

I let him go. The wreck which remained of him fell away into the clouds, spinning slowly as a substance like dark sand spilled from his shattered torso. Then I focused my will, and flew up and out of the well, feeling it ignite behind me as I stepped down to the deck of the

Valor Eternal.

Numb. Empty. There was no joy in the thought of Sinder lying broken on the open mountainside, too dried out and cold even for the scavengers...

As soon as my feet touched the ground all the fight went out of me. Weariness settled across my shoulders, driving me to my knees.

"We're sorry. But we needed him to die," said a whisper in my head, coming up out of the well. *"Will you forgive us? Will you let us rest now?"*

I felt the Keel lurch under me as the millstones forced the dead into servitude again, running on automatic. This was their voice, and it seemed much more calm and rational now that they had fed.

"I don't think either of us will be satisfied with the servant while the master still lives," I whispered. There was a powerful urge to vomit rising in my throat, and my vision swum with red and purple flarelights. "Serve me for a little longer, and I'll give you the Thearch himself."

"Ohhhh, but it hurts, cruel one! It hurts us like knives and fire!"

"What's a little more hurt against the pain of a God? The Thearch, and Esau himself after him."

The voice laughed, an oily little chuckle with definite traces of madness.

*"A bold claim, warlock. Shall we say either the Thearch and his God – or **you**?"*

I could see the draken landing now, coming down like the blackened pages of a burned grimoire, their wings folding as they came in to roost on the deck of the Keel. Angan soldiers plunged screaming over the side rather than roast in their fires.

"Me or him, then. Me or him. Just keep this rock airborne until we reach Urexes, and we'll make the bastards suffer."

Then the cold grey waters of fatigue took me under, and I heard no more. But deep in my flesh, down where muscle welded to bone, I felt quite distinctly the first few threads of transformation spreading... the cost of sorcery turning my body to the same dry, fibrous husk which Sinder had become before he died.

The mageblight had me – and soon I would be the same as he had been, body and soul.

"Long before the age of man, it is disquieting to note, there are layers in the stone which speak of a time of scaled and massive beasts. Some were like draken in form, and may even be their great-great-grandsires many times over. Others vary wildly in shape and size, from the tiny and scuttling to the huge and lumbering. What is more disturbing still is that some of them - the equivalent in mind, if not body, to modern men - built halls and statues and palaces, and temples to Gods now forgotten. What is most chilling of all is the fact that, of this entire teeming vastness of fecundity, all that is left today are the draken of the Hiledoran (be they other than myth), and the so-called Coldblood of the Akhazi, if indeed that vile deity is more than just the fevered dream of savages..."

The forbidden book of the Orelord Charnost Draul,
engineer of the West Delvings, Ythe.

THERE FOLLOWED A period of darkness. Cold, fever - icy water and the smells of sickness, wool and sulphur. Figures moved in the haze like ghosts, carrying bowls of blue radiance. Sometimes Elion Morekh's face loomed over me, sometimes that of Imkhantu, or countless others. Names, at the time, eluded me... as did most of the rudiments of reason and sanity.

I walked with Sothara, his head caved in and one eye lolling on his tattooed cheek, through glades of dead autumn leaves and bodies hanging like swollen fruit. I sat on the lip of an ice-island in the utter north with Gernish Maudrin, and listened to him speak of the Nine while leviathenes whistled and lowed in the twilight.

And I stood in a tunnel huge enough to dock a war-Keel, hundreds of fathoms deep in the roots of the mountains, looking up at the head of a draken so old and vast that it filled the stony cleft from edge to edge. Each of its eyes was wider than the well at the heart of the Angan keels, and it spoke directly into my mind, with a voice like whole continents grinding together down in fire.

Not all of it was dreams. Some of it may have been more real than the room you sit in right now, reading the words of an evil madman on some dusty scroll. But while I slept and raved with visions, my allies were hard at work.

I had given them a Keel, but not the means to use it. True to their bargain, the dead in the stoneship's well had kept it aloft, but without a crew of trained acolytes to man the chantries and galleries it could not steer, or even move. Elion told the Zengaji about the leviathenes, and forty-two great pairs of wings towed the crippled Keel deep into the mountains, to a hidden place high above the clouds.

I learned later that I was delirious, babbling about mathematics and light, weeping and laughing at the same time. A mixture of superstitious dread, old-fashioned racial prejudice and the outright bullying of Elion Morekh kept the Murathic surgeons from my bedside – a good thing, as they are to this day known for their zealous use of cold baths, leeches and foul-smelling narcotic herbs. I believe he told them I was keeping the *Valor Eternal* off the ground, which made my fate somewhat political. My allies had plans for the stoneship which whipped his Faeroan crew into a frenzy of activity.

High in a hanging valley, between sheer walls honeycombed with cave-houses and draken eyries, Elion Morekh began to craft the weapon of our revenge.

It took acres of sailcloth, miles of rope, and spars cut from the tallest trees in the stormwood. All these tasks gave the Skyborn plenty of scope for stealing, raiding, and otherwise vexing the Angan foe, preying mercilessly on their supply lines as they straggled north through the Bloody Gates and the narrow gullet of Burned Hand Pass. Autumn was closing in, and Elion was keen to be ready for the winter storms, which he planned to ride like Anghul's bone-white huntsmen.

I awoke well before the Keel was properly finished – at about the time when Jenan returned from the north, with the wheel and the bell of the old *Shadow of Blades* lashed to her draken's back. Not because I was healed, either in mind or in body, but because a greater power than I had commanded it.

It found me down in the deeps again – in a great fissure which zigzagged deep into the mountain's heart. A little stream churned along in its stony bed here, but the rest of the cavern was dry, floored with cold black sand. Though I should have been blind a ghostly blue light flickered around me – sourceless, gentle and quite unsettling.

Aeons ago, some stonemason had crawled all these miles beneath the earth to carve twin statues on the slopes of the fissure. They framed an immense hollow space where the stream plunged over a precipice and into darkness. Both statues shared that eerie glow, and by its light I had studied them before. Each was a humanoid figure, robed and armored, with long gauntlets and a chestplate of beaten gold. But their serpentine necks supported heads like those of the draken – slim-snouted and fanged, with polished amethyst cabochons for eyes.

It was through this gateway that the Archaeon came.

Or at least- the *head* of the Archaeon. The rest of the titanic beast was so huge that it filled the chamber beyond the door, and its horns (each one the length of a ship's mast, and thick with ornamental bands and chains) nearly scraped the rune-etched lintel when it leaned forward to address me. The hot carnivore stink of its breath blew past me, and I wondered (disquietingly) exactly what – and *how much-* a thing like this ate.

"We have very little time left," rumbled the voice of the great wyrm in my mind. "And you are so untrained! I never foresaw this in the skrying pools, but fate is relentless. You must awaken."

"Awaken and do *what?* Sinder is dead. Makara is lost, along with my people. Why don't I just stay mad and let the world go on without me?"

The Archaeon huffed, bathing me in a cloud of noxious fumes. The true horrors of a draken's digestive processes are only known to a sorry few naturalists, many of whom are quite insane.

"This business with your little tribes is just part of a larger game. The pawns are cleared from the board, and the Nobles, Thrones and Principalities are being maneuvered far to the south. You are needed there."

"So what am I? Am I a pawn as well, to be thrown away in some reckless gambit?"

The beast narrowed its huge violet eyes, and what passed for laughter bubbled up through my mind.

"You are one of those rare pawns which makes it all the way across the board, Kuhal da'Hurik Moer. Where you can become whatever you wish."

"And if I wish to go home? And give up? What then?"

"The thing with this rather strained analogy," said the Archaeon "Is that *nowhere* is off the board. The world may be likened to a game of chess, but the Gods who play it do so with knives out, too."

"What do you care for our human Gods?" I asked, with all the bravado of someone who thinks they're still dreaming. "And what do they care for your kind?"

This time the harmonics of the great draken's voice conveyed a deep and hollow sadness.

"*They* don't. But there are others. The Akhazi serve the Coldblood, and the Coldblood serves the dwellers in the outer dark. You have seen them, though your mind is such that you could not comprehend them. I know, because you can talk without drooling and screaming."

"I can sometimes go for whole minutes without doing either."

"Then know that Anganesse holds the means for them to step over the threshold and feed. The hubris of the White Empire has given the Akhazi and their lord an excuse, and they march north to seize that power. It must not be."

"I'm not here to help the Thearch," I said, trying to appear grim and fierce. It's *hard* to measure up to a mountain-sized predatory wyrm when it comes to such qualities; but I persevered. "I'd quite like to see him destroyed, in fact. Won't the Gods be able to stop your... *dwellers* from crossing over? They did it before."

"Not if the voices which scream in the void can unite as one. They were once of a single mind, those wretches – but I must never recall the name they chose for themselves. We stopped believing in *that* name long ago."

Now the blue glow flared, and I caught a sparkle of metal and crystal high on the spiked brow-ridge of the Archaeon's left eye. A crystal point, wrapped in a filigree of silver, and more than eight spans long... it had been screwed into the titanic beast's skull and bolted into place with bands of riveted black iron.

"Rather than have that entity walk the world, we Draken gave up our sentience. All higher thoughts erased. An entire nation bludgeoned back to the condition mindless beasts – all but I, Gnaar'Usuul Koraxiss Threyn, the Archaeon, who enacted the great incantation of erasure *forty million cycles of the sun and moon ago*."

Now the passion in the old wyrm's words had ignited its inner fires, and those of the mountain beneath. The stench of sulphur rose up along with a sullen red glow, and jagged shadows underlit its face.

"Only the Coldblood survived, and he was diminished, condemned to crawl in filth on his belly for aeons. *Your* revenge is a candle before the firestorm - compared to the hatred which he has nursed for so long."

Sudden cold gripped me. A shock ran the length of my spine, and lights flared before my eyes, white and blue as ice. The cavern began to blur, as if seen through tears, and I felt the sharp, slippery mind of the Archaeon falling away, lost in the background rumble and seethe of the fires beneath the earth.

"Look beyond the Thearch, Khytein," came the last hooked whisper of the draken's voice. "There is far more at stake here than a crown and a throne..."

Cold slapped me hard in the face, and I felt little trickles of ice crawling over my skin. Now I could see hunched, inhuman forms wavering above me, and feel the rocking and swaying motion of...

"He's awake! By the stars, the Gods and hogshit - he lives! I suppose you'll be wanting those skins of firemead, Jenan?"

"If his mind's gone, you'll be wanting to drown your own sorrows," said another voice. "Maegister Corvo said he'd gone far too deep, and that the Archaeon would either save him or spit him out."

"More water! We have to get airborne before those southern mother-rapers can break the warding walls!"

This time I saw it coming, and I sat up spluttering and gasping. The water was colder than death, poured over my head from a rough wooden ladle by none other than Elion Morekh. The old pirate clapped me heartily on the back, dislodging what felt like a handful of ribs.

"See? Nothing to be afraid of! I'd gladly pay any amount of that horse-piss you Skyborn drink to have *this* one back among us. You know what the Anganesse are calling him?"

"A pawn," I slurred, with tongue which felt like week-old sausage. "Right across the board."

It came out as mumbled, drooling nonsense. But my words would have gone unheeded anyway. Because at that moment Elion, Jenan and the quartet of robed Murathic Zengaji acolytes who were carrying my entire bed between them came out into sunlight, and I beheld the high valley of the Skyborn under siege.

I think they all understood perfectly well the obscenity I shouted next.

"The Gods are all-knowing and omnipotent; yet our creed declares that they do not exist.

Sure in the knowledge that they themselves do not exist, they are guilty of sowing false hope in the hearts of the credulous, thus causing tears, strife, war, and disorder in the affairs of men.

So I say to you, my brethren - for the crime of non-existence, we must sentence these fractious Gods to death!"

Attributed to Yissus U'l, Antipriest of the Murathic Zengaji, some few minutes prior to his anathemization by the conclave of the Elders of the Unseeen Blade.

TO UNDERSTAND THE high eyrie of the Skyborn, you have to understand a little about their clanfather, the long-dead master of assassins, Yissus U'l.

All Zengaji loathe sorcery. There are those who say this is because they fear it – though people foolish enough to insinuate cowardice to the face-mask of a Zengaji often turn up headless soon after. No; their hatred is utterly pure and abstract. Their leaders are the cadre of the Antipriests for this very reason – men who nurture an iron-hard disbelief in the Gods.

No Gods, no power. No power, and the cackling archmage is suddenly nothing but a sad old man in piss-stained robes, staring in horror at the three foot *khirang* sword thrust bloody through his ribcage.

It takes a very stubborn kind of mind to remain atheist in a world overburdened with witches, demoncallers, pyromancers, thaumaturges, alchemists, soul-binders, warlocks, scourges, night-thegns and at least one aged and cynical necromancer.

And it took a kind of genius just short of physical brain damage for Yissus U'l, at the generational conclave of Murat (hitherto an unremarkable fishing village in peninsular Ghuram) to suggest that the surest way of ensuring the non-existence of a fictitious pantheon was to do away with them, in the manner for which the Zengaji are famous.

In the Zengaji language, the words for 'vigourous ontological and theological debate' and 'bloodbath' are a mere inflection of a single vowel apart. There is a reason for this.

Murat became famous for the horror discovered there by the outriders of the local magistrate's garrison. Yissus U'l fled, pursued by the most skilled agents of death ever to walk the night in Sarem.

And something in his mind drew him, like iron filings to a lodestone, to a place where the deicide he had mused had actually once been perpetrated. The fact that he gathered a cult around him - and that they became known for such ferocity that the Zengaji elders quietly rescinded the contract against his life – was almost immaterial.

Here, in this narrow, twisting gullet of a valley, halfway up the most treacherous mountain range in Sarem, sorcery couldn't skry the children of the Antipriest. They and their draken - and their draken's unspeakably ancient master - were hidden from the myriad eyes of Anganesse, and spared the wrath of their sorcerous cadres and engines of war.

The floating cities of Faeros had been shattered by the incantations of the Thearch's Chantries and Circles, commanding mountain-sized detonations of raw power from half a world away. Twice, the lord of Anganesse had sent forth one of the three Excoriators Major, those floating necropolis-pyramids which were said to have reduced whole city-states to fine grey dust. In Ythe you can still see the lagoon which was once the free port of Mharabaat, its glass beach etched with the shadows of the incinerated.

Not so here. Either the latent power of the Archaeon - or echoes of what it had done when it severed a divinity from the world – prevented the Thearch from avenging Sinder's death with a battery of magecraft. Instead he had sent his fleet.

The valley of the Skyborn breached the wall of an ancient crater – the rotten cusp of a mountain hollowed out by fire and ice. To the north the rim of the great bowl fell away, letting the waters of the crater's central lake cascade down a torturous canyon, and finally out into sunlight, where they plunged over a mile-high drop. Nothing but drifting spray ever hit the ground.

To the south the walls became rotten with layered, honeycombed caves, some natural, others carved into the rock so long ago it was hard to tell the difference. An ornate gothic monstrosity of wind-smoothed spires, domes, statuary and pillars reared up over a smoking maw beyond the crater lake – the lair of the Archaeon itself, though there was no way that the great beast could ever exit the way it had entered. Wind and water had erased most of the detail from this hidden city, but what remained was both utterly alien – ferns as tall as stormwood pines, bat-winged creatures with the heads of birds, serpent-necked beasts wearing armour like warhorses – and just slightly too *large* to have been crafted by men. Maybe a tenth of this cyclopean place was inhabited by the Zengaji outcasts, while yet more had been hollowed out and expanded for their draken mounts.

Now it was burning.

Three great war-keels hung in the air above us like arrowhead stormclouds, raining down death from their batteries of bonepowder cannon. The stench of dead souls and sorcery assailed me as I watched another rippling broadside stab out from the belly of the nearest Keel, shattering a row of pillars. Down went an entire gallery of frescoed cavern-halls, billows of oily fire licking up amid the rumble of destruction.

People were screaming, and the itch and pressure of death assailed my mind, but most of the city was empty – the core of the Zengaji defense was here, with us. It rested in the hands of a tiny figure, out at the tip of a pier of stone.

We had emerged from the warrens beneath at the shoulder of an immense headless statue – a drakonic figure two hundred spans tall, robed and mailed. A broad avenue lay across the statue's shoulders like a ribbon, and led on down its outstretched arm – then on again, down the flat blade of a sword it held at guard. The entire immense structure was crazed with shards of rainbow, and for a second my vision swum, tottering on the brink of darkness.

Then Elion and Imkhantu grabbed me by the arms and lifted me bodily from my sickbed. I saw, as they half-dragged me out onto the tongue of ancient granite, that the sky was rippled and curdled by an immense magikal shield, one cast out from the hands of that tiny man in black. Even as I watched, a barrage of iron came spearing down from the keels, only to be evaporated against the great warding. The entire statue shook, and I was certain I could feel the stone cracking and groaning beneath me. Sparks blew past us in a great roiling cloud.

"He's holding them. But for how much longer?" panted Elion, as we pushed into a milling chaos of ropes, bales, people, animals and crates.

"The Archaeon is feeding him power. It all depends on how long his brain can keep from boiling in his skull," answered the Zengaji with a grim smile. "We need is long enough for our great admiral to launch his vessel, after all - then *apparently* we'll be saved."

Elion snarled, and lurched forward with a renewed burst of speed, almost dislocating my arm.

"If it has sails, boy, I can make the bastard *sing*. You'll see. These Angans will see, too! We only need..." he gestured with one hand "THAT!".

The *Shadow of Blades* had been eclipsed by the broad flat of the sword we traversed, but now its great fang-shaped bulk came into view, hanging in the air just below the edge. I was barely awake enough to stand, but when the power of the ossuaries flared in my brain my thoughts sizzled like bacon-fat on a skillet.

Ahhhh... he comes to keep our bargain! We are ready, Khytein. We **hunger***...*

"Beautiful," said another voice – this one not echoing in my skull. "You boys and your little toys! I thought you wanted to fly this thing, Morekh, not just look at it?"

It was a woman, all in green, from her long outrider's boots to her hooded woolen half-cloak. Even her hair was dyed a deep viridian hue. The smile she flashed over her shoulder at Elion was coy and mocking.

"Well, I'll... that is, you can go and..." spluttered the Faeroan captain, all trace of his usual wit deserting him.

"If you oafs don't get aboard soon, we'll leave you here for the Southmen," said the lady in green. "Don't keep me waiting."

"I think she likes you," I said, staggering back against a wall of casks. The heady rush of power had settled back to a thumping ache – I could hear the millstones of the Keel grinding in my head. "Although *why*, I couldn't possibly imagine."

"God's bollocks, the wretched thing speaks! And here I thought we were going to have to lash him to the mast!"

"It's good to see you too, Morekh," I said, taking the hand he held out to me. "And Imkhantu. And, in fact, even those persistent Anganesse. Is there *really* a giant draken forty million years old under this mountain?"

The look on the Zengaji's face became all but reverential as he took my other hand.

"We see it in dreams, Khytein. And we try very, very hard not to worship it, for all its power. If you have seen the Archaeon, then..."

"Then we still need to cast off and *fight*," growled Elion. "Come on!"

We ducked and twisted our way past cranes and swinging nets of provisions, past bleating sheep and great cubes of wax sealed around stolen cylinders of bonepowder. At last we passed over a thin gangwalk and onto the stolen Keel *Shadow of Blades*, stepping lightly over a killing drop. Elion took charge as soon as his feet touched the deck.

The Faeroan stood taller in his silver-toed boots, casting off his weariness and regaining, I supposed, a little of the arrogant certainty of command. He adjusted the angle of his hat and strode ahead of us, up ramps and through doors, down corridors echoing with arguments and the scrape and thump of cargo, until at last we came to what had once been the stone keep at the stern of the vessel.

Now the entire bridge-deck of the old *Shadow* was mounted atop the sheared-off tower, complete with a map table, telescopes, braziers, a chilled keg of spiced rum, and the immense brass-banded wheel and bell of the original ship. From this vantage I could look down the spine of the Keel, and see just how much work Elion's men had done while I slept.

"How did you do it?" I asked, feeling a rumble of power thrumming through the wood and stone beneath me. "Didn't they put up a fight when you told them we were keeping their Keel?"

"Oh, they fought. Just very, very badly. Without Sinder to terrify them into slavery, half of the crew came over to our side in any case."

"I still don't trust them," growled Imkhantu. "It is better to die than to betray your people."

"That's just it! They were Rasuul, Ontokhi, Ghuram – pressganged recruits. Getting them to turn pirate was easier than seducing a fat merchant's youngest wife!"

One of the more striking additions to the *Shadow of Blades* was a vast, ramified and meticulous thicket of masts and spars. At a bellowed order from Soap (who stood with his huge hands clamped tight around the rail, his cannon slung over one shoulder on a length of anchor chain) they bloomed with acres of canvas, expanding like a cloud to the sound of crisp whipcracks.

"See, Cap'n? Clean white sheets!" leered the giant. "After all, this is her maiden voyage..."

"Tell those ashore to jump or be left behind," roared Elion, his eyes flashing with savage joy. "And don't forget that old fool Corvo! It's time we showed these louse-infested Angan pedophiles how to sail, and how to fight!"

He drew his cutlass, and for the first time I noticed that the Faeroan's left had had been replaced by a gleaming silver sickle – a serrated hook which winked evilly in the sunlight. He used it to snare a speaking tube from its brass-inlaid rack.

"Mister Orduvis, are the gun decks armed and ready?"

A muffled reply made Elion crack a wicked smile.

"And so we will! Mister Ricketts, are we ready to cast off?"

The wiry, flame-haired man who clung to the wheel snapped off a sharp salute, grinning with a mouthful of ivory teeth.

"Mister Kuhal, you have control of the spirits. Tell them that this might be a bumpy ride."

Well, in truth I had as much power over the Keel's soulbound dead as a songbird has over a hurricane. But I smiled, and nodded, and gripped the rail with both hands as the shouting, cursing and bleating both aboard and on the pier reached a fevered pitch. Cranes and gantries swung away, gangwalks fell, and as yet another rolling fusillade was deflected by the sorcerous shield above us, the *Shadow of Blades* began to move.

Those lines and hawsers still connected to pier snapped. Stone ground on stone for a long second as the sails bellied out, and then the Keel began to build up speed, heading for the wavering heat-haze of the warding. The figure at the end of the statue's sword shot a glance over his shoulder and saw us pulling away, and he shouted an incomprehensible curse.

The Angan gunners saw the warding fail as he turned aside, hitching up the hem of his black and white raiment. The crack and whine of their small swivel-guns followed at his heels as he ran to the edge and stepped off into empty air. A large bird rose flapping from his shoulder as he disappeared from view, cawing raucously as it followed.

But this was no ordinary old man. He rose into view again an instant later, weightless as a dandelion seed on the wind, to land on the bridge next to Elion. Up close, he resembled a feathered turtle – wattled, wrinkled, liver-spotted and ancient, with eyes like chips of frozen diamond.

"A little warning next time, perhaps?"

He raised one eyebrow, extracting a long horn pipe from somewhere inside his robes. It was obvious that they were sewn entirely from feathers – and that they had never, ever been washed. "And perhaps you'd also best unleash the draken? I suspect you're going to ask me for some wind soon, and the currents up here in the mountains can be quite treacherous..."

Now the Angan crew had reloaded and aimed their larger guns, and I could see part of Elion's strategy. We had pulled away hard to starboard, putting us in the shadow of one of the Angan keels... but blocked from the view of the others. It seemed a small mercy as the great wolf-muzzle guns began to belch flame, but it may have saved our lives.

"Imkhantu! Has your sister prepared our little diversion?"

"I'm sure the southmen will find her just as diverting as you do, captain."

"Then let's light the fireworks. You have my leave to fly, Skyborn."

"And you have mine to stay alive, Faeroan. Good hunting."

The bald-pated old sorcerer in the feather cloak had stoked up his pipe now, and smoke leaked from the gaps between his sharp little teeth as he smiled at me.

"Necromancer, eh? I'm glad old Stormsong and his friends didn't have to awaken Sothara. You seem a lot less...mmmm, *decomposing*. Excuse me for a second."

This time nothing stood between the Angans' heavy iron shot and the *Shadow of Blades*. Cannonballs skipped and cracked across her decks, cutting down a score of the men and women who still laboured to stow provisions and munitions into the great vessel's holds. The screech and stench of draken wafted up to me as curses rang out, desperate.

But my new companion simply rolled his eyes back in his head and exhaled a smoky breath, seeming to shrink down into his feather cloak. A magpie the size of a carrion crow chose this moment to land on his shoulder, ruining the drama by voiding its bowels down half his back. But when he raised his hand, palm up, then clenched his ring-finger and thumb together...

The end of the sword broke off. Granite carved in the ages before man splintered and fissured as ice spread across and within it, finding some ancient flaw. A shield-shaped tongue of stone as big as one of the *Shadow*'s sails began to fall, and then the sorcerer slashed his hand sideways and upward, letting loose a little grunt of effort.

The stone shard blurred, spinning. It neatly sliced through half of the enemy gun-deck, carving into the side of the nearest Keel with a sound like an avalanche. I could see white-clad acolytes within, tiny insects scrabbling in a shattered hive.

"Stop showing off to the boy and get us *moving*, Corvo - you old fraud," said a voice on the ladder. It was the woman I had seen earlier, though now her hood was thrown back to reveal a slim, cinnamon-coloured face and startling opal eyes. Her smile was genuine, though, and she looked at me with open curiosity.

"So... this must be the one who Gernish Maudrin told us about. He's still so wet behind the ears I'm surprised they didn't send him with a towel!"

"Bonesigner, isn't he?" asked Corvo, rolling up his feathered sleeves one by one. His arms were entirely covered with tiny metal piercings – silver tubes of no more than a fingernail's length, arranged in rows from wrist to elbow. "They start 'em young in the north, Tishande, and it's a good thing they do. He's the one keeping us airborne."

Of course I'd heard (in the drunken, feasting-hall boasting of warriors who had never ridden more than a mile beyond the Stormwood) that the people of Ythe weren't as pale and white as we other folk of Sarem, and that their women were the most beautiful in creation. But I only realized I was openly staring at Tishande when she winked one opalescent eye at me, grinning.

"No offense, Kuhal. It's just that in this kind of situation, I'd much rather laugh because of my friends than weep because of my enemies."

"Speaking of which..." muttered Corvo.

"Speaking of which, the two of you *could* leave the Khytein alone and pay for your passage with a little sorcery," said Elion, snapping closed the brass and bone telescope he'd been using to spy out the carnage. "A fine shot across their bows, Maegister, but that's not going to get us out of here alive."

"I'm not a nautical man," said Corvo, clenching his pipe between his teeth. "But aren't the bows the front part? I sort of hit them on the side..."

"Tishande, if *you* could take the lead?" sighed Elion. "We have butcher's work to do before we sleep tonight..."

Then his voice was drowned out, because the draken had been released.

It would have been suicide for the great beasts to take wing into the teeth of Corvo's warding, but now the Skyborn and their mounts leaped from the broad back of the Keel in perfect synchronicity, with a sound like the hissing thump of a chemical explosion. Copper-coloured scales flashed in the cold sunlight as two score of the beasts curved up and around, forming a series of arrowhead ranks in the sky.

They descended on the crippled Angan Keel without mercy, and even from the bridge of the *Shadow of Blades* I could hear the brittle screams of the dying. Curtains of white flame roared from the broken stoneship, and it began to list in the air, its gun decks angling up uselessly toward the clouds.

The Skyborn didn't have it all their own way. A hail of bolts and swivel-gun shot peppered the flying draken, ripping through membranous wings and eliciting screeches of rage. One of the huge creatures was struck full in the chest by a red-hot iron cannonball, and it spiraled to the ground broken, turning end over end until it plunged into the waters of the crater lake.

"They won't underestimate us a second time," cautioned Ricketts, pointing up above us. A second Keel now eclipsed the first, and it was angling down steeply to pass across our bows.

"Aye," said Elion, plucking the pipe from Corvo's fingers and taking a long drag. He coughed. "What in the foetid hells is *in* this thing, Ontokhi? Dried guano?"

The sorcerer shrugged.

"Among other things," he said. "I suppose it's time for our party piece? Tishande?"

The opal-eyed Ythean sorceress laced her fingers together and cracked her knuckles with a series of small pops.

"Watch and learn, old man. I've worked out a new trick to cut down on the dissonance feedback, and the reflections are going to look *amazing...*"

Normally, to use sorcery aboard one of the keels was to tempt impact and gravity. But our stoneship was powered by acres of taut canvas, and levitated by a seething whirlpool of vengeful spirits. What nobody had told me was that *I* would have to take up the strain when the incantations started flying.

Tishande unlaced a small velvet pouch of crystals and poured them into her palm. The hot-iron scent of magik filled the air. Little sparks skipped and crackled across the shimmering stones, and I felt the spirits pressing up against the veil of reality, ravenously hungry.

Ahhhhh! The warmth! The light! Give them to us, warlock! Let us taste life, the merest shred, the swiftest instant...

I felt cold sweat break out across my skin. Sudden pain tied knots inside my chest. But my will held them. This was the reason why sorcery stopped the millstone wheels of the stoneships - it was a *conduit*, a path to freedom for the captive souls within.

I imagined my hand, closing around the breach. Slowly, painfully, I forced my fingers shut. I felt something burst inside my head, and a trickle of blood dripped from my nose. But damn it, *I held them.*

When I opened my eyes again, the sky was full of draken.

Not just the ravening which seethed and boiled around the crippled Angan Keel – no, this was a swirling tesselation of wings and bodies, as dense and full of malice as a swarm of hornets. It whipped the southmen to terrified madness, and I watched as tiny armoured figures flung themselves from the underslung turrets of the stoneships, screaming down to their deaths.

Now all three of the keels were under drakonic assault, and this time the explosions which tore through them were even more fierce, shattering towers and reducing siege engines to ashes. The Anganesse didn't know where to aim amid the storm of scales and teeth, but the Skyborn knew *exactly* what they were doing.

I watched one come looping around the *Shadow of Blades* in a controlled spiral, rider and mount in perfect harmony. The red-tattooed Zengaji crouched over the draken's heaving back had a bandolier of wineskins in his hand, and a long leather cord between his teeth. He ripped it loose as he and his aerial charger powered up toward the second, unbroken Keel, and a mist of burning white droplets told me precisely what was inside.

Seconds later he peeled away, twisting into a dive, and I watched a tiny speck arc on to fly though an open gunport. The detonation which followed blew open the side of the Keel, sending cracks skittering across its starboard flank.

"And you called *me* a show-off?" said Corvo, who had retrieved his pipe and was watching the battle with smug satisfaction. "Sure, you can just throw power at an incantation, but I thought a *lady* would be far more subtle."

"You're a fine one to talk of subtlety, old man! I'm surprised your storm-God isn't half starved to death every time you mumble out the tiniest little cantrip!"

"*Old man?* I'm at least three years younger than you, Tishande! I just don't waste my damned vitae on cosmetic vanities!"

Power was building behind reality now, making the air taste hot and slippery. The cost of keeping the spirits chained to their sacred bones was a dull pulse in my temples.

"If the two of you don't stop arguing, we'll be following the Angans down," I grated. "And I, for one, don't feel like taking a bath today."

Tishande opened her mouth, no doubt to criticize Corvo's sanitary habits. Elion shot her a look which stopped her cold.

"Both of you, be ready for the first maneuver – the one we talked about," he said, holding the wheel hard with his serrated hook. "Or else Kuhal will be right. And I don't want to die like that..."

Below us, the shattered hulk of the first Angan Keel had gone into a flat spin, billowing towers of black smoke. It punctuated the Faeroan's warning by slamming sideways into the crater wall, obliterating itself in an explosion of pale green witchfire. With its ossuaries gone it was nothing but a vast hunk of rock, and it tumbled down the slope shedding towers, wood and rune-etched metal, until it finally plunged into the waters of the crater lake and was gone. A war Keel of Anganesse carries a crew compliment of near to three hundred, and not one of them floated to the surface.

"That's one down, but there are two more! The three of you, ready on my mark!"

I could read the runes etched into the second great vessel's flank as it came powering down toward us – its name was *Fury of Angels*, and its captain was obviously no fool. Keel had never fought Keel in all the long history of the White Empire, but this man must have learned his craft on the sea before he took to the air. If he was able to present three decks of broadside guns to our vulnerable bows, then he would rake the *Shadow* with chainshot, snapping off masts and stays like a scythe through grain.

Elion roared some incomprehensible Faeroan curse, and the howl of the dead clawed its way through my mind.

Corvo's feather cloak billowed out from his scrawny shoulders, and his magpie familiar pricked blood from his pale white skin with its claws as it held tight. Because the little Ontohki was gathering in the winds, weaving them into a swirling, ice-flecked ball above us. Guttural phrases whipsawed through the agony in my head – an incantation calling on the Stormlord, Auruvasz, Corvo's chosen God. Tishande was working, too, spooling in power from her own facet of the great Divine. A spiral of linked crystal shards spun between her palms as she invoked the Lady of Hallucinomancy, Erys.

Both sorcerers let go at once, and the sheer pressure on the fabric of reality was enough to hammer me to my knees. In the same instant the entire sixty-gun broadside of the *Fury of Angels* was unleashed, a rippling fusillade wreathing the Keel in bonepowder smoke.

But the cloud of spinning chains and runic iron never touched us.

Instead it ripped apart a perfect illusion of the *Shadow*, splintering it into fragments of rainbow-tinted light. The real stoneship had come about during that cataclysmic working of power, driven by a supernatural storm which hung in the air behind us, fed by the sweating, trembling figure of Maegister Corvo. Under its influence Elion and his crew had swung the entire immense Keel up and around, sails slackening for a heartbeat and then bellying out again with a series of thumps almost as loud as cannon-shot. Down on the deck, teams of men worked at capstan grinders, tautening ropes and letting others run slack. Soap strode among them, bellowing curses and offering gulps of spiced rum from a cask gripped in one huge hand.

"Mister Orduvis, stand ready to fire the port-side battery," purred Elion, cradling the leather speaking-tube down to the gun decks in his hook. "At your command, sir..."

He had locked the wheel hard across, and brought us around and behind the *Fury*, looking up at her great inverted underslung castle-towers; the chantries of her acolytes.

Orduvis picked his moment perfectly. The first thunder-roll of guns obliterated the masonry of the Keel's stern, carving it open all the way down to the great millstone chamber at its heart. The second broadside was of hollow shells, filled with white drakenfire, and it roasted hundreds alive - including the acolytes of the watch, incinerated at their lecterns.

The third broke its back. It was solid ordnance from the biggest of our guns - the top deck seige-belchers, with wolf-faced muzzles wide enough for a man to crawl inside. Their runic shot was designed to shatter fortress walls, and at least one of the gunners managed a direct hit on the grinding wheels around the *Fury's* ossuary well.

A chain of explosions tore through the great vessel, spearing out as plumes of witchfire and flame. One of the millstones tore loose, and it bounced upright between our masts, gouging a furrow in the solid stone of the *Shadow's* deck. The last I saw of the *Fury of Angels* was its corkscrew death-plunge into the mountainside, a ruined hulk trailing sparks and screams.

But it was the third Keel which had us.

I was reeling drunk with power when it came swimming up through the smoke, a mountain of ancient and frost-rimed stone aswarm with tiny figures. This was – according to the runes – the *Thearch's Fist,* and it was one of a handful of Angan keels designed to smash apart castles and cities.

The Acolyte-engineers on board had seen our sorcery, and their captain was all but desperate. He must have assumed that it was the sheer saturation of power in the aether which allowed us to fly while our adepts worked their chants. Indeed, each breath I took was as heady as moonshine and sweet with cinnamon and honey - thick with death and the imminence of the divine.

So he gave them leave to work. The steersmen closed their wardings and let the Keel fly unbound, bending their power to darker magiks.

A cloud of churning grey spewed from the arched windows of the chantry as they prayed. It formed a nimbus around the *Thearch's Fist,* plucking Draken and their riders from the air and casting them aside like motes of dust. And it blurred the vast, knife-blade shape of the Keel, running fast and sure with the howl of the damned behind it. It hid the captain's intent even from Elion Morekh, until it was far too late for us to evade.

"Brace yourselves!" bellowed the Captain - and his crew, who had seen cataclysms like this before on the shallow sea, raced for cover. Tishande's sorcery flickered and died with a sound like breaking harp-strings, and her eyes grew wide with horror. Corvo tried to manhandle his globe of winds around through sheer will, but the blade of rushing air he cast was not enough to slew the *Fist* from its course.

The ramming spike of the Keel split the clouds first, followed by several million tons of Angan artifice. It struck us amidships, and all of us were knocked from our feet amid the grind and crack of breaking stone. A series of bonepowder detonations rung out, followed by a score or more of wrenching impacts. Chains clattered and groaned as the two ships were pulled into a tight embrace.

"They've got us with the grapples!' shouted Ricketts, the navigator, hanging out over the bridge-rail with one hand on his hat. "Hundreds of 'em, Cap'n, and they're ready to board!"

"The Draken can't help us," said Tishande. "If we bring down that Keel, we fall with it. This is sword work, and bloody."

"Then I hope you've kept yours sharp," cackled Corvo. "I, of course, don't have to bother with steel..."

Elion Morekh wasn't looking at either of them, though. Both he, and Soap, who had come up the ladder with his cannon tucked under one arm – and indeed, the entire Faeroan crew – were looking at me.

Little pops and cracks of witchfire sizzled at the tips of my hair. My mouth was locked in a savage grin, and blood leaked in thin trickles from my nose and the corner of my eyes.

"I never told you what the Southmen are calling you now, Kuhal," said Elion, while behind him the whack and clatter of gangwalks being thrown across the gap was joined by the sound of screams and curses.

"Oh? Exactly what title have our Angan friends dreamed up for me?"

"They call you the Soulflayer. The Scourge of the North - enemy of the light of Esau."

I had come this far – through delirium, waking dream, battle and death and flame, without a single thought about what I was wearing. But as a barbarian, and a saga-song hero with a head full of bard's lies, my hand went for my sword without even knowing it was there. The pommel was smooth and cold, and it drew from its scabbard with a musical ringing sound, melodic and unsettling at once. The blade had been Jerrold Sinder's.

"Let's give them something to talk about then," I said – and with that I leaped over the rail.

I felt hands grasping for me; heard Corvo's laughter and Elion's cursing. But I had to get away from them.

"Stop him! If he dies, we fall! *Come on,* damn you!"

I landed in a crouch, a shock of sudden pain numbing my legs. I was out of shape - but then of course I'd been *asleep* for almost two seasons. First under the mental knives of Jerrold Sinder, and then... well, I suspected that the Archaeon had been performing exactly the same kind of experiments, in the name of its own obscure cause. I was angry, and the sword in my hand was part of the reason why.

They had *dressed me.* I was all in black, in a mockery of the black scaled armour and tattered robes of Sothara the Bone Collector. They had given me Jerrold Sinder's swords – spares, I supposed, as the original pair were ground to dust along with most of his body. They had made me into something for the Anganesse to fear.

I half-suspected that Elion Morekh himself had dreamed up those pretty names for me... *Soulflayer,* indeed!

All it meant was that I was still being used – part of some grand scheme which none of my so-called friends would let me in on. Corvo had even said that *Sothara himself* was my replacement; that Aerik and Maudrin had known...

Which made me even angrier - and more appalled at my own naivety. How far back did it go? Was I being groomed as a necromantic weapon when I was still too young to know what that meant? Too young to walk, or talk, or shit anywhere but in my pants? *Why did they want an accursed warlock, anyway?*

It *worked*, damn them. I ran for the edge of the Keel, and people scattered before me. Our own soldiers, clad in mismatched armour, or the white-lacquered helms of Anganesse defaced with a crude red 'x'. Fear boiled up from them like smoke in the Dark Sight, and they recoiled from my shadow.

But the enemy didn't just fear me. They were utterly terrified.

Hundreds of Angan warriors came swarming over the iron gangwalks from the Thearch's Fist, and they had already pushed deep onto our own decks, carving a foothold through flesh and metal with their wicked boarding axes.

Two score of the hardest, most scarred and ruthless of the Thearch's marines... and they let out a groan of mortal dread as they saw me pelting across the deck towards them, alone. Sinder's blade was held out to my left and his long knife to my right. Elion had remembered everything – I felt a squirming, clicking presence inside my cloak, and then the pinprick of claws up my back as Sei bound himself together, emerging at my shoulder.

"It's him! Anghul's Son! The vengeance of the North!"

"Retreat! Sound the horns!"

"Gah, you cowards! He's but one man! Hack him down, curse you!"

At least they'd called me a man, and not a child. I was smiling as I closed in, and perhaps that scared the bastards more than anything.

Time seemed to slow down. I saw, with pinpoint clarity, the mixture of drunken rage and bowel-clenching terror in the eyes of the Anganesse as they faltered, whipped on by their grizzled Sejant. And I saw myself, as if in a dying dream – a pale white figure surrounded by a storm of darkness, my cloak billowing out on a wind of ash and sparks.

Elion Morekh was right behind me, his hook and cutlass winking in the light. Soap was reaching out for me with one immense hand, his cannon gripped by the barrel in the other like a club. Tishande was just a blur of green, sliced up by rainbows. And Corvo still stood at the rail, smoking his pipe and laughing.

So, they wanted a bloody *warlock*, did they?

I'd show them what they'd created, and damn them all!

I had never learned to fight like Conn, or even like Ulkar and his kind – I was no warrior, not by the reckoning of my own savage people. But Sothara the Bone Collector *was*, and my anger gave the shadow-memory of him control. I saw, with piercing, painful clarity, how a warlock should fight.

There - a Faceless swordsman, his bones laid bare in the Dark Sight. An old wound, healed wrong, a *weakness* – snapped and shattered to splinters by the power of my hatred. I took his pain and drove it sideways into the temple of the man next to him, making him scream and drop his shield. Then both were down, and I was into the gap before their comrades could rally, both swords a blur.

Death enervated me. Death twisted the sinews of my power almost to breaking point. I didn't even hear my own feral war-scream as I butchered into the terrified Anganesse, unsplicing souls from flesh left and right. Sinder's blades cut through mail like silk, and though bone like hot tallow, singing their own one-note slaying song. And the darkness deepened around me, the light shifting to cold, empty blue.

This was the core of Sothara's brutal style. The ultimate form of necromancy. I was animating *my own* bones and tendons, muscle and flesh, just like I would the cadavers of the slain. And like that dead, twitching meat, I was able to push my body further and harder than I had any right to.

Time trickled and dripped like water underground - dark, pressurized and slow. Clumsy, sweating apes gibbered and drooled, eyes wide, guts uncoiling in slow, bloody arcs, limbs hacked clean from spurting stumps, organs pumping and bulging from severed torso smiles...

And I could see how it all worked. Blue shifted to black, tunneling my vision down to a bright, far-off coin of light and horror. Souls billowed like ragged smoke from the dead, drawn into the vortex of my power. There was no way out for them – no rest, no respite. Without my permission they were bound to reality, living inside the last terrible moment of their pain.

I could bind them to their bones for centuries, fill their mouths with clay and ashes. I could use them to raise me up, burn them away to nothing to fuel my own internal fires – or I could nail them screaming to their own dead flesh.

I stopped, swords held out crossed in front of me, blood dripping from both. Around me lay a circle of the slain, bodies cross-hatched with savage cuts. And I slammed both swords back into their scabbards, spitting out the sharp syllables of a terrible incantation.

They rose.

The sheer power of the spell wrenched me back into the here and now, blue shifting to red all around me. The pain - when my nerves caught up with my mind - was terrifying, but I pushed it aside, feeling my will spread out in all directions. My hands came up, fingers spread, and I flung my new harvest of bodies at the enemy, just in time for Elion and his crew to join the charge.

It broke them. Utterly broke them, mind and body. Between the thunderous impact of Soap's cannon (wielded like an ogre's club, and smashing six southern spearmen at one blow), the shimmering blur of Tishande's rapier, the wicked precision of Elion Morekh's hook and cutlass, and the assorted boarding axes, machetes, panga, polearms, maces, glaives, yari and bludgeons of our mismatched crew, we forced the Angans screaming from our decks, sending dozens of them reeling over the edge at once. The momentum of our charge carried us right up to the boarding planks of the *Thearch's Fist* – but there was no respite there for the routed conscripts. Their way was blocked by a thicket of spiked shields, locked into formation by the Faceless.

My wights knew no mercy. They butchered the cowards to a man, only to be hacked apart in turn by the half-moon axes of the Thearch's elite guard. Dead men toppled without sound or scream from the gangwalks, still grasping with bloodied fingers for their former allies' throats.

"Who am I? *What do you bastards call me?*"

I was raving like one of the Touched, utterly ignoring the arrows and quarrels which whipped past on either side. It's some kind of dark miracle that none of them skewered me.

"Come on, you castrated dog-rapists! Come and give your souls to the monster!"

As I stood there on the edge, panting and bloody, I felt a hand on my shoulder. It pulled me away from the drop, and into the cover of a roll of wrist-thick rope, now bristling with arrows.

"You know if you risk your life again like that, I'll have to kill you myself." It was Elion Morekh. When I turned to confront him he was smiling, all gold teeth and wild eyes. "We can't have..."

"*What?* Your precious cargo getting damaged in transit? Your pet warlock finding out about your plans for him? Do you know about the legend of Winter's King, Elion?"

The pirate looked stunned – not by my question, but by the anger behind it.

"Who? Is this some kind of Khytein history lesson? Because now is not the place for..."

"Back in the stone times, when Ciermakh was among us and great beasts ruled the Stormwood, we would gather each year to pray for the end of the dark season. On the black of the moon, in the cold of winter, we would sacrifice a young man who had been anointed as the vessel of the wolf-God. He was tied to a tree and disemboweled, to ensure that the sun would rise again."

"I know," said Tishande, appearing next to the Faeroan. Her green cloak was spattered with blood, and her opal eyes burned with latent sorcery. "Anghul took him in place of Ciermakh, and the cycle was made whole. In old Ythe, in the times of the empire, we had a similar ritual. And you think..."

"I think *I've* been anointed as Winter's King. I think that you, the Archaeon, and even Aerik Stormsong himself wouldn't tell me what was at stake in this game, because in the end it's my *life*."

Behind me I could hear the crack and whine of arrows deflected from another or Maegister Corvo's shields. Under his protection teams of men were heaving the Angan gangwalks over the side, and hacking through the chains which bound our keels together.

"You think it's just *your* life that's forfeit?" asked Tishande. "We're *all* not coming back from this one, child. Come on! A handful of powers against an empire? What can we hope for, except a glorious death?"

There was no bitterness in her words – just sorrowful resignation.

"There's no such thing as a *glorious death*. Just shit and blood and grief."

"And yet it must be done," growled Elion. "You know about the Coldblood. We *all* do. And if we can free our peoples at the same time, then I, for one, will gladly die. What is life but more ale, more music, more women and more battles anyhow? I'll have all of those in the next world, Gods willing."

Gods willing indeed. Even *I* didn't know where I was sending those dead souls to, after I freed them from bondage.

"I owed you Jerrold Sinder," I said. "But you once told me, Elion, that nothing comes for free. I'll want payment for the Thearch's head.

And if you think it's going to cost us all our lives, I'll want paying in advance."

The old reaver nodded, and I knew he had caught my meaning. But before he could answer the Keel lurched under our feet, pulling up and away from the *Thearch's Fist*.

Elion spun around, waving his hook up to Ricketts at the wheel.

"Don't let them come about! Tell Orduvis that if he values his poxy hide, he'll have those damned guns reloaded *now*!"

He had. The stuttering rumble of a full sixty-cannon broadside at such close range was deafening, and it carved craters from the Angan Keel's deck. Whole squads of Faceless were blown to mist and chips of bone as chainshot whirled and skipped across the decks of the *Fist*.

But it wasn't their intention to flee. The entire immense blade of the stoneship was heeling over, presenting the eye of its ossuary well to us. The wounded scrabbled and slipped from her decks, screaming. And beneath reality I could feel something building – a power distorting the world as it was worked.

"Sweet blood of Erys, they *wouldn't*!" hissed Tishande, as our own Keel slewed up and around, struggling for height. I was thrown to the deck with Elion holding me down, and above us in the rigging I could see men leaping among the ropes and spars, adding more and more sail.

"Come on!" whispered the captain, and I knew he was talking to the *Shadow of Blades* itself. "You can do it, old girl! You can outrun the wind, you beautiful, evil bitch!"

I struggled to turn my head, and I saw the witchfire inside the *Fist*'s ossuaries flare, a gyre of green flame forming between them. Cracks ramified through the stoneship's hull, and huge sections of the Keel's towers were sucked down into that annihilating light, only to flare into ashes.

"They can't hold it. Not like this. The whole damned thing is going to cut loose!"

We were moving, running before a storm of Corvo's making. I could feel the ice in it as it spun along the length of our Keel, chilling me to the bone. But we were moving far too slowly. When the acolytes of the *Thearch's Fist* released the power of all those souls they would fall. But *we* would be incinerated.

I closed my eyes tightly, waiting for the blast. I prayed - to whichever Gods cared to listen - that it would be quick and painless.

But I had forgotten about the Draken.

They came past so low across our decks that I could actually smell the chemical stench of their breath, and feel the massive downdraft of their wings. Swallows the size of warships, with whooping, screaming Zengaji Skyborn on their backs – all out of their incendiary fireskins, but ready with their bows and the furnace breath of their mounts.

First a pair of them, and then a dozen more slammed into the upraised side of the Angan Keel, trying to force it down through sheer weight and impact. Still more crashed into the tottering towers of the stoneship, raging and flaming as masonry and rock gave way beneath them. The crews of the *Fist*'s siege engines were too busy trying to hold tight to offer any resistance. They burned, lit up like wax candles and screaming for death.

It still wasn't enough. The seething eye of the ossuary well was almost eclipsed, but even a glancing blow would break the back of our Keel.

I felt the final phrases as they left the lips of the Angan high priest. Ten thousand glass tombs shattered, and a pair of gargantuan millstones fused into one solid lump of rock.

But in the instant before cataclysm overtook us the greatest of the draken came down like a hammer, black and copper scales reflecting fire. It was Imkhantu's mount, the beast he called his soul, and it was a sire half as large again as its cousins. The huge creature flared its wings at the last possible moment, over the ossuary well itself, and it slammed into the lip of that circular chasm with a force which almost tore the Keel in two.

A heartbeat later it was incinerated.

For one terrible instant the entire world flashed white, and even with my eyes tightly shut the image of Imkhantu's draken was branded into my mind. The Dark Sight saw beyond the sheer heat and light of the blast, and it made me witness the flesh unspliced from around the creature's skeleton. Scales cracked and spiraled away, membranous wings melted like wax... it blazed until nothing but blackened bones remained, hanging amid a cloud of fire.

Imkhantu fared no better. I heard his unhinged scream turn to laughter as his soul was stripped away.

But he had his victory. The blast of energy which raved from the core of the *Thearch's Fist* missed us entirely... or at least did nothing more than char the edges of our sails.

Now there was nothing to stop master gunner Orduvis from unleashing hell against the Angans, and he was surgically precise.

His gunnery crews may have been deserters and outcasts, but they knew their opportunity for revenge when they saw it. A devastating broadside ripped into the enemy Keel, crushing fortifications and shattering stone. It was almost an afterthought, for without the dead souls of the ossuaries to keep it airborne it was doomed.

The *Thearch's Fist* came down hard, plowing a furrow across the valley floor. Its acolytes had prevented it from falling like the stone which it was, but I feared they would be powerless to protect themselves from the enraged Zengaji who swarmed from their warren of caves toward it, blades winking in the light above a tide of bodies.

"Kuhal!" Said a voice above me. I opened my eyes and saw Tishande there, with Corvo at her side. "We did it, Khytein. We're clear of them!"

I struggled to sit up, pushing Elion Morekh away.

"Aye, free for now," agreed the Faeroan. "But we must run before this storm while we can. The Thearch will want to make us pay for the work we've done here today."

"That's not... *exactly* what I meant," said the sorceress, reaching for my hand. It was clenched into a fist, my fingers wrapped tight around the tiny skull of Sei.

Corvo gestured with his pipe, smirking with grim humor. Elion turned, and the look on his face went from wonder to horror in an instant.

Because the war Keel *Thearch's Fist* had fallen from the sky, but Imkhantu's great draken had not. It still burned, its muscles and scales scrawled across its blackened bones as a boiling cloud of witchfire. Smouldering corpse-lights shone where its eyes had been, and it stood rampant in an expanding cloud of its own ashes, wings outstretched like twin aurorae. The other draken circled it in a wheeling halo, crying out their reverence and terror.

"If you're really doing that, then I'm truly glad that you aren't Sothara the tyrant," said Corvo. "He'd already have plotted ten ways to use such a thing for conquest. *You're* still showing off."

"It's horrible," whipsered Tishande. "All its hatred. All its despite... You have to let it *die*, Khytein."

I smiled, and it was a grin of utter madness. If they wanted to hammer me into a sword, they would damn well have to learn which end to hold.

"Sei likes it. *I* like it. And Imkhantu was laughing when I let him go. What will the Anganesse think of me now, Elion?"

The old reaver was visibly shaken, his face as white as ash.

"More to the point, what do you think his *sister* is going to do to you, child? This is an abomination."

I staggered away from him, my head throbbing and echoing with the laughter of the dead.

"*I'm* an abomination, Captain. If I wasn't, you wouldn't need me at all. And this abomination has a special request for you, if you want things like *this* -" I gestured behind me at the undead draken, as it soared up across the face of the sun, scattering crazed shadows. "If you want things like this to happen to your enemies."

Elion's face was grim as he brought his hook within a whisper of my throat.

"So. *Leverage*, then. I won't call it blackmail, because I still want to like you, boy."

"Call it what you like," I said, as Corvo cackled amid a cloud of smoke, and Tishande sank to her knees, weeping quietly. The Keel's crew were watching, and I drank in their revulsion. "But call it payment, as well. We're taking this ship to Korisal."

Korisal? What can I tell you of that doomed kingdom? Perhaps it would satisfy your morbid curiosity to know of the curse which befell that land - the war of the Clockmakers and the Guild of Artifice, so long ago that it is now less than a memory.

Both factions were so righteous in worship that they gave themselves up to certain arkane processes, blessedly now lost. In seeking to emulate their deity they became engines of brass and fire and flesh, undying but unfeeling, dwindling in number as the priests who created them grew old and mad. At last the two great conventicles disagreed over a line of scripture - a single word, if the scholars of Saradrim are to be believed. And then the crazed half-men of Korisal broke themselves against each other in war, leaving only one to lament their folly...

THERE WAS LITTLE argument, even after I released Sei's soul from that of the draken, letting it blow away to dust on the mountain winds. I think that the whole crew were besotted with the doomed romance of my quest, as well as utterly terrified by my newfound power. This meant that I spent the voyage which followed in a little bubble of isolation, despite sharing quarters with over two hundred free men and women of Sarem. Their babble of languages, petty arguments, personal odours and the scents of strangely spiced cookery passed me by, and I was an outcast once again.

Elion Morekh had command, and he knew that this flight was my soul-price, his payment for revenge against the Thearch. I think that the poetry in his Faeroan soul agreed entirely with my purpose, while the anger in him lusted to see me unleashed upon his foes.

So we sailed north, into the cauldron of war and woe which had once been my homeland. As part of the grand plan enacted by the Free Powers – a conclave of three ancient Warbards, one Archaeon, a cabal of Faeroan Captains, the five remaining soul-sworn of Erys, Maegister Corvo, and sundry other sorcerously gifted or temporally powerful pariahs – rebel armies and mercenary companies from all over the conquered north had descended on Khytein, seeking to crush the Thearch's legions while they were overstretched.

Ephris, the exile of Ravenstrand, led his Silver Company against the Angan First and Ninth Legions to the west, assisted by wild skirmishers from the ice of the utter north. They turned the snow crimson with Angan blood, decimating the First and killing the Ninth to the last man.

In the south, the dispossessed Rasuul nobles-turned-bandits known as the Blackened Brotherhood exacted a grim toll, using Ghuram firestone to bring down the walls of Burned Hand Pass. Half of the Angan Third Legion was buried alive, and the remainder were picked off by Ontokhi mountain scouts, unerringly accurate with their horn bows and blowdarts.

But it was my own poor, doomed people who took the fight to the southmen most viciously. We picked up survivors whenever we could, descending from the clouds to ransack burned towns and villages for food and supplies, or to take on water from abandoned wells and pools. They told us that the last Warbard, Ukarion of the Roege, had enacted the rite of Sorrow, and that the entire Khytein nation was at war.

The Path of Sorrows is a hard one, and even I was unprepared for the sight of Khytein mothers dead in the snow, with their babies lashed to their chests full of arrows. Man, woman and child alike, we savages had taken to the Stormwood, and the grisly victories we had inflicted were marked out in cairns of Angan helms, trees groaning under the weight of the hanged, and whole fields of limbs, hacked off and planted upright in the snow as if grasping for the aid of the Gods.

The winter was our ally, and with the passes closed the Angan annexation forces were desperate. Sometimes we passed over marching columns of them streaming south, abandoning their processing camps and heading toward the supposed safety of the trader's towns on the edge of the Stormwood. But those walled sanctuaries – established in centuries past by Ythean caravans – were charnel pits now, for there was worse abroad in the north than simple slaughter.

Some of those we rescued from what became known as the Red Winter were utterly mad, staring blankly, rocking and babbling and refusing even a mouthful of food. Others raved about horrors far more dire than war. And the few who were still sane told us the terrible truth.

The Nine had been unleashed against Khytein, and against all the rag-tag forces who had come to her aid. But they were wild, unbound – one old man spoke of hiding in a hollow tree as he watched what could only have been the Shining One and the Black Shepherd tearing an entire battalion of Faceless limb from limb. He said that the little glowing child's feet had never touched the ground, and that the thing in the long black cloak with the thorn-wrapped crozier had taken its time, harvesting the eyes of the dead.

The Burning Dark had been seen to the south, where it had flayed the faces from every living soul in the town of Arnsford, then stitched them together into a great banner which it flew from the spire of Ciermakh's temple.

That Which Walks had come in the night to a processing camp by the shores of lake Rhyva, and the single slave who survived to tell the tale swore that it had simply pushed whole buildings and handfuls of people into its chest, drowning them in black fire.

Other stories spread like a fever among the crew. Tales of evil and excess which made the horrors of battle seem warm and friendly by comparison...

But we were headed east, ever east, towards where Mr Ricketts' maps gave out into pictures of sea-devils and draken. To the peninsula of Korisal, which Maegister Corvo assured me had been damned for centuries before I was even born.

Corvo was my constant companion during our flight – not because of any love for me, I think, but because alone among the hundreds of people on board he knew what it meant to be an outcast power. As a servant of the Ontokhi stormlord he had seen his temples thrown down and his brethren crucified. He harboured a deep, cold hatred of

Anganesse beneath his facade of elderly merriment.

I would often find him perched with his great magpie, Rain, on the chantry decks beneath the Keel, both he and the enormous bird huddled in a cloud of feathers. It was here that he told me what he knew of sorcery – not how he could work the winds and call lightning to his hands, but the lore that sages had gleaned over the centuries about why it existed at all.

"They say that there was one Divine, back in the dawning age. He wrought the world – or *she*, if you believe Tishande – with his own hands. But in order to give things life, the Divine had to shatter himself, and give little pieces of his mind to every living thing. Tiny pieces for the insects and crawling things, shards for the beasts and birds, and for us... well, you must have met people, Kuhal, who seem to have been given sharp and jagged souls."

I nodded, looking down at the snow past my dangling boots, three hundred spans below.

"We started believing in Gods just as soon as we could dream. And those big pieces left over, out there in the Unmanifest – they turned to mirrors, see. Or the facets of a jewel, as old king Harmensis used to say. *We* gave them faces, and, because people are people, whether they're black, white, mad or sane, a lot of those faces were quite the same. Anghul, the Harvestman, Ogrun, Shadowmask – they are all part of the same thing, boy, and they reach back through the veil to those who believe in them most."

I thought of Sothara, trapped in his prison of time, and how he had become the image of his God, all thorny antlers and darkness beneath his cowl. And I couldn't help but think of Gernish Maudrin, as wild and hairy and savage as our own bear-God Theyr, brother of Ciermakh and guardian of the Stormwood.

"I feel Auruvasz behind me when I draw down power," said Corvo, taking a long drag on his pipe. "His face is always shadowed, but his wings eclipse the sun, and I can taste the ice wind when I breathe in his power. He gives me strength, and with that strength I make people believe in him. A blizzard or two, a couple of bolts of lightning – that does a whole lot more for the faith than any number of dreary old hymns." He laughed. "But it must be a fearsome thing, to feel the old reaper working through you. He and I, as you can see, are almost on speaking terms, what with my age and all..."

I thought of the times when I had unleashed my power, and I shook my head.

"All I feel is *anger*, Maegister. A vast, endless anger, which I can hardly contain. And I don't see the face of Anghul, or Ogrun, or Shadowmask. What I see is a great stone door, miles high. Two pillars of stone, and a lintel of black iron. When it cracks open the power comes into me, and it feels like water flowing into the world."

I had never thought about it – not really. I spoke in a hollow voice, picking out the shape of that black portal from memories my mind had tried to repress. Corvo's smile disappeared, and his pipe stopped halfway to his lips.

"Are there runes on the stone? Figures carved into the lintel?"

"No... nothing. At least, not that I remember."

"And what's beyond the door? Does it speak to you?"

"*Speak to me*? No! It's just some kind of metaphor, isn't it? Something my mind has dreamed up to explain where the power is coming from – a tomb, a barrow, some kind of illusion..."

I hoped with all that was left of my heart that I was right. But even then my denials seemed perilously frail.

Corvo's lips twitched into a semblance of his former smile. He laid his pipe down with a tiny click against the stone, snuffing out its bowl with one callused thumb.

"Oh... oh yes. Just a dream of the collective grave, I suppose. Better for you, boy, that the Harvestman doesn't show his face."

Rain fluffed up his feathers and shifted on his perch, fixing me with one beady eye. Something I had said had shocked the little Ontohki, and his discomfort was almost palpable. Below us the flat white plain had turned to rumpled foothills, blanketed in freezing snow. I stood to leave, suddenly all too aware that Corvo could hurl me from this ledge, and nobody would ever find my body.

A withered hand grabbed my wrist before I could take a second step.

"You'll tell me if you ever hear that voice, boy. Tell me what it says, and what it promises."

It wasn't a request. I swallowed, hard, remembering the dismissive gesture of this same liver-spotted hand which had torn open the side of an entire Keel.

"I... I will, Maegister. I..."

He let go, and huddled into his robe of feathers, the very shadow of his familiar.

"Go. We are almost there, Kuhal Moer. I know what waits for us in Korisal, so believe me when I tell you that you'll need your rest."

I chanced a look back past Corvo as I walked away, into the echoing cloister which bracketed the stern of the Keel. The sky behind us was a wall of thundercloud, riven with crawling arcs of lightning. Beneath it the southern plains of Khytein spread crisp and white, and under the snow waited whole frozen armies of corpses, carrion to rot in the spring.

I thought I saw, there in the boiling darkness of the storm, the outline of vast wings, a crowned head lifted for a moment above the anvils of cloud. But from the dead, nothing.

I walked alone through the crowded halls of the Keel to my quarters, and when I slept I dreamed of a vast stone door, standing open on a field of bones.

Comes to us a barbarian... a southman of what calls he the Anganesse, some upstart empire of these latter days. Like the others come before he is - full of pride, full of pity for poor old Urzen the mad. But he comes to bargain, and what needs we have must be sated! Commands he - commands, I laugh, to think that such a worm should speak so to a Forgemaster of Korisal! - nine examples of my peerless art, nine wrought from the servants of fallen Gods to act as the hidden scourge of his master. So it shall be, and in return - the Great Work can continue. Wary we must be however, that this one plays us not false. Like young Sothara the Khytein, who stole the tomes of the Guardian Engines under a masque of false flattery and reverence - he has that same mischief in his eyes.

The journal of Urzen, last Forgemaster of Korisal

KORISAL BURNED.

A pall of ash hung over the land as we approached, spewing from the craters of a whole chain of volcanic crags, some weeping great sullen streams of lava, others boiling with sulphurous gases, and all spiked and gnarled with spires of black obsidian.

This, Corvo assured us, was the work of the Guild of Artifice and the Clockmakers, who needed immense power to forge their sorcerous creations. As a result of their hubris the peninsula of Korisal was cut off from the mainland by a massif of smoking mountains, and the interior was a waste of pumice, ash, and slowly cooling rock. Corvo insisted that the brave and foolish who had ventured beyond the Demonspine (for such the volcanic range was called) had found the towers and spires of ancient cities protruding from the plain, all buried under a great vomitous outpouring of lava long ago.

Now we drew near to the place Jerrold Sinder had told me about, seconds before he was torn apart. Urzen's keep, the Hammerforge, its pillars and arches carved into the side of a basalt cliff three hundred spans tall. A long, seemingly unsupported tongue of black glass stretched out from one of those arches to meet an upthrust spire, the top of which had been razed flat to form a docking place for keels. Obviously Sinder – or some other catspaw of the Thearch – had need of much discourse with this old, old sorcerer. Both Corvo and Tishande were adamant that he was quite insane, and perhaps ten times older even than Sothara himself.

"He hungers for steel, and other metals. Rare gemstones, flammable oils from within the earth, ores and acids... but the traders won't go near this place. Even they can tell it's accursed. And the story goes around that..."

"Those who visit don't come back?" hazarded Tishande, her hands gripping the rail tightly. A hot, foul wind blew her green hair away from her face, and I saw the flash of her opal eyes. "I know. We tried to kill him, you know – myself and my sisters, before the Anganesse came north to Ythe. I've seen what's inside there, even if it was only through the eyes of a shade. The damned creature *takes them apart*. He's trying to build something, and I think he's forgotten how."

Corvo nodded, clenching his pipe between his teeth.

"I don't know if Urzen was a Clockmaker or a Guildsmith, but I think he wants his body back. His, and those of his masters. Ontokh remembers the war between them, even if it is only in campfire tales."

"Stories are one thing. Life is quite another," said Elion. "And sorcery tends to blur the line. But Kuhal says that this Urzen *created* the Nine. If he's right, then they are flesh and bone like us. We can kill them. The question is – who's going with him?"

There was no question of trying to stop me. I think Corvo had talked to them all... and in any case, the plan dreamed up by their outcast cabal called for a necromancer. I was the only one they could count on.

"I'll go alone," I said. "there's nothing for any of you here. And if I don't come back..."

"That's *exactly* why I'm coming with you," said Jenan, tightening the sash which held her swords. "You're not ready to face a thing like this Urzen in a duel of powers. But we Zengaji know *all* there is to know about cutting down sorcerers."

I tried very hard to ignore the look she gave me – there was still the fate of her brother between us, for all that he was hailed as a hero.

"I'm going too," said Tishande. "There's a matter of honour here, and I have my own dead to lay to rest."

"They'll sleep easier with their murderer in pieces?" I asked.

Tishande frowned down several centuries of High Ythean culture at my barbarian sensibilities. I shrugged.

"It's not that I have any particular problem with the concept... my father used to take the scalps, ears and fingers of everyone who wronged him, after all."

"I suppose our noble captain will be joining us as well?"

Elion looked decidedly uncomfortable as he peered up through the drifting smoke at Urzen's citadel. But he would never allow himself to seem a coward – especially not in front of the Ythean sorceress.

"Four against the darkness, then. At least it'll make a great saga-song. And if we can plunder some supplies from this evil old wretch, so much the better. I'm getting heartily sick of easting salt beef and hardbread for every meal."

We disembarked down a long gangwalk into eerie silence. The crew of the *Shadow* lined the rail, watching as we made our way across the bridge toward Urzen's home. Down below us a river of molten rock bubbled and churned, turning great metal wheels which glowed red-hot in the gloom.

"What do you suppose those are for?" I asked, watching the immense mills grind through another rotation.

"Power," said Tishande. "All the engines and traps of the citadel are driven by them – some say even the lord of this place himself needs winding up like a clock..."

We passed into the shadow of the gatehouse, and I couldn't help but notice the little runnels of metal which had cooled and solidified on the lips of Urzen's gargoyles – if he had wanted to, the sorcerer could have rained down molten lead from their mouths. But the portcullis was raised and the gates were open. We came into a shadowy hall, lit from below by slits in the floor, and still there was no sign of either the keep's master or his slaves.

"I don't like this," said Tishande, hefting her pouch of crystals in one hand.

"What's not to like?" whispered Jenan. "We aren't being eaten by anything big and hungry... yet."

"Why did you have to say *yet*? I..."

"Quiet!" hissed Elion, and I felt the hairs on the back of my neck prickle. "Someone's coming!"

We split apart and hid in the shadows of a row of pillars, their capstones carved to resemble faceless angels. Something was descending the stairway at the end of the great hall, shuffling and clanking as if encased in baroque Ghurami platemail.

It was a grey-skinned giant of a man – as big as Soap, if not quite as wide across the belly. But its head was encased in a cube of featureless black iron, and its hands were stumps, ending in a pair of metal rings. These were locked into the handles of a vast copper chest, spilling over with lengths of chain. The thing clumped onward, unseeing, and disappeared through a doorway – though my last glimpse of it revealed that its back was flayed open, and metal whirred and clicked beneath its polished ribs.

"Drudge," whispered Tishande. "One of his little projects. That one was a servitor, but there are others..."

"With blades?" ventured Jenan. Her tone made it apparent that it would be a novel and interesting thing to try to kill one.

"With *all kinds* of nasty additions. That's why people don't come back from this place."

"The drudges kill them?" asked Elion, slipping around the pillar to check for any signs of movement.

"No. Urzen uses them to *make more drudges*."

I shuddered. Even necromancers have their horrors, and that poor shambling thing had been a twisted ruin in the Dark Sight.

"Come on. If it was headed down, we're going up. Hopefully we can take the old monster by surprise."

"You don't think he's noticed the Keel, then? It's sort of hard to miss, Morekh."

"Perhaps he'll think it's his butt-boy Sinder," growled the Captain, motioning us forward. We scampered up the stairway and into a long gallery, hung with moldering portraits of grim-faced clerics. "In any case, he doesn't seem to be laying on a grand welcome, does he?"

He certainly wasn't. We passed through halls big enough to dock the *Shadow of Blades*, past iron crucibles the size of houses bubbling with liquid metal. We traversed crosswalks over rivers of lava, and slipped though forges gone cold, their titanic trip-hammers and rollers silent. Here and there we caught sight of drudges toiling in the shadows – they had no need for sight, it seemed, and they worked on even when their tasks were futile.

Some, like the giant we had seen earlier, simply carried and poured and piled supplies – ingots and black sand, crushed glass and buckets of smoking acids. Several of these had kept piling and stacking even when the hoppers they tended had overflowed. One or two walked in circles, or tried in vain to push their way through solid walls. In other places human pumps and cranks slaved in the ruddy light of molten rock – some headless, their necks fused to segmented pipes and tubes which disappeared through holes in the walls, others with missing limbs, or simply torsos bolted down to plinths, repeating the same tired motions on and on without thought or feeling.

Tishande led us. By now the rest of us were mazed by a combination of fumes, heat and revulsion. Jenan, I think, would have stopped to put each of the drudges we passed out of their misery. But Elion forbade it – it was a miracle we had come so far into Urzen's fastness without being discovered as it was.

We had climbed to what by my reckoning was the twenty-third level when we found the first signs of carnage.

The door from the spiral stairwell into the hall beyond was splintered, and a spray of blood and other liquids crusted the smooth-hewn stone. When I peered through into the gloom beyond I saw two huge bodies lying slumped across the wreck of a marble table – obviously dead, as the living tend to have more in the way of limbs and heads attached.

Tishande pulled me back from the doorway, her opal eyes flashing.

"*No.* They may seem dead, but things like this aren't properly alive to begin with."

I was about to protest that life and death were pretty damned clear-cut to the likes of me, but before I could the Ythean conjured a sphere of light from her hand and let it drift into the room. The words choked in my throat.

"*Ironhands.* Big ones. Whatever killed them wasn't taking any chances."

The light revealed the true extent of what the things had been – and what had been done to them. Like the Slaughterborn I'd raised, Urzen's Ironhands were built from more than one body, with ropes of muscle and stitched-together skin stretched tight across a frame which was part bone and part wood, shot through with wires and metal. Their heads were globes of iron with a single round portal in front – a lens of segmented crystal like the eye of an insect. And their arms – three in number for the first, four for the second – were waist-thick pistons of necrified meat and metal, ending in a selection of hooks, blades, maces and flails. Glass tubes inside their hollowed-out chests spilled reeking fluids, and there were gears in there, still and silent among a ruin of organs, crystals, wires and bellows-pumps.

"Somebody's doing our work for us," said Elion, pushing past us both. He prodded the wreck of one Ironhand with the toe of his boot. "How gracious of them to clear our path."

"*Somebody*," said Tishande, "Has crushed a pair of five-hundred pound monstrosities with what looks like their bare hands. And they might still be in here with us..."

Jenan knelt by one of the corpses, dipping her finger into its shattered chest.

"This was done days ago. Whoever wrought this butchery is long gone."

"And Urzen?"

"I suppose we'll have to find out for ourselves," growled Morekh, leaving the two felled Ironhands behind him.

The further we climbed, the more scenes of bloodshed we found. A hacked-off limb still crawling down an empty corridor on its fingernails. The heads of a dozen Ironhands piled in a crude cairn at an intersection of two crosswalks. Piles of bones and twisted metal in a blackened circle on the floor, beneath the bucket of a monstrous lava-mill. Here and there were the signs of sorcerous warfare – drudges turned to statues of ash beneath a thin skin of glass, whole walls neatly cut through with otherworldly fire, and the after-image blur of bodies hanging in mid air, burning.

"Such power!" breathed Tishande, as we skirted around yet another hulking Ironhand corpse, this one encased in what had once been liquid steel. "If Urzen has burned up this much vitae defending himself, he may even be in torpor. We can take what we need and be gone before he can wake from under his healing wards."

"But who could have done this? And why *now*? Every power north of the Akhazi border has taken sides, and if it isn't with the Empire, then it's with *us*."

"If we knew that, Elion, then we'd be begging them to join us too," said the sorceress. "That is, if they survived. I told you a circle of Hallucinomancers tried to kill Urzen once before... and that was in my youth, when the temple of Erys was almost as strong as Esau is now. He spit us out in tatters."

"Perhaps those beasts of his finally went wrong," said Jenan. "I wouldn't blame them, from what we've seen."

Tishande shook her head.

"There's not enough left of them to rebel. This was something else. And it feels wrong. It feels... *old*. Old magik, perhaps as old as the Archaeon itself."

"Could it have been?" I ventured. I could certainly imagine the great beast's shade swimming through underground seas of magma and into Urzen's keep. *I* had seen the size of its teeth.

"No. If the father of draken could do that, Anganesse would be a smoking ruin. We'd all be drinking chilled rum on some Faeroan beach right now!" Elion smiled at that. "This was something new. We must tread carefully."

After that, we did. If our progress before had been skulking and silent, then our new efforts at stealth would have put a hunting spider to shame. Tishande even risked a breath of Hallucinomantic sorcery, cloaking us in a haze of shifting shadows and dust.

But there was no sign of the cabal who had wrought such carnage in Urzen's stronghold. As we climbed, leaving the forge levels behind, we saw fewer and fewer drudges, and even less of the bizarre living engines which cranked and pulled and heaved in the gloom. The air became cold, and a thin rime of frost crunched underfoot as we traversed galleries carved into the open cliff-face – pillared halls looking out to a dizzying view.

There below us was the war-Keel *Shadow of Blades*, and beyond it the scrub wasteland of the Demonspine's foothills, straggling away to dirty snow. Boiling across the immensity of the eastern plains as a backdrop came the storm - the one which had followed at our heels all the way from south Khytein.

"I'd wager that one doesn't belong to old Corvo," grumbled Elion Morekh as he passed by, absently tugging me away from the edge with one hand. "Hard weather to run against, when we're done in this cursed warren."

"Hark to the jolly old sailor! As if we'll dare the storm in a rowboat with paper sails! I'd wager..."

But Tishande's voice faltered and died as she chanced a look through the next doorway, into an airy space with pillars like spreading trees of stone. She motioned us to keep back, and we obliged, pressing up hard against the wall.

"He's there!" she hissed, in an all-but inaudible voice. "Urzen himself! I don't think he saw me..."

Jenan produced a small round mirror from somewhere on her person, and flicked it out in one hand, almost too fast to follow.

"He's not moving. Does a thing like that ever sleep?"

"He could be in... what was it you called it?"

"*Torpor*. It's a time manipulation, and not an easy one. The healers of Estaron still know the weaving of such a work, but for a creature as old as Urzen it's only a matter of *hours*, not weeks. And you said that whoever killed all those Ironhands has been long gone."

"Just how powerful *is* he, anyway?" I asked. 'If he's anywhere near as cunning as Sothara, then he already knows we're here..."

That was an unsettling thought. The four of us looked at each other in a kind of sickened realization.

Then Jenan was gone.

The Zengaji are said to know no fear – though this is likely another of the good doctor Xeng's academic falsehoods. The assassins of that savage race certainly know fear quite intimately, as they inspire it on a regular basis. And the instant, feral reaction of a born-and-bred Zengaji killer to the first stirrings of such an emotion is to fly into violent and bloody action.

We all piled through the doorway behind Jenan – Elion brandishing his sword, Tishande drawing in power so that the air around us grew suddenly dry and cold. I caught myself wondering just how well necromancy would fare against a thing half-dead for longer than accepted history.

I need not have worried.

The figure hunched at its rough wooden workbench was only child-sized – robed and hooded in grey homespun. Its hands were the only thing which marked it out as more than human - each one had fingers of intricately wrought brass, bifurcating like the branches of a tree, so that rather than ten digits, Urzen the soul-binder had a thicket of metal tendrils, some grasping quills and ink-pots, others tipped with tiny blades.

They didn't even twitch as Jenan's *khirang* sword swept his head clean from his shoulders. She was ready for this to be less than fatal, however – her follow-through was a backhand which chopped both of Urzen's arms off at the elbow. Still, the little man didn't so much as tremble.

The Dark Sight showed me why, as his head bounced and rolled to land at my feet. Urzen's face was a mask of elaborately rune-carved brass, nailed to skin so wrinkled, liver-spotted and cracked that he made Corvo look like a springtime maiden. Two sightless eyes stared out from crusted hollows in the metal, unsprung lenses clicking and flashing from tiny insect-leg armatures at its brows.

"He's dead, Zengaji. He's been a dead a good long time."

Jenan stood there panting, her eyes wild for a second. Then she slammed her *khirang* back into its sheath, and pushed a trailing strand of hair away from her face.

"Just... just making sure," she said. "So. What exactly does this mean for us?"

"It means that there's something loose in the world that can destroy powers of the second tier," said Tshande, "and not have the shockwave felt by every sorcerer and cantrip-weaver in Sarem."

She pulled the robe from around Urzen's shoulders, revealing the truth of his transformation. The ancient thing was human from the waist up – though plates of metal and deep-socketed crystals were bored into his sunken chest. But from the waist down there was nothing to him – just a fat skein of bandage-wrapped pipes and tubes, coiling under the table to a mortared well in the centre of the room. Whoever had killed the soul-binder had propped him up at his desk, resting on the flaccid coils of his artificial body.

"It means that Makara is lost," I said, staring numbly at the remains of one of Sarem's most feared monsters. In death, the poor composite thing looked pathetic; its gruesome augmentations a feeble attempt to cheat mortality. "This was where Sinder said she'd been taken. But there are no prisons here, and now there's no master for me to bargain with."

"*Bargain with*? You were going to..."

"I was going to do *whatever I had to*," I snarled, turning on Tishande. And she was afraid – more afraid, I think, in that moment than she had been at any time since entering Urzen's dominion. "You might not think of me as a human being, but there's some of my soul left yet."

"Kuhal, I..."

"*Save it.* There's nothing for me here...obviously."

Elion Morekh coughed into his hand, glancing up at us with a worried expression on his face.

"Umm – actually, Khytein, there *is* something here for you. A letter, and a box. They're made out in your name."

I looked back at the table, and at the book which had been laid open in front of Urzen's corpse. The vellum was spattered with dried blood, but the meticulous sketches there were very clear. They showed a grotesque cutaway of the Silence, that bloated and vile thing which Makara had killed in the necropolis.

Marking the page was an envelope, and holding it flat against the cold wind which whipped through this workroom aerie was a rosewood box, about a handspan to a side. Inlaid in the polished wood was a sigil in plain steel – the stylized thorns-and-antlers rune of Anghul.

I picked up the envelope between trembling fingers. I hardly dared to breathe. Indeed, there was my name, scribed across the paper in flowing cursive. I turned it over in my hands, and slipped my thumbnail under the crease, peeling it open.

Inside was a letter, on paper so fine and thin that it seemed almost weightless. That, and a single lock of black hair, tied up with a twist of lyrecaster string.

I felt something break, deep inside my mind. Chains and hasps across that ancient door of stone gave way – chains bound with old Khytein spirit-fetishes and devotional ribbons to ward away evil.

Well played, young warlock, read the words on the page.

But played nonetheless - for life and death are all part of a great and wondrous game. Urzen has discovered this; he has fulfilled his destiny, and completed his three finest works.

Firstly, he has perfected me. He has laboured mightily to give me form, and for this I thank him.

Secondly, he has given me the Nine – too fine a plaything for the stuffy old Thearch, you must agree.

And thirdly, he has wrought something truly special for you. A gift from us both, Kuhal Moer, in the name of the strife we will both bring to this fly-blown and rotten world.

Enjoy.

Your friend,

Dirge.

The box on the table shuddered, moving just a little against the vellum page. It lurched again, as if a living heart was trapped inside.

This time there was no creaking of old, old stone. This time the door in my mind didn't just open a crack. The great slabs of rune-scored granite slammed aside, and what was within vomited forth like a flume of freezing water, gushing between ribs and skulls and shattered bones. The whole room grew dark around the edges, and I could feel the temperature plummet. Little sparks of witchfire tapered from the points of Urzen's high-backed chairs, from the unlit sconces on the walls – even from the blade of Elion morekh's hook.

"Leave," I grated, in a voice thick with self-constraint. The old, old suffering of this place was being drawn into me from every stone and crevice, and I ached for an excuse to unleash it. Sothara's memories flickered through me – spells of execration, of blasting, of scourging... I barely held them in check.

"Kuhal! No! *You can fight this!* It's what Sinder would have wanted you to do!"

Tishande's face was a tiny thing, far away down a swirling tunnel of darkness. And Corvo had been right. There were voices in that tide of shadow, muttering and laughing just beyond hearing. I forced my vision open, just enough to see the horror in her eyes - and Elion's one good hand on her arm, pulling her away. Jenan stood between us, her *Khirang* at guard.

"No," I said, forcing the words out between my teeth. "I *can't*. Now RUN, damn you, because if he's done what I think he has, I'm going to bring him back. He'll tell me where to find this Dirge, even if it takes me *centuries* to wring it from him."

Elion's eyes widened.

"Bring him *back*? *Sinder*? I thought you said that you destroyed him?"

Now I could see the strands of Sothara's great Instrumentorum, lit up in just the right places. With this kind of power, and the right pressure on the world *here* and *here* and *here*, I could wrench Sinder's shade from the nether-hell he deserved, and flay him inch by inch. So what if Urzen's keep and all things in it were rendered down to dust in the process?

"Elion," I panted, raising hands which boiled with green and gold fire. "You're still. Not. *Running*."

Gods help me, but I didn't even wait to see if he heeded my warning. I let the power go, and it made of me nothing but the pinch in the hourglass – the fulcrum between two raving infinities of madness.

Urzen's keep had endured for more than four thousand years, and in that time it had seen death and misery on a staggering scale, from the war of the Guild and the Clockmakers to the mad experiments of its latter-day master. I felt my will go down through the endless levels of the place like the roots of a stormwood oak, a hundred springtimes in a second. The power heaved stones asunder, shaking the whole damned edifice to its foundations.

Drudges died, their souls torn from dead flesh. Once-human machines gave out as I burned them away, feeding a growing conflagration inside me.

Oh, I could see his mocking smile. I could see his pale and perfect face, laughing at my naivete.

But now I had it within me to reach out to Jerrold Sinder, wherever he was, and crush that smile to bloody ruin.

I felt my hands weaving the power. I felt my tongue, heavy and thick in my mouth, spitting out the syllables of the great incantation of recall. And I saw what happened next from outside of myself; perhaps to have remained tied body-to-soul would have blown my reason to shreds.

The top three storeys of Urzen's keep bulged out from the mountainside, swelling and stretching with agonizing slowness. Then the colonnades and arches of the fortress exploded in a spray of fire, whole statues and spires cartwheeling down into the snow, or plunging into the lava moat. A lightning-flash of dirty green energy followed, stabbing out through every crack and crevice, sending long beams of power raking into the dusk.

And then came the spell itself. A core of intense white flame, surrounded by a nimbus of blurred, anguished faces – it punched out from the ruin of Urzen's workroom and flew up into the sky, trailing sparks. Then it drew out into a single strand, piercing the wall of stormclouds which bore down on the keep.

Something inside the storm answered it.

I felt a great, heavy head come up and around, like a hound scenting its prey. I caught a glimpse of a thick black cowl, and beneath its shadow, the razor-slash of a smile. Then the presence hidden in that wall of clouds opened its hand, and I felt something deep in Urzen's fastness crack open.

I didn't have time to stop it. A tight knot of power came slithering up through the rootwork of my will, clear through my body, and out along the flickering line scored across the sky by my incantation. The creature in the storm closed its fist, and I felt the force of it, twitching like a fish-hook in my soul.

"Sinder. It wants one called Sinder. Doesn't it know that such a creature is dead and gone?" The laughter which followed was oily and menacing, accompanied by a rumble of thunder.

"Foolish human. It hasn't even opened the box."

I dropped back into myself then, almost collapsing to the floor with the aftershock of the working. I struggled to the side of Urzen's worktable, roughly kicking his corpse aside, and reached out for the box. Above me, the clouds boiled purple and black, poised over the keep like a wave about to break.

My hands were shaking as I wrapped them around the rosewood cube, and the Dark Sight told me the truth. The Mageblight was advancing inexorably down from my fingers to my palms, turning them white and numb with spiderweb traceries. When I brushed my thumbs over the rune of Anghul those webworks of blight tingled, and hidden mechanisms inside the box clicked open.

Within was a tiny version of the Incantus Instrumentorum – a sphere of iron woven around a sphere of gold, with glistening flesh at its core. The miniature incantus levitated, never touching the red velvet lining of the box. And, like a fool, I reached out and grasped it.

Two things happened as I brushed the spinning ball with my fingers. The stormclouds bearing down on the keep convulsed, sending a blast of stinging rain and wind skirling before them. It blew across the ruins of Urzen's workroom, moaning in the great smoking hollow carved out of the keep. A voice carried on the wind whispered-

"We have you now!"

At the same time I heard a grinding noise behind me, and a shadow fell across the table. I turned, the incantus connected to my fingertips by glowing threads of witchfire, and saw an iron pillar screw its way up from out of the floor. It was steaming cold, inset with eye-watering glyphs in brass and jade.

But it was the soul inside the incantus which ripped a scream from my throat. It poured into me like water, finding little memories and binding tight to them with a thousand thorny roots.

It was Makara.

"When the blight takes you, you become just like the Gods you've slaved and sacrificed for. You become a mere reflection of the Shard and Facet which gave you all that wonderful, beautiful power. And that means you have to live like them - live on belief, or fear, if that's enough for you. The Gods can't walk the earth, see, but they can shape us into their tools. And if you think I'm just an old fool, know this. I've seen sorcerers mightier than I'll ever be fall literally to pieces because of the scorn of children. I've watched Gods become nothing but tiny little voices, whispering to madmen as they fall into the Outer Dark..."

From 'My discourses with Corvo of Ontokh', compiled by the traveling bard-scholar Arus Li'and of the Greater Saradrim Academiat.

IN A SINGLE convulsive instant I *knew* her.

Every happiness, every pain, every hope, every tragedy... visions of ritual fires, fingerbones swinging on chains, of Gernish Maudrin in his guise as archpriest of Theyr, young and strong and naked but for his black bearskin cloak and ocher warpaint. Sunlight and shadows. The smell of pine needles and smoke. A vague, warm blur of dreams.

I saw a life in that fractured heartbeat, and I reached out for my place in it, hungry for an answer. But now...

Now all she could think were *my* thoughts. All she could feel was what I *wanted* her to feel. Makara was dead, and all that remained of her was twisted by my own desire. I plunged into the incantus, frantic, searching for the night we had spent together on a barge full of refugees and sorrow, the solace of warmth and passion cast against the darkness. But my very presence warped her memories. They became what I wanted to see, what I wanted to know, even as they withered up and blew away beneath the flame of my will.

She was mine at last. But she was just an echo of her living self.

That - and the body which lay within a pillar of iron before me; a sarcophagus for one of the Nine Now Nameless.

I damned myself. I opened the doors.

I couldn't leave her in there. Not when I knew that she was still alive, at least in some way. I tore open the iron hasps and locks with a sickening lurch of power, then sank to my knees in the rain, numb with horror.

Urzen had *completed* her. Urzen had remade the last warbard of Theyr as one of his Nine, and she was beautiful and terrible to behold.

He had spared her face – and for that I almost wanted to kiss the twisted wreck of a thing which had been the soul-binder. Her eyes were closed, and a sly little smile played on her lips as she slept, cradled amid copper and steel. Urzen had made for her a beautiful suit of armour, all sharp angles and wicked spikes, as ornate and gothic as the most lordly Ghuram plate, but inset all over with a golden pattern of thorns. A finely worked chestpiece followed every curve of her body, giving way to scaled steel corsetry, a belt of linked golden rings, and long, segmented boots trailing ribbons of black and green.

It was her arms and her hands which the soul-binder had mutilated. Urzen's ideal of beauty was wedded to the dealing of death, and he had made Makara into a killer to rival even That Which Walks or the Burning Dark.

From between her long, pale fingers, all the way up her naked forearms to the elbow, Urzen had split Makara's flesh and bone apart. Now there were three long grooves running across the back of her hands, and separating radius from ulna. A third tube of bone had been grafted in, along with clockwork gears, shards of crystal and spiderwebs of wire, tight between tiny pulleys and cranks. Three metal drums, each about a handspan in width, depended from the armour of her back, and thick braided wires disappeared into each one. The wires ran through her bones, ending in a trio of arrowhead barbs clenched between her fingers.

Urzen had completed his work by inscribing a shoal of red tattoos across both hands and arms – a tight-packed swirl of script which made it look as though Makara had plunged elbow-deep into a cauldron of blood.

Inside that beautiful shell, within the ornate armour and under the pale white skin, she was no longer human. What appeared to be sleep was a dreamless nothingness – the patience of a sword in its scabbard, waiting for war.

I believe this was the last time I ever wept. Now, so long after, it seems like a kind of waking nightmare, so I have no idea how long I knelt there in the rain, waiting for my despair to turn to anger.

At last I stood, slowly, cradling Makara in my arms. A hissing spray came in through the ruin of Urzen's workroom, drenching us both and erasing the tears from my cheeks. Out there, I could see tiny figures swarming over the *Shadow of Blades*, pulling down acres of canvas and lashing down a spiderweb of ropes and stays. But there was something else - something out beyond them, moving across the pale white immensity of the plain.

There were four of them, and they weren't trudging through the waist-deep snow. They flew in under the wings of the storm, as swift and weightless as Corvo himself, and tearing the clouds to tatters in their wake. In the Dark Sight I could see their power curdling reality around them, and I knew them for what they were – the things which had destroyed Urzen, returned.

I suddenly regretted sending Tishande, Elion and Jenan away. I gently laid Makara's cold body out on Urzen's table, watching her eyelids flicker and her fingers clench into fists. Hidden machinery inside her hands clicked and ratcheted, and I was gripped by a pang of utter, desperate anger - one which sent crazed images of bones and black skies wheeling across my vision. Her incantus fit perfectly into a concave socket in the armour's chest, locking tight with a snick of hidden teeth.

I unfolded myself from over Makara and let the lightning silhouette me in the arch of the windows. *Let them see me.* Let them feel the power which was building behind my eyes, concentrating cold and heavy in my hands...

They felt it. They stopped, hanging in the air before Urzen's keep - a quartet of shadows, cloaked and hooded in the pouring rain. A blue flash of lightning illuminated the ragged hems of their garments, but nothing could penetrate the gloom beneath their cowls. Darkness writhed within them like smoke.

"What are you?" I whispered. "And who in all the hells sent you?"

The next flash of lighting cast a shadow across the walls, and Tishande answered me.

"It's a trap, Khytein. Can't you feel the pain in them? They hate this place, and yet they are called to it. They were *born* here."

It was true. In the Dark Sight the four hooded wraiths were wounds in reality - festering gashes of red and black power distorting everything around them. My macabre gift stripped away their disguise, laying bare their true forms.

The first was tiny - nothing more than a child, really, with pale, pearlescent skin. She was clad in a ragged white dress hemmed with lace and silver. Her hair was bone-white, too - an albinotic tangle which all but covered her face. But her eyes were bleeding pits, cored out to the size of a grown man's fists. Black gems spun within those dripping hollows, flashing with cold, cold despite.

The second was armoured from head to toe in scarred and battered plate, rimed with verdigris and rust. No two pieces of armour matched... some were from the high age of old Ythe, others from the burned lands of the Akhazi, and yet others scavenged and gleaned from a hundred battlefields. The creature carried no blade, however - its hands were massive, rusted fists, clenched inside gauntlets wrapped in lengths of smoking chain.

The third was tall and twisted, its spine bent over into a curve which left its head hunched down below its shoulders. Its body was wrapped tightly in strips of leather, the ends flapping and jingling with little brass bells. A long, rune-embroidered scarf covered the lower part of its face, but the ruin above marked the thing out for what it was. The creature's head was sawn through just below the bridge of its nose, and only a skullcap of bone remained. The effect was as if a strip had simply been erased from its face, neatly cauterizing its eyes. Blue and green flames boiled out from the resulting gap.

The last... The last appeared exactly as it did to my mortal sight. A cape and a cowl, soaked through with icy rain; but this was the thing which spoke.

"Hello, Kuhal Moer of the Khytein. We *do* hope you like our little gift." It raised one armoured hand to its lips, stifling a mad giggle.

The cloaked figure gestured with its other hand, and I heard Tishande gasp behind me. We both felt the spike of power which it sent down into the river of molten rock below us, raising a spire from the red-hot lava.

"But even if you don't," it continued, "courtesy dictates that you should know our titles. After all – they may be the last you ever hear."

The spine of basalt cracked and cooled as it rose, and when it had reached the height of Urzen's sanctum the figure stepped down onto it, boot-soles smoking. It flourished one claw-tipped gauntlet as it bowed.

"This is the Shining One. This is the Devouring Wind. And this delightful fellow here is called the Eyeless." The thing chuckled. "As for myself – my name is Dirge, and I am here to offer you *immortality*. Or at least the next best thing."

The creature cocked its head to one side, and I caught a glimpse of an utterly mirthless smile; a rictus of bloodless lips and sharpened teeth.

"You and your dead Khytein witch will make such a pretty couple!"

This time I didn't wait. There was nothing I wanted to say to such a vile creature, after all. The power which arced from my fingertips was my last, and if it didn't blow Dirge to ashes then I was certain I would be dead seconds later.

He *caught* it.

Damn the truth, but he caught my bolt of black fire in his hand, crushing it down to nothingness. The spell which should have ripped his soul to ribbons spilled from between Dirge's fingers as a spray of black sand, and he laughed.

"If you're quite finished, little one? I have so much to do, and no time to waste catching cantrips from the air."

I stepped around the table, putting myself between Makara and the quartet of Nameless. But Dirge wasn't here to witness pointless heroics. He snarled, a animal growl deep in his shadowy hood, and he gestured to his minions.

"Take him alive. Kill the rest. I've already gotten what I came here for."

The Nameless obeyed.

The thing known as the Shining One cast off its disguise first, and came flying at me, its tiny pale hands crooked into talons. But Tishande was up to the tabletop before I could even draw Sinder's sword from my belt – and she was blazing with power, a halo of crystal shards encircling her in a flickering storm.

"This one is *mine*, Khytein," she said, blurring even as she spoke. For an instant the Ythean sorceress appeared to have too many arms, too many eyes and faces... and then she was airborne, leaping up to collide with the tiny Nameless in a spray of sparks. Her hands flew out wide as she caught the Shining One a terrible blow – and lucky that she had, for the deathless thing let out a scream as Tishande's boot connected with the side of its head; a scream which toppled an entire tower from the crown of Urzen's fortress.

Tishande was merciless, though. Her hands came together in a blur which seemed to flow around and through itself, and a handful of crystal points burst into flame, tearing at the Nameless like crossbow quarrels. They left searing blue trails behind them as they pierced the thing's lacy white dress in ten places, but there was no blood. The Shining One righted itself from a flat spin and screamed again, cracking a vast swathe of flagstones as it tracked the Ythean's fall. The rain was blown to mist as it attacked again.

"Don't just stand there!" shouted Tishande, drawing her rapier. "RUN, you little fool! There's no place here for your lack of discipline!"

She was right. I was drained from the great working I had attempted- the one which Dirge had apparently swallowed up whole. Sinder still writhed in some nether pit, but that was small consolation as I turned to gather up Makara... and found the Eyeless behind me.

The creature appeared from nowhere, stepping out of its own shadow amid lazy coils of darkness. Its hands moved almost too fast to follow, and a long black whip whispered past my cheek. Its edge was serrated and sharp, and as I dove and slid on the slick flagstones it squirmed like a live thing, biting closed in a loop where my neck had been.

I dodged a second coil of darkness, trying to put the table between myself and the horror, but when I chanced a look over my shoulder it was gone. Tishande had her hands around the Shining One's throat and was squeezing with all her strength.

When I looked back I saw the Eyeless slide out of the shadows, taking on a third dimension again as easy as slipping on a cloak. It brought back its hand, liquid darkness licking out from where its wrist met its palm, and it laughed, dry and sickly.

Then Elion Morekh's hook was around its forearm, and the Nameless froze, hissing. Its terrible sundered face turned, vertebrae clicking and popping, until the blazing cavity in its skull was pointing right at the Faeroan pirate.

"Look down, before you think of doing anything clever," grinned Elion. "I'm willing to bet that you used to have balls... and even if Urzen took them, there's still plenty down there to be worried about."

The notched blade of his cutlass twitched a little, right between the nightmare creature's legs.

I heard a scream behind me, tapering off into an anguished gurgle. Tishande had spitted the Shining One on her rapier, following through to pin the demon child to the wall, like a butterfly to a collector's board.

"Jenan! Take the damned Khytein to safety! If he doesn't get to Urexes then all this will be for nothing!"

The tiny Nameless looked Tishande directly in the eye, its black-jeweled gaze drawing in the light until reality itself began to waver. This time its scream clawed its way right up the scale into agony, dropping me to my knees. Elion had the presence of mind to draw his hook across the throat of his captive, but the Eyeless had already folded in on itself, sliding back into the shadows in a cloud of coiling smoke.

Tishande's rapier shattered. The crystals surrounding her dropped from the air, smashing against the wet stone with a sad little chiming patter. And the force of the Shining One's scream flung the Ythean sorceress backwards, spinning end over end to strike the far wall of the gallery with a crack of broken bones.

The hideous little thing turned its head toward us, and its lips peeled back in the semblance of a smile. Too wide. Too many teeth. *Rows* of them, like the gullet of a hungry shark...

"I'd like you to know that I've never run from battle," said Elion Morekh, his eyes twitching left and right. We could both *feel* the Eyeless closing in, slipping from shadow to shadow between the flickers of lightning. "But sometimes there can be such a thing as an honourably strategic retreat..."

Jenan was there before we even saw the Nameless One levering itself back into the world, hands outstretched to throttle us. Her *khirang* sword was a silver blur, and the next flash of lightning burned the image of her into my eyes, locked in a clinch with the leather-wrapped ghoul. Three feet of consecrated steel protruded between its shoulderblades.

It laughed again, waving a single finger in mock admonition. Then it made to pierce the Skyborn with one of its serrated whip-blades, a hand twisting up under her guard.

Elion's hook took that hand off at the wrist. The Eyeless shrieked, jerking its body back and off Jenan's sword, clutching at its stump.

"Now we're even, hey?"said Morekh, spinning his cutlass in figure-of-eights. "Come and dance with a real man, you slippery little bastard. I'll take care of the ladies myself."

"What about your *strategic retreat*?" asked Jenan, circling warily, back to back with the Faeroan. Her sword dripped with black slime where she had pulled it clean of the Eyeless, but her attention was on the Shining One, which came gliding toward us through the rain, its dark eyes reflecting fire.

"Sometimes the only place to retreat to is *behind* the enemy." He shrugged. "And once you've gotten them out of the way, they don't tend to follow."

"In that case…" said Jenan, reaching into her cross-body bandolier. "You won't mind if I leave this to you?"

She didn't give him time to answer. Before either of us could move she took a running leap off the side of the parapet, spinning in midair as she disappeared from view.

We hadn't followed her hand, though. And neither had the Shining One. Because a heartbeat later it shrieked, staggering in the air. Three knife hilts had sprouted in a tight circle on its chest, and this time there was blood – black, viscous stuff, but blood nonetheless. Zengaji steel is anathema to sorcery, and the Nameless clawed at the three blades, frantic, tearing its own fingers to tatters.

"What in all hells is she *doing*? They may be tough, but this is no time to think of suicide…"

All this time Elion's cutlass had been warily following the Eyeless, and all this time the thing had been putting itself back together. Strips of leather wove and writhed like snakes as it bound up the wound in its chest, and as for its hand…

"Urgh! Why do demons like this always have to resort to *insects!* Isn't the whole claws-and-teeth thing bad enough?"

Indeed, the husk of the Eyeless seemed to be empty, filled to the brim with a solid mass of many-legged worms. The segmented things crawled from the stump of its hand, knotting together, and as they took on the form of fingers and a palm they began to weave pale white thread from their mandibles, creating a semblance of skin. Within seconds the Nameless One was cracking its knuckles and smiling, the scarf fallen away from an emaciated face whose lips were sewn shut.

The Shining One was just the opposite – its mouth hinged open with a series of sharp little clicks, far too wide and *far* too full of teeth. A shimmering glow of sorcery burned deep in its throat.

"I can't say it's been entirely a pleasure, Khytein," drawled Elion, a grim little smile on his lips. "But then again, there are probably people who'd like this kind of thing."

I felt the power building in both of the Nameless – immense wells of energy focused through their mutilated flesh, wild enough to tear Urzen's keep stone from stone. I realized, in that instant, that the things had been playing with us.

"The bards call it *adventure*, Captain. Funny how they always leave out the part where you're about to shit yourself and die."

The Shining One drew in a breath to scream. The face of the Eyeless split open, its whole skull coming apart in a jigsaw confusion to reveal a globe of searing fire.

And Dirge stopped them both with a gesture of one hand.

"*Alive*, you fools! *Alive!* I despair, sometimes, that you creatures are as stupid as you are cruel!"

The pair of demons snarled and hissed, but they came no further. In the Dark Sight I could see the chains which bound them to their master, stretched taut as bowstrings and groaning under the strain. If they had been mere steel they would have surely shattered.

"I think there's a way I can convince our recalcitrant little warlock to change his mind. Do you see the Keel, child? Your precious friends, your allies, all so safe and snug behind walls of stone?"

I stepped forward, a curse ready for the cowled shape atop its spire of rock. But I couldn't help but look. Down below us hung the *Shadow of Blades*, its decks swarming with tiny figures. The draken were out of their pens, and Skyborn tugged at their halters and chains, trying to soothe them in the face of the unnatural storm. Then I saw the third of Dirge's servants, standing on the air just above the great stoneship. The one all in armour – the Devouring Wind.

"Yessss," hissed Dirge, and there was something unwholesome in his voice which I recognized. "You know what it does, don't you? And you know enough of me to be certain I'm not mistaken when I say *it will slaughter them all.* Join us, or the Wind will be unleashed."

I *had* heard enough, both in half-forgotten witch-stories and during our doomed flight north. I knew what lived inside that rusted suit of plate, and I'd seen what remained of the towns and encampments it had visited. Whole glades dripping red, houses and hovels smouldering amid a mile-wide stain of crimson...

"*Stop!* I'll do it! Just... just let them go. Elion, Tishande... my people. Let them go, and I'll do whatever you want."

Elion grabbed a fistful of my cloak, spinning me around.

"Are you *mad*, boy? He'll find us all soon enough. Us, and every other living thing in Sarem!"

I tried to keep my mind blank, imagining a smooth stone wall. I could feel Dirge prying at it with his will, skrying out any deceit with spells the Bone Collector himself knew rune by rune.

"I have to, Morekh," I grated, pushing him away. "Now – get the hells out of here while you still can. If I can't save Makara, I can still save you."

He stared at me, open mouthed, and then spat.

"Then you're a thrice-damned fool, Kuhal Moer. Next time we meet you'll be one of them."

I let my defenses slip – just enough to feel the first razor tendrils of Dirge's power come sliding in to the meat of my brain. Just enough to distract him, because neither he nor Elion Morekh had seen what I had seen. A tiny spark, curving against the boiling ceiling of clouds. The flicker of a draken's wings as it folded them against its flanks, ready to dive on its prey.

I grabbed a double handful of the Faeroan's coat, and flung him to the ground an instant before the whole broken gallery was drowned in flames.

Jenan's draken struck Dirge with the force of a falling star, impacting talons-first behind a wall of raving white fire. It cast him from his perch and hammered him into the side of the mountain, clear through a great black statue of one of Urzen's forgotten Gods. Tearing and ripping sounds followed as the beast raked him with claws and fangs – an attack so ferocious and brutal that it shook the whole keep, dislodging gargoyles and pillars from above.

Jenan's mount drove Dirge a full ten spans into the enduring rock, powering him down and down in a storm of splinters and smoke until they reached the boiling lava of the moat. Just before they went under the great beast gave a final lunge, thrusting Dirge into a molten hell.

The Eyeless and the Shining One caught the edge of the blast, and they shrieked in agony, reduced to stark black shadows against the white. The image was burned onto my eyes even though they were tightly shut, and I felt my armour heating up, pungent with the smell of burning wool and leather.

Thunder rolled, breaking the silence which followed. Elion Morekh coughed and staggered to his feet, his hat charred away to nothing but a brocaded brim.

"Well, it seems your little friend there wasn't so tough after all. Perhaps we can even salvage something from this piss-soaked ruin of a day."

The clatter and slither of shifting debris made us both jump, but it was only Tishande, hauling herself from under a shattered urn. The Sorceress had taken a beating at the hands of the Shining One, and her left arm hung limp and bloody. But she was smiling through the pain.

"Either we won, or I've died and gone to the worst of the nether hells. Otherwise why would you two be standing there with your fool mouths open like that?"

She was carrying Makara, armour and all, as though the poor dead girl was no heavier than a child.

"I think we must have..." began Elion... but his declaration of victory was short lived.

To this day the events of the next few heartbeats are still a blur, but they are all the more terrible for it. First came a sound like a gurgling scream, utterly inhuman. Then Jenan and her draken came level with Urzen's workroom, thrown skyward by an immense blast of power. I caught a glimpse of burning black robes and flying hair as the creature howled and snapped at a thing wrapped around its neck, its hands ripping through scales and tearing loose chunks of flesh and muscle.

It was Dirge, and he hung in the air with the writhing beast's throat clenched in his fists, Jenan clinging to its back. Then he held it aloft in one hand, clenched his fingers tight, and snapped its spine. The draken's bones were as thick as the pillars in Urzen's halls, but they broke like matchwood. Dirge gestured with his other hand, and a jagged spire of obsidian sheared off from the castle walls above us. He brought it up over his head and hammered it down, clear through the Zengaji and her mount. They fell, tumbling and bouncing from wall to wall until the lava swallowed them up.

At the same time a shadow gaped open beneath Elion Morekh, and a snarl of serrated whips burst from inside it, biting deep into his skin. The Eyeless rose up from out of the darkness right behind the Faeroan pirate, and behind it came the Shining One, still trying to draw the daggers from its chest. Elion had enough time to reach out one hand to me before it was entangled in sharp, chitinous tendrils... and then the Eyeless pulled them tight.

For a second the Reaver Admiral stood there, unbelieving, as lines of crimson sketched their way across his neck, his torso, his belly... then he simply fell to pieces.

Tishande screamed, dropping Makara to the floor. I drank in the pain of Elion's death, coiling it into a spike of power between my fingers.

But before either of us could move, Dirge was there. His metal-clad fingers were hot around my throat, still smoking from his immersion in molten rock. Now his cloak was burned away, and I could see him for what he was.

"Ahh, so my secret's out," purred Jerrold Sinder, once-human Pontifex of Anganesse, Warmaster of the Khytein Annexation and ruler of the Nine. "How sad that everyone who knows the truth about to become either very, very dead... or thoroughly enslaved."

Facets of the Shard of Death - From the Old Ythean Deck of Divinations, otherwise called the Dark Tarot

Living shards -
Ogrun, Rasuul'i avatar of death and dreams
The Harvestman, Ontohki avatar of death and time
Anghul, Khytein avatar of death and punishment
Shadowmask, Ythean avatar of death and deception
Mas'ri, Ghuram avatar of death and rebirth
The Lady of Storms, Faeroan goddess of the drowned

Dead shards -
Knifesplinter, ancient Zengaji assassin-God (dethroned)
Zael - Angan avatar of death in battle (dethroned)
Khoso - pre-Empire Akhazi tribal death-deity (devoured)
Arkhan - Estarene avatar of rebirth (devoured)

WHAT I FELT at that moment had nothing to do with healthy, honest hatred. You may have heard of the expression 'it made my skin crawl'? Well, the hot touch of Sinder's gauntlets made my skin want to burst into flames.

Little good it would have done, seeing as he'd just come back from a dip in a moat of lava, but still – I knew he was in my mind, so I concentrated my loathing into a weapon, driving it deep into his thoughts.

"*Excellent*," he said, as he dragged me bodily to the edge of the drop. "At least you've finally learned to hate me with some Gods-damned balls and backbone, child! I had begun to think that your northern stoicism was born of sheer stupidity."

Urzen had changed him. More than he had done to Makara, and more, even, than he had done to himself. This must have been the pale Angan lord's last contingency plan; rebirth through the lost arcana of Korisal.

"See what your defiance has wrought, Kuhal? From the very beginning, you couldn't just lay your head on the block for me like a good little peasant. You had to squirm and struggle so! Anyone who's seen an execution can tell you that the axe is prone to make a mess when the condemned still dares to hope."

The millstones had taken him diagonally across the chest, biting off everything from his left arm, down in a razor-straight line to his right hip. Now black, crystalline roots burrowed through his alabaster flesh, spreading across his chest and fusing to a densely coiled mass of the same stuff which made up the rest of his body. It was thorny and dark, neither stone nor metal, and it glistened unwholesomely in the firelight. Beneath the web, Urzen had rebuilt his final supplicant with cinnamon-scented mummified flesh, stitched up with copper wires and bolted with plates of rune-forged armour. The roots and thorns which bound it all up seemed to writhe and flex as Sinder moved, dangling my feet over the parapet.

"Yes, I can hear you in there. And no, it's not *Sinder* any more – that one really *is* as dead as your precious little warbard bitch." He laughed. "I should thank you, I suppose. It was you who sent me to meet my new masters, and you who gave me the power to transcend my petty ambitions. To think, I would have settled for the throne of Anganesse! Now I fully intend to devour the hearts of Gods."

It was obvious that he was quite mad. I struggled to look past Sinder's hulking new form, back to where the Shining One and the Eyeless were closing in on Tishande. From their previous display of ferocity, it appeared that they were no longer interested in playing with their food.

"It's *Dirge*, imbecile!" said the thing which had taken that name. It punctuated its snarl with a ringing slap, sending purple starbursts cartwheeling across my vision. "Or at least, that's one translation which mortal tongues can pronounce. Those in the Outer Dark named me 'Song for the Ending of All Things Under Light', which is far more poetic – but a bit of a mouthful, don't you think?"

He loosened his fingers a fraction. I felt myself slip, and I grabbed at his gauntlet with both hands.

"Dirge, then..." I croaked. "But you still have Sinder's memories, don't you?"

"All them and more. I know things now which even the Coldbood and the Archaeon dare not contemplate..."

I cut him off.

"Then you'll remember that I told you to *go fuck your mother?*"

Dirge's face was still beautiful, in a cold and androgynous way. It twisted up for an instant, and I thought he would drop me to my death, but then he laughed.

"Almost clever, boy. I suppose you think that if I grow angry enough, I'll make another mistake?" He shook his head. "Not this time. You can rue your own mistakes for a while, and suffer for them."

From behind Dirge came a series of bright blue flashes, shaking dust and grit loose from the keep's vaulted ceiling. Tishande was holding back the Nameless as best she could. But my eyes were on the *Shadow of Blades*, and the tiny figure in armour which stood directly in front of its bows.

Orduvis hadn't waited for his dead captain's order. There were only a few guns at the fore of the *Shadow*, but they were big ones – seige-breakers and bombards which flung shells the size of cauldrons. Now they spoke, in a thunderous drum-roll like the beginning of the Wild Song. Clouds of bonepowder smoke billowed, and for an instant I thought that Angan nekrology had beaten the Nameless – nothing could survive a direct hit from those murderous cannon.

Then the smoke blew out in a whirling gyre, and I saw the truth. The Devouring Wind had stopped the shrapnel and shot in midair, not three spans from its body. The iron was glowing red hot, and as I watched it *melted*, falling like rain down into the lava below. A grinding sound, like saws on steel, may have been the creature's laugh.

"And now to work," giggled Dirge, shaking me like a ragdoll. "What a lovely day for genocide! Then again, *which day isn't?*"

The Nameless One's armour began to come apart as the crew of the war Keel frantically reloaded their guns. A few draken took to the air, kicking aside the sailors and refugees who clung to them, wailing.

But it was too late.

Inside, the Devouring Wind was nothing but hot shards of metal – broken pieces of weapons glowing white-hot like a cloud of stars. They slipped out from the gaps between helm and pauldrons, chestpiece and belly-plate, coiling like snakes through the air. Then they began to quicken.

There was far, far too much metal inside that hollow suit of armor for this to have been anything but sorcery. Soon the Devouring Wind was a tiny metal mannikin at the heart of a tornado of steel; all sizzling hot, and still accelerating.

"Now. Now we'll see." crooned Dirge – and he pointed with his free hand. "Make them die, Benharu d'al-Suul. By your lost name I command you!"

The deathless creature didn't hesitate.

A storm of shards flew at the *Shadow of Blades*, grinding into the stone and shredding the vessel's bowspirit, snapping ropes and cutting canvas to ribbons. But before it could sweep down the decks, turning them into a charnel-floor of bloody meat, the storm came up hard against an unseen shield.

It was Corvo, and he was bedecked in the full raiment of his priesthood – his cloak flung back to reveal lightning-bolt tattoos and copper charms pierced through his flesh. The tiny silver tubes on his arms had been filled with the quills of innumerable black and white feathers, giving him the appearance of wings, and there was a staff in his hands, blazing with crackling electrical discharge.

He held the shield with one hand, and pointed the staff with the other... right at Dirge. Despite being old, and small, and far away, his voice echoed in the hollow ruin of Urzen's workroom, booming like thunder.

"I watched you try to control the storm, dead man. Clumsy. A child could have done better. But your theatrics are about ninety-nine percent of your power, aren't they? Silly little southern fop. You were doing it WRONG!"

With this last word Corvo unleashed a flickering coruscation of power, sending it spearing up into the belly of the clouds. They answered him an instant later.

The bolt of lightning lifted Dirge from his feet before it flung him backwards – to this day I have no idea how the old Ontohki managed to leave me unscathed. As it was, I watched in slow motion as Dirge's fine silver hair stood on end, each strand sizzling with energy. Then the hammer-blow struck him from above, blowing us both in opposite directions.

This meant that Dirge was driven back through a row of pillars, collapsing a vast ruin of stone and statuary down onto his head. But I was propelled out over the drop, arms and legs windmilling as I screamed. I could feel the heat of the lava moat against my cheek, smell the stench of brimstone rolling up in a gaseous exhalation...

And then I landed across the broad back of a draken, knocking the wind from my lungs. The Skyborn standing in the beast's stirrups glanced back over her shoulder to see that I still had wits enough to hold on, and then she wheeled her mount in a tight circle, stooping on Urzen's keep with an arrow nocked to her bowstring.

I felt heartily and thoroughly sick. Beneath me the *Shadow of Blades* spun by, and I caught a glimpse of Corvo, driven to his knees as the Nameless pressed its attack. Steel ground on stone with a sound like teeth as the Skyborn let her arrow fly.

It went clear through the Eyeless, lighting that evil thing up with drakenfire – but the black-clad demon paid no attention. Its head was cracked open, and a lance of searing flame licked out at Tishande's shield once, twice... deflected away as a rain of sparks. The Ythean sorceress was crouching over Makara's body, protecting them both. But each blow diminished her shield, and it was melting like ice in springtime.

I gulped down a lungful of achingly cold air as we reached the very apex of our flight. For an instant we hung there over Korisal, and I tried desperately to draw in power... but there was close to nothing. Fleeting shreds and scraps of energy, flaring wild from the edges of the Nameless Ones' assault – hardly enough to even scratch their skin.

But enough, perhaps, for me to do something utterly, recklessly heroic. What can I say? The bards have a lot to answer for.

Just before the draken folded its wings and began to fall, I grabbed a pair of arrows from its rider's quiver, and rolled over the side. The air was freezing cold as it rushed by me, and the sorcerous vitae at my disposal was nowhere near enough to craft an incantation of flight – this was a barely controlled fall, aimed at the craterous hole in the wall of Urzen's keep. Through streaming eyes I could see the regular flashes of power which chipped away at Tishande's wardings, and I used them to guide me in, praying to Clermakh to help me in this most foolish of saga-drunk last chances. After all, it was definitely in the wolf-God's idiom...

The Eyeless turned as if it had felt my intention. But there was no stopping me – not from that height, and not at that speed. I barked the runes of an old assassin's cantrip just before I hit home, and the energy of my fall flared out in a shallow dish below me, heating the air to red-hot with a sudden thunderclap. All of it struck the Eyeless, and I felt its immensely strong bones shatter as my boots connected with its chest.

Even with the spell to slow me the impact shook me from my heels to my teeth. I tasted blood as I brought my hands down, left and right, driving two Zengaji arrowheads deep into the Nameless One's broken head.

The fire couldn't harm it – not a thing which was filled to brimming with sorcerous power. But it could crack that fractured jigsaw of a skull open, and when it did...

I thrust my hand inside. There was pain there – terrible, cold, searing pain, but I gritted my teeth and pushed deeper, up to the elbow in the shallow pan of the thing's lower jaw. It should have been impossible. Indeed, by the laws of any sane creator it *was* impossible. But there, at the heart of the fire, I found the knot of withered muscle I was groping for. And with a scream I tore the heart from the Eyeless, ripping it from its mountings in a spray of pale blue fire.

Sothara knew. Sothara the Bone Collector had been here, when he was as young and reckless as I. He'd seen the books in Urzen's great librarium – the preliminary sketches for a thing just like the Eyeless. I bit down on the heart, ripping off a piece of dry, spiced flesh between my teeth. I swallowed, almost gagging on the sickly sweetness of it, the way it seemed to writhe and slither in my throat.

And the Eyeless disintegrated. Many-legged worms burst from its shriveling skin, scuttling in circles until they, too, curled up and died, dissolving into puddles of ichorous slime. I threw aside the husk of its heart, and it crumbled to ashes before it left my fingers.

Then I turned my stare on the Shining One.

"And then there were eight," I slurred, wiping a trickle of blood from the corner of my mouth. I felt drunk with power, filled with the terrible flame of the Eyeless, and in my thoughts I was already imagining the door of stone, the chains which had held it shut now writhing like tentacles from their deep-sunk mounts, alive with witchfire. The bone-field before it was burning.

The Shining one had just managed to work the last of Jenan's daggers from its chest, and it looked pathetically weak – a little dead girl with cored-out eyes, hissing and scrabbling away across the flagstones. Black, bilious blood bubbled from a neat circle of three wounds... the Skyborn Zengaji's last living act on this earth.

"I'm afraid that if I tear you open like your brother there, I'll not have room for a second course," I said, completely failing to stop my words from turning into a deranged little laugh. I could see Tishande staring at me in horror, lying across Makara's lifeless form. Whatever the Eyeless had thrown at her had used up all her power, and her opal eyes were dim with pain.

"Kuhal... you..."

"Not this time," I said, pointing at the Shining One with a single outstretched finger. "I know you value mercy, but this thing... this thing deserves every ounce of suffering I can conjure."

"No! Khytein, don't..."

I spun the incantus in my head. Traceries of witchfire lined up, forming a great arcane sigil before my eyes. And I unleashed the power, a bolt of raving energy wrung from the heart of the Eyeless.

It never even reached my fingertip. Just as I spat the last runes of the incantation something exploded from the rubble behind me, sending a billowing cloud of dust rolling out into the night. Thick black chains lashed out through the swirling grey, and they bound up my arm tight, jerking me from my feet. All the vitae I'd crafted and woven was leeched away by the utter cold of them – not quite metal, not quite stone, but all glistening with a slick organic *wrongness* as they dragged me into the cloud.

To the feet of Dirge.

"I have tried *so hard* to be patient with you, Kuhal da'Hurik Moer," he said, horrifyingly calm. "Even now, when your life is worth nothing to me, I'm gracious enough to offer you a place in the new world to come. But you and your so-called *friends* keep on trying to *inconvenience* me! What am I to make of *such. Ungrateful. Stupidity?*"

The chains collapsed into oily liquid as he laid his boot across the side of my head. Whether it was leather, armour or nekrologikal flesh was hard to discern anymore – the viscous black stuff which had formed the chains melted back into Dirge's heel with an obscene sucking sound, growing into a tendril of thorns around his ankle.

"The Akhazi are coming, boy. The Coldblood is with them. But in me, the dwellers in the Outer Dark have found a champion more subtle than that antediluvian fleshpile. When I tear open the veil and let them have this world, they will give all the useless parts to me."

"Useless? I thought... I thought you were a monster of *ambition,*

Sinder?"

"Dirge," grated his voice inside my head. "And only useless as far as *they* are concerned. They are dead and living, mountains and insects, flesh and fire all at once, Kuhal. They have no need for land and sky and human lives... not when they can feast on the Divine."

"You're as shite-brained as you are ugly, then," I gasped, feeling him bear down with all his unnatural weight. "The Akhazi have *legions*. Your little force of abominations is down to eight."

"But *you* will give me an army, boy. An army even the Coldblood will choke on. Why do you think your dear warbards cared for you so? Did you think it was your *charming character?*"

I couldn't answer. My head may as well have been clamped in a vise, for all that I could move. Behind me I heard Tishande scream.

Dirge shifted his weight, and I could just make out why – the Shining One had reached through the Ythean's wardings, and now held her off the ground in a choke-hold of glittering blue light. Even from behind I could see the little monster's head stretching and splitting open, revealing that unholy maw full of sharklike teeth...

Then Corvo's voice was in my mind, all ice and rage.

"Use this, boy. Watch, and honour what we all do for you now. When this creature is dust, go to Urexes. Make his masters suffer!"

Then the pain started. The dying started. Because at that moment Corvo let his sorcerous shield fall, and the Devouring Wind fell upon its prey.

The old Ontokhi had opened the conduit; every death, every piercing by flying hot steel was mine. I screamed until my throat was raw, and Dirge laughed, thinking that Corvo had failed and fallen. But even as I twisted under the Angan's boot I felt a knot of power surge through reality, the opening of a naked Shard of the Divine into the world. I would learn later...oh, how I would learn! - that such excess made the mageblight burn, charring away the human flesh which it was marbled through.

But Corvo was desperate. The very taste of his mind was bitter and sweet with the anger he felt... and the same kind of broken love for Tishande which I felt for my poor doomed Makara.

He disappeared from the foredeck of the *Shadow* in a swirl of ice, his after-image blown apart by the metal storm which followed. And he burst into existence again right next to the Silent One, just in time for it to turn its head a fraction before he struck.

The Nameless still had Tishande in its grip, and the detonation of power carried both of them along with it – a solid rod of blue-white force three armspans wide, boring an ice-rimed hole clear through the heart of the mountain and into the open air. Corvo alighted for a moment, all vestige of old age gone, and his eyes turned on Dirge, as hard and cold as aeons of winter.

"You. Next." he said – and then he was airborne, shrugging off the entire roof of the keep as if it was a thin drift of snow across his shoulders. Up above I heard a shriek as lightning ripped the sky.

All this I heard, and all this I saw – but all through a haze of pain.

The Devouring Wind came down on the *Shadow of Blades* without mercy, driving a hurricane of steel before it. Broken shards of metal tore through limbs, heads, chests – a handful at a time, or in spinning swarms and eddies, flensing and grinding, seeking out hiding places and making them tombs. Those on the decks had a choice – leap to their doom in a river of boiling rock, or stay and be punctured, skinned, and dissected by the whirling tornado of death.

Those who took refuge below – their fate was even worse. Can you even begin to imagine what a red-hot storm of broken knives will do as it bounces and grinds against stone... in a warren of corridors choked with flesh? Blood poured from the gun-ports in torrents. Blood painted the white sails red to half-mast.

Even the draken were caught up and overwhelmed. Some made it into the air, beating their great wings frantically against their tethers. Others were sliced from the sky or simply died in their roosts, snuffed out by a hail of blades.

Orduvis the master gunner perished, laughing madly as the bonepowder magazine exploded, severing half of the Keel's underdslung chantries. Ricketts, the navigator, died at the wheel, a prayer to the Faeroan sealord on his lips. Solland, the Estarene healer and ship's surgeon, died holding the door of his surgery shut, trying to protect the wounded.

Only Soap managed a single strike back against the Nameless. He had torn one of the great iron doors from a siege-gun port, and he used it like a shield, pushing through an ever-intensifying storm of metal toward the armoured figure of his foe. The Devouring Wind had come down to walk the blood-slick decks of the Keel now, and it regarded this defiance with a tilt of its helm, gesturing lazily with one gauntlet. A spiral of hissing blades ground against Soap's shield, throwing sparks, but he gritted his teeth and advanced, ignoring the nicks and gashes on his arms and shoulders from the metal which had caught him in passing.

Now he was twenty paces from the Nameless, and it brought both hands forward, sending even more of its power against the Faeroan giant. Now he was ten paces away, and each step was a feat of titanic strength.

Now he was within arms-reach...

There was no way for the expressionless helm of the Nameless to show surprise, let alone terror. But it tried to jerk back as Soap's massive hand closed around it, fingers pushing into the steel to leave five deep dents. The huge pirate threw his shield aside and clamped his other hand tight, squeezing with all his bulk and muscle.

But he was unprotected now. Seconds were all he had, and the Nameless knew it. Before its helm could be cracked open like an egg the creature brought its own hands up and around in a spiral, conjuring a cloud of hot metal. The shards coalesced, forming a tight helix in the air above Soap...

Then they fell. The jagged drill-bit of steel was ten times his size; he had no chance at all. It obliterated the giant with a scream of metal on stone, then exploded outward, taking every scrap of his flesh and bones with it. The Devouring Wind was left with ten deep finger-sized gouges in its helm.

Dirge was ecstatic.

"Oh yes! That's my sweet little slave! See how they die, Kuhal Moer! And all because you were foolish enough to come here, and mad enough to give me back my soul."

I was in shock. Even a necromancer – and remember, at the time, only a lad of sixteen – should never have to experience so much violent death, all in the space of a few hundred heartbeats.

"I knew you'd try to call me back. And when you did, the old Clockmaker lost his hold on me. No matter that he was dead... a soul is a very useful thing, boy. You'll see when I take yours! Now..."

He kicked me over onto my back and turned his head skyward, gesturing with both hands. The hole in the roof on Urzen's keep, so recently excavated by Corvo of Ontokh, became a gaping chasm as Dirge brought his palms out, toppling the entire crown of the mountain.

Once again I felt something painfully familiar in the working – a taste of cold and foulness which I found all too commonplace. But I was in no position to stop him; once again, I had been used, predictable, *stupid!* The incantation of recall had found Sinder, of course... and it had given him back whatever Urzen had kept as collateral.

Up above us both the night flared white and silver. The air tasted of iron and snow, slippery with power. But despite his rage, Maegister Corvo could not strike the Shining One down. His assault washed over it like rain, sending barbs and planes of ice shearing away into the dark, their edges sharp as sorrow. Dirge measured up the Ontokhi, preparing some vile sorcery of his own, and I felt the earth lurch beneath us. Cracks skittered across the stone as I struggled to rise, calling in power from the dead aboard the *Shadow of Blades*.

It was an uneven contest. Dirge and I were drinking from the same ocean of pain, but his thirst was vast, unquenchable.

"Say goodbye to them, Khytein. Your new brothers and sisters are far lass fractious, or so you'll find..."

His hand crooked into a claw, fingers splayed around a ball of sizzling purple radiance. But Tishande didn't wait.

"Corvo! Stop holding back to spare me, and *kill* this little bitch!"

She reached out as she spoke, and plunged her fingers into the wound in the Shining One's chest, wrist deep. She *twisted*, and the Nameless One screeched, jaws snapping open and shut in agony. Then the power Dirge and I were fighting over was gone, absorbed utterly by the tiny child in blood-soaked lace. The Nameless seemed to swell up, ripping at the seams, and then...

Tishande smiled as the death-scream of the Shining One tore her apart – the sound was a physical thing, as sharp and deadly as the Devouring Wind itself, but charged with so much vitae that even metal and bone could not endure it. In a heartbeat all that remained of the sorceress was a glittering shower of falling stars – motes of mageblighted flesh unwoven and burning.

Corvo's howl of rage was almost as visceral. His staff came around in a blur as the Shining One spun in the air, its stone eyes hard and cruel. The little smile on its lips concealed the vortex of teeth and power inside.

"By the Lord of Winter's Gales I condemn you!" raged the Ontokhi, his hair streaming out in a white mane. The image of vast black wings flickered behind him in the almost constant detonation of lightning, bolts dancing from crag to crag. *"A' sundokh Auruvaszii na'kalim maundahk!"*

The air froze in my throat. Down below us, the ever-churning moat of lava hissed and cracked as it skinned over. Frost bloomed silently across every surface.

And the Shining One caught a hair-thin beam of utter cold, right through the chest – a tendril of power descended directly from the Elemental Shard, through Corvo, and into its corrupted flesh. The expression on the demon child's face tried to change, but it couldn't; the thing was frozen, immobile... and doomed.

It was the echo of its own scream which destroyed it. The high-pitched howl which had flayed Tishande came back from the whole great half-circle of the Demonspine at once, followed by a thunderclap which shook my teeth in their sockets. When the sound struck the Shining One it shattered, sure as a block of ice smashed with a war-hammer.

Corvo didn't wait to savour his revenge. He immediately turned his staff on Dirge, calling forth a storm of lightning. At the same time the master of the Nine released his own incantation, and the powers clawed at each other, splashing fountains of unnatural fire and twisted skeins of aurorae amid the ruined towers of the keep.

For a second it looked as through the two were evenly matched. Jagged blue lightning danced, stabbing through the glassy blades of Dirge's violet fire. Neither sorcerer could seem to push aside the other, and they bent all their concentration on the white-hot point between them, just as Aerik and Gernish Maudrin had done on that half-forgotten battlefield of my youth.

"Why won't you *die?* The things you serve take you, Sinder – you won't have this world, or any in it."

"They took me already, old man! The twilight of the Shards is upon your kind, and all I ask is that you go into the darkness quietly..."

"Quietly? And what about *him?* Do you feel strong enough to swallow up the entire Shard of Death?"

Dirge chuckled.

"*He* was the one who showed me the way. Shadowmask and his ilk can reap themselves at the end... Kuhal here has no more connection to the Facets of the Dark Harvest than you do."

"*Then he truly doesn't know...*"

The smile on those pale, bloodless lips was one part cruelty to another part madness. Dirge giggled.

"Your caution has bred a fool, Ontohki. My masters don't care from *where* your precious little necromancer obtained his power – only that we can use it. It's your fault for considering the bastard whelp at all human... you would have been better served to feed him to Sothara when you could."

I groaned. I knew they were talking about me – but I was beyond caring. All this talk of Shards and Facets was, exactly as Dirge had said, beside the point. What the albinotic maggot understood was *power* – and while I was nowhere near as strong as he in a battle of sorceries, I knew one way to even the odds. I let Sei loose from his pouch and sent him skittering away across the rain-slick stones before Dirge could notice.

Deep below me, in the cold halls of Urzen's keep, the dead began to rise. Touching them, even with the tendrils of my necromantic power, was like plunging my hand into a stew of sewage and corpse-grease – utterly foul, reeking of decay. These things had not died natural deaths, or easy ones. For a fleeting instant I understood why Urzen the Mad had been numbered among the most feared monsters in Sarem.

Then I gritted my teeth, and did all I could to eclipse him.

Eyeless heads lifted. Arms tendoned with wire shuddered, flexing hands like wrecking balls and shears. Pieces crawled on fingertips, flopped like beached fish, met in dark places and *merged*…

I felt a sudden wash of heat, like draken-breath against the stones, and I looked up just in time to see Dirge's sorcery break, the violet flames solidifying and falling like glass. Corvo's skeins of lightning wove together and reared back like a serpent, striking almost too fast to follow, and the thing which had once been Sinder was blown backwards, driven clear across the gulf above the moat and into the side of a neighbouring mountain. The hole he left in the rock crawled with little tendrils of electricity, billowing smoke.

"There! The damned thing *had* to run out of vitae sooner or later…"

Corvo's hands were smoking too – his flesh blackened and charred. The mageblight was marbled deeply through his arms, all the way to his chest, and ugly red burns stood proud from his skin, some already blistering in the cold.

"I should have guessed this was a trap," he grumbled to himself. "Damned Urzen, and all his bloody works! At least the world is rid of that old basta…"

He stopped, not three paces from me, his blackened hand outstretched to help me up. And we both felt it – a tremor in the ground, accompanied by a massive surge of power.

"Oh, you have to be…" managed Corvo, before the Devouring Wind shimmered into sight behind him, its gauntlets gone, crusted over by two long serrated blades. They crossed around the Ontokhi's throat, and each edge was made of hundreds upon hundreds of glittering steel shards, locked together like draken scales.

The Nameless didn't waste time with words. It brought its blades together with a sound like a vast pair of scissors, cleanly lopping the head from Maegister Corvo's neck.

Blood fountained and pattered down as what was left of him fell to its knees, then collapsed, feathers blowing away from his cloak in a black and white cloud. The look of irritated surprise on his face was no less acute for the fact that it was his last.

I heard three crunching footfalls, like boots full of broken glass. Then the Devouring Wind loomed over me, bringing back one blade over its head...

And I snarled, releasing the power I had been weaving. A hand punched up through the floor beneath it – a composite thing made of flesh and wire and gears and bone, the broken pieces of Urzen's slaves. Fingers fashioned from whole arms and legs crushed the Nameless like a little tin soldier in a vise, making its metal skin squeal and pop. Rivets flew. Seams tore open. And as the slaughterborn I had called up raised its hideous head from the flame-lit wreck of Urzen's home, I watched the lights go out inside its helm.

It was not enough. The great beast was sheer agony to control (*all those terrible years of suffering! All those experiments gone wrong!*), but it was *mine* – I raised my hand, laughing, and the giant undead did the same. An arm of fused-together torsos and limbs unfurled against the stormclouds, haloed in witchfire.

Then I cast the Devouring Wind down, watching it tumble from the slaughterborn's hand, down into the depths of Urzen's moat. It punched through the thin lava crust and deep into the molten rock, dissolving into a swirl of liquid metal down below.

"Six. Now... only six..." I slurred, trying to retain some semblance of a mind as the slaughterborn bellowed and screamed inside me. I staggered to the edge, taking in the horror of it all.

Urzen's fortress was gone – I was perched on a hanging platform which clung to a tottering section of wall, exposed to the rain. The heart of the keep was torn open, and my beautiful slaughterborn wallowed and flailed in the abyss, the sum of all the dead flesh Urzen had hoarded to himself. Below me, the *Shadow of Blades* hung at anchor, still airborne but burning, its chantries severed, its decks awash with gore.

They were all dead.

In all this vastness of ruin and rain and fire, I was the only one left alive...

I laughed. It just came bubbling up from inside of me – counterpoint, perhaps, to the agony of the slaughterborn. It was either that, or lose my mind entirely; an option of some considerable solace, to many who have found themselves in similar circumstances.

But I was not alone. Makara's body was lying in the rain a few spans distant, cold and white and perfect. Her eyes were open, and the raindrops splashed against them as if they were glass; as if she were nothing but a grim life-sized doll. I collapsed next to her, heedless of the slaugherborn's fists as they pummeled another tower to splinters.

"I'm sorry," I whispered, gently pushing a strand of hair from her cheek. It was as smooth and pale as porcelain. "I couldn't... couldn't do it. I couldn't save anyone – not even you."

She couldn't answer. Without the right incantation she would never wake, after all. But someone was listening. Behind me I heard the clap of slow, sardonic applause.

Dirge was a huge and twisted shadow in the rain, the roots and tendrils of darkness which bound up his flesh seeming to pulse and writhe as he moved. The ragged remains of his cloak and cowl were still smoking, but his face was as inhumanly beautiful as ever, his long white hair hanging in dripping strands over his eyes.

"Such wonderful theatrics! Worthy of the grand opera house in Urexes - if only you knew what the hells *opera* was," he said. "Still, this little tragedy has reached its final act, Khual Moer. You've proven to be harder to break than I would have hoped. But now your friends are beyond helping you. Give up, and I will make this just painful enough to teach you *obedience*."

He reached the edge of a ruined section of parapet and a clutch of shadows unfolded from his flesh, splitting and stretching until they became many-jointed spider legs, all glistening wet darkness. Dirge floated over the chasm between us with his hands outstretched, his boots touching the stone again as the shadows collapsed into black liquid.

"Come. There's no shame in defeat, child – not when you see what I will bring to this world..."

I didn't bother to answer. Instead I came up swinging, Sinder's stolen sword in my fist. Rage focused my will through the flesh of the slaughterborn, and its wild strike mirrored my own, its huge hand coming down palm-first to crush the lord of the Nameless.

Dirge sighed.

"Again? Very well. But I'm going to be very vexed if you damage yourself, Khytein. You'll make a much prettier slave if I'm able to keep your face intact."

He blocked the blade with a shimmering burst of tendrils, encysting the steel and wrenching it from my grasp. Those roots of darkness were burning cold, and they came down over my hand, holding me in a viselike grip. As for the slaughterborn...

"Now you'll see!" breathed Dirge, his tiny pinprick pupils not a handspan from my face. "*This* is where you sent me, Kuhal. This is where you sent them all!"

I felt the power inside me break, as something slippery and vile slithered through my mind. I saw, for an instant, a sky-scraping door of stone and iron, standing alone in a field of bones.

And then the door exploded.

Dirge held out his hand to the onrushing fist of the slaughterborn, and a thin line of darkness skittered across reality from his outstretched fingers. It was a crack – a crazed tracery of cracks, in fact, and where they met and fused pieces of the world fell away. It was as if we – Dirge, myself, Makara, Urzen's keep, all of Sarem – were simply painted images daubed on the cheap porcelain of an urn, and someone had struck it with a hammer.

The rift sucked the breath from me, along with the warmth. It grew in an instant into a jagged-toothed maw as big as the *Shadow of Blades*, both completely flat and at the same time curved, bent around itself in a mockery of geometry and reason. The slaughterborn's vast momentum carried its whole arm through the rift to the shoulder, and I felt the pain as it began to unravel, devoured by what was inside.

Ahhh... *what was inside.*

It was enough to make Dirge howl in triumph, even as whole flagstones and tons of masonry whirled past us and out of the world. It was *hungry* – that I can tell you true, because it snaffled down the vast bulk of the slaughterborn in a vortex of unspliced wood and metal and muscle, peeling it layer by layer until it was gone. A bellowing wind tore statues from their mountings and spun Urzen's books and scrolls into the air, while through it all I clung grimly to Makara, feeling the rift tugging insistently at my soul.

"Look at them, damn you!" screamed Dirge, his thorny tendrils gripping the stone so he could stand. "This is where you sent me, Kuhal – me, and every other poor doomed bastard you killed. Look on the face of our masters, and be assured of their supremacy!"

Gods help me, but I couldn't stop it. I felt my head turn, my eyes opening against my will... and I saw them.

The things in the Outer Dark were just as Dirge had promised – fluid as fire, soft and bloody as flesh, insectile and gigantic, all of them (if they were indeed separate; if they were not one vast melange of ecstasy and suffering!) locked in the throes of copulation and self-devouring. The most vast were preyed upon by countless swarming parasites, broken things all, with human faces twisted and fused, limbs pumping and mandibles sawing meat... But even the smallest were ravaged and infested in the very same way, so that in an eye-watering inversion the tiniest of the Dwellers in Darkness were the most immense, and the greatest among them nothing but lice on the parasites of still greater entities.

Madness clawed at me. Strands of Sothara's incantus broke, whipsawing through whole galleries of my memory. But what I saw was *eyes* – whole galaxies of eyes, from pinpricks to oceans in size, and all of them turned on me.

"You thought you were sending them to their rest, Khytein," said Dirge, lit up by the flickering blue glow of the Beyond. "But all the while you made us stronger. This is where the Facets of dead Gods go, and where the Coldblood sends its sacrifices of hearts and heads. This is *reality* – the rest is just a foolish dream, conjured by the madness of the Divine."

"You're insane! You... you can't let them in! I won't..."

"*You won't let me?*" He shook me. "How will you stop me? In fact, how will you stop yourself from joining me, after you've tasted their beautiful suffering?" Dirge lifted me from the ground and held me aloft in one hand – the hand which had broken a draken's neck between its fingers.

"Call me mad if you wish, Kuhal, but this is the deeper truth. This is the sanity behind a world of madness. My masters feast, and fuck, and *feel* - all without the burden of morals or philosophy. Such things twist us into more and less than beasts, and *I will do away with them.*"

"You   mean...   you   mean   we'll   all   be...?

"Pure," he said, and his smile was so simple and joyful that it sickened me. "Innocent again. The Divine made us fall, when he gave us the tangled ruin of his mind. When such irrationality is burned away we will be *happy*. We'll know that even agony means that we are *alive*."

"I'll never serve them! I'd rather die!"

This time the smile on Dirge's lips was one of sly certainty.

"Oh, I suppose you would. But I didn't intend to give you a choice."
And with that he threw me into the rift.

I spun out of control, arms and legs outstretched, but nothing stood between me and the Outer Dark. Then I saw the shadows rise up behind Dirge as I plunged out of reality, and I saw the thin strand of silver which shot out from them, wrapping itself around my boot.

"You stupid, sad little puppet," said a voice I instantly recognized. "You can have the rest. But this one is *mine*."

It was Makara, and she slammed me back to earth with a twitch of her humming wire, letting it whisper back into the space between her fingers. Like the Shining One, the reborn warbard of the Vhaur seemed to glow with an inner light, and her eyes were blazing green with witchfire. Dirge turned.

"So, you finally decide to wake? And you've chosen the wrong side, too. A pity. I always thought you were the most beautiful of Urzen's creations."

Makara let all six of her arrow-tipped wires loose, unspooling them with a sizzling, humming vibration. Drops of rain blurred to mist as they coiled, like lazy strands of water-weed on the air.

"Spare me the compliments, and *die*," said Makara. Dirge snarled, thousands of black tentacles boiling up from his skin...

It was all over in an instant.

The two Nameless clashed in a burst of hard white light, accompanied by a thunderclap which sent whole ruined sections of Urzen's keep tumbling down into the abyss. Both of them moved far too fast for the eye to follow, but I caught a glimpse of jagged dark tendrils and singing wires looping and swirling, describing calligraphic spirals and jags before Makara and Dirge landed, facing away from each other.

He slid to a stop in a shower of sparks, boiling the puddles on the stone to steam. She turned a delicate somersault in the air and alighted on the tips of her toes, six glittering arrowheads snicking back into place between her fingers.

For an instant, neither one moved.

And then six black lines appeared across Dirge's chest. Dark, bubbling blood began to drip and ooze from the woulds, and he tried to scream, though whether from rage or agony I will likely never know. The cuts were deep; all the way through the Nameless One's torso, severing his arms, his waist, his legs...

"Tell your masters that this world is not for them," said Makara, and she leveled her fist at the Angan. Power built up, turning the air slippery and hot. Then she spread her fingers, and Dirge came apart.

There were great sticky ropes and webs of shadow inside him, and these prevented the creature from flying completely to pieces. But he was caught up in a blast of raw energy which sent him spinning backward, over my head – a knotted, membranous mess of flesh and darkness, teased out into a long thin strand by the pull of the rift.

There was a taste of copper and snow. There was a sound like continent-sized slabs of metal being hammered in a furnace. Hot black velvet suffocated the world for an instant. And the rift slammed closed, swallowing up Dirge and his so-called masters like the jaws of some storybook monster.

I came to with the taste of wet wool and blood in my mouth, and Makara was there. Her eyes no longer blazed with fire, but her hands were cold where they touched my face, as if to remind me of what she had become. Along with that thought came a tide of guilt, and I struggled away from her, pushing my back up against a shattered merlon.

"Dead. All dead. You as well... all of them..."

"*I know*," she said, kneeling next to me. "You don't have to say anything. Just take this."

Her hand went to the ball of black and gold wire between her throat and her chest, and she pulled it free with a sound of tiny metal teeth. The miniature incantus was warm to the touch, and she pressed it into my hands, smiling as all the life drained out of her.

I grabbed at her as she collapsed, and I suppose I must have screamed. Once again I saw myself from outside my body – a tiny, bedraggled figure in black, cradling a dead girl in my lap and holding a tiny star between my fingers.

Then the incantatus bloomed inside my mind, silent as an exploding sun, brittle and beautiful as a snowflake. Makara's life, in every detail, right down to the brass-and-bone face of Urzen looking down at her...

I knew what I had to do, then.

Everyone was dead. Aerik and Maudrin, Corvo, Imkhantu, Tishande - all of them. But here, in this place, had lived a creature who scorned death as a mere technicality...

I had a lot to learn before I could claim the same kind of power.

And then... Then Dirge, and his masters, and the Thearch, and *all of them*...

I stood, cradling Makara's body in my arms, and I walked into what remained of Urzen's keep, slamming the great iron doors behind me. I would not open them again until winter had turned to spring, and a whole year had rolled by beneath the uncaring stars.

What came out, alas, was far, far less wholesome than what had entered.

Five

Pariah's Crown

They say that love can redeem the heart of a monster - but of course, the old wisdom states that 'to love a monster, you must also become one yourself'. In any case, such emotions have never been proven to truly exist within the strict definitions of logic and science... more likely madness is the root of this trite superstition.

Nyvar Xeng,
- Supreme Redactor of Saradrim

THIS TIME NYVAR Xeng was right. Madness took me, and despair. As if in sympathy with my dark mood – or with the death of Corvo, perhaps – the skies descended, and blizzards locked the Demonspine in ice, driving me deep into the haunted halls of Urzen's keep.

What I found were his great libraries and scriptoria – those, and the urns full of grey, flavourless hardbread he used to keep his drudges alive.

So, as winter gripped Korisal I began to study.

At first it was for Makara's sake. Without vitae to feed into the Incantus at her throat she slept the open-eyed sleep of the dead, and that was too much for me to face. So I hauled down the dusty tomes which spoke of engines, and telluric currents in the fire beneath the earth, and how to harness them. I unearthed cracked and faded maps of the keep itself, and carried Makara through a nightmare labyrinth, down to levels where great wheels churned endlessly, grinding out a skein of power.

I fed the Incantus – which Urzen's books called a *Cerebrex*, and one of many – until Makara woke.

I remember feeling utterly numb as she wrapped her mutilated arms around me. I remember her kiss being as cold as graveside charity, and the hard metal of her armour biting into my chest. But she was *alive*, or at least as close to life as I could bring her. And we were together at last, in a cruel mockery of everything I'd dreamed of.

At first I strove to reverse whatever sorcery Urzen had wrought, but even with the shade of Sothara to translate the runes of old Korisal there was nothing in the Forgemaster's libraries which offered any hope. I may have been able to revivify Makara's flesh, but by the artifice of Urzen she was now so much more than human - and so much less.

She didn't need to eat. She never slept, except in a blank-eyed torpor which resembled death, and only then when I took the incantus from her throat to study its inner workings.

But beneath the cold dark armour and the scars there was still a flickering shadow of the fey, sly witch-girl of the Khytein Vaur. I lived for the moments when Makara's old self shone through. And I hated myself for distrusting the devotion – even, dare I say it, the love – which this demon of the Nameless showed me. After all, the bond we shared was not one of young lovers, bound by blood and whispered vows in the sight of the goddess of the moon. What we shared – or so I told myself, in my darkest moments – was the bond between a sorcerer and the summoned, a necromancer and the dead.

But sometimes, late at night, I'd awake from my studies, my head cradled in the pages of a dusty grimoire, and I'd hear the echo of an old Khytein children's song echoing up through the deeps. Or I'd see Makara smile a sad half-smile at one of my jokes. Then I'd feel that old familiar tightness in my chest – the one which had nothing to do with the spreading mageblight. Then, hope hammered against the walls of my cynicism, and the stones shifted, just a little each time.

She helped me. By and by our work became grisly and cold and hard, as I unearthed the means to begin crafting my revenge. We ventured out into the winter gales to hack corpses from the ice. We trod the decks of the *Shadow of Blades*, frozen red, and we harvested pieces; heads, limbs, bodies, all butchered and rimed with frost. We uncovered friends torn to pieces, and I told Makara tales of them in life – of Elion Morekh's braggadocio, of Soap's massive strength and even bigger heart, of Corvo the storm-caller and his pipe of foul, smouldering weeds...

The day we chipped Corvo's head from the ice a great magpie, bigger than the largest of carrion crows, alighted atop the walls of Urzen's keep. It was Rain, and he watched us with beady little dark eyes as we carried his master's body down into the depths. Makara took to feeding him, and he shivered up among the merlons all through winter, keeping vigil.

I fed the souls in the ossurary well of the Keel. Gods help me, but

I had no choice – without them we would never see the marble walls of Urexes, or its dreaming towers. So I called back the spirits of my poor dead people, one by one, binding them into their cold flesh and throwing them into the well, where a storm of green fire obliterated them. I remembered the spirits' bargain – The Thearch, his God, or me.

I learned how the Angans had made such things as the Keel in the first place; how their vast engines of nekrological art functioned, grinding power as penance from the souls of Esau's faithful, bound in death to rune-etched metal and glass until they were finally frayed away to nothing.

My studies were fruitful. I began work on my own Cerebrex, the black-spiked globe of iron which accompanies me to this day. Many happy hours I spent with Makara, sawing the crowns from skulls and plunging human brains into vats of bubbling tinctures, propagating a strain of the crystalline mageblight through soft tissue.

The forge-hall began to resemble an abattoir. Pieces hung on hooks and chains, while discarded limbs in barrels and buckets awaited the furnace. I wondered, in moments of sudden clarity, if this was madness – this sheer hard, bright brittle purpose of mine, so logical and sweet that it blinded me to the horrors of what I was actually doing.

I dismissed such thoughts as squeamishness or nonsense. Our experiments continued. And, one cold, clear night, when the stars flickered above the keep like chips of diamond, we brought back Elion Morekh.

It had taken a lot of stitches. It had also taken a great deal of power, but now my Cerebrex was the size of a man's head, and growing daily. I spent hours in meditation, peeling the tendrils of Sothar'as influence from my mind and imprinting them into the glowing ball of iron and gold, and I was quite appalled to see just how clumsy I had been in the past.

Despite our care and attention, I don't think Elion was glad to be back. In retrospect, we may have gotten some of the organs wrong, or perhaps the rites of embalming. Makara had to pry the Faeroan's cold dead hands from around my throat before his eyes rolled forward in their sockets and he realized where he was.

They couldn't speak, of course. Not he, nor Solland, nor Corvo, or any of the others I called back from beyond death, binding them into their frozen flesh with old arcana. But they *understood*.

I told them that I was sorry for my failings – sorry, too, that I had brought them forth into this vale of tears for a second time. I didn't want to know if my friends had been condemned to the hells or exalted in the heavens, but I knew the road ahead of us was more like the former than the latter. I told them that this was what they had wanted, that we were sailing for Urexes, the eternal city, and that by the end I would have severed poor doomed Esau from his crucifixion tree and from the mortal world.

I knew that they hated me. I felt their resentment, hot and dark in the back of my mind. But their living brains had been encysted in crystal, bound into the Cerebrex, and they had no choice but to obey.

Days passed in darkness and blood. Weeks passed, as I paced the workrooms of Urzen the Mad, sleeping fitfully among tomes and hacksaws, hooks and body parts.

Until spring came.

One morning I stood atop the tallest tower of Urzen's keep, the wind from the south carrying a scent of salt, sap, and honey. I was wearing a great black cloak Makara had made for me; bearskin, like Gernish Maudrin's, but lined with silk, and thrown over a suit of leather and copper scale. I lit a shallow brazier under a dish of oil, blood and water, and watched as the rainbow sheen on its surface bubbled into a map of Sarem. Then I plucked a human eyeball from the tiny clay pyx which had preserved it, and transfixing it on a golden needle, I broke the surface of my liquid map.

A sorcerous vision assailed me, and suddenly I was flying over the plains of Ghuram. Below me spread a hot ocher hardpan of dust and stone, crawling with insects.

No – not insects. *Men.* Legions of Angan warriors, conscripts and Faceless running in rout, war machines overturned and burning...

I saw the ziggurat-shaped hulk of one of the Thearch's Excoriators Major lying in a crater, smoke billowing up from its shattered side. The crater walls were skinned in glass, sand fused to a glossy sheen by the force of sorcery unleashed against it.

I saw the place where two armies had come together, and the bodies piled in drifts like snow. On one side, the ragged remains of white-clad Anganesse legions, butchered horses, and the splintered bulk of fallen keels. On the other, the forces of the Akhazi; men of the utter south with purple-black skin and crocodile-leather armour, warrior women clad in feathers and bones, pale, thin sorcerers with bound feet deformed into hooves and long, tapering skulls...

They had brought their own engines of war, and beasts to pull them – great, mindless hulks almost as big as the keels of Anganesse, with low, squat bodies and thick limbs, scaly hides and drooling jaws big enough to crunch up whole regiments. Several of these creatures were browsing on the dead, slobbering down whole graveyards full of carrion at once.

At the heart of the victorious Akhazi horde was a palanquin as wide as the fallen Excoriator, carried forward on a living carpet of slaves. How they could bear such an immensity of carved wood and copper I could not fathom, but they inched forward at a crawl, whipped on by armoured men on long-limbed riding beasts, half lizard, half bird.

It was the Coldblood.

I only caught a glimpse of the vast, loathsome thing before it saw me with its mind, and the agony it leveled at me made my vision reel and blur. But what I saw was vast and cancerous – a bloated and rotting serpent, curled and knotted in on itself, with the squamous face of a toad and a body all swelling growths, bedecked in jewels and plates of runic gold. This was the thing which the Silence was a shadow of, that much was clear. And the reality was enough to blast my wandering sight up and away from the battlefield, spinning out of control.

Up through the ragged clouds, and into the upper air, where stars burned even at noonday. Up until I could see the true form of our world, and look down into the heart of the Divine.

The scholars of modern-day Ghuram teach their children that the world is a globe, spinning in space, and they do so with the same self-satisfied certainty with which earlier scholars taught children that the world was flat, or bowl-shaped, or carried through the endless night on the back of a raven.

But the truth is far stranger.

From up above the blood-soaked plain I could see the fragment of the world which carried Sarem, from the polar seas to the deserts of the south. I could see the glassy, near-invisible blades of force radiating from the exposed core of the planet, neatly slicing this vast segment of the globe away. And I could see all the other shattered fragments of the world, hanging isolated in space, their oceans hemmed in by shimmering veils of power, veins of molten rock seething up from beneath, where they were heated in the sorcerous forge of the core.

The Akhazi had invaded Ghuram because Ghuram represented the very limit of Sarem. Standing on the severed edge of the desert a man could look down into an immensity of nothingness, or look across the gulf at a wall of rock, falling away forever into the furnace of the Divine. And if he stepped out, through the shimmering barrier – well, he may very well end up across the divide, safe and sound in the Protectorate of Akhaz. But it was equally likely that he would find himself buried under rock, drowned in the salt sea, or falling from a great height. The facets of the shattered globe did not match up, and only a few small apertures allowed a person – or an army – to stride from one fragment to the other with any chance of success.

The Coldblood had found such a place. Even now, more of the Akhazi baggage train came pouring through the flat, sky-spanning pane of the divide, sending little wisps of auroral light swirling across its surface.

From here, it was only a few short months march to the gates of Urexes, perched on its arch of stone by the shores of the Shallow Sea.

I shook off the vision, drained, and my mind folded itself neatly back into my body again, taking up the aches and strains of flesh. I plucked the eyeball on its golden needle from the hot oil, and held it up to my shoulder, where Rain gobbled it down gratefully.

"Makara. It's time. Make the others ready, and tell them to prepare my Keel. I know where Dirge has gone, and what he plans to do."

My beautiful dead warbard nodded and turned away. I looked out, to the south, as if my mortal eyes alone could look into the heart of Urexes, where the thing which had once been Jerrold Sinder knelt before an old man on an alabaster throne.

"I'm coming," I whispered, licking the oil and blood from my fingers. "And this time, I'm bringing an army..."

There is a saying, "and the rest is history". You may be familiar with it.

History certainly recalls the flight of what the Young Nations call the *Graveyard Ark*. There is poetry, of course, interminable sagas concocted by bards with more romance in their souls than they have brains in their heads. One aspiring young fool in Ythe actually wrote a *play* about it, or so I hear – my own soliloquy runs to half an hour, I'm told, and has often moved audiences to either tears or to strong drink.

But there is a wealth of real history, too. History of the kind which is measured out in small, nondescript stone monuments commemorating particularly impressive sites of massacre and suffering. And at the end – oh, yes! The Desolation may very well be my most enduring legacy, especially as none of you will thank me for three centuries of peace and prosperity.

We harvested the spring thaw on the plains of southern Khytein. That was our first destination.

I had set out from Korisal with a crew of only forty dead men, Makara, Corvo, Elion and myself. But we had extensively modified the old *Shadow of Blades* to better serve our purposes. Our captain may have been a mute grey wight with stitches running clear across his face, but he had enough respect for his poor old ship to hack the name from her side, long before we fitted the boiling vats and the great underslung doors, replacing the shattered chantries with all the tools of a slaughterhouse.

It was these which gave the vessel her third and final name – the *Graveyard Ark*, bearer of sorrow, the black wings of ruin... an icon for the superstitious to fear. And when Esau's priests couldn't banish that fear, or the Thearch's armies destroy it, my hope was that Sarem would rise in rebellion.

There were armies interred under the snow, whole battlefields of them, left for the crows as the Red Winter closed in. My crew of undead sailors dug them up, chose those with the least hideous injuries, then sent them aloft into the belly of the Keel on long hooked chains. Up above more wights were waiting, with knives and pincers hot, to flense the rotting flesh from the bones of the dead. We boiled them in reeking cauldrons filled with lye, exactly as Urzen's books instructed – there was much written by the scholars of old Korisal about disease, and I did not want to be a bearer of plagues; only a minister of vengeance.

How can I explain what it felt like to open the wardings of limitation about my new Cerebrex for the first time? How can I convey to you, who lack the Dark Sight, the rapture of becoming a thousand times yourself, of the utter potency of command which a true necromancer feels? It would be both trite and false to call upon sexual innuendo, or even to evoke communion with the Divine. It was, instead, like taking control of a vast and complex machine, one which rumbles with the power of great turbines sunk into underground rivers, or windmill blades thrashing a winter gale. To grasp that power and ride it was to invite obliteration, but it came with an exhilaration greater than any I had ever known.

I sent my will out from the Cerebrex in waves, standing at the prow of the Ark, and the great runic spirals of bones which my minions had laid amid the spring wildflowers of the plain began to rise. It was like one awakening after another, the feeling of eyes within eyes opening to a cataclysm of intricate light – and this time the dead were entirely mine. I floated in the centre of the Cerebrex, a soul without flesh, and in every direction my mind's eye glimpsed spinning shards of people's lives – children crying, lovers and parents and friends, grief and joy, disease and piety, hunger and lust and...

I opened my eyes – the real ones, sunken into a face made old beyond its years. My hair was bound back with a silver circlet of thorns, and I had taken up the war-paint of Anghul, the black traceries of spiked antlers curling out from my eyes, and inverted down across my cheeks. The hank of fire-red in my hair had been bleached white by the mageblight, and it hung crooked as a frozen splinter of lightning from my brow.

Ten thousand dead men stood up.

Their bones were scoured clean, their skulls inset with black runes, and their souls were bound within the Cerebrex, where their memories couldn't chip away at my own expanded mind. I clenched my fist and raised it above my head, and ten thousand fleshless hands drew their swords, with a sound like a scythe whispering through a field of grain.

There was no need for me to control each one. Urzen's long-dead compatriots had shown me the way, and the merest push with my will urged the whole vast engine of living bone forward, first one step, then a second. Ten thousand shields came up to form a curving wall, just as we of the Khytein had done since the dawn age, when Ciermakh walked the Stormwood with us.

It felt *right*. It felt as natural as breathing – as effortless as marshaling each nerve and tendon in your arm to raise a horn of ale, or pluck an apple from a tree. I laughed, and the sound was lost amid the silence.

So I sat encysted at the core of my bone machine as we began to move. Elion Morekh stood to my right, grey and expressionless, his eyes milky white and his mind grinding out an undertone of hate. Makara stood at my left, cold and graceful, a queen of the damned. And Corvo could still call power, despite his burned and withered hands. The bloodied sails of the Keel bellied out as I slid a command word into his mind, and with a creaking, snapping rush of tiny sounds the horde began to march.

From the throne I had stolen I looked down on a sea of animated bone, glittering with sharp steel, and I began composing eulogies for the cities in my path...

"Almerre will stand forever! These walls are built not of stone and mortar, but from the courage of my Ontokhi knights, the strength of my loyal soldiers! So let them come! We will see them drown in the Iceflood like all those who have dared to come before them!"

Tzar Andrei Kharold Idris, last free ruler of Ontokh, before his reign was swiftly ended by assassination, in the 1322nd year of the Light of Esau, Angan reckoning.

THE SKY WAS yellow with stormlight as the steppes of Ontokh rolled out below us, a pattern of fields and low stone walls cross-hatching the landscape as I looked south, toward the city of Almerre. Behind the tattered sails of the *Graveyard Ark* loomed a wall of churning clouds - sick green and bruise purple, writhing with lightning. Beneath the storm everything was still. Every bird had flown, and the wild horses and bison of the plain had fled, leaving an unnatural silence behind them.

The Ontokhi knew what was coming. Outriders had escaped from the chain of trading forts and villages I had already taken, bearing tales of carnage and horror. I had let them live - it would have been pathetically easy to hunt them down, but complete destruction wasn't my purpose. Now the aldermen of Almerre knew that a horde of the dead were marching toward them, and that my minions were only hungry for the flesh of Angan loyalists.

In Scarn they had fought to the last man, Southerners and Ontokhi together. In Ortar it had taken only a single assault to topple the palisade walls, and when the spearmen atop the parapet saw the glowing green eyes and grasping hands of the dead coming for them they turned on their Angan masters, completing the butchery themselves. By the time we reached Czanthe, the gates were already thrown open, and I walked through the silent streets in silence, between two rows of hanging corpses in white. The people of Czanthe watched, frightened and cold, as I accepted their grim tribute, and I left the fortress town on its hill with a band of hard-bitten Ontokhi rangers at my back. It seemed that there were many among the vassal states of the White Empire who would rather ride with the dead than obey their living masters.

I had never seen a city before Czanthe. I had thought that the fortified shanties of the Ythean trader-camps were mighty conurbations, and that even Urexes itself would be the same again, if more beautiful. But Sothara had seen them. He whispered to me at night of the great walls and towers of Almerre – the southernmost reach of his old empire, and I saw visions of that crowded, festering warren of stone and warped wood, a cloud of deathly power churning up from it day and night.

At the time I had refused to believe that men would live in such a place. But as the Graveyard Ark swung south we encountered larger and larger towns, monuments to Esau on a colossal scale, and tower-keeps bigger than my entire village straddling the high-road just to exact tolls and tariffs. We crushed them all.

We tore down chapels and cathedrals, burning the effigies of Esau. By the light of flaming pyres I accepted the offered swords and shields of bandits and deserters - some of them Angan conscripts with crude red crosses daubed across their armour. An army of the living soon followed in the wake of my slow and silent horde, and the fear of me stopped them from looting and raping after each victory.

I was surrounded by a great shambling, bleating, stinking nation by the time we cleared the Plainsea and drove into the underbelly of Ontokh. And though my mind was woven through the bones of countless wights, I was utterly alone. I spent most of the march brooding on my scavenged throne, there at the prow of the Ark, my ragged cloak billowing out from my shoulders as I watched through the eyes of the dead. I watched men drinking and whoring and gambling - all the saga-hero pastimes which my father would have not only approved of, but would have joined in to uproarious excess.

But there was nothing left in me which felt anything but contempt for the flesh. The chill of ice-splintered bone was under my skin, and it made me remote, as cold as the storm-wind which drove us onward. As cold as Makara, who slept like a perfect, frozen statue, waiting for carnage to give her a reason to wake.

And now we came to the capital of Ontokh, its high walls bright with banners and bristling with seige-engines. The city itself stood encircled by a bend in the Iceflood, the swift-running river which coursed down through the steppes from the high Hiledoran. To this formidable natural defense the old Tzars of Ontokh had added a hundred-span curtain wall, and a double barbican on the landward side encircled by a moat. Now the great sluice gates which fed the moat were open, and icy water lapped at the spiked casements of the city's gatehouse keep.

Water wouldn't stop the dead. They would be the hammer which struck hard against the walls of Almerre - thirty thousand strong, all animated by my will and my power through the focus of the Cerebrex.

I had divided them into two great companies, as easily as a Ghuram goldsmith might push beads about on his abacus. Half formed an implacable shield-wall, with immense wheeled battering rams and hide-covered mantlets between them. Their task was to push through to the gates and cast them down, making a path for my living forces. The dead were cold and resolute, but quite stubbornly stupid; it would take speed and bloody skill to seize the complex of towers around Almerre's gate, the Crow Tower and Bell Tower with their high drawbridges out to the barbicans beyond the moat. My plan was then to turn the seige-engines of the gateway bastions against the Inner Ward and the Citadel, high up the slope of the city. Living hands would be needed to arm and fire the towering trebuchets and iron-banded siege ballistae there.

The second company were only five thousand strong, and their task was one which no mortal could accomplish. The third I kept waiting, cold and inert, as nothing but a pile of jumbled ribs and skulls deep in the holds of the Ark. If all went according to plan, their job would be to sow terror among the bright chapels and mansions of Almerre's upper city, where the tongue of land which supported the Ontokhi capital rose up sharply to a precipitous drop.

Fear had become the most brutal weapon of the horde. My living commanders had taken to wearing the savage warpaint of Anghul in imitation of myself, and their men delighted in cultivating the aspects of demons, all spiked armour and horned helms, skin daubed with ocher and soot-blackened fat. Loose bands of similar warriors had formed, and they adopted banners depicting horrors to wake dread in the foe – the flayed head of my Czanthene outriders, for example, or the leering horned skull of my bandit archers from the forests of Rasuul.

At night I let my legions of bone and steel collapse where they stood, and the plain beneath the Graveyard Ark twinkled with kindling fires. Wagons, tents and a whole straggling village worth of livestock, stone-grinders, prostitutes, hawkers, cooks, thieves and illegitimate children caught up in our wake, and I learned another very important fact about human nature – marching with an army of the dead seemed utterly wrong and terrible at first. But with each victory, (and soon, it seemed, with each mile) more rebels flocked to my banner. Because no matter how awful it seems, the winning side is still *winning*.

My commanders had been briefed the night before – the living, of course, for there was no need for me to issue anything as crude as spoken commands to my beautiful dead. Now we rode the yellow storm-light, a shadow sliding across the plain and casting it into darkness. The bells of Almerre were ringing, an incongruously merry sound above the tramp and grind of bony feet and seige-engine wheels, and as we closed to just outside of ballista-shot we could see the men on the walls and atop the towers standing fast by their regimental standards, a thicket of pikes and halberds glittering in their hands.

I could feel them with the edges of my will – almost a living thing, coiling through the square-formed regiments of the dead like a tangled thicket of thorns. Every man defending Almerre was terrified, and most were blind drunk to mask that terror. I smiled, and gave the command to advance.

Toward the gates of Almerre marched twenty thousand dead men, clad in rusting chain and plate, bearing swords forged by a handful of warring nations but all striding in lockstep, driven by my will. Two-span long iron quarrels began to rain down from the siege bows, but they were useless against a force of fleshless bone – even those which chanced to smash into a ribcage or clip an armoured scapula only slowed the dead men's advance, as chips and shards of bone knit back together, and green sparks re-kindled in their hollow eyesockets. On the rare occasion that a quarrel shattered the skull of one of my minions I felt a brief spike of ice-cold pain, and one of the facets in my vision winked out. But there were a hundred more for every one which fell, and now came the burning fire-pots of the trebuchets, the tumbling boulders of the catapults...

Twenty thousand grinning skulls didn't so much as flinch as hell rained down on them. I made a subtle motion with one finger and their shields came up, deflecting the splash of naptha fire. The boulders, on the other hand, skipped and rolled clean through whole ranks of the dead, splintering them to useless ruin. Still, they came on. And now the siege engineers were tiring. The shots came slower, the hail of iron and stone a mere shower.

It was time to answer them.

I gestured to Elion Morekh, and the grey-faced wight who had once been Admiral of the Free Reavers raised a curling draken-horn to his lips. He took his first breath in several months just to sound it, and the mournful bellow set the first stage of my attack into motion. Down below us Master Orduvis lashed his whip, his mummified lips drawn back into a rictus grin. And a crew of undead gunners manhandled bonepowder charges and runic balls into their weapons, aiming them at the barbican fortresses outside the gate.

At the same time my skeletal horde broke into a shambling run, arrowing deep into the killing ground bounded by those twin towers and the gatehouse. A huge, iron-clad mantlet was passed from hand to hand atop the crush of fleshless bodies, and behind came the rumbling wheels of the rams, their arm-thick chains jangling.

The defenders didn't have time to stop the dead from reaching the moat. The battery of guns aboard the *Graveyard Ark* spoke, and my whole vast arrowhead-shaped vessel was consumed by a pall of smoke. We had heeled around broadside to the gates now and were cruising slowly toward the south of the city, hundreds of undead labouring in the rigging above to make the great Keel come about.

Through the smoke I saw flashes of orange flame, and heard screams of dismay and horror. The Almerran guard had just found out what that wide, strong mantlet was for – a makeshift drawbridge to span the moat. Now long siege ladders were raised against the barbican walls, and skeletal warriors with daggers clenched between their teeth swarmed up, along with another little surprise I had concocted...

I focused through the eyes of the first undead to breach the parapet, and my vision was shattered as a silver-bladed axe took its skull from its shoulders. The second, however, skewered the axeman on its gladius, and the third scuttled over the man's corpse to hew into the Almerran line, sinking its yellowed teeth into the throat of a white-clad Angan officer. That's when I took control of the fourth wight's hand, and pulled the ring on the glass bonepowder shell bound up inside its ribcage.

Green fire flared, and a score of living men had their souls stripped away. Burned and smoking, they rose and turned on those who had survived. Men threw down their weapons and fled, screaming. Men jumped from the high barbican into the Iceflood, dragged to the bottom by their armour. And the Angan commander of the gatehouse walls did exactly what I had expected – he raised the high drawbridge which cut the barbican off from the city's defenses. Now it was an island tower amid a sea of ravenous corpses, and behind my legions came the living – cadres of deserters and seige engineers from Czanthe and Uldara, galley-slaves from the high reaches of the Iceflood and quarrymen from the Hiledoran, where Angan slavers oversaw the carving of new keels from the mountainsides.

They turned the siege batteries atop the towers on the gate itself, and a short, vicious exchange broke out, punctuated by the flare of naptha and the crunch of immense boulders. The long-necked trebuchets were at too close a range to assist, but they began raining rocks and fire-pots down on the upper city; the high wards and the Citadel. We were drifting over streets of mansions and town-houses now, tacking against the wind to circle back toward the highest part of the city's walls.

I felt the rams bite into the gate. I saw cauldrons of boiling oil and pitch sluice down, utterly useless against animated bone.

And then the conventicle of Angan priests atop Almerre's cathedral struck the *Graveyard Ark* with a storm of sorcery, and I lost sight of my horde altogether.

That first blast was raw, raving power – a fist of violet fire crackling with magikal discharge as it slammed into the side of the Ark, throwing us sideways in the air. I had nothing with which to retaliate-it took all of my will to control an army of the dead, Cerebrex or no.

"Makara!" I screamed, holding onto the arms of my throne as the Keel lurched violently, hammered by a second blast. "Stop them! Kill them! Now!"

The flat spin of the Ark didn't seem to affect my beautiful demoness. She opened her eyes and unfolded, lithe and graceful in her spiked armour, a playful little smile on her lips.

"And their souls? I'm thirsty, Kuhal. So very thirsty..."

I shuddered. I knew what it meant, now, to be fed whole to one of the Nameless. The vertigo and madness of the Outer Dark still waited in my dreams.

"Yes," I said, watching the cathedral's spire spin slowly past again. A crackling detonation from belowdecks told me that one of the preist-mages had managed to ignite some of Orduvis' precious bonepowder ordnance. "You can keep them. Just... just make sure the people down there see them die."

Makara gave me the same exasperated look she'd reserved for me since the day we met.

"This is going to be very hard to miss... *Master.*" She loaded the word with no small amount of irony. "Just make sure your little pets leave some alive to tell the tale."

She had a point. Through the after-echo of sorcerous discharge I could feel the advance guard of my army, and see that they had lain waste to the gates of Almerre. Already fires were spreading in the gateside slums of Brokeluck Town and Gallows Corner, and a frightened mob of citizens hammered on the portcullis of the Inner Ward, watched by impassive ranks of Angan Faceless. I have never understood why the dead desire human flesh, but without my will controlling them the wights gave in to their craving. My vision reeled with images of bloodied blades and bony claws, viscera-deep in bucking, writhing victims, of strewn limbs and scattered chunks of flesh...

I lashed them into control. I burned them with the image of the Outer Dark. And like curs whipped to heel they came, forming up in the square of the lower town with their fleshless hands dripping red. Behind them, the living were equally savage. Crosses were lashed together, and Angan hands and feet were driven through with nails. Nooses jerked tight around Southern necks. Prayers turned to screams and inhuman sounds of agony.

But the Ontokhi, seeing their own people enacting such butchery... well, there has never been a more efficient recruitment campaign in the history of military arms. Red cross-marks were daubed upon the armour of my new recruits, using fingers dipped in the blood of their hated Angan officers.

It seemed that the inner gates would fall within minutes. The Ontokhi themselves brought baulks of timber and hammers to tear the portcullis down. Archers fired point-blank through the metal bars, throwing the Faceless back and pinning them to the walls, while I held tight to the sorcerous chains which restrained the dead.

I saw all this in the seconds between watching Makara stalk to the very prow of the Graveyard Ark - and watching her leap out into the air over the city.

She didn't so much fall as *fly* toward the gothic spire of Almerre's cathedral, silver wires licking out from between her fingers. A blur of sorcery surrounded each thread, and they framed her tiny armoured figure as it sped in toward the tower, spinning in the air until she was falling feet-first.

Three wires cut into the stone, and I watched chips of marble spin away amid the smoke, gargoyles and effigies of saints toppling to crash into the streets below. Too late, one of the chantry priests realized what was coming. He let loose an anguished cry, sending a blue-green bolt zagging across the sky toward Makara.

She dodged it with contempt, using her momentum and the pull of the wires to wrap in tight to the spire, coming in fast. She shattered one of the tower's stained-glass windows as the wires reached full draw, and then she was among her prey.

Flying shards sliced through priestly flesh, eliciting a chorus of screams. Then the bloody work began, claws flashing out left and right, armour-blades loosing sprays of arterial crimson. Before the rain of blood could patter down across the cold white marble Makara had one of the priests – a short, fat subdeacon – by the throat, and she was back out in the air above Almerre, falling.

The priest squirmed in Makara's grip, but the cruel metal talons which Urzen had given her bit deep, choking the words in his throat. As a crowd of Ontokhi nobles in the cobbled street below pointed and yammered, my beautiful Nameless squeezed her fingers into a fist, popping the Angan's head clean from his shoulders. Blood fountained, along with thick, auroral skeins of soul-stuff, drawn into Makara's open mouth like a breath of Corvo's pipe-smoke.

Then her fall was arrested by the single thick bass-string wire which played out from her other hand, and every last one of the Angan coven were dragged screaming from their chantry, strung together neck to neck like slaves on the saleyard block. Makara reached the end of the wire, and tension bought her back around the spire in a looping spin, tautening the coil and making all six of the white-robed acolytes dance on air, clawing at their throats.

The wire bit into the corner of the tower. A twist more tension sent it carving through muscle and between vertebrae, beheading the whole frantic gaggle of men and letting them fall. Then Makara let go, sliding to a stop along the spine of a tiled rooftop, her armoured boots plowing twin furrow in its terracotta surface.

A noise from the bell tower made her turn.

"Truly are the damned given great power by their corruptors. But such cursed gifts are anathema to the light of our Lord, and must be shunned, punished, and purged from this world."

The High Priest – the one who had loosed that bolt of violet flame

– was still alive. I saw him pull back his sleeves, smiling as he turned to face Makara, drawing in the death-energies of his Faithful to weave a killing blow. The blight was marbled through this one like fat through a side of bacon, and his thin, creased face was as sharp and cruel as a hatchet.

"Perish, demon!" he snarled, spreading his hands around a ball of sizzling blackness. "In Esau's name I cast you out – you, and your grave-crawling master!"

That, I felt, was hardly fair. After all, the dead who now hammered on the gates of the Inner Ward hadn't been hacked from sanctified earth. Makara was similarly unimpressed.

As the sphere of killing power flew from the priest's hands it uncoiled into an intricate, fluid knotwork of black tendrils, the tip of each one an eyeless serpent-head. But they were met by a fierce exhalation of flame – a beam compressed between Makara's cupped hands. The geometric writhe of serpents blew away to a spiral of ash as the beam lanced upward, missing the priest by a whisper and striking the great bell in the carillon over his head.

"Foolish hell-spawn," spat the priest, tearing the icon of Esau from around his neck. In his hand it began to glow with a silvery light, building up power until the world around it began to bubble and shimmer with heat-haze. "You missed! But I won't be so gracious as to give you another chance..."

Makara simply stood firm amid the ruined tiles, her hands gently smoking.

"I'm sure you won't," she said. She raised one eyebrow.

And then the thick hempen ropes which held the bell burnt through. The priest had barely a second to look up before the vast red-hot tonnage of the thing crushed him, smashing through floor after floor all the way down into the undercroft of the cathedral. When the dust cleared I could still clearly hear his screams – far more resilient than a mere mortal, the Angan hammered against the walls of his burning metal prison until he was cooked inside it.

Ricketts wrestled against the wheel, and the *Graveyard Ark* heeled over, coming back onto heading with a creaking of rope and canvas. But Makara wasn't finished.

As I watched, she loosed all six of her singing wires, wrapping them tight around the steeple-spire of the Angan cathedral. Archers on the other towers and amid the crenelated merlons of the Citadel were firing at her now, but their arrows skipped harmlessly off the tiles, or shattered on her gleaming armour without so much as a scratch. I heard her voice whispering in my ear, a little purr of laughter, and the hairs on the back of my neck stood on end.

"Don't we have better things to do," she asked, "than to humor these weak Ontokhi peasants? Our business is with Urexes, not Almerre."

"*I'll* handle strategy," I sent back, including just a little ice and steel in my reply. "You are my right hand, Makara – the one which holds the sword."

Her laugh was far, far too coy and mocking to belong to a dead girl – but I had to remind myself that this was exactly what she was.

"I *know* what you do with your right hand, Kuhal Moer. And as to holding your sword – I have weapons *far* more effective at my disposal..."

I heard the rising chord as it shimmered down the wires, and felt the bone-deep snapping sound as the cathedral tower broke. Then Makara leaned her weight back against the load, and the entire eighty-span, copper-sheathed steeple ripped loose, wrapped in a spiderweb of silver filaments.

"Oh, no! You can't be..."

"*Watch me.* And hope that Dirge is watching too."

It should have been impossible. Armour and all, Makara still weighed much less than even I did, and I was considered a gaunt and unhealthy whelp by Khytein standards. But she leaned back on her heels and swung that ungodly tonnage of sanctified stone like a ball on a length of chain, scattering fragments of stained glass, gargoyles, bricks and assorted carillon bells behind it. Once, twice, she spun the spire in a wide circle, and the whole city was silent as they watched its immense shadow flicker across the rooftops and cobbles.

Then she brought it down, the statue of Esau on his cross atop the spire first, like the largest battering ram in Sarem's history. The metal-clad steeple drove clear through the stout walls of the Citadel, sending men on the battlements flying like tiny dolls. Blocks of stone the size of cottages pulverized rows of shops and houses, and the disintegrating spire plowed on, collapsing whole floors of barracks and armouries behind it.

The rest was almost a formality.

On the southern flank of the city my second division marched resolutely into the waters of the Iceflood, building a ford of living bone. Siege ladders were carried across by the men of my Ontokhi rebel skirmishers, but when the defenders on the walls saw them raise the triple-crown banner of the old Tzars they did exactly what the garrison of Czanthe had done. Soon a score of Angan nobles kicked their heels on long ropes attached to the merlons, and those who had once stood ready to withstand a siege helped their attackers up and over the wall.

I brought the *Graveyard Ark* in over the burning remains of the Citadel just as the last defenses of the Inner Ward collapsed, and a churning mob of people – some looting, some drunken, some terrified, some weeping and praying or laden down with religious icons – burst into the narrow streets of the old town, followed by marching regiments of the dead.

So proud Almerre fell, taken by an army of darkness.

I entered the city in triumph as the sun set, a vast red cabochon seething on the horizon. The wall of unnatural cloud which had followed the *Graveyard Ark* wrapped the sky from the north all the way around to the east, and beneath its low ceiling rain hammered the plains. It was the perfect backdrop for my victory, and I dressed for added effect. After all, Makara may have been right. Dirge *may* have been watching. Even Elion Morekh, my master navigator and commander of the Ark, seemed to approve of my newfound sense of theatre. My raiment was certainly a far cry from the workaday black robe I had worn all through that long winter in Korisal.

The dead lined the streets for me, swords upraised at guard, and the people of Almerre overcame their fear long enough to decorate them with chains of paper and ribbons, little votive offerings of flowers and strings of beads. After all, my minions were as still and unmoving as statues, and it was they who had put out the fires which had spread through the lower city. Perhaps it was traumatizing to be rescued from a burning house by a grinning, fleshless skeleton. But I was willing to bet that *not* being rescued was more traumatizing still.

I landed before the gatehouse on draken-back, amid what was partway between a vigil, a religious rite and a carnival. The silver-barded undead beast stirred up a cloud of dust as it furled its wings, and people staggered back from the sudden rush of air... or more likely from the cold, hungry stare of its witchfire eyes. There were screams, but there were a fair few cheers as well, and not a little drunken bellowing of the old Ontokhi Tsarist Anthem.

Makara and Corvo landed on either side of me, their mounts just as vast, armoured and cold as my own. Then the three of us dismounted, and marched toward the ruined gates, the mob drawing back to allow us passage.

It was a strange procession. I led the way in my ornate black armour; a scale hauberk and finely wrought Korisali chestplate depicting the bones and muscles inside a human chest. A great black bearskin was my cape, clasped at the shoulders by brooches in the form of leering skulls, and my pauldrons were the baroque silverwork of old Ythe, swept up into wings with raven feathers worked in jet. I hid the mageblight beneath long black gloves, and my hair was, as ever, bound back by a silver band of thorns, my face masked by the grim warpaint of Anghul.

Corvo walked in all his priestly finery, and for all that it was apparent that he was grey and dead the people of Almerre bowed to him. After all, hadn't they seen the cathedral of Esau cast down? And now, who came to collect their tribute but the last acolyte of their old God, the Stormlord Auruvasz?

Makara was... Makara. Despite the fact that she was pale and beautiful, walking through a city full of drunken fighting men, not one dared to whistle or growl at her, or offer any ribald jest. Perhaps it was the fact that her form-fitting body-sheath of armour was still covered with dried blood.

None of us spoke as we walked through Brokeluck Town and Gallows Corner, past rows of hanging Anganesse gone black and purple, then past the crucified, some still alive and raving, others hacked to ruin by vengeful Ontohki swords. We reached the portcullis to the Inner Ward and saw how it had been torn from its arch of stone, cast down and trampled. Up the winding incline to the old city we went, and the air was filled with the sound of singing and prayers, weeping and the tolling of bells.

The great and the good of Almerre waited for us in the ceremonial court before the Citadel – now a ruin of toppled statuary and overflowing fountains. Behind them reared a cliff of masonry, intricately carved and inlaid by some of the finest artists ever to grace the Ontokhi capital. It was shattered as if by the blow of a giant's hammer, and twists of verdigris-green copper littered the ground. This was where Makara's thrown steeple had struck.

To their credit, the rulers of Almerre put on a brave face. They came in their finery, or such of it which had survived – the Council of Gold and Steel fussing in their merchant's robes of satin and velvet, the Arch-arbiter of the Judiciary, attended by a school of flitting black clerks in their severe black cassocks, and of course the supreme secular powers of Ontokh itself; the Lord Regent Vyrim Chaar, and the Angan Provincial Governor, Sinder's equal, Lord Balthus Schresse.

This last was all cold dignity in his overwrought Angan finery. But Chaar simply looked sick to his stomach, and the merchants had the look about them of fat hens who have seen the shadow of a fox outside their cozy little coop.

It was the Arbiter who spoke first, describing a courtly bow which almost saw his immense periwig topple from his head. Outlying clerks scuttled in to peel away his ermine-trimmed cloak as he stood, fixing me with a watery smile.

"Welcome, my Lord of the North. We have anticipated your arrival for some time, and...'

"Welcome?" erupted Balthus, the Angan, his face mottled white and red. "You actually WELCOME this... this *creature* who has defiled our..."

I only saw Vyrim Chaar's hand move out of the corner of my eye, but I knew from the look on his face an instant later that the mustachioed Ontokhi noble had pricked the Governor's side with a hidden dagger. He shut his mouth as beads of sweat broke on his brow.

"So sorry, dear guest," went on the Arbiter, in tones of oil and vinegar. "So much is lost in translation between the tongues of we northern tribes and the outlanders of the South." He fumbled in his robes for a pair of pince-nez spectacles, found them, and tightened them with a tiny brass clamp to the bulge of his impressive nose. "But cordial greetings aside, My Lord, we must also inquire why... that is to say, for what reason... you..."

The old judge's attempt to remain polite - while broaching the subject of an assault by thirty thousand dead men and as many stinking, drunken rebels - was torture in itself. Chaar rescued him.

"The chief hangman here wants to know why you've come knocking on our bloody castle doors with vast chunks of architecture," said the Ontokhi, twisting the knife-point into Schresse's side to elicit a whimpering little squeal. "That, and all those dead bastards out of the ground tends to make the judiciary a little worried. Around here, they've tucked quite a few evil sons of whores under the dirt, and they don't want them coming back for an appeal, y'see."

I decided I liked the Lord Regent. The merchants of the Council certainly didn't – they shrunk back, as though convinced that I was going to flay his flesh from his bones with a glance, and them soon after.

So I laughed.

Corvo joined in, hacking up dry, muffled spasms which counted as mirth from a dead man. Makara's cold lips twitched into a smile. And soon, with a kind of nervous, forced humor, the whole court were chuckling along with me. I stopped suddenly, pointing one black-nailed finger at Balthus Schresse.

"What exactly do *you* find so funny," I asked "About losing an entire principality of your empire? Would you care to let me in on the subtleties of the joke?"

Everyone else fell silent. I could clearly hear the click and ratchet of the wires between Makara's fingers as all of them held their breaths. But I'll give the pompous old Angan this much – he had more bravery between his legs than he had hairs left on his head.

"What's so funny? *You!* An upstart little barbarian, not much more than a boy... and you think that a few small victories will shake the foundations of Anganesse? Pah!"

Now the merchants were all trying to hide behind each other. Chaar spread his hands and backed away, showing that he did indeed have a glittering bootknife in his left.

"What our dear emissary *means* to say is..." began the Arbiter, but I held out a finger to silence him.

"No. Let the man finish. He has the right."

Schresse drew himself up to his full height, a blue-veined and trembling figure lost amid the geometric folds of his white robe.

"I knew what you were, and I knew you were coming. I was commanded to hold you here, by the power of Prelate Lothar and his chantry circle, and with the help of our *loyal allies.*" Here he cast a withering gaze across the assembled Ontokhi, and even I was forced to wince. "We have faced worse than you before, necromancer, and we have triumphed. What I hadn't expected was that you were just a beardless little boy!"

One of the merchants spoke up – a round-bellied man whose tabard bore the insignia of three crossed hammers.

"This *beardless little boy* took apart a whole legion of your faceless, Balthus! Why should we pay tribute to the Thearch if he can't protect us against wild children from the North?"

I felt that this lack of respect had gone on long enough. I remembered what Aerik had taught me long ago- that most sorcery is done in people's heads, and the vast bulk of it is done by the enchanted themselves.

"Silence!" I grated, and the Cold Voice convinced the fat old merchant that my claws were clenched deep in his chest. "I look down on you from nine hundred years of winter, from the cold memories locked in the heart of Sothara Roege, the Bone Collector. I have seen Urzen the Mad lying dead at my feet, and taken his forty centuries of arkane knowledge. Do you not think that a power such as I can appear as *anything I choose?*"

I used a whisper of Gernish Maudrin's hideous face-shifting illusion, then – a mental image of skin stretched tight and leathery across a dark-eyed skull, of twisting roots of mageblight advancing across cheekbones tattooed in writhing black...

The merchant sunk to his knees, clutching at his heart. I leered knowingly. And, amazingly, Balthus Schresse gave me a senatorial little nod of approval.

"Quite. Your conqueror answers you well, Olmaris. His power is an *anomaly*, and it falls upon us at a time when our dear Thearch is otherwise engaged, saving us all from Akhazi slavery. The Empire endures." he turned to me, all anger subsumed beneath an icy calm. "And I would remind you, Kuhal of the Clan Moer, that *Almerre is not Urexes*."

"Indeed it isn't," said Vyrim Chaar, sitting himself down on a broken statue of some martial saint. He uncorked a hitherto-hidden bottle of spiced liquor and took a long pull. "For one thing, we don't rape little bo..."

"Ahem!" coughed the Arbiter. "Perhaps we should move on the matter of *surrender*. There are precedents, you know!"

"Of course," said Balthus. "Then allow us to open with a most generous offer. If our young bonecaller here removes himself beyond the Hiledoran within a month, then we will only have to execute the traitors in Almerre's garrison, and this whole sordid business can be forgotten."

The Ontokhi were stunned into silence by the audacity of it. I, on the other hand, decided that I almost liked the pompous old Angan as much as I liked Chaar himself. At first I had thought this Provincial governor to be no match for Jerrold Sinder. But if they met in the debating chamber and not on the battlefield...

Chaar spat a mouthful of fiery spirits and offered the bottle to me with an expansive wave of his arms.

"Of course, you could always accept our backup plan. I'll gut the windy old Southman, and raise the banner of the triple crown over what's left of our bloody noble citadel."

"And who would stand in for the Tsar?" asked another of the Council of Gold and Steel, this one as tall and thin as Olmaris was short and fat. "This would seem a very convenient turn of events for the house of Chaar, in my opinion!"

"Well, it wasn't *my* great-grandfather who knifed poor old Adrei Idris, Gods rest his soul!"

"And it wasn't *my* family who made their fortune selling their swords to both sides in the wars which followed! I should..."

Makara silenced them all. There was a blur and jangle of music in the air as her wires unfurled, whipping through the air to ensnare each and every one of Almerre's rulers. Humming tension pricked tiny beads of blood from necks and wrists as she looked up at them, her eyes huge and dark.

"I say we should let the *people* decide," she said, in a voice so low and silky that every one of her captives had to strain to hear it. "These are fools, traitors, fops and failures, all of them. And as the dried-up old Angan said, Almerre is not Urexes. Let me have them, and this land will tear itself apart behind us."

Not one of them dared speak, or even move. Only Balthus Schresse met my eyes with any shred of defiance – he looked ready to die for his Thearch, then and there.

But martyrs are potent symbols. And all the stubborn idiocy in the world could not quite qualify him as truly evil.

"I am not here to loot. I am not here to rape, or plunder, or even to make a grand saga for my memory," I said. "I don't want any of the things which you will assure yourself that barbarians want – especially ale-swilling savages like my dear departed father. I am here to offer you *freedom*, because that is far more convenient to me than simply killing you all, man, woman and child."

I walked among them as I spoke, and only their eyes moved – every other muscle held taut as the wires which bound them.

"It's up to you what kind of freedom you make of it, because there are so very, very many kinds. Right now, it looks like you'll enjoy the utter, boundless freedom of a man swimming alone in the middle of the ocean. But the choice, of course, is yours."

I called out with my will, and a shadow fell over the courtyard. My undead draken had been perched on the triumphal arch to the west this whole time, and now it spread its ragged wings and extended its long armoured neck.

"Can you ride?" I asked Balthus Schresse. He nodded, making the wires cut into the wattles of his throat. But he also dared a tiny, imperious smile.

"I was taught, a long time ago, one of the most useful lessons of any barbarian warlord. *Always leave one alive to tell the world just how savage you are.* No sagas ever got sung about battles with no survivors." The great beast landed with a thump beside me, and I swung up into the saddle just as Makara let her wires fly loose, pulling them back between her fingers with a hiss like tearing silk. "So you'll give this man a horse - a fast one – and you'll tie him in the saddle and set it on the road south. I want Urexes to know what's coming. I want a battle you can really *sing* about, with a chorus you'll remember even after two barrels of ale."

Makara's mount and Corvo's alighted next to mine, and my companions climbed aboard, settling into the high-backed saddles of leather and ironwood. I turned to Vyrim Chaar, who was still sitting on his downed statue, a bottle of cinnamon fire-water in his hand.

"Raise the banner of your Tsar if you want to, Ontokhi," I said, as the great dead Draken pawed at the marble flagstones, chewing the bit between its dagger teeth. "But why raise it here in peace and quiet when you could raise it over the walls of Urexes? I'll be headed there next, and I hear there's a few good generations of Northern tribute to plunder back."

I didn't wait to hear his reply. Instead I sunk the spurs of my will into the Draken's mind, and all three beasts leaped skyward with a thunderclap of downdraft, knocking the assembled nobility of Almerre on their privileged arses in the dust.

Because Makara was right.

Time was growing short, and Urexes was our destination. There, all the plans of those who had sought to use me came together. And there, I swore, I would shear through the knot of their entanglement, once and for all.

"Nothing grows around the edges. And there's something burning down there - that smoke don't smell right. Nobody knows how the damned thing got there, neither... I suppose because if you'd been anywhere near it when it happened, you wouldn't be in any shape to be tellin' folks about it, would ya?"

Warden of the Desolation Harvel Szorn, on the
great crater known as the Hellmouth.

CITIES FELL.

Suluun with its sunken temples and its great crater lake. The red-stone walls of Eriyth. The tall spires of the monastic enclave at Yoru, where I left a generation of Esau's priests impaled, pages from holy books nailed to their eyeless faces…

The cold inside me deepened. I began to see death and horror as mere collateral, a necessary part of my advance. Subtleties – like the great auto-da-fe I arranged at Cyvenne – became more important to me than the sheer body count exacted. Terror flew before me, faster than Rain ever could, and my calculated cruelties made men tear down the white banners of Anganesse before I could see them flying over their holdfasts and hovels.

Other than such little diversions, the march south was pure hell.

Makara's presence tormented me. My hands were numb with cold and the blight. I could no longer sleep, and I spent whole days slumped on my throne of steel, ragged cape billowing out behind me like a thunderhead.

My horde crept across the land like a plague, crushing spring's harvest under tens of thousands of marching boots and creaking wagon wheels. The living trudged mile after mile at the same slow, relentlessly plodding pace as the dead, and from above the cloud of banners, pennants and standards lofted above the mass of warriors made the whole thing seem like some grim carnival – one which promised far more than just the usual curiosities and freaks.

After Almerre the Angan armies of the north were in full rout, and they stirred the countryside to panic as they raped and slew their way south, enacting what they thought was a terrible retribution on the land of Ontokh. Few of them realized that the very definition of terrible retribution was gliding silently through the skies behind them – at least until the *Graveyard Ark* hove into view on the horizon, dragging a cloak of sickly clouds behind it. Then, those Anganesse who failed to flee were cut down, rendered, boiled, resurrected and chained to my will. My army grew with every bloody victory.

No keels came. They were busy in the South, where all of Ghuram was now aflame, trying to stem the Akhazi tide. I often flew aloft in the mind of Rain, and I saw the terrible squat form of the Coldblood dragged inch by inch toward Urexes, leaving a trail of emaciated and broken slaves behind it. The Nine gave better fight than the Thearch's armies – I saw the aftermath of their assaults, the plains burned black with unnatural frost, the piles of human and saurian bodies crawling with flies… but the sheer power of the Coldblood and his sorcerous cadre drove them back. Even Dirge, I suppose, for some of the scenes of slaughter were on a scale which lesser demons could not conceivably have wrought.

We were all headed for the same destination. Urexes the proud, capital of the White Empire, the many-spired city on its arch of pale stone… a city where the dead slaved beneath the marble streets, and a tortured God bled power into the world for men like Jerrold Sinder. If the Coldblood reached those glittering towers first, he would have the power to unlock the Outer Dark. And if I was triumphant? I supposed that I would have to take my revenge, for the father I barely knew and the nation I hardly mourned - but mainly for Makara. Having her stand next to me all those long miles, cold and empty as a statue… it filled me with a terrible ache for what could have been.

Many times I let my mind fall into the Cerebrex, and watched from outside a memory I longed to erase. It was a single night, on a barge which stank of death and hopelessness, traveling under a sickle moon toward Sothara's city of tombs…

I knew that I could have that night again, deep in the heart of the Cerebrex, in the encysted ball of tissue which held Makara's mind. But I knew with equal certainty that to give in once would make me an addict. And that the dark-haired girl with the jade-green eyes in that memory was just as dead as the monster who had walked into the pyre at Cyvenne, to bring me the still-burning head of the Angan master-at-arms, fingers twined in his smoking hair.

If I reached Urexes before the Coldblood did, I swore that I'd release

Esau from his torment, and send him back into the Unmanifest. But I'd only let the martyred God go if he agreed to take Makara's soul with him. That much she surely deserved, even if the thing she had become... well, she was no more or less a monster than I was, by then.

And that was the truth of it. We shared this one thing, in spite of the love and intimacy we could never have. We plucked hearts and heads for each other like other lovers plucked flowers. We gave each other burning tower-holds and towns as trysting trinkets. And I found a heat beyond the cold in my heart – a brittle, ice-blue flame kindled by my desire. We turned our mutual and frustrated lust to carnage, and promised each other – in the soul-deep embrace of the Cerebrex – that the slow dismemberment of Dirge would be our night of wedded bliss.

Three weeks out of Almerre I finally collapsed into a fitful sleep, after pacing the decks in the dark, listening to the creak and groan of the Ark around me.

I found myself back beneath my Father's hut of idols, with shafts of dusty summer light stabbing down all around me. This time I wasn't a nine-year-old child, and my brother Rordan was nowhere to be seen. But Sei was there, curled up on my chest, once again a ragged bundle of fur and bone. Out of the corner of my eye I could see the steel-masked carving which had leered down at me on that long-ago day, its inset human teeth all yellow and cracked.

I tried to move, but I couldn't. Despite his size, the little dead cat weighed as much as worlds, and his eyes were hypnotic sparks of amber.

"You're going to think this is just a part of your poor mageblighted mind talking to you," said Sei, lazily kneading my chest with his claws. I looked down at the cat as best I could, and noticed that I was wearing the white woolen sacrificial robes of Winter's King. "Or perhaps something out of that cobbled-together Cerebrex you've made. It scarcely matters, really. All that's important is that you *listen*."

Sei's voice was unmistakably that of Aerik Stormsong. He had my undivided attention.

"When you get to Urexes – and we have every faith that you will – you'll find Esau in the place they call the Capitoline Deep. It's under the palace arch, right beneath the Thearch's throne. Your power won't work there, such as it is... and if we're right about it..."

"If we're right about you *at all*, you don't want to be just cutting the poor doomed little godling down from his killing tree. There'll be feedback. Nasty. You might end up feeding him to those things in the Outer Dark after all."

This voice belonged to Gernish Maudrin – bellicose and rough as ever, elbowing Aerik out of his way. The thought of the two of them sharing the inside of a dead cat's skull for all eternity brought a smile to my dreaming lips.

"You'll have to kill him with your own hands. Collapse him back into the Shard he came from. But lad... it will take all of your strength."

"ALL of your strength," said Aerik, and there was a grim undertone to his voice. "We won't lie to you. Not after all you've been through. This is the part which you were never meant to survive."

Sei's eyes were as deep as the void between the stars, and the little amber lights inside flared bright. I heard the sound of wood scraping on wood, and through the knothole in the floor above me I saw the idol move. It revolved slowly on its base until its eyes bored into mine, and its mouth seemed to stretch, in a grin wide enough to unhinge the top of its head...

"Wait!" I shouted, as I felt the dream collapsing around me. "There must be something I can do! Makara – can he take her with him? Is there..."

My eyes snapped open in the dark, and I found myself laid out on my pallet bed, still clad in my armour and cloak. Something gnarled and slippery flickered away from the grasping fingers of my consciousness, down into the depths of the great Cerebrex which hung in the air at my bedside, sizzling gently.

Then came a flat, bright burst of light, and the Keel lurched in the air. I flung myself from the bed and upright, staggering to the doorway and bracing myself across the frame with both arms.

There, again – a titanic burst of power, painting the whole world monochrome. I could feel the dead souls in the Keel's ossuaries shrinking back from it, holding on to reality as the detonation of raw magik punched holes through the world.

"Elion!" I shouted. "Makara! Corvo! Are we under attack?"

There was no answer. My Soultaken were nowhere to be felt, no matter where I searched. I reeled down the corridor and flung open the locks to the Keel's upper deck just as a third flash split the night. This time I saw from whence it came.

We were riding at anchor north of Urexes, above the low foothills of the Arem Sidhar. The tallest spires of the Angan capital were still far over the horizon, but I was certain that this was where the detonations of power were coming from – I saw one build and weave with my own eyes, meshing together into a geometric tangle of glittering silver and blue.

This was the work of the Grand Chantry; city-breaking sorcery on a scale to dwarf any other I had seen. Shafts and skeins of killing light leaped upward into the vault of heaven, where they formed great spheres and astrolabes of runes, condensing tighter, shell on shell, until they were nothing but a pinpoint high over the Angan city. Then some commanding intellect chose its target, and the pinpoint became a jagged crack across the night, searing white, leaving an after-image behind it as it fell in a great curving arc.

When it struck, the earth convulsed. A shockwave of sorcerous energy went racing out, creating that star-burst flash. And now...

"Mage war," said Corvo, appearing at my side. These were the first two words the old man had spoken to me since his forced resurrection, and they echoed in my mind, without his ever having to move his mummified lips. "The Coldblood endures, however. And now we will see its counter-gambit."

"It endured *that?*" I asked, incredulous. "How in the world could anything..."

This time the Keel didn't just stagger in the air. We dropped for a heart-stopping second or two, and I was forced to take hold of a twist of rope to avoid being flung over the side. But I still saw the great deaths-head burst of ruby-red which lit up the southern horizon – a roiling, angry bubble of force skinned over with lightning. It downshifted to purple, and then deep blue as the air-shock raced away from Urexes, but even here, so far to the north we felt the furnace-blast wind of the shockwave passing over us.

"Ahhhh..." chuckled the old Ontokhi. "The towers fall. I can feel those pious Angan fools burning! But our Akhazi friends have over-reached themselves..."

I am no skryer. Binding the dead is my power, and it is one which the other Gods shun. I cannot see the future.

But even I knew that what was coming next would make the previous assaults seem like childrens' fireworks.

"Bring her up! Ricketts, Elion, get this Keel moving! We have to ride before the..."

They must have managed. They simply *must* have, for I am here to recount this sorry tale today, and able to remember quite clearly what happened next.

This time the power didn't come from the spires of imperial Urexes, where even now the chantry halls were thick with the smoke of burning hair and flesh. This time it came from beneath the earth. I felt it swim below us in deep seas of lava – a living incantation crafted by a being far older than humanity.

A pillar of orange fire reared up against the stars to the south. It was the trunk of a tree of flame; a rod of pure force slammed up from the core of Sarem, where the Shards of the divine shattered the world and heated stone to incandescence. We were miles away, and I still felt the raving, unquenchable heat of it. A plug of rock – part of the Urexian plain itself – rode atop the fountain of lava for a handful of heartbeats before it turned ponderously in the upper air and began to fall.

So slow. So *very* slow. It must have been the size of the Angan capital itself, that slab of tumbling stone, but it flipped like a coin from a gambler's thumb. And then it slammed down again – upside down, its surface glowing sullen red.

A wall of dust and topsoil, flaming trees and fragments of farmsteads flew out before the blast. Cracks ramified through the ground, through the hills below us, and boulders tore loose, tumbling down into the valleys.

Then the air-shock hit us, and I was knocked reeling, darkness blooming silently inside my head. My arm, tangled in that trailing rope, was all that kept me from being plucked from the deck by the gale of hot earth, gravel, dust and smoke. We spun wildly, until finally Elion Morekh and his deathless crew regained control.

As for my poor landbound armies...

"The Archaeon has played its hand, then." said Corvo, still standing in the same spot, hunched in his feather cloak. "But to little avail. The Coldblood lives. It has been weakened... but it lives."

I could do little but croak obscenities in return. The enormity of what had just happened was one thing – it left me feeling weak and sick, kneeling on the deck of the Ark and shaking. But that the Coldblood had survived... that was truly chilling. And what of its armies? What of those loathsome, lumbering saurian beasts, the high-stepping mounts of the Akhazi lancers, the numberless hordes of warriors in their scale armour and bright feathers?

"All it's done is buy us time," leered Corvo, stumping away toward the bows, hunched against his staff. "There are more Akhazi where those came from. Look to your own armies, great Warlock – you'll be needing them."

He was right, damn him. We were three days march from the walls of Urexes, and the horde I dragged in my wake was now at least three hundred thousand strong, not counting all the human flotsam and wreckage it drew along behind it. Now the whole seething mass encamped below me was in panic, tents collapsed, wagons overturned... a wailing, cursing throng beneath a gentle rain of ashes.

I sighed. The living were such *children*.

With a thought I called the Cerebrex to me, and at my touch tens of thousands of pale, fleshless warriors rose from were they had fallen. Runes carved into bone flashed sickly green, and sparks kindled deep in countless empty eye sockets.

It was time to regain some measure of discipline. It was time to reassure my mortal commanders that my power was equal to any pyrotechnic excess cooked up by a desperate enemy.

Most importantly, it was time to convince *myself*.

Because, in three days time, we would assault that source of killing power head-on.

The Battle of Urexes -

One of the least understood, most lauded, most reviled, most oft-falsified and almost eternally recounted clashes in military history. Of records, troop dispositions, orders, tactics and over-arching strategies we have none. But of drunken ale-house stories, usually professed by madmen missing various bodily members, we have a great surfeit.

All we know is this - the ale-sodden veterans who claim to have fought beneath the walls of Urexes are lying. Because we do have one statistic which puts the whole sorry exercise into perspective.

Casualties, alas, were absolute.

The Ghuram scholar Parmar Jihani, Lord Tactical of the School of Light and Shadow, the Kalif's military academy.

THEY CAME WITH their Keels in the grey hour before dawn – when the short scrub-grass of the Urexian plain still glistened with dew, and the sun had not yet broached the eastern horizon. Only five, out of the grand fleet of thirty-three commissioned by Thearch Osiryan Trasse – but five were all that remained, the rest wrecked, ruined, broken and obliterated by the machinations of myself and the Coldblood.

They came with their Keels, stripped and rigged for a kind of battle they had never been built to face. Not the crushing power of Angan 'diplomacy' - not this time. The wolf-muzzle guns stacked in battery at the bow of each flying stone fortress spelled out their intent... victory through sheer excess of firepower.

I was ready and waiting for them.

Rain had been aloft since the constellation of the Harvestman had sunk beneath the western hills, and his bright eyes had seen the huge shapes rise up from behind the walls of Urexes, buoyed up by the pillars of choking, underlit smoke which roiled from the city's foundries.

Five against one. The badly damaged *Shroud* took the left flank, while the ancient, three-century old relic *Glory Arisen* rode high on the right, smaller and less heavily armed than her sister ships. But the core of the Angan formation was formidable indeed – two great Keels of the line, the *Invictus* and the *Intrepid,* each one the equal of my own stolen stoneship. My beautiful Ark had once been the possession of a Pontifex of Anganesse, after all, and these two grim arrowheads of stone would well befit a man of Sinder's stature.

The last of them was the greatest. It held the centre like a cruising leviathene trailed by sharks; an impossible mountain of granite and steel sliding through the air like a knife.

This was the Thearch's Own, the greatest show of sorcerous and temporal power in Sarem – almost an equal in its bulk and wondrous terror to the grand palanquin of the Coldblood.

Osiryan Trasse would not be on board – he was an ancient, if my sources were to be believed, a withered thing kept alive by decoctions of Esau's living blood. But the Keel which bore his banner of an eagle-winged wolf was perhaps a more potent symbol of strength than even he himself; three times the length of the *Graveyard Ark*, the *Redemptor* boasted not one central castle-keep but a whole layered ziggurat of fortifications, and the ossuary well at its heart could have swallowed my home village whole.

They came riding against the wind, flying into the unnatural storm which powered the *Graveyard Ark* with banners and pennants cracking. The first flash of sunlight caught the glass and copper of their great ossuaries as they came, and glinted from the metal of their guns. I could make out the tiny figures of men standing at their posts, and behind them the massed ranks of soldiers who would try to board us, should the cannonade fail.

"Elion," I said, reaching out to my left to grasp the Faeroan's cold, dead arm. "Do you think we can get past them? Or will we have to pick them off one by one?"

I was musing to myself, really – my undead captain hadn't spoken a word since the night I had brought him back to the mortal realm. But he surprised me, drawing the serrated dagger from his belt and holding it up to catch the light. For an instant I feared that the spells which bound him had failed, and that he would try to plunge it into my chest. But then he drew the cruel steel across the stitches which held his lips shut, parting them one by one.

"If it has sails," he soughed, dark eyes twinkling with a measure of his old vitality. "I can make the bastard *dance*, Warlock."

I grinned, reckless and foolish and feeling every one of my seventeen years old. Was I naïve enough to believe that this was just some saga-song adventure – that my destiny was only to craft a beautiful, poetic revenge? Perhaps. For at that moment the sun crested the horizon, and the city of Urexes was laid out before me, all stark and monochrome, hashed out in monolithic lines of light and shadow.

Once, it had been an island. Once, when the Shallow Sea had been a true ocean, waves had crashed against this thousand-span arch of stone, and on the gnarled teeth of pale rock which thrust up from the deep around it. When the sea fell it left the vast, fertile Urexian Plain, and the arch itself high and dry. Men had lived here since the days when we were all just wandering tribes, huddling in caves for shelter and wearing the skins of animals for warmth.

But it was the Anganesse who had made this natural wonder into a place of awe and power. They had carved the arch itself into a religious symbol; a model of the world supporting citadels, cathedral towers, domes, temples, armouries and palaces. The two ends of the arch were fashioned into clusters of robed and crowned statues – the rulers of the old empire, sages and warlords. There were six supporting the southern end, and ten the northern – though the tenth figure was by far and away larger than the rest, a muscled titan in armour, depicted holding the curve of the arch's central span over his head by brute force. His face was that of Esau, serene and haloed, though his raiment and weapons were clearly much older than the Martyred God's reign here. The arch itself was carved with a map of the heavens – planets, constellations and moons wrought in immense scale. And all through this colossal statuary, throwing its titanic size into dizzying perspective...

There were *windows* in the folds of those great robes. There were balconies and stairs cut into the arms and faces of each vast statue, and in the vault of heaven carved in stone between them. The mansions and towers of Urexes rose to knee-height around them, like surf foaming about the legs of fishermen, and those lesser pinnacles of rock, girding the great central arch, had been linked by a tall, thick curtain wall, its entire surface sheathed in gleaming bronze. Beaten murals depicting the three thousand and thirty-three parables of Esau faced out onto the plain, and atop the walls countless towers bristled with seige engines and bonepowder bombards, as well as huge wheel-and-cross icons of gold and copper, agumenting the city's sorcerous defenses.

This was the prize. This, and the great many-domed palace at the northern end of the arch itself – the seat of the Thearch.

I had been preparing for this day for more than a year now. Others had been sharpening me up for this moment for even longer. And if I survived, I told myself, I may even find it in what was left of my heart to forgive them.

"Let us dance, then," I said, gripping Elion's forearm tight. "Sound the drums! Sound the Horns! Let my legions form up and await my order. We go first to clear the path!"

From behind me, on the open decks of the Graveyard ark, the drums began to sound. I had a surplus of human skin with which to build them, but none consecrated with the blue spiral tattoos of the Touched. Instead they were immense wide-bellied kettles stretched tight with cow-hide, and their sonorous pulse played counterpoint to a chorus of horns - long draken-horns and brazen trumpets, skirling pipes and bellowing ox-horn drones.

On the ground below, the sound of a similar hell-chorus answered me. The dawn light showed the whole Urexian Plain moving, seething with marching soldiery in their motley armour, banners raised high and hulking engines of war creaking along behind them.

This was what two hundred thousand dead men looked like when they went to war. They were clad in scraps of mail, fragments of plate, boiled leather and spiked copper, pauldrons of ornate brass and bronze, half-helms from Ghuram with leering demon faces inset in jet and ivory, old Khytein iron from the days of Sothara himself, and Korisali steel even older. In the neural web of the Cerebrex I had organized them into units, ranks, phalanxes and battalions – based almost entirely upon which rusted, bent or scavenged weapons they carried. Perhaps they had their own preferences. Perhaps they had borne such instruments of war when they were alive.

All I knew was that the front ranks were made up of square formations of heavy-shielded hoplites, their spears, pikes and halberds sharp. Following them came a heaving mass of infantry – the rank and file of the dead, holding a rusty scrap-yard's worth of axes, maces, swords, sickles, bardiches and clubs at guard.

The dead made poor archers, and worse horsemen – find me a mount which will tolerate being ridden by a wight or a ghoul, and I'll show you a horse which has long gone insane. So these positions in my order of battle were taken by the living – Rasuuli and Ontokhi bowmen, rowdy lancers and skittish ranks of horse-archers, to the rear and flanks of my undead force respectively.

Makara led the dead on the ground. I planned to join her as soon as we dispensed with the Thearch's keels. And the living – those mad, drunken bandits and nobles sharing firewater and preening their long mustachios – they were led by Vyrim Chaar, who could no more resist the temptation of plundering Urexes than a fly could resist a fat ripe turd.

The Nameless were there in the back of my mind. They would come, and their master with them – of that I was certain. Corvo hadn't spoken to me since the night of the great cataclysm, but I knew he sensed it, too; if such an excess of power hadn't killed the Coldblood, then it could not have stopped Dirge, either.

As for the Akhazi themselves, they dared not advance without their hulking demigod. Rain could fly no nearer to the site of the Archaeon's great working than I could – the Coldblood and his cadre had woven the smoke of that mighty conflagration into a seething wall, behind which they and their army gathered their strength. It covered a hand's-span of the southern horizon, even from here.

Clearly, the Anganesse had decided to divide and conquer. First crush the upstart warlock from the North, then launch an all-out assault against the Akhazi, pushing them back through Ghuram and out of Sarem altogether.

I was most enthusiastic to ruin their plans.

"Release the Draken! Elion, keep out of range of the *Redemptor*'s guns, and focus all fire on the *Shroud*. We'll take out the weakest link in this chain first."

The grey-faced captain simply nodded, but I noted, as I swung down from my throne and took up my new helm and sword, that he had procured from somewhere an entirely new tricorne hat. It sat atop his lumpen, stitch-crazed head at a rakish angle, feathers whipping back in the breeze.

I strode across the deck, pushing undead sailors and crewmen gently aside with my will. Then on to the Draken pens, where my mount awaited, two skeletal Skyborn holding its chain halter and saddle-step. The immense creature huffed and snapped as I swung up and aboard, checking the leather belts which held my wargear tight.

One final thing – the helm I had forged, deep in Urzen's foundries during that long, cold winter. I slid it over my head and felt the cunning clasps I'd wrought click into place, narrowing my vision down to a t-shaped slit. But something else unfurled inside the layered steel, bone and brass as I took the draken's reins – the vast spiderweb burn of the Cerebrex, tethered to my mind through the circlet of silver thorns bound into the helm. With this, I would not need to carry the great sphere of gold and iron into battle – it could remain here, in the relative safety of the Keel's heart.

Ahh, yes. *Relative* safety, indeed.

Both Elion and I had misjudged the range of the *Redemptor*'s great seige-cannons. They spoke in the same instant that I leaped from the deck, twin thunderclaps pealing almost in unison. Dear Gods, the *size* of those things! A whole mortuary full of sinners must have gone into each bonepowder shell, and the cannonballs they fired were runic chain-shot – mast-snapping munitions which spun across the sky screaming.

My Faeroan captain was as good as his word, though. I plunged down toward the plain with my wing of undead draken, looking back to where I was sure I would soon hear the crack and snap of shearing timber. But instead the whole ponderous hulk of the Ark came around, neat as a smuggler's skiff before a storm-wind, and the two great spinning chains did no more than gouge furrows from her iron-clad belly.

A whole cloud of new sail had been ready and waiting. Cut loose at Elion's command it transformed the slow, ponderous Ark into an arrowhead beneath a storm of black canvas. Vast sections of the machinery beneath fell away, lightening the load.

Then I could look no more, because the ground was rushing up at me fast. I hauled back on the reins and cast out my will, arresting the other draken in mid-stoop, flaring their ragged wings wide to skim above a thicket of spears and pikes.

They shouldn't have been able to fly. Not now, with their immense wings torn and tattered, their great muscles reduced to sinewy strands over gleaming bone. But a feral, wild hunger burned in the Draken, a sensation my human mind dared not touch, even with them enslaved to my will. It skinned them over with seething witchfire and they turned, graceful as swallows, to arrow up again, up toward the crippled war-Keel *Shroud*.

Hell rained down on us from above as the horns rang out again below. I saw faces contorted with fear and hatred at every window and merlon across the mass of the burned Keel, archers and crossbowmen letting fly, while others hurled urns of burning pitch, rocks, cannonballs and even chamber-pots full of filth. We came up on them hard, and my Draken flew through the storm untroubled, great wings beating the cold, thin air. Then we wheeled and skimmed sideways along the *Shroud's* flank, keeping below the level of the decks, and the carnage started.

The fire of undead Draken is not like the white-hot chemical flame of their living kin. Much dire arkane research had gone into re-kindling the fury in the bellies of my pets, and what spewed from between their jaws now was more akin to the pale blue fire of the Eyeless... focused, hot and unquenchable.

It melted steel like wax. And as for flesh...

Twelve lances of blue death quartered the side of the *Shroud*, re-opening cracks in the stone which had been hammered shut with metal staples and plates. This war-Keel had seen action against the Akhazi, and one of their terrible sorcerous weapons had all but clawed it from the sky in pieces. Now my draken came to finish the job.

From bow to stern we went, leaving a cloud of ashes and greasy smoke behind us. Inside the Keel men were roasted alive, screaming and burning, some throwing themselves from its windows on fire as they tried to escape the flames. We described a tight loop around the underslung chantry towers, then we sped up the rear slope of the Keel, putting its bulk between us and what I knew was coming.

Elion had been right.

This was his moment – his battle – and though he would go down in history as a monster, a dead thing with a crew of skeletal ghouls, he would at least be *remembered*.. Years later I'd hear tales of the Ghost Captain, who rode the night sky in a ship of bones, and I would see his grinning, stitch-scarred face in my mind.

The *Graveyard Ark* effortlessly outflanked the *Shroud*, coming up and under the doomed Keel on the line my ravening of draken had just followed. A panicked stutter of gunfire lanced out from the Angan's batteries, but it was too little, and far too late. Many of the gun crews had died at their posts, incinerated. And far too many of the Keel's bonepowder cannon had been moved to the bows, anticipating a slow and wallowing foe.

Orduvis and his crew of skeletal gunners made them pay. The iron hatches clanged back in unison all down the flank of my Ark, and wolf-muzzled murder-guns ran out to the thud and pound of the drums. Through the helm, to the Cerebrex, to Elion, to Orduvis and into the minds of two hundred fleshless, grinning artillerymen... I gave the order.

And the weakened *Shroud* was torn apart.

What the Akhazi had begun, their broadside finished. It slapped the entire Keel sideways in the air, shearing off towers and shattering stone, opening vast heat-stress cracks all the way through to the ossuary well itself. When the runic stone circle of the well was shattered, it was over. A silent burst of green fire boiled up from above and below the disintegrating Keel, and it split in half, the front spinning down like a sycamore seed to glance off the bulk of its sister Keel *Invictus* before crashing to the plain. The heavy, fortified rear simply dropped from the air as dead weight.

Screams rang out where it struck the empty plain. A heat-haze shimmer rippled out from where the vast ruin of stone carved out its impact crater. And all across the beaten-bronze walls of Urexes I caught a glimpse of glassy shadows moving, rainbows hues twisting like oil on water...

"Makara!" I managed, fighting blackout as the draken spun into a sharp and savage turn. "They're not inside the walls! They've come to..."

And then something blotted out the light with a great unfurling of wings, and earth and sky began to tumble over and over.

Darkness bloomed behind my eyes, and my head slammed against the back of my helm, crazing the witchfire threads of the Cerebrex. Through a haze of pain I saw what had attacked us – a woman all in black, hunched and feral in form-fitting leather, with thousands of colourful ribbons streaming back from a galaxy of bright piercing rings. Her face was beautiful and empty, her eyes blazing white, but her hands and feet were nothing but steel hooks, metal bolted to still-bleeding stumps, and from her shoulders grew a pair of impossible wings – vast, glittering pinions as wide as those of my draken mount. Each feather was a slim, curved knifeblade.

Right now, those serrated hand-hooks were punctured through the chest of my draken, and streamers of blue fire seethed out around them, wisping away in our slipstream. The beast snapped at its attacker as we spun out of control, but to no avail – she blocked its serpent neck with the curve of those nightmare wings, and all it could do was lacerate its mummified lips against the blades.

I was stuck in the saddle. Panic hashed my will to ruin, and I could only look behind me as the upper decks of the *Invictus* spiraled in, growing larger and larger...

Sei snapped me out of my death-trance. The little dead cat bit down hard on the leather mantle between my helm and my cuirass, and his needle teeth drew blood. It was enough to shock me into action.

An instant before the Nameless demoness – Sister Pain, the Angel of Carnage – drove us both clear through a tiered terrace of towers and galleries, I reached out with my will and tugged at the minds of two of my other draken, furling their wings in tight to their sides and letting them fall.

She turned, hissing, on the first as it rushed past, loosening one of her hooks to score a deep gash through its belly-muscles and scutes. But this turned her back on the second, and its jaws snapped shut around her body with an audible crunch, ripping her away into the sky.

There was no time for my mount to recover. But it did manage to twist in the air so that I wasn't crushed beneath it on impact. It was a small blessing.

Leather straps snapped and sheared as we bounced and rolled down the stepped side of the Keel's central fortress. Bones broke, and membranous wings tore, but all through the grinding, crashing plunge I managed to remain unhurt. At last the wreck of my noble beast came to rest on the deck of the *Invictus*, thrashing weakly with blue fire dripping from between its jaws. I was flat on my back, breathing heavily inside my hollow helm, and I knew that any moment now the Angan crew would overcome their fear and close in to finish the job.

I can't say that it didn't hurt. But then again, I have always found that a pain shared with one's enemies is a pain far more than halved...

I called out to Sei with my mind, and found him – a slippery, arrowhead-shaped little ball of fury and instinct in the Dark Sight. Now it was time for what we had practiced so many times in the depths of Urzen's forge-halls. I only prayed that my studies had been thorough enough. One mis-spelled engraving, and...

But there was no time for hesitation. I felt Sei slither back into his rabbit-skin pouch, and my armoured fingers deftly plucked his skull from amid the tangle of bones, socketing it into a hollow in my chestplate. It snicked into place between the strakes of steel and bone like a heart behind the bars of a ribcage, and it brought my armour to life.

Sothara's attempt at creating what the Korisali Guild of Artifice called *Azhem-Ghuulan* had been crude and barbaric. I knew that now. The Pale Armour had been nothing but copper wire and the bones of murdered gladiators, hung with charm-stones and bronze totem rings to bind it together. I had tried to surpass the old monster, even while he mocked me from inside my own head – my armour was a suit of ornate plate found deep in Urzen's storehouses, bound with runes by a demoness of the Nameless, and inset with sigil-etched bone taken from hulking Ironhands and Drudges.

But for speed and savagery, I had added my own peculiar twist. Now my every nerve sparked and seethed with barely suppressed energy. My vision narrowed behind the slit mask of my helm, and colour bled out of the world. As a circle of Angan spear-points formed up around me, I let Sei's sharp, instinctive mind take over.

It was a beautiful thing. It was a *dance*, and the poetry of it almost erased the horror.

I spun to my feet with my sword already heavy in my hand, and a circle of Angan soldiers were lopped off at the knee, howling in sudden pain. Up, and I sheared through the spears of the second rank, resisting the urge to use claws I didn't have. Instead I swung the blade in great reaping arcs; a broadsword in the Ontokhi style, twin-edged and as wide as two open palms, made to be wielded double-handed from horseback. I gripped it in my left as I rushed the horrified Angans, and my right was free to weave power, the thick, sweet death-energy which boiled up all around me as I slew.

An axeman swung at me, teeth gritted, eyes wide and mad – I took him across the chest, shearing him in half, and I drove the pain of his demise into the mind of the spearman who came charging in behind me, bursting some vital vessel in his brain. A twitch of the fingers and he rose, spear blurring to impale one of his comrades before he, too, was hacked down. Three more white-clad soldiers tried to hem me in with shields, but I simply leaped over them, rolling as I landed, sword licking out left and right... They fell, butchered, bleeding and gurgling their last breaths. And now I was at the foot of the Keel's central tower. Now I was atop the first tier wall, vaulting ten spans in a single impossible leap.

That, I hadn't expected. Sei took it in my stride for me.

Crossbowmen loosed their quarrels, panicked, close enough that

I could smell the stink of fear and sweat on them – but the iron barbs couldn't penetrate the layers of bone and steel which wrapped me in their embrace. My blade unspliced them, dripping red.

Black shadows whipped past, spitting flashes of fierce blue – my draken, avenging their fallen brother. I watched as one of the siege-platforms above me rattled around on great wooden cogs, frantic men atop it winding back the crank of a vast ballista. An undead draken sliced through the smoky air above them and they let fly, piercing its chest with a harpoon on a length of chain.

I took another leap closer, preparing to smash the great engine to kindling, but the Angans had underestimated their prey. The draken reached the full run of the chain and turned, dropping below the Keel – it likely didn't even feel the five-span barb sunk through its flesh. But the siege-gunners felt the pull of all that flying weight. The entire wooden platform they were on lurched as bolts sheared and greasy wooden gears snapped. Then they were ripped away from the Keel, holding on to their weapon and screaming.

The draken performed a loop, coming up on the leeward side of the Keel, and the luckless ballista-crew were thrown out into space as the chain jerked taut. Then it ripped clear across the deck at neck-height, gathering up a harvest of southmen to send them plummeting to the ground below. The draken reared back its head and bit through the chain just as the swinging platform smashed against the Keel's belly, leaving the metal harpoon deep in the muscle of its shoulder.

I felt a sudden surge of pride – a savage feeling which may have been more Sei's than mine. Even a creature as proud as a cat respects a display of such elegant predation.

But then the draken staggered in the air. A blur of glittering silver and black whispered past it, and one of its wings was torn bodily from its flank, with a sound like a knife through wet leather. The beast twisted and snapped, but its other wing was sheared off a heartbeat later, and as it fell from the sky...

Sister Pain came up on the falling draken in a spiral, her wings formed into a sweeping teardrop all bristling with razors. The doomed creature was torn to ribbons as she powered clear through it, and it was only Sei's keen reflexes which saved me a similar fate.

The harpoon threw a shower of sparks as its flared head scraped across my cheek, scoring steel and bone. If I hadn't twitched left at just that moment, it would have pinned me bloody to the wall.

"Ahhh, a slippery one! How delightful! My lord Dirge was right about you, warlock. You will make good sport before you die!"

The Nameless One's voice was a sibilant rasp, like a whisper from behind me. But the demoness herself alighted atop the highest turret of the Invictus, her steel-blade feet making two tiny sharp noises on the stone. Her hook hands slithered together in gleeful anticipation.

"Did Dirge tell you the rest, Sli'shandara Istivaari? Did he tell you that I have studied the black scrolls of Urzen, and that I know your True Name?"

There was one Angan crossbowman atop the tower with Sister Pain, and his hands were shaking as he brought his weapon to bear on the black-clad Nameless. No doubt he would have stuttered out a prayer to Esau if she had not casually flicked out one of her hooks, taking him through the cheek and gaffing him like a salmon.

"You think *that* gives you power over me, here and now?" laughed Sli'shandara Istivaari, once high priestess of Asuraa, sister of Erys and goddess of the dark of the moon. "Perhaps, if my sweet lord Dirge were dead and gone. Perhaps then I would show you the nature of... *submission*." She paused to bring her other hook around in a blur, ripping apart her captive's skull like a ball of wet paper. "But what you know is immaterial, Kuhal Moer. We know *your* true name as well, and now we want to see the colour of your marrow!"

She leaped to the attack, wings swept wide, knifeblade feathers driven before her in a storm. Sister Pain, the Angel of Carnage, a thing which had devoured the souls and shredded the flesh of countless thousands...

But she was wrong.

What I knew meant *everything*.

I met her onrushing assault with the flat of my blade, and it caught her clean across the jaw, flattening out the side of her skull with a hideous wet cracking sound. Then, rather than trying to vainly shield myself from the slicing blades of her pinions, I came in close, wrapping my armoured fingers tight around the juncture between wings and shoulders. Unnatural, spliced muscle writhed in my grip, and I brought my helm up close to the creature's snarling face, as intimate as a lover.

"You were always just a *test*, Sli'shandara. He says so in the Tomes of Making. The Devouring Wind was the final perfection of what you were supposed to be, and Urzen kept you only because he enjoyed your cruelties."

I felt bone and muscle creaking as Sister Pain's hooks scrabbled and thrashed at my back. The runes etched into my armour glowed red-hot, and bone began to smoke as I pushed the bindings to their limit.

"Damn you, Khytein! Dirge will eat your soul!"

"Look around you, priestess. I'm damned already. But *you're* the one who's about to die."

I made sure that the Angans were watching. I held the Nameless aloft, smoke wreathing my skull-faced helm in a choking cloud.

And I tore the wings from Sister Pain, drawing out thick, barbed strands of segmented metal from deep in her chest. Black, clotted foulness spewed from the wounds as she screamed, and her hooks beat out a frantic tattoo against my back.

"I commend you to your goddess, fallen one," I whispered, seeing for an awful moment a glimpse of the poor, abused human being who had been wrought into such a monster. And perhaps, too, a little of myself. "Be assured that Dirge will follow."

Then I turned, gripping the demoness in a one-handed stranglehold, and cast her down into the ossuary well of the *Invictus*.

It was pure theatre. It was awe and grandiosity.

It was also *exceedingly* stupid.

The detonation threw me from the walkway between the Keel's towers, and I only just managed to catch the edge of the stone parapet with my fingers. Behind me, my sword tumbled end over end into an ice-green maelstrom, flashing to molten steel before the witchfire devoured it.

Pieces of the *Invictus* blew out below it in a rain of stone and metal. Gutted, it spun in the air, shedding turrets and statues, a shower of shattered stained glass from its chapels...

And then its wide-swinging stern came about hard, and I saw exactly what would happen next. I looked down past my feet, and as the tilt of the stricken Keel threw them out and away from the seething well I decided it was as good a time as any to let go.

I saw the impact as I fell, helpless in the clutch of gravity.

The *Invictus* swung stern-first into the side of the mighty *Redemptor*, dashing itself to ruin against the armoured bulk of the Thearch's Own. Such was the size and grandeur of the Angan capitol Keel that even the raving explosion which followed seemed a tiny thing – a spark struck against a wall of granite. But as the tumbling, blackened chunks of the *Invictus* fell away I could see that a whole craterous wound had been gouged from the side of the huge vessel –

palace-sized cathedra and fortifications raining down on the Urexian plain below.

I had expected to be snapped from the air by draken claws before I hit the ground.

Like many expectations, this proved to be the seed of a grave disappointment.

I fell – uncaught - with the deluge of other debris, crashing to earth amid smoking rubble and the bodies of the slain. The impact should have killed me; it was testament to the craft of Urzen and his kind that I lived at all. But it was thanks to Sei that I landed on my feet. Cracks radiated out from where I struck, and a I rose from a crouch, flexing my armoured fingers and smiling.

Oh yes. *This* was power. This was what all the saga-striding heroes of my childhood dreams had felt, I was sure...

Reality came back to me in a rush, along with the vision of rank upon rank of white-lacquered shields, raving priests lofting religious icons, flagellant monks brandishing thorny whips, horsemen with banners of silver and cream, and all along the endless files of them, the glitter and grind of sharp steel.

"Him! He comes! The heretic! The abomination! He dares to face us, alone in his foolish arrogance!"

There must have been almost three hundred thousand men ranged against me – the Capitoline Legion, the Orders of the Burning Wheel and the Ibis, the militant ecclesiarchs of the High Chantry – and I faced them alone, in a clear and ringing silence, sure that my own forces had evaporated with the morning mist.

I could hear the flutter and crack of banners. I could hear whetstones slithering against blades. I could even hear the mumbled prayers of drunken conscripts, the foaming, muttering fervency of the Anchorites...

In truth I had landed between the two armies, but the gap was soon to close. Through the blur of pain in my head I watched the front rank of Angan Ibis Knights dip their lances, slamming shut their white-enameled helms. They quickly brought their mounts to a canter, and then to a full charge. A pall of dust flew up behind the war-horses' hooves, all but choking the phalanxes of infantry who followed.

I forced back a wave of dizziness and nausea. I cast about for a weapon – *any* weapon – with which to resist the Angan charge.

Then the ground beneath my feet began to rumble, and trumpets rang out, brazen and harsh in the dawn light. Horses in studded leather barding thundered past me on both sides, whooping, ululating warriors high in their stirrups, brandishing long-bladed lances of their own, all streaming with pennants in red and gold.

It was Vyrim Chaar and his Ontokhi plainsmen, and the old Regent hauled back on his reins as he saw me weaponless, pulling up his great warhorse in a rearing, snorting slide.

"Here! Khytein! It's called a *mace*, and you hold it in your hand! Don't drop it!"

He threw the great bladed head-crusher from its saddle-scabbard, and I snapped it out of the air, touching the fingers of my other hand to my helm in a sardonic little salute.

"Next you'll be telling me how to wipe my arse, your courtly southern fop!"

He smiled, brandishing his lance.

"Are we going to stand here all day bantering like washerwomen, or are we going to spill some Angan blood?"

He didn't wait for an answer – instead he hauled his horse's head around by the bit and dug in his spurs, loosing a terrible, howling war-cry, which I'm sure the Thearch himself heard on his cold marble throne.

I turned to follow him, muttering words of power under my breath.

"Aligning the seal of the Black Gate. Balancing the vitae flow to the seven cardinal sigils. Cerebrex bindings locked by the praxis of the Horned Eye, with restraint now unlimited to the second level..."

The first had been woven into my armour – the incantations and runes which augmented my strength with that of Urzen's half-dead slaves, and my speed with Sei's predatory reflexes. Now I called upon the hidden knowledge of the Skyborn Zengaji, the secret forms and techniques of war which that savage sect had learned from their master, Yissus U'l.

The fingerbones of dead Skyborn were knotted into my long, dark hair. Zengaji minds and souls boiled in the depths of my Cerebrex, imparting to me the Way of the Killing Strike, bone deep and instinctive.

After this, there was just one more level of power I could unlock. But for now, this stolen knowledge and skill would more than suffice.

Within a handful of heartbeats I had caught up to the charging Ontohki horsemen. Each stride covered ten spans, twelve, more... I left cracked and cratered boot-prints behind me as I tore across the Urexian Plain, the runes etched into my bone-laced armour glowing bright. Now I could see the thundering white wall of the Ibis Knights, their tall helms snapping with bleached horse-hair, their cloaks of white feathers blowing in the dust – and their lances leveled, an onrushing thicket of steel.

We Khytein are not a race of cavalrymen. Our wars were always fought on foot, in the shield-wall, and many other nations have tried to break the bronzewood ramparts of our warriors in vain. So this was the first time I had ever witnessed two massed ranks of cavalry collide at full charge – and I saw it all from ground level, right at the point where wood and metal and bloody flesh struck home.

Lances ripped through armour and muscle, skewering men and beasts before their wooden shafts smashed to matchwood. Splinters flew wide with a rain of bright crimson blood, and I saw men lifted clear from their saddles, impaled, some reeling in the stirrups, chests run through, heads crushed to pulp inside their helms. I was just behind the first shattering impact of the charge, and I came in from below the Angan Sejant-at-arms, dropping my shoulder to strike his rearing war-horse as it thrashed the air above me with its spike-shod hooves.

Ribs shattered. The beast screamed like a dying man as my strength and momentum lifted it bodily from the press, slamming it down on its rider. His legs broke with the twin crack of snapping boughs, and he flailed uselessly with his sword before I followed through with my borrowed mace, reducing his head to a gore-slick crater.

Now it was every man for himself. The charge had devolved into a vicious melee, and I lashed out with my will, a raw burst of anger which staggred Ontohki and Angan alike. An Ibis Knight sliced down at me with his sword, but I turned the blade and grabbed the man's arm, hauling him from the saddle before I brought my mace around to stave in his chestplate. The blow sent him flying – he must have been able to see his home over the walls of Urexes before he died.

"They're finished! Ride them down!" screamed Vyrim Chaar, off on my right flank – I saw him hack down an Angan knight with his double-headed axe, grey beard and mustachios dripping with crimson. "Kill the whorsesons and fall back, before those spearmen can bog us down!"

I hauled myself up into the saddle of a white Angan charger, narrowly missing the swing of another knight's morningstar, then battering him down with my mace. Despite the armour, and despite the seething death-energies flowing into me from all around, my head was pounding, my mouth dry and filled with the taste of dust and blood.

But the Angans were doomed. The Ontokhi were falling back. My horse wheeled, rearing up, and its hooves lashed out, splitting the skull of a crawling white-armoured survivor. In mere minutes we had reduced the proud Ibis Knights to a ruin of twisted metal and meat- though at a terrible cost. More than half of Vyrim Chaar's riders lay motionless, side by side with the bodies of their foes.

"Come on, warlock! I know your poxy barbarian battles are over as soon as the first savage loses his balls, but these southmen have such a thing as *strategy*!"

I spurred after Chaar, just as arrows began to patter down among the corpses. But something was wrong.

"Khytein! It's only going to take them so long to range in those catapults, and then..."

There. Through the swirling dust, between the foot-slogging spear phalanxes... a dark, twisted distortion in the world. A single man, unarmed, clad only in beggar's robes, hooded and marked as a leper, with chains of brass bells wrapped around his stooped and twisted frame.

The dust blew aside for him. Even the ranks of soldiers didn't seem to see him there, shuffling between them with a long, lantern-topped staff in one hand.

He stopped as soon as I noticed him. Down the thread of my will came a sick, oily laugh – one which drilled clear into my mind, prying and gouging with sorcerous hooks.

"*You.* You, who have had the temerity to pity my sister as you killed her. You are marked for death, and worse, by the greatest and most fell of the Nameless." It cast back its hood, revealing a ruined face; half a skull, all driven through with hundreds upon hundreds of crucifixion nails, of every shape and size. They covered the bald dome of its head like a rust-caked stubble.

The thing cackled, drool spattering from its black teeth. It pointed at me with a gnarled and yellow-nailed finger.

"You now face *That Which Walks.*"

The strength of the Khytein berserker (or the Touched, as that primitive race call these madmen) is not in his sheer size and bulk, even though among all the races of Sarem the men of the North are by far and away the largest. No - it is the unpredictable, unfeeling, relentless blood-thirst of the berserker which sets him apart from other warriors. They have been known to fight on after being hewn limb from limb; some are even said to have throttled their killers after being beheaded. All we know is this - it is a distillation of herbs and fungi which brings on the berserk state, chief among them the purple hellcap, found only in the Stormwood forests.

In the interests of pure knowledge I have experimented with this ingredient alone, but I can report that after ingesting two standard measures of dried hellcaps I have not felt in the least bit possessed to kill or maim. I have, to the contrary, enjoyed such waking dreams as would recommend this substance to poets, philosophers and other libertines as sovereign even above the liquid sap of the Ghuram poppy.

The Alchemist Chion Suldarin
- Apothecary Royal of Faeros

BATTLE WAS JOINED around us. A grim tide of the dead rushed past me on either side, shields held high and blades flashing in the sunlight – animated by my will for revenge, but utterly out of my control. For them, this was the shadow of the wars they had died fighting; it was catharsis, and they met the enemy with a savagery born of hopelessness. From behind That Which Walks legions of Angan warriors came charging through a churning pall of dust, bellowing pious war-cries as they flung themselves into the fray.

Bone splintered and muscle sheared. Steel shattered and wood was hewn apart. Across a front as wide as the Urexian wall the Thearch's legions hammered home their fury, and my army of the dead held them.

"Does the dying taste sweet to you?" asked That Which Walks, leaning forward on its staff. The lantern which swung from its hooked tip was without wick or candle; it was a brass cage around a human skull. "Is this whole great game of slaughter some kind of necromantic banquet? Or some *other* form of satisfaction?"

The leer on that ravaged face was horribly knowing.

"I don't question how it works, demon. I just use what power I have to put down *things like you.*"

The Nameless laughed, once again sending cascades of foulness dripping from his ruined mouth.

"Dirge said you were a pompous little fool. You *are* things like me, Kuhal Moer. In a way, I'll be sorry to have to kill you."

The melee swirled about us, parting on either side as if we were rocks in a river of carnage. Shadow memories drove my dead men on – they locked shields and met a furious charge of flail-wielding Anchorites, bearded, ragged men with pages of Esau's book sewn to their chests and limbs. The holy men died screaming the name of their lord, kindling sorcerous fire which blackened bone and shattered skulls.

"I know your true name, Akiim u'Skraye. father of shadows, high acolyte of the Court of Knifesplinter – you have no secrets from me."

"You're wrong," it laughed. "So wrong! Even now, you're already dead"

A chill crept in, through my armour, rising like frost from my feet, up my legs...

I looked down, and saw that I was sinking into the shadow of That Which Walks – a shadow which had become a bubbling, oozing pool of tar as the sun crested the walls of Urexes.

"Dirge is afraid of me, you know," purred the demon. "why, even

Urzen was a little bit frightened of what he had created. But *you* have the empty-headed bravado to think that..."

"Enough talk, demon! Time to suffer!"

The creature's head napped around, with a speed even Sei would have envied. And the black iron staff of Akiim u'Skraye, last worshipper of the Zengaji lord of death, caught three hissing, crackling wires an instant before they pulled tight, slicing its lantern-pole to pieces.

What happened next was a blur of ringing noise, a mere few heartbeats of crystal-bright slow motion.

That Which Walks threw itself backward, bending and twisting in ways which were far from human. Its chain of bells caught the dawn light as it cartwheeled back to its feet, throwing its skeletal lantern high. At the same time I saw Makara coming down from a leap which had carried her over my head – the oily black shadow-stuff was gone, the spell broken, and she fell in to the fray swinging a great bladed staff, like the crook of a bishop sharpened to a razor edge.

The deadly crozius missed, slicing away a ribbon of dirty sack-cloth from the demon's robes. A second blurring swing shattered its chain of bells, before the hand of the Nameless One snapped a two-span shard of broken lantern-haft from out of the air and tried to drive it through Makara's chest.

She staggered backwards, but kept her footing.

The brass-caged skull reached the apogee of its flight. And That Which Walks smiled a sickly smile.

"Goodbye," it mouthed, in the flat, bright flare of sorcery which followed.

Then it stepped backward into his own shadow. Akiim u'Skraye, and every man, living or dead, who so much as touched the dark shape streaming out behind him – they all vanished, falling through the shadow as if it were the surface of a bottomless black pool.

"This," said Makara, as pale and cold as ice-statuary, "isn't good *at all*." She lifted me bodily from the ground; my boots were still sunk a hand's-span deep in the arid soil. "I think you had better leave this one to me, Khytein. I've read the Tomes of Making too, you know. I know what he does."

"And miss the fun? I'd probably regret it."

Makara fixed me with a hard, black-eyed stare, and I bit my tongue. It was the gaze of a creature which could welcome death or leave it, just the same.

"I tore this crozius from the hands of the Black Shepherd, Kuhal.

I've just fought my way through a thousand stinking, praying Southmen to save you, *again*, in what is becoming a very tedious habit of mine. So this time *you* get to be the sword in *my* right hand." She paused, looking back to where the shadow of That Which Walks lay boiling and twisting on the ground, pulling loose around the edges.

"So history will record that I hid behind a woman?"

"History will record us *both* as stories to frighten children with," she said, "if we're lucky." One great hand tore loose from the dirt, and an arm made of utter night swept clean through a rank of Angan levies, obliterating whatsoever it touched. Men, armour, horses, corpses and fallen weapons – all spun away into the bottomless dark. Makara hefted her stolen crozius and fixed me with a look of grim defiance.

"But it will also record that right here, right now, I held off That Which Walks single-handed. And *you* brought me the war-Keel *Redemptor*, so that I could finish the undying bastard for good."

Now the staggering, man-shaped hole in reality lurched upright. For all that they had girded themselves with courage to face the living dead, the men of Anganesse were terrified of this fresh horror – not knowing whether it was conjured by their own priestly cadre or by my own dark magik. They scattered, breaking ranks and screaming.

Akiim u'Skraye wasn't particular in his destruction. A hand the size of an ox-cart reached out after the fleeing Angans, swallowing them up greedily as they ran. I didn't have to tell the dead to do the same. The waves of ice-cold, slippery sorcery which radiated from the Nameless were enough to drive my wights back, as they felt the will which bound them fraying and tearing apart.

Makara turned to face the thing, grown as tall as the Urexian walls now, a faceless, ragged-edged nightmare walking in daylight. And she leveled the crozius she'd stolen from the Black Shepherd, the only one among thousands to stand her ground.

"Shadowfather! Chosen of Knifesplinter! I enact the Rite of the Crucible, and call you to face me!"

From out of the walking darkness came a hollow peal of laughter. There were no words, but we both knew that the Nameless had accepted her challenge. It turned to regard her with a pair of eyes like bloated, dying suns.

"And witnesses?" it asked, spreading its fingers wide to take in the whole churning battlefield. "Will all of my people, and all of yours suffice? They will be the sacrifice, after all..."

Above us, the *Redemptor* blotted out the sun like a thunderhead of stone. Cannonfire cracked across the heavens, and as I looked up I saw the *Graveyard Ark* rake the stern of the *Intrepid* with shot, pulverizing its chantries and galleries. The Angan Keel was burning, listing in the air, but the sails of my proud ark were a ruined tatter, the mainmast was sheared clean in two, and black, acrid smoke boiled up from deep craters in its belly and flanks.

"Kuhal Moer," said Makara, in a voice of barely contained fury. "I wasn't resurrected as a damned monster to wait for you to pick your scabs and count the clouds. Call your draken. Finish this. *Now!*"

She was in my mind; in the Cerebrex, which even now was beginning to calcify with the mageblight. I saw her plan unfold behind my eyes, and it was a thing of simple, savage beauty.

I have always been a hopeless romantic, I suppose. But words tend to fail me on the sharp end of the moment.

"Just don't die," I said - and then I cast out my will, calling down one of my draken from the smoke-hazed sky.

The great scaly beast plucked me from the battlefield just as That Which Walks attacked, hammering both its fists together down at Makara. Through a swirl of dust and wings I saw her blur sideways, avoiding the blow, but I never caught the counterstrike – just a howl of outrage, as Akiim u'Skraye learned that my beautiful demoness was far from tender prey.

Then I was airborne, spiraling up above the bloody plain as the *Redemptor* grew to fill the sky. I risked a glance behind me, taking in the full scope of the horror I had unleashed.

All across the northern walls of Urexes, the legions of the Thearch were pressed hard. It had been a brave strategem to try to break my army of the dead, avoiding a siege – and in truth, there was no way for the Thearch to have known that the Coldblood and I were not brothers in arms. But it hindered the cannon and war-engines atop the beaten bronze walls. It made those walls an anvil, against which my relentless infantry were the hammer. Vyrim Chaar and my horsemen were the pincers and tongs which pushed and pulled the enemy force, denying them escape.

Higher now, and I could make out the broken Grand Chantry steeples of the bright city, the smoking pillars of stone where the Thearch's mightiest priestly cadres had worked. The Coldblood had torn them down days ago, but thick, unwholesome smoke still boiled from the jagged stumps, and multi-coloured fire flared up beneath.

South of Urexes the coast road was a crawling mass of refugees – the simple folk of the Angan capital, fleeing for their lives before invaders' swords.

Just as *my* people had done. Just as had happened across the entire North, city after city and tribe after tribe, as the White Empire brought 'civilization' to Sarem. I hardened my heart to their fate, then, knowing that when the walls came down, thousands of innocents would burn. I told myself it was revenge, the will of destiny, the caprice of the Gods. But I knew that I was wrong.

I also knew that it was far too late to turn aside.

The *Redemptor* was ponderous and slow, but it had come about now, outflanking my army, and its guns were in range of my siege engines, the great trebuchet and wheeled towers which would allow me to breach the city walls. Even as I watched one of the mighty bombards at the bows of the Keel belched flame, lobbing a stone ball the size of a cottage on an arc which connected with a row of covered wagons, crushing them to matchwood.

I knew what I had to do to take the Keel. *Urzen* knew, and he had written much on the subject of Angan nekrology in his endless, human-skin-bound tomes. But to fight my way through the thousands of soldiers and fanatics aboard the lumbering sky-fortress, I would need somewhat of an edge...

My fingers found a tiny bottle, tucked into a loop of my belt for just such an emergency. The liquid within was inky black, bubbling, and when I pulled the stopper from its neck I could smell a mixture of earthy, dark decay and the ozone tang of summer lightning.

The helm would have to go. I felt the kiss of cold air against my face as I pulled it away, my hair streaming out behind me in the wind. The circlet of silver thorns between the helm's horns unclipped, and I wrapped it tight around my brow, reconnecting to the star-hung web of the cerebrex. Then I held my breath, closed my eyes, and drank.

I had to pray that the cerebrex, infused with my will and my mind, would keep the dead fighting after I swallowed. Because this was a tincture of bonebark, draken's-claw root, hookthorn berry and hellcap mushrooms... the Black Draught which Aerik Stormsong had once prepared solely for the Touched.

My last coherent memory was of leaping from the back of my Draken mount, landing on the arrowhead bow of the Keel with enough force to splinter the stone. Then the divine madness took me, and the pulse of my own heartbeat became a thunder as deep as oceans, the sound of great drums under the earth, echoing in the court of Anghul.

Power raved through me. I believe I must have screamed. And the first Angan soldier who ran at me, sword held high, was blasted to bones and molten metal by a bolt of black lightning from my fingertips.

I giggled, utterly unhinged. A blur of colours wheeled across my vision. Then the laughter turned to a howl, the animal fury of the true berserker, and I began killing my way toward the stern of the *Redemptor*.

The poor bastards didn't stand a chance. The next half-hour, for me, was nothing but the intoxicating scent of blood, the sweet sound of screams. All I recall is an endless, red-tinted, pulsing nightmare – my hands swinging Vyrim Chaar's mace until it was bent and useless, then picking up swords, axes, chunks of stone, metal poles, nail-studded baulks of timber ripped from the walls...

I battered men to pulp, leaving them as faceless mincemeat. I made whole corridors run red with gore, and I felt bone crack under my fingers, felt chunks of warm flesh still trailing clotted hanks of hair and flaps of skin. I beat men to death with the limbs I had torn bloody from their comrades seconds before. And when they tried to shoot me down with arrows, I swept them from the air with sorcery. When they manhandled bonepowder cannon into the warren of stone, intent on shredding me with chain-shot, I was on them before they could prime the hammers, running on the walls, springing from arch to ceiling to pillar in a storm of screams and gurgling death-rattles, steel and madness.

The mageblight burned. I was out of my mind, and I channeled every single death through myself, pushing for more power, more speed, more destruction... it was a feeling like gluttony, like carnal ecstasy, a howling emptiness at my core demanding MORE...

I saw the face of Anghul. The antlered God looked back at me, and he shrank back on his throne of bones and swords, holding his hands up before his cowl and trembling. The old butcher was *afraid* of me, and I gloried in his fear, bursting through the wall of the Keel's well chamber with a sword in each hand, and a nimbus of writhing witchfire haloing my head.

But at that moment the madness boiled away. My mind crash-froze back into reality, severed from the Shard of Death by the sheer proximity of such power.

And oh, the power here. It had taken a whole empire of the pious dead to gather it in.

The ossuary well of the *Redemptor* was wide enough to swallow a town like Czanthe whole, and the wheels which ground out the suffering of the dead were vast, kept in motion by a chantry of two hundred acolytes. I had blasted my way through into the chamber near enough to the cardinal altar, where ten of the most exalted of Esau's faithful attended a spinning, mirrored pillar, eight feet tall and blurred with sigils.

I saw myself reflected, in the instant before the grey-robed priests turned to face me. And I realized that I had become everything the Southmen's stories had made me.

Somewhere along the way I had lost my chestplate and hauberk of mail. My arms were still clad in Korisali steel, inlaid with bone, and my legs from the waist down were similarly armoured. But my head and chest were bare, my gauntlets were gone, and from head to toe I was spattered with fresh bright blood, splashes of it speckled with chips of bone, scraps of skin and human teeth. My hair hung in a dripping, dark tangle, and my eyes were blazing white, without iris or pupil, set deep in bruise-purple sockets.

My skin was unnaturally pale, tight across my chest and belly, and every muscle, tendon and scar stood proud, lit up by a galaxy of blue swirls and knots – the sacred tattoos of the Touched, burning under my skin as the mageblight took on the shape and colour of those ancient symbols. My hands were blackened claws, burned by sorcery until they were long-fingered, taloned horrors of exposed muscle and bone, crackling with witchfire.

"Run," I slurred, trying to regain control of a tongue which felt like a hunk of mouldering leather. "*Run,* and you might just live."

I took a step forward, unsteady on my feet. Traceries of green fire licked out across the chantry hall, earthing themselves against the millstones with a flash of sparks.

"*Hold!*" shouted the archpriest at his lectern – a bald-pated slug of a man, his face tattooed with cross-and-wheel icons on both cheeks. "This demon holds no fear for we, the righteous! Hold your stations, and abide in your duty! I will *strike this abomination down!*"

With these words he hefted the holy book of Esau from its eagle-winged stand, brandishing it like a weapon. And from his other hand he unleashed a fury of silver flames – fire which coalesced into blades as it flew, becoming a storm of spinning knives.

The shock of such powerful sorcery rocked the Keel – even a vessel as vast as the *Redemptor* was not immune. But this close to Urexes where was no way we could fall from the sky; the souls trapped in their bone prison could feel the presence of Esau, heavy and urgent behind the world.

So I was free to retaliate with as much force as I could muster.

I let the whirling cloud of blades slice past me, deflecting them with a shield of power cast out with my will. Then I turned to the millstones, dropping my swords, and extended my hands, palm to palm, speaking the words of an incantation in the wicked gutturals of old Korisal.

The pressure was immense, but I forced my palms apart, gritting my teeth as I spat out the last few syllables.

And the millstones snapped open. Still spinning, the monolithic gears at the heart of the Keel recessed into the floor and ceiling, letting in a furnace-glow of green light. It painted the assembled priesthood in stark black and white, tinted with violent jade, and it showed them running – abandoning their posts to scramble for the exits. They knew exactly what was coming next.

To his credit, the corpulent Archpriest stood his ground. Martyrdom is foolish, selfish, superstitious and trite – but I will grudgingly admit that it smacks of a certain idiot nobility. His circle of priests stood with him, though out of petrified fear, honour or simple shame I will never know.

Because at that moment I called a thick, writhing skein of souls out from the ossuary well – a blurred melange of screaming faces, grasping hands and ragged, translucent ghosts, all slithering through the air like one of the Silence's Void Wyrms. I brought my hands up above my head and cast the whole gibbering mass of them at the Archpriest, who barely had time to utter a prayer to his God before he was obliterated.

It took all of them. The tortured souls swept through the gaggle of priests as a firestorm, cold and all-consuming. For a brief instant the holy men flared white, a glow which picked out their bones, teeth and pious jewelry. Then nothing was left of them but a hazy after-image, and a drift of swirling ashes. The souls split apart as they raved through the Keel, fraying away to wisps of nothingness, but their job was done.

Now, nothing was keeping the awful bulk of the Thearch's Own airborne.

The deck lurched beneath me as gravity took hold, but I was ready – I leaped through the open millstones into the silent ossuary well, then up its walls, feet landing lightly on the copper endcaps of those bone-stuffed glass coffins. Up, and to the flying bridge of the stoneship, a place abandoned by its crew and captain.

Now I called out to my draken, and one of them peeled away from its harrying of the war-Keel *Intrepid*, a ruin all but broken in the air. Now the undead beast arced high over me, reaching the zenith of its flight and folding its wings...

Far in front of me stretched the arrowhead point of the *Redemptor*, angled down toward the battlefield below. Men were pointing, screaming, fleeing, desperate to be out form under its shadow. Away to starboard (for I had learned such nautical accuracies from Elion Morkeh) I could see the burnt and blackened circle of earth where Makara and That Which Walks dueled. The Father of Shadows still raged and bellowed, though he was cut in several places, bleeding a tarry black ichor which crusted the ground with frost where it struck. Makara was a tiny, darting figure in silver and black, weaving snares with her wires, avoiding the sweeping blows of the Nameless One's fists.

But she saw me. And her thoughts touched mine like a burst of sunlight, hot and savage after years of darkness. The last of the hellcap brew burned away, and I saw, with terrible inevitability, just how her plan would play out.

My draken plunged into the cold ossuary well with a scream, just as I slammed the millstones closed again and spun them into motion. The soul-shock, as titanic energies ripped the poor creature's spirit from its bones, was enough to send me reeling. But there was just enough time for me to slide one final command into its head.

For an instant I felt a rush of confusion, anger, pain... radiating up from the stone beneath my feet. For just long enough, the entire vast war-Keel *Redemptor* was possessed by the spirit of a wild Draken – one which I controlled.

The gilded figurehead at the prow of the Keel came about, a statue of Esau bearing a golden sword in one hand and his own holy book in the other. The tip of that sword was aimed squarely at Akiim u'Skraye, That Which Walks. Before the demon could sense the looming danger Makara twisted around behind him, her wires licking out to score a line across his cheek.

Then she fell.

Makara's foot slipped on a frozen slick of Nameless blood, and she tumbled to the ground, the Black Shepherd's crozius flying from her hands. She tried to rise, but it seemed that she had broken something – her ankle wouldn't support her weight, and she collapsed again, crawling in the dust.

That Which Walks roared in triumph. It rose over her like a wave about to break, its fist held high, ready to slam down in obliteration...

But all this meant that its back was turned.

Just before the darkness swept down on her Makara rolled over, splaying all of her fingers wide, in a fan aimed through the Nameless One's chest. Six silver threads licked out, piercing Akiim u'Skraye clean through. But those six tiny puncture wounds were not her purpose. Indeed, the hulking Nameless seemed hardly to feel them.

No - those wires came on, whipping out taut at the very extent of their reach, and they bit into the stone and steel of the *Redemptor's* bows. Each one locked tight with the snick of spring-loaded barbs. Urzen was nothing if not a consummate weaponsmith, after all.

Now *I* had to run. Now I was grateful of the skill and agility I'd borrowed from little Sei. Because as soon as those barbs bit home, Makara took up the strain, and the nose of the Thearch's Own arrowed downward, pitching the whole stoneship into a suicidal plunge.

I sprinted up the incline of the deck, dodging falling bodies, braziers and map-tables, censers and chains, cannon-shot and bonepowder shells. The Keel wasn't just falling now – it was being *reeled in*, shuddering with the speed of its descent, and I sprung with desperate grace from deck to deck, past wailing Angans hanging on for dear life, through clouds of burning pages from holy books aflame...

I leaped from the very back of the Keel as the statue of Esau at its prow pierced the nebulous void of That Which Walks. Arms and legs windmilling wildly, I watched the Urexian Plain rush up to greet me, braced for the pain of impact.

This time, it didn't come.

This time there was a Draken to catch me, and I swung up into its saddle with the momentum of my fall, hauling the reins around to watch the doom of Akiim u'Skraye.

The *Redemptor* was vast – as large as the arch of Urexes itself, a mountain carved into the likeness of a great arrowhead, then bound with sorcery to cruise the clouds. It was swallowed up by the darkness of That Which Walks in a single, impossible thunderclap of noise –

stretched out thin and tight so that it could be devoured by the void of u'Skraye's being. It was like watching a man being run through with a battering ram... but nothing burst from the chest of the Nameless, even when the last towers and trailing chains of the mighty Keel were sucked beneath its living surface.

Instead the demon froze, coiled ready to strike. Makara rolled to her feet as soon as her deadly wires snapped back into place – her fall had been a ruse, and one so childishly simple that it had taken all of Akiim's pride and hubris to believe it.

In Urzen's scriptoria I had read the Tomes of Making; those black volumes in which the mad Forgemaster detailed his creation of the Nine. So I knew that it was a cunning manipulation of the Mageblight which gave the things their power – a power based on belief, fed on terror, sustained by the very stories which peasants whispered in tones of dread.

I also knew, from painful experience, that blighted flesh can only sustain so much power. Makara had just fed That Which Walks a meal it would choke on.

It began slowly – first the creature's head seemed to crumple in, as if it was being crushed inside a giant's fist. Then its right arm collapsed, becoming a black, twig-like scrawl with spider-leg fingers. Piece by piece, That Which Walks was compacted in on itself, falling to the ground to writhe and jerk in agony.

Soon it was man-sized again, and the darkness drew back across its skin, bubbling and hissing as it went. Finally, all that was left was the leprous ancient who had first faced me, his skull studded with nails, and a black circle steaming cold in the middle of his forehead.

He was still alive. Even after the web of blight inside him had been burned to ruin, he still had enough strength to claw his way to his knees, holding out his hands to Makara in supplication.

"Sister!" he shouted, in a voice of utter despair. "Why? We could have killed them all! We could have brought down the heavens themselves, and lived in ecstasy, forever! *Why did you have to turn against us?*"

It wasn't the pain in his words which cut me to the bone. It wasn't the betrayal, either. It was the sheer, incredulous *disbelief* – the fact that he could not fathom a soul which rejected the Dwellers in Darkness.

Makara said nothing. She ran.

Because a heartbeat later the vast bulk of the *Redemptor* came back into the world of life and light, vomited forth from that tiny black hole in Akiim u'Skraye's forehead.

His body was not up to the punishment. Obliteration has rarely been so absolute.

But the Keel, in all its mass and weight, could not easily be squeezed through such a keyhole, either. I am largely ignorant of the mathematical laws which I am assured govern such things, by the wisdom of the Divine. But later studies would indicate (if the scholars of Saradrim are to be believed) that most of the stone, flesh, metal and wood which made up the Thearch's Own was transmuted to elemental energy as it strove to force its way back into the world. The resulting, almost solid rod of sorcerous power was enough to utterly erase That Which Walks from reality - and that was just blowback, like the muzzle-flash from a bonepowder cannon.

The rest struck the walls of Urexes head-on, a tangled spiral of grey, silver, green and gold fire, and it punched through the twenty-span thick copper-sheathed stone like a burning brand through paper. A furrow deeper than the ridge-pole of my father's longhouse was carved from the plain behind it, and beyond the wall a vast swathe of homes, forges, factoring houses, granaries and slums were instantly incinerated, all the way up to the lower end of the city's great arch. Bricks – some weighing more than a laden barquentine – tumbled end over end through the sky, glowing red hot. The ground-shock made all the temple bells of Urexes ring, a manic carillon out of tune.

In the rumble and echo of the aftermath, every man on the battlefield held his breath. I believe that even the dead tried to, out of some latent sense of the memory of flesh.

Then a great cheer went up from my living soldiers – Vyrim Chaar's men, my bandits and outriders, my free Ghuram archers and my Ythean spearmen – while a moan of horror rose from the Angan ranks.

Because the walls were down, and nothing now stood between my horde and the Capitoline Deep but a few doomed regiments, even now dropping their weapons and pleading for a quick death.

The city was mine.

IT WAS NO easy road.

There were no flowers strewn in my path as I entered through the ruined gates of Urexes; no banners flown, or hymns incanted, or even dead foes hung in chains. Vyrim Chaar's men set to despoiling and looting with a vengeance – literally, in many cases – leaving me to gather up Makara and march on the Imperial Arch alone.

Well... alone, apart from ten thousand fleshless, grinning warriors, who fanned out through the city around us, exterminating any of Esau's fanatics and the Thearch's loyalists they found.

The sun stood high above the burning city, a copper disc behind a pall of smoke, before we reached the foot of the nearest marble colossus.

I had seen too much horror in the past six hours – more death in that one terrible morning than I had witnessed in all my years. It may surprise you to learn that I felt each one of them – every arrow as it pierced mail and flesh, every ragged sword-cut fountaining blood, every crushing blow of mace and hammer... *all*. It was the price of leading my legions, and one which I had started the day willing enough to pay. Now I was all but dead on my feet.

Bloodied, dust-caked and staggering toward victory on Makara's shoulder... I was not sure, any more, if my mind would ever heal from what I had suffered through. To this day scholars debate whether it ever truly did, and grow fat on tenure explaining just how mad I am. Makara, for her part, questioned nothing.

We had watched the towers crumble. We had seen the fire leaping hungrily from the upper arrow-slits of the gatehouse bastion. We had seen the *Intrepid* fall, a lifeless wreck, to slew through the lower city, ploughing whole streets to rubble as it came apart.

And we had watched as the *Glory Arisen*, that old relic of the Rholian Secession, had fought a last, bitter engagement with the *Graveyard Ark*, now drifting rudderless, its sails ablaze. The *Glory Arisen* was gutted by cannonfire, but not before it forced Elion into range of the great Urexian Cathedral. The priesthood were waiting – their barrage of sorcery was too far away for me to stop, and too powerful for Corvo to deflect.

As his command was torn stone from stone beneath his feet, Elion Morekh stayed at the wheel, cold dead hands unflinching. He set the Ark on a collision course and rode it all the way down, shearing the towers from the cathedral in his last moments, before the ossauries burst, and that vast explosion almost cracked the arch itself in two.

There was no escape for the holy men who had doomed him. Deep in the Ark's belly were the vast cauldrons which had once hung in Urzen's forge. Now they were filled with churning acid and lye afloat with still-dissolving chunks of meat; the abattoir hell-broth in which I turned corpses into soldiers of the dead. As the *Graveyard Ark* disintegrated, a slurry of caustic, boiling foulness was loosed through the chapels and precincts of the cathedral, drowning, choking and scalding the faithful.

More horror. More final memories of pain, branded into my aching nerves. We climbed the spiral stair inside the colossus as my warriors went ahead of us, driving the last of the Thearch's defenders before them.

At last we came to the fifty-span-high doors of the Thearch's palace. The courtyard before them was a charnel pit; I picked my way through ankle-deep blood, while heads bobbed merrily in the ornamental fountains, and from somewhere in the cloisters came the sound of hysterical weeping and laughter. I pushed myself upright from Makara's shoulder, heaved in a great breath, and leaned with all my weight against the twin slabs of gold-inlaid stone, so like the black portal in my dreams.

Inside, the Urexian Capitol was a perfect sphere – a dome so wide that clouds were said to form among its upper frescoes and hanging monuments, and a tiered basin of seats and desks, where the Senate would meet to determine the fates of such disparate, unimportant vassals as starving Ghuram farmers, fractious Rasuuli noblemen and brutally repressed Khytein savages. They were also known for their exquisitely composed poetry.

At the very centre of the room, upon the turquoise-and-jade

inlaid map of Sarem which was the lowest tier of the pit, sat the throne. Ancient, ugly, cold and uncomfortable, it stood for everything pertinent about the Thearch himself. Bright rays of sunlight speared down from the cupola above, stirring gold-flecked motes of dust, illuminating the masterworks of painters, sculptors, tapestry weavers – all wrung out to make this single room the very focus of a continent.

But the Thearch wasn't on his throne. Any stinging words I may have composed for him choked in my throat. Because his body lay at the stepped foot of that ornate and massive chair, his neck twisted around much further than was humanly possible. The look on his aged and leathery face was one of considerable affront, and his vast, brocaded, pearl-encysted robes were spattered with blood.

Ahh, who else could it have been? If not for him, I would be the villain of this piece, after all.

On the throne itself – slouched insouciantly, an apple in one hand – sat Dirge, all radiant and beautiful in white, as calm as if the empire he had just usurped was not falling down around him.

He took a bite of his apple. It was red, as waxy and perfect in appearance as his own powdered face.

"What are you *doing* here, Kuhal Moer?" he asked, stretching like a sun-drowsed cat. "Really. Think before you answer, please."

It was wariness as much as sheer bone-deep fatigue which stopped me from throwing myself at him. My skeletal minions prowled down the tiered steps of the chamber to encircle the Angan lord, green witchfire eyes glittering the the gloom.

"You know as well as I do, Sinder," I said, spitting the name he had rejected. "I've come to avenge my father, and my people, and everyone you've slaughtered to sit on that throne. I've come to end you, and all your works."

I could, perhaps, have forgiven him a full-blown, unhinged peal of laughter then. It was certainly the time and place for one. But instead the white-clad creature perched on the throne giggled, taking another bite of his apple. He wiped the juice from his lips with the back of one silver-ringed hand.

"How long, do you suppose, before some upstart young hero spouts the same tired speech in *your* ear, Khytein? I'll tell you why you're really here. You're here, in this place, right now, because this is where *I need you*. Your purpose is mine, as it always has been."

I took a step forward, shrugging Makara's hand from my shoulder. Two score of fleshless wights raised their blades, leveling a thicket of steel at Dirge.

"You think this whole fractured world revolves around you, do you?"

He arched an eyebrow.

"It's never shown any indication of spinning for any other."

"I seem to recall killing you once. Was *that* all part of your master plan?"

"Dead things tend to stay in the ground," he replied, gesturing expansively with his apple-core. "present company excluded. It all just goes to show that fate has a higher purpose for me."

"Betrayer? Usurper? *Song of ending for all things under light*?"

"Oh, bravo! The savage remembers my name! But no, my erstwhile masters erred on the side of poetry there. Think of me as the father of a more enlightened age."

"Only if you can get out of this room alive," I grated. My soultaken moved in, blades flashing golden in the dusty air. "Personally, I don't think fate has any further use for you."

This time he actually applauded. The clean-picked core of his apple caromed off the helm of one of my wights, skewing it aslant.

"And *so* dramatic, too. For the pride of a people who wanted to dash your feeble brains out, and the memory of a father who never loved you more than his next horn of ale. What a dutiful little fool! It's no wonder that you've proven so easy to manipulate."

Dirge was on his feet before I could so much as blink, dropping down from the throne to stand over the corpse of his Thearch. His nose wrinkled in disgust as he looked down at the old man's body.

"Just like this one, really. All I had to do was mumble pious nothings, kiss his fingertips, and promise never to tell a soul that we, between us, wielded the power of the Nine. A small wisdom, Kuhal, which you will never get the chance to use... every empire needs a plausibly deniable butcher. The smart ones, however, never let them hone their blades *too* sharp..."

"Enough! I didn't come here to bear witness to your treasons, Sinder. I came to make you pay for them."

Now the shadows seemed to coil about the white-clad Angan lord. Now the sun-dappled hall grew cold, and as the thing which had been Jerrold Sinder looked up at me I saw something bulging and slithering behind his night-black eyes.

"Careful what you wish for, peasant," he said. "You might just make me angry..."

He cast back his cloak of white ibis feathers, revealing the simple, undyed cotton robe of a warrior monk – a belted, half-sleeved garment adorned with the wheel-and-cross in black, and hung with a plain pair of swords.

He didn't draw them, though. Instead, the master of the Nine held up his right hand, palm splayed, and made a complex gesture with the fingers of his left. The air shimmered, like a veil pulling away from something hidden behind reality...

"And when I get angry, I have a *definite* habit of breaking pretty little toys like these."

It was the Cerebrex.

I felt a blade of cold stab through me as Dirge clenched his fingers. It ramified through the web of magblight inside me, and I felt my undead falling away, souls unbound, returning to bones and dust. A sad little clatter and chime of empty armour let me know that my protection was gone. And Makara...

"Not one more step, little witch," hissed Dirge. "Your soul is at the very core of this thing, and I'd have to shred it to pieces to destroy you. What would that do to his mind, do you think? No – you'll just watch this time. And think about what you've done to my beautiful Nine!"

The pain of it was immense, world-heavy, and it drove me to my knees. I felt something give inside my head, and hot bright blood dripped from my nose, spattering the white marble floor.

He could have demanded anything of me then. At full strength I would have perhaps been able to seize the Cerebrex back, but as I was now all I could do was grit my teeth and curse. He must have snatched the sorcerous device from the wreck of the Ark – it was all but indestructible, after all, and even the explosion of an entire Keel's ossuary would barely have heated its black iron surface.

What he demanded, however, was exactly what I wanted.

"Get up and fight me, Khytein," said Dirge, drawing his swords with a rasp of oiled steel. "Right now. Just the two of us, for all of Urexes and Sarem to see."

I could hardly believe it. The aftershock was fading, and I pulled myself to my feet with a grunt of effort, smiling bloody.

"We danced that dance before, Southman. And as I recall..."

"But this time is *very* different, Kuhal. This time there'll be no necromantic trickery. Just light and darkness, the old story... the one they're all expecting."

"And which one are you?" I asked. I wiped one hand across my lips, leaving it dripping with crimson.

"Why, I'm the *hero*, of course. The very image of our dear founder, Ulriq Trasse, all done up in white. You, however, are the greatest monster of this age – at least to those poor fools who have not yet looked upon the Coldblood. And when they watch me destroy you..."

I understood, then, exactly what he planned.

"*Belief*. The mageblight feeds on it, just as the Gods do."

"Exactly. You're not so slow a student after all, Kuhal. When they witness my ascension, they will believe. Between that faith, and the power I wring from your lifeless corpse, I will tear reality in two!"

It would have been quite redundant to remind Dirge that he was utterly mad. Instead I held out my right hand, palm open, and looked him in the eyes.

"You put too much faith in stories, Sinder. In real life, the monster usually wins."

"Kuhal! No! You mustn't let him..."

I risked taking my eyes off of the Angan lord for long enough to look back over my shoulder at Makara.

"He's not giving me a choice. You'll not sacrifice yourself for me again, girl, and *somebody* has to end this insanity."

Dirge chuckled.

"Now who's putting all their faith in stories, Khytein? The damsel and the warrior – how trite! Come on! Strike me down if you can. What are you waiting for?"

High above us, section of the Capitoline dome exploded inward, showering us with chips of marble and gold leaf. A solid rod of darkness punched down, tracing a line from the sky to my open hand. I clenched my fingers tight.

"I was waiting for *this*, Sinder. You're not the only one to pluck new toys from the wreck of my Ark."

It was the Cryptfeeder – that immense black blade of Sothara da'Urgon Roege, seven spans long and three wide, a slab of dark iron inset with twisting red runes. It was only by the power of my sorcerous armour that I could lift the thing.

Dirge smiled.

"Excellent! Just one last thing, Khytein..."

He hit me. Faster than I could follow, darting in to catch me a blow in the chest with both sets of knuckles. Had he used his blades, I would have been skewered through and through. Instead I was propelled from my feet, flung back against the wall of the capitol, twenty spans from the floor.

I saw his follow-through coming – barely – and had time to brace myself for the pain. The pale Angan's spinning kick took me high to the left, and it landed with such force that I was driven clear *through* the wall of the immense building, flying amid a shower of stone and mortar-dust.

"My. Fucking. Name. Is. DIRGE!"

In that instant of free-fall and agony I had time to acquaint myself, once again, with the disciplines of sorcery Sothara had perfected so long ago. Cut off from the tangled web of witchfire and bone which had recently been the greater part of my body, I had to grapple with my own slippery nerves to gain control.

It all fit together just in time. I arrested my flight and reversed direction, feet touching down for a heartbeat on the minaret of some noble's palace before I came back to meet Dirge, the Cryptfeeder leaving a trail of darkness behind it in the air.

He fell in on me like a comet, sparkling white and grinning madly, his blades flashing silver. When we met, the shockwave tore out across the city as a visible sphere of force, cracking stone and sending a hail of roof tiles flying. It was brute strength against unnatural speed as we hung in the air above Urexes, trading blows which shook the city to its roots. Each time our swords crossed, bursts of green and purple fire scattered a rain of sparks, with a ringing peal heard far across the plain.

I could feel the eyes of millions on us. Refugees turned from their trudging progress to watch the clash of powers. Warriors - the wounded, captives and the dying, along with Vyrim Chaar's victorious men. Slaves, trapped in their pits and pens, abandoned by their Angan masters. All watching. All *believing*.

And the focus of that power wasn't me. It was the white-clad angel who faced me. The living hammer of retribution, trailing burning ibis feathers as he pressed his assault. No doubt many of them thought he was Ulriq Trasse come again, and sent their prayers for salvation up to him. But the reality was quite the opposite.

Dirge's blows came faster. I felt him driving me back, and his silver blades carved deep notches in the edge of the Cryptfeeder. At last I couldn't hold the cantrip of levitation which held me pinned to the air, and I let myself fall, springing from rooftop to rooftop as blasts of quicksilver fire licked at my heels. Weathervanes and chimneys fell, sliced through.

"Come back here and *die*, you upstart little worm! Or have you forgotten that I have your damned Incantus?"

I jinked and sidestepped to buy time. I ran on the marble skin of a shattered chantry tower, circling all the way around to leap back at Dirge, black iron singing in my hands.

He blocked me with contempt. Between his crossed swords his face was twisted with rage and ecstasy, his pupils pinholes in immensities of bloodshot white.

"And if I have your Korisali trinket, I have Makara. I can do with her whatever I..."

This time he'd gloated for too long. The Cryptfeeder flew underhand, biting into his side just above the hip. But there was no tearing of flesh before its razored edge – there was not even a drop of crimson to mark the wound. Instead my blade shuddered, as if I had hewn into the flank of some great Stormwood oak, and the blast of power I earthed through it propelled Dirge halfway across the arch of Urexes. His tumbling body smashed through a chapel bell tower, setting it to pealing and clamouring.

He was right though. With the Cerebrex in his grasp, every one of my dead was Dirge's to command. Granted, he knew nothing of necromancy, and had no connection to the source of my power. But he *did* know how to control Urzen's creations, the Nine – of which Makara was assuredly one. I would have no help from my demoness this time.

I had to finish him – fast.

I dragged the Cryptfeeder behind me as I pelted across the rooftops, throwing up a roostertail of shattered tiles in my wake. Faster, pushing my own flesh and bones through sorcery, until the mageblight lit up under my skin in the swirling knotwork of the Touched.

Dirge met me halfway, blurring across the sky in a streak of white. In the instant before we struck each other I swung the Cyptfeeder in an overhand arc, aiming to cleave him in two. No matter how tough the bastard was, a blow so mighty should split him from crown to arsehole... or so I reasoned.

But I hadn't reckoned on his speed. The bastard had been *playing* with me, spooling in all the sweet belief and prayers of the watching multitudes. Now he unleashed it, showing his true form.

I remember that instant in agonizing detail – in the icy, blue-shaded slow motion of deep sorcery. As the Cryptfeeder descended on him Dirge laughed, bringing one of his blades up over his head to block me. *Pathetic* – it would shear through like a reed before my strike. But then something convulsed under his skin, like a pulse of dark, viscous ichor swelling every artery and vein.

Every tendon stood proud beneath his skin as his arms ballooned outward, swelling to three times their normal girth. Spikes of wet, glistening darkness erupted from his back, tracing the curve of his spine as his vertebrae separated with sound like cracking knuckles.

His eyes bulged, blazing white. And suddenly that long, slim sword of his looked like a toy dagger in the hand which held it.

This time the detonation as our swords met wasn't just a shockwave in the air. It was a spherical wavefront of fire, followed by a chain of thunderclaps which rolled out across the plains behind it. Buildings cracked to their foundations. Stained glass windows blew out in glittering clouds of colour. Those unfortunates who remained within the city – Vyrim Chaar's men among them – were tossed through the air like matchsticks before a hurricane, dead before they hit the ground.

But Gods be damned, I *held* him. This ogre in the rags of a warrior-monk's robes, his veins writhing thick and black under his skin, his limbs grown grotesquely large with muscle... *I held him.*

But only until his free hand came around in an unstoppable haymaker punch, connecting with my jaw like a hammer striking an anvil.

I felt bones break. I thought of Sothara, and the elk's femur scored with runes shattering his skull. I thought of my brother Rordan, and the day he came at Ulkar from behind in the training circle, a dagger in his fist... I remembered, most vividly, the look on his misshapen face after Ulkar backhanded him, hard, with the edge of his bronzewood shield.

All these things passed through my mind as my neck snapped to the left, and my teeth flew wide in a spray of blood. Cracks ramified through my skull like brittle lightning. And I fell.

Well – not so much *fell.*

It was more a flat trajectory, spinning through the air until I struck the side of the ruined cathedral. I went through the first wall, demolishing a fresco of saints judging the impious. I went through the second wall, and clearly felt my spine snap clean in two. The third slowed me down, as both my legs were shattered to splinters and agony. But the fourth stopped me cold, with a blow that must have burst several vital organs of which I knew little, let alone their names.

I felt them now. The pain was like nothing I can commit to parchment and ink. It would require the skill of several master torturers to convey the pitch and intensity of my suffering, and I have already made my opinion clear on of men of that profession.

I struggled upright, pushing myself up against the rough stone wall. I could feel nothing below my waist, and nothing but pain above it. I heaved in a racking breath, fighting against my own ruined flesh to hold onto life.

It was no use. Darkness crowded and swarmed at the edges of my vision, blurring the image of Dirge as he laughed, framed on the disc of the blood-red sun.

I breathed out, and it came with a spray of blood, and a rattle in my throat which I recognized all too well.

It was the last breath I ever took.

The darkness rose up over my head, and I let go.

I was dead.

"I enjoin you, brothers, root out this vile pagan practice with all your power! Find those who still practice the rites of Zael and put them to the sword, in Esau's name. Though the corruption has spread far through our legions, even unto the upper echelons of the Strategium, it is our holy task to carve it out branch and stem.

I find it hard, myself, to believe that the practices of Zael have survived so many centuries after his casting out. But he was, after all, a God of war and battle - suitable sentiments for the crude men of the old Republic. Our legionaries and centurions share such rough but useful sensibilities. No wonder, then, that they still cling to superstitions to appease the old God.

We cannot blame them, I suppose.

But we can punish them. It is, happily, the mandate of Esau, the one true God made flesh."

Envigilator Dornic Navonne
- Lord Inquisitor of Anganesse

ANY CAREFUL OBSERVER will tell you that the Gods enjoy irony more than almost anything in creation. The rest of that list may very well include plagues, natural disasters, war and a good sunset, but irony seems to take pride of place.

It was not lost on me, then, that despite being a necromancer, and commanding a legion of the dead greater than even that of Sothara the Bone Collector, I had no idea at all what the afterlife would look like.

331

Well – I did have *some* idea.

It's just that, with the last ounce of foolish hope left in me, I had assumed it would not be *this*.

I stood on a plain of bones, beneath a curdled sky the colour of beaten copper. Hideous shapes swum and flickered behind the clouds, half-glimpsed, massive, and utterly alien. The bones underfoot were bleached white, brittle and cracked.

Before me stood the door, and it was open.

Despite having no more depth than the twin monoliths which framed it, the door let onto a deep hall of green-black stone, slick and glistening. Through the windows of that impossible room I could glimpse the Outer Dark, in all its vile and maddening glory.

It was all so much *clearer*, without the veils of mortal sanity to cloud it. I could see details which I really wished I couldn't.

And I could see, slumped on a throne of human skulls before the portal, the figure of a man all in armour.

He was old, and hunched, his hair a straggle of grey, his arms thin and sinewy, loose in their cladding of mail and leather. But as he looked up at me, I could see that his face was half-masked in steel, and that his eyes were completely red, glowing from within with furnace light.

"Ahhh. The necromancer. Just like my prodigal son Ulriq Trasse – but *so* much more loyal to my cause."

I recognized him. And at the same time I recognized the way in which he seemed to bend the light around him, as though his very being weighed heavy on the world.

"You... you're a *God*," I said. "The one from my father's shrine of idols. The one who..."

"Who saw a scared, snot-nosed little boy with the touch of my brother Anghul upon him, and offered him a taste of my power. Or rather, the power I've found here, just short of oblivion. Do you know, the soldiers of the White Empire still sacrifice a ram to me on the eve of battle? They divine their strategies in its entrails, just as they used to do. But then they burn the damned thing to Esau, instead of *me*. I ask you! Why would that milksop little shepherd want a slaughtered sheep?"

The God's voice was reedy and cracked, strained with unimaginable age. And that, in itself, was wrong. Things like this – shards of the Divine – were not supposed to age like mortal men.

"So... you were their God before Esau. You were Zael Kataphraxis, the iron-bearer, lord of death in battle. You..."

Just the sound of his name seemed to make the aged God stronger. A cloud flickered around him, blurred with the image of a much larger man, his skin shining like beaten brass.

"I AM Zael Kataphraxis, ancient lord of Anganesse, and *you* are dead. You should be cast through that accursed gateway behind me and into oblivion, just like your dear friend Dirge would wish. But... despite what the little bastard says, *I* was the one who gave you power, and *I* was the one who brought you here. It takes a necromancer to undo the foolishness of a necromancer, and I've waited *centuries* for someone to rid me of that whining Estarene."

"But Sinder..."

Zael smiled.

"Cast his own divination in the entrails, just as every other Angan soldier does. And if I showed him a power growing in Khytein lands, and foresaw his predictably bloodthirsty response... well, it brought you to the place where you were needed. It hardened your heart for what must be done."

"*You* want me to kill Esau? And, I suppose, to build you temples, raise you monuments, the whole worship and sacrifice show?"

Zael laughed, and it came out as a broken cackle. I wondered how long he had been exiled here, starved of belief, and if he was still even within spitting distance of sanity.

"No. I'm here to help you, Kuhal Moer. You're a dead man, but you yet live. A few more seconds, perhaps, back in the world of the Manifest. And in that husk of flesh you hold so much power! Power enough to let me walk the world again, at least in the city I helped them build. Ungrateful bastards!" He spat, leaning forward on his throne. "Don't you want *revenge*? I can eradicate Dirge from the world, and I can let you watch."

I considered for a second. But only for a second.

I knew that the creature was right. I was done for. And if Dirge won, all we had fought for, all my friends had died for... it would all be for nothing.

"But if you set me on this path, why should I help you? It's been nothing but misery, death and loss, the whole damned way! How long have you been pulling my strings?"

Zael rose from his throne, slowly, hesitantly, his back bowed with immense age. He tottered forward, and reached out a hand to silence me.

"Look at me, Khytein. I'm using my battle-blade as a cripple's cane. I leech what power I have from the very threshold of oblivion, and I'm held just on this side by the mumbled superstitions of drunken soldiers. I may have set you in motion, but it was others who shaped your path. It was Dirge, more than any. Why not let me give him what he deserves?"

"And my mortal flesh? Do you suppose you'll just possess a broken thing like me?"

A flicker of flame ghosted across Zael's eyes as he looked up at me.

"No. Never that. But I *will* choose the form of one of your dead. That will suffice to bring the Dwellers' champion down."

I waited for what would have been a heartbeat, had that long-suffering organ not stopped beating to send me here. Zael had no patience,

"Choose, then – or pass! Those in the Outer Dark have no love for you, Kuhal, and an eternity to play with you."

I looked over the ancient God's shoulder, into that hall of skewed geometry and nightmare shadows. And I chose.

No heartbeat.

No rush of blood in my veins.

No breath. No crack and sizzle of nerves, no flood of chemicals heralding dread or ecstasy...

I was truly dead.

But I opened my eyes nonetheless, and there was something else missing.

No pain. And no power, burning in the mageblight which marbled my body through.

Zael had taken it all, as he promised. And I was left in a pile of rubble, beneath a cathedral which Dirge must have demolished – ever the meticulous one – to utterly finish me off.

I was strangley emotionless about my condition. There was no anger, no sorrow... just a very precise, very detailed plan in my mind of what I should do to put myself back together.

I was just flesh and bone. Calcium, chemicals, mageblight and meat. A machine to house a naked soul, and one which could be repaired, like THIS...

Bones knit together, down there in the dark. Flesh healed shut, creating a web of cold scars across my body. And I found that, just like the bones of my legions, I could push my dead muscles far beyond what living tissue would endure. I shrugged off half of the cathedral's west nave as easily as another man would brush away a light dusting of snow.

An instant later a blast of sorcery threw me from my feet. I tumbled down a slope of broken marble and cracked statuary, the world spinning end over end. In the small glimpses of the sky which I managed to apprehend I saw a gyre of ink-black clouds, crawling with green lightning.

This was, perhaps, a sign that all was not well.

The next indication that Zael's return was far from an occasion for joy was the impact which tore a furrow in the crest of the arch beside me, glowing red through the stone. Substantial hunks of masonry whirred past my head with the sound of startled pheasants. I struggled to my knees just in time to watch a burned and blackened figure drag itself from the end of the trench.

It was Dirge.

The Angan lord was wild-eyed, hunched and bloated with muscle, but one of his arms hung limp at his side, and half of his face was peeled open like some grotesque fruit, revealing a web of tendons and darkness. He didn't even notice me kneeling there – instead he strode from the ruin of his impact, muttering the syllables of a terrible incantation. He pointed his open palm up into the boiling skies and let it loose, flattening me again – the sheer overspill of such magik was enough to fuse the ground to glass for spans around him.

I blinked the after-images of fire from my sight and looked up, to where his bolt of energy tore apart the clouds. It shattered against an invisible shield of force, spiraling away as streamers of lightning. Then the thing behind the shield answered.

Six searing rays of light lashed out, plucking Dirge from his feet. They tossed him into the air, a tiny thing, his scream of outrage dwindling as he arced up over the city. Then they came curling back in, faster this time, to slice clean through his body in a series of razor-thin glowing lines.

The darkness inside him boiled out, knitting him back together as he fell. But before he could hit the ground the whips of light were on him again, serpent-quick, tossing him skyward and bisecting him at the waist.

I followed the trails of white-hot light back to their source. I stood, gathering in what residual power I could from the shimmering backlash of such destructive sorcery.

And I saw which of my soultaken Zael had chosen as the vessel for his rebirth.

It was Makara, of course – for the idea of gender had little meaning to an ageless Shard of the Divine. All Zael Kataphraxis cared about was *strength*, and the last surviving demoness of the Nine had more than enough. Now she was possessed by the spirit of an awakened God, and the mageblight in her burned, punching out through her armour as a pair of red-hot, glowing wings, each feather traced in flame. Her whole body was wreathed in a swirling conflagration, which sketched out the image of a larger, more masculine body around her own – a body arraigned in ancient Angan armour, crowned and haloed.

Damn me, but I could *feel* the raw power of belief flowing into her, and into the God who rode her. It was like a roaring wind, fanning sparks into a wildfire. From out across the plain, where a whole city's worth of refugees shielded their eyes and fell to their knees, it must have been a stark religious revelation. They could not have seen the broken, black-armoured Khytein girl pinned to the air at the heart of it. They would only have seen the old God of Anganesse rising up from the smoke and flames of his burning city, to utterly destroy the champion of Esau.

Utter destruction was just what Zael delivered. In that, he was as good as his word.

I was already running for the Cerebrex as the wires lashed out for the last time. I could feel Dirge's mind scrabbling for it too, searching for the very core of it, where Makara's soul burned bright with agony. He didn't stand a chance.

Those filaments of singing metal were white-hot from root to tip, and they came in at him from six directions at once. Two punched into his flesh at the wrists, coiling around radius and ulna, binding up his bones until they bored their way between his ribs, clenching tight. Two more pierced the soles of his feet, twining around his femurs beneath the flesh, roasting it as they went. Another drove up through the base of his spine, puncturing each vertebra in turn as it slithered up into his skull.

And the last...

The last searing wire swayed before his eyes like a cobra, counting out Dirge's torment as his bones blackened inside him, and flames licked out of his open mouth. His eyes burst before it finished Zael's work; his skull cracked open, spilling blue-green fire from inside the furnace of his brain-pan. Only then did the lord of death in battle wrap his final thread of flame around the usurper's neck, and cleanly lop off his head.

The wires convulsed. A massive surge of energy was drawn into the vortex of Zael's material form as they retracted. And the fiery skin of the God began to grow opaque, imprisoning Makara inside the image of a brazen-skinned giant, leonine and half-masked in steel, his flame-crown tapering up through a halo of blades.

The huge apparition looked down at me, as patronizing and smug as only divinity can be.

"BOW," it suggested. **"Bow before me, dead man. Be anointed as the first of my prophets. Witness what ruin I wreak upon the Coldblood, and record it as the first chapter of my holy testament."**

The need to prostrate myself before the physical manifestation of Zael was like the weight of all Sarem pressing down on my shoulders. Had I still lived, I believe I would indeed have fallen to my knees and worshiped the figure who stood before me, stern and mighty in his power.

But I was already dead. No God could promise me a glorious afterlife. I was forced to make my own. So I stood, defiant, and raised my hand, building up a charge of power.

"No! You have no right to her, Kataphraxis! Give her back! That one is *mine!*"

A look of mixed confusion and amusement flickered across Zael's huge face.

"You seek to split words with me *now*, human? I have chosen one of your dead. I have taken the vessel most apt to my purpose. What you want means less to me than you could possibly imagine!"

I loosed the incantation. A bolt of pure darkness leaped from my hand, strong enough to eradicate armies. The mageblight within me burned cold, savaging me with pain.

But Zael hardly felt the blow. It blew past him as a cloud of sparks, and he laughed.

"And now you try to *attack* me? Perhaps the shock of your demise has driven you insane. A pity. You would have made a fine prophet. The mad ones always do..."

The God turned, utterly ignoring me, and strode away across the arch of Urexes, his footfalls shaking the entire great span of stone.

I fell to my knees at last, but not in prayer. There was only one thing I could think of doing which would stop a being like Zael – only one other power I could call on in my extremity.

I clenched my fingers into a layer of rubble and ash, and felt the warm iron of the Cerebrex against my cold, dead skin.

It was time to end the age of Esau, and enact what would come to be called the Desolation.

FOR ALL THE Keels, all the sorcery, all the perversions of Urzen's art, and all the machinations of the Powers of Sarem, it came down to this.

One knife, one hand, one strike... that was all it would take to sever Esau from the world, fulfilling the purpose Aerik and Maudrin had set for me.

The one I was *not supposed to survive*, of course.

I had other plans.

It was cold in the Capitoline Deep – a place you are already familiar with, I'm sure, for this is the very same sanctum where the unfortunate Zuris O crept at the beginning of my tale. It was - and still is - a vaulted cavern, tapered and columned with glittering limestone, at the heart of which stands a black pyramid, the prison of Esau. Ulriq Trasse built the place as a power-focus, a trap for the essence of a God, using the necromantic power he'd been granted by Zael himself.

Now I ascended the steps to the black gate, and passed beneath the lintel, carved with the winged wolves of the house of Trasse. A stolen dagger weighed heavy in my hand, and I could feel the hearbeat of Esau through the very stones themselves, a tectonic shiver which set my teeth on edge.

At last, the cross. That great wheel of ancient iron, counterbraced with thick beams of Estarene cedar. And spread-eagled across it, nailed at the wrists and ankles... a figure in radiant white, bleeding thick and oily darkness. Reality was crushed and twisted out of true around him, faceted like crystal.

"**I have awaited you,**" said Esau, the Martyred God, lifting his head from his chest. Behind a curtain of long dark hair he was grotesque in his perfection; too finely made for this mortal world. "**And I forgive you. You know not what you have done.**"

Once again, if I had been a living being, the look of compassion and pain in those deep, star-flecked eyes would have driven me to my knees. Instead I bristled with indignation.

"*You* forgive *me*? You, whose people have raped and butchered mine? I thought that you would be begging for *my* forgiveness, Estarene."

"Yet who holds the knife, warlock? I speak not of the murder in your heart. The *deicide*, to be exact. I mean the calling of Zael Kataphraxis. The undoing of my great work."

A cold feeling slithered up my spine. The depths of Esau's eyes glittered, cold as the oceans of space.

"But Aerik Stormsong... The Archaeon..."

"None of them knew. None of them *could* know. My martyrdom supplanted Zael, and put an end to his madness. Though even that I can forgive. He only acted out of fear, after all."

"And what would a God of death fear?" I asked. Though a part of me already knew the answer. I had seen beyond the door. I *knew* what lurked in the Outer Dark.

"The cold. Oblivion. The *dwindling*, the death of belief, until one is no more than a whisper in the shadows of ruined temples. *That* is what he feared. That, and what comes after."

"The Dwellers in Darkness."

"Indeed. The elder ones, first children of the Divine. To be devoured by them, and to *become* them – that is what all of the Aziphem fear. He tried to bargain with them instead. He fed them mortal souls, in exchange for pacts of binding and constraint."

"So... you *meant* to be captured? You *wanted* to be tortured? You let Ulriq Trasse build an empire on your suffering?"

"Better that, than see all Sarem fall under the power of such as Zael. I was chosen by the Shards of the Aziphem to bear this fate. I accept it gladly."

"Which means that I've just unleashed a mad God into the world," I said. "And if I destroy your mortal form..."

"He will have utterly free reign. I have usurped his holy places, and that is all which tethers him to Urexes. Send me back to the Unmanifest, and he will have the freedom of Sarem, and the world."

"Then... can you stop him? If I pull those nails, can you send him back to where he came from?"

Esau shook his head, infinite sadness in his eyes.

"I am a peaceful God, Kuhal Moer. If your Ciermakh or Theyr was here in my place, things may have been different. But there is only one way to master the Iron-bearer now. One which comes at a terrible price."

The knife fell from my numb fingers as he explained it to me. I had hardened my heart to do what must be done – yes, just as Zael Kataphraxis had wanted. And now I chose another path; one which has seen me wait out three hundred years in this lonely tomb.

It began with the Cerebrex.

I held the globe of gold and iron above my head as I rose up out of the Capitoline Deep – out through the open point of the pyramid and up, past dripping stalactites and rune-carved arches, through the marble-lined well under the Thearch's throne, up through the flame-lit sphere of the capitol itself, and into the smoke-filled sky above Urexes.

From here, I could witness what Zael had wrought in the short time he had been manifest in the world. It confirmed Esau's opinion of him no end.

Every icon of the martyred God had been torn down. Chapels and temples had been crushed to ruins, and the city below the arch was a sea of flame, licking at the waist of the mad God's new, more potent avatar.

It was the statue which had once stood at the northern end of the arch itself – the armoured titan head and shoulders taller than its peers. I had thought, when I first glimpsed the colossus, that its face was wrong, the work of later, lesser masons. I had been quite right. Now the statue's original features were restored, and I saw it for what it was – a titanic icon of Zael himself, the warrior-God of the Republic.

This would have been terrible enough if he were only cold, dead stone. But this was no mere carving – not now. Makara stood on the statue's right shoulder, her face slack and her eyes blazing red. All six of her wires were drilled taut into the pale white stone beneath her, and through her Zael Kataphraxis had animated his vast effigy, sending it striding through the burning city.

As I watched, the colossus kicked apart a section of the Urexian wall, sending blocks of stone and siege-engines tumbling across the plain. It opened its mouth and bellowed a sound of formless rage, red light issuing from between its lips to paint the belly of the clouds.

It was going for the Coldblood.

I should have been elated. After all, the two great powers were no friends of mine, and their clash could only end in destruction. Instead I watched with a mixture of awe and horror as the vast colossus lumbered up to a charge, slamming into the veil of smoke and power which wreathed the Akhazi demigod.

Fingers of stone tore into the wall of force. Arms as wide as fallen towers strained against the load.

The barrier was ripped asunder, with a sound like tearing silk. A blast of raw energy flew from the gap, striking the great statue in the chest and staggering it back on its heels. But there was no way that Makara's possessor would let it fall. Zael regained his balance and retaliated, shredding the remnants of the Coldblood's warding and striding forth, his stone feet cracking the surface of the plain.

The Coldblood was alive, despite the Archaeon's massive assault. But it had assuredly seen better days. Perhaps this was the first true pain it had felt for millennia; not since the cataclysm which had driven its kind to extinction.

None of this had improved its mood.

It was burned and charred, its damaged skin half sloughed away from a body all bloated and glistening. Its slaves had all perished – the great palanquin of carved and inlaid wood was still smouldering around the edges, streaked with splashes of freshly cooled lava.

But the hatred in its tiny dark eyes was adamant. And the hell it unleashed upon Zael left me in no doubt that if the Archaeon had not moved when it did, Urexes would even now be a charred ruin under the Akhazi banner.

The sun itself seemed to flicker and grow dim as the Coldblood focused its power. A disc of pure white opened in the air before it, centred on its scaly forehead, and from this portal spewed a rod of almost solid power – a flame beyond flame, the stuff which the Saradrim say lies at the very core of stars.

The beam struck Zael full centre, landing like a hammer-blow against his crossed arms. It drove him slowly backward, grinding him down into the plain, span by span. A corona of actinic fire splashed out around the colossus, trailing back behind it into a teardrop point.

But even a thing like the Coldblood has limits. I have no idea how deep the mageblight runs inside the vast, necrotic body of that serpent-thing, but it *is* mortal, its power finite. The blast tapered off to a shimmering thread of white, then a scatter of sparks... and Zael Kataphraxis still stood.

He laughed, a hollow booming sound echoing up out of his furnace mouth. And then he struck back.

The statue brought its hands together, palm to palm, and drew a blade of darkness from out of nowhere as it pulled them apart. This was not just black iron – it was a sliver of the night sky, speckled with constellations, and when it moved the stars within it remained fixed, as though this was no so much a physical weapon, and more a portal into the deeps of the void.

Hands larger than castle keeps brought the blade back over Zael's head, pinpoints of light wheeling past inside it.

And the Coldblood cut its losses.

The great serpent could not move – not without its living carpet of wretches to drag it along. But now it wove a cage of violet light about itself, a thing of weird angles and inside-out geometry, tracing the form of two pyramids joined along far too many planes.

Before Zael's sword could shear it in two the Akhazi wyrm completed its incantation, folding in on itself as the cage collapsed, then winking out of reality altogether.

The blade bit deep into the still-smoking surface of the plain, embedding itself in stone. But the Coldblood was gone – escaped through sorcery, back to the swamps and jungles of its native land.

I tried very hard not to think about what I had just seen. I tried even harder not to consider what I was about to do. Esau had been very specific.

I could not destroy his mortal form – not without unchaining the mad God's full power. But I *could* use Esau's faithful – the pious dead who ground the mills and worked the pumps beneath the streets of Urexes. I only hoped that there would be enough of them left.

I held the Cerebrex up over my head, holding back a tremor of fear. Yes – even without a life to lose, I was afraid. I knew full well the consequences of what I was about to do.

"Iron-bearer!" I shouted. "Kataphraxis! Hear me!"

Far away across the plain the colossus raised its head. Blank red eyes like volcanic vents bored into my own.

"I…I call you to the test of judgment before the Divine. I lay claim to that which you have stolen."

The roar of incredulity and anger which came rolling in across the plain was enough to topple several burning buildings. Sparks spiraled up around me where I hung in the air, Cerebrex in my hands.

"I enact the Rite of the Crucible," I croaked -

And then I awaited my inevitable destruction.

"They say that dead men tell no tales.
Funny, then, that priests seem so damned
sure what the afterworld looks like."

Roriq de'Thraye
- Founder of the Ythean philosophical order of Cynics.

THERE WERE *THOUSANDS* of them, trapped in their glass and copper tombs. The bones of whole generations, families laid to rest together, bones scrimshawed with psalms and verses, wrapped with gold leaf, scented with rose oil and incense – then set to grind out their suffering for centuries, turning the wheels which made Urexes the capital of an empire.

The common people had no idea. Even the bulk of the priesthood saw it as nothing but a necessary penance for a life of unavoidable sin – the gateway to an afterlife of bliss.

So few of them knew that their God was bound in torment deep beneath the streets and houses of Urexes, bled for power. But I knew. And I could call out to them, just as I had done to the souls in the Graveyard Ark's ossuary well. I could offer them freedom – at a price.

So, as countless tons of God-possessed stone came striding toward me, hefting a blade made of sharpened night, I drove my will down through the earth, twisting through pipes and conduits, flooding through bone-choked catacombs and mausoleums.

The dead answered. They saw the truth of Esau's torment in my memories, and knew that they had been deceived. They came to my call.

From the great hollow warrens and undercrofts beneath Urexes came a storm of bones – ribs and skulls, femurs and fingers, spines and shins and broken fragments without names. They came on a rising tide of wraiths, a witchfire web flowing like water under pressure, seeking out weaknesses until it could burst forth into the light.

From the graveyards and the churches they came, punching up from the ground in twisted spires, bone on bone, curving in toward the magnetic force of the Cerebrex. Where I was waiting.

It had always been my purpose – at least, in the plans of the Archaeon and its cabal – for me to free these spirits. But it was supposed to come as a conflagration, a seismic soul-shock heralding the death of Esau. Now I called them to me instead, wrapping them

344

about me in a whirling gyre. Bones locked together, binding tight. Witchfire earthed itself through the mageblight in me, blurring my consciousness to a star-flecked blaze of green.

I opened my eyes.

I stood, from the stooping crouch I had been in.

And Zael Kataphraxis stopped short, bringing his blade up to guard. There was a look on his pale stone face which I will always cherish. It was a look of pure dread.

I stared down at my hand, and saw fingers a long as a warship's masts, each built from a tangle of bleached bones. Palms wide enough to uproot fortresses. Arms as mighty as the Urexian arch itself. Hells, I could *feel* the form which swallowed up my mortal flesh, and it was a thing of terrible beauty – a thousand spans of consecrated bone, fused by witchfire into the figure of a man.

A man with a blazing-eyed skull for a face. A man with antlers of bone, in an echo of Anghul himself, and the incandescent green sphere of the Cerebrex burning on his brow.

I smiled, deep within the tangle of bone which was his hollow skull. I clenched my fingers into a fist, and I felt the dread titan do the same, hefting countless tons of calcified remains.

"One will stand, and one will fall, Iron-bearer!" I shouted. *"Come and face your brother's son! Come and face the judgment of the Aziphem!"*

I have no idea where the words came from. But they were a mere formality. We both knew that this would be finished in war, not conversation.

Zael's answering bellow told me all I needed to know of his intentions.

I remember little of the next few hours – though they tell me that the sun had sunk to kiss the western horizon before victor and vanquished staggered apart. There are none alive to tell me of the thrusts and counterthrusts, ruses and stratagems which defined the battle between my titan of bone and Zael's stone colossus. But fragments of memory surface, sometimes – half imagined glimpses of horror.

I see visions of Urexes burning – of vast, flame-lit figures wrestling and heaving amid what had once been streets and houses. I remember the grim satisfaction of driving my immense fists of bone again and again into that serene, mocking face, fracturing the stone with sheer, unbound wrath.

I recall being thrown through towers and shattering spires as I stumbled. More than once Zael pinned me up against the bulwark of the arch, hammering blows at me with his heavy stone fists. I know how he lost his sword, as well – wrested from his grasp in the first frantic seconds of our clash, and hurled beyond the horizon before he could use it against me.

We were evenly matched, he and I. One a God, but freshly reborn into the world, starved of belief for centuries, and only a shadow of his former self. The other a dead man, grim in his desperation, borne up by the limitless fury of the dead.

In time we both weakened. The white-hot blur of rage which had sustained me began to fail, just as Zael himself began to tire. My blows became leaden and slow... but the Iron-bearer was too weary in his turn to evade them.

At last we broke apart, reeling – he to collapse against the south face of the arch, and I to totter on my feet, barely able to keep from collapsing. We both knew that the next assault would be our last.

"Submit!" rasped Zael, his voice echoing up from the depths of his hollow chest. **"You can never best me, warlock. You know that in your heart. Even if this body fails me, I have your soultaken. I will be worshiped again, while you rot in the earth."**

Not, perhaps, the most finely reasoned argument. But one which was far too close to the mark. Indeed, with the mageblight so far gone within me, and none left to so much as fear me, I would soon crumble into dust. I didn't even warrant a childrens' story like the Nine.

"I'm not beaten yet," I snarled, defiant. "And it's *you* who will submit, Zael. Your place is in the Outer Dark, and they're waiting for you there."

The mad God laughed.

"My throne may have stood at the threshold, but there is *power* in such places. The Dwellers won't have me, Kuhal Moer. Not now, and not ever!"

We came together with an impact which leveled the remains of the Urexian wall. The Ghuram say, with all their wisdom, that the continents of Yrde float about on a sea of lava, heated to boiling by the Shards of the Divine. They say that mountains are thrown up when two such plates of rock collide, forced miles high in a cataclysm of stone and fire.

If this is true – and it is, indeed, a terrifying prospect – then I have some reckoning of how it must feel.

We grappled and clawed at each other, trading blows which shook the entire ruined city. Through pillars of choking smoke and gouts of flame we staggered, until my back slammed up against the arch, and Zael's stone hands wrapped tight around my throat.

It should have meant nothing at all. I was dead, without need of blood or breath, and the neck he strove to snap was a construct of animated bone, nothing more.

But I felt it. My hands scrabbled against the balconies and statues of the arch, clawing them away as rubble. I couldn't break free. As my vision began to swim with purple and black starbursts I caught a final glimpse of Makara, there on the shoulder of the colossus, her face smeared with soot and ashes.

For an instant she looked directly through the tangled thicket of bones, and into my soul. And I heard her voice come up out of the Cerebrex, whispering inside my head.

"He hasn't taken all of me, Kuhal," she said. *"Not every last piece. That toy of yours began with me – with Dirge's gift. Now let it end with me. Let me go."*

I saw it, then. As clearly as a revelation depicted in a stained-glass window – a light shining down from heaven to bathe some mad old saint in glory. I saw what I had to do.

The fingers of my bone titan were already unraveling as I brought them up to my forehead, ossified fragments raining down amid sparks of witchfire. They scrabbled at the cracks which spread across my skull, digging deep as my antlers fell away, shattering to dust in the streets below.

But they found the Cerebrex. They plucked it from my brow, burning, and thrust it into Zael's open mouth.

For a heartbeat nothing happened.

Then the colossus reared back, throwing its arms wide. It sunk to its knees and roared at the heavens, loosing a pillar of blue-green flame from its throat. And then the cracks began to appear, ramifying across its limbs and chest, crazing its face into a patchwork of pale stone and fire.

It clawed at its own throat. Pieces of its limestone skin fell away, letting beams of emerald light stab out to the horizons.

Then came the detonation, and my whole world was swallowed up by the sheer immensity of it.

I was thrown far from the ruins of Urexes by the blast, my tangled husk of bones disintegrating in flight. The great cracked skull of the thing bounced and rolled across the plain with me inside it, shedding fragments of the dead like chaff, until it collapsed completely in a slew of consecrated pieces.

It was from there, outside the circle of the blast, that I witnessed the Desolation.

The clouds spun open, like the iris of a great eye. Lightning scourged the earth, shattering the few remaining structures which still stood, silhouettes against a wall of flame. And the figure of Zael Kataphraxis, the rebel Shard of the Aziphem, rose up above his holy city, a blazing shape in green. The spiraling winds tore at him, bending reality, warping it sideways until his screaming, contorted face was a nightmare of clashing planes and angles.

"NO! WE ARE BOUND BY PACTS OF SACRIFICE! I WILL NEVER JOIN YOU! I DEFY YOU! I..."

I never heard what other trite legalities the mad God tried to level at the Dwellers in Darkness. I knew enough, at that moment, to draw in every shred of power I could, until the scrub-grass for fifty spans around me crackled with frost.

This time the blast wasn't something you could see or hear. This time it was something *felt*, soul deep, a wind of hooks and razors tearing at the mind as well as the flesh. The shield I threw up against it was the best I could muster; I was still driven waist-deep into the plain by the force of it.

The entire city of Urexes flashed white-hot. Stone melted instantly. Sand and ashes fused to glass. And the entire Urexian plain, for miles around, described a sickening *twist* – slower and more subtle at the edges, but sharp and savage at the centre. The arch was tapered upward into a blackened spire of rock, sheathed in blades of obsidian. Buildings and statues, fountains and aqueducts whirled up into the air, vaporized.

And Zael became a pillar of fire, then a line, then a thread, then a razor-cut in reality...

Then nothing.

A second later the soul-shock of mass extinction washed over me – every last refugee and deserter from the Angan capital had just been blasted to wind-blown ashes.

I dug myself from the ground, laughing. I looked down at my hands, and saw blackened claws of bone. I threw back my head and laughed a little more; after all, it couldn't hurt.

Then the thunder rolled, and the rain began to fall, pattering against my face like tears. I didn't stop laughing for a very long time...

even when the glass-crusted soil around me became a mire of black mud.

There are those, I'm sure, who will tell you that this is exactly the kind of thing a madman would do.

Then again, they have probably never had to do what I did next.

"Stories only start because fools like to put 'once upon a time' in front of their version of history. And stories only end because other fools like to rule a line under the really big battles, then call it even."

The collected teachings of Old Mother Aeveris

EVENTUALLY I FOUND my way back.

Surely you must have pieced together the rest by now.

I found Makara. Or at least, what remained of her. Despite being right at the centre of the Desolation – or perhaps *because* of this fact – she was still alive, after a fashion. No man ever said that the work of Urzen couldn't take a little punishment.

I dug her out of the glass-crazed sand of what had once been the merchants' quarter, cradling her head in my lap as I knelt amid the ruins. One of her arms was gone – sheared clean away, and in places whole strips of her flesh were missing, revealing a knotted tangle of dark metal tubes beneath. There was no blood - just a pale, gelid fluid which dripped from inside, pooling on the glazed earth.

"I'm sorry," I said, for it seemed the right thing to do. "It should never have ended this way. We should have left these Gods and powers to their games, and just..."

Her eyes flickered open. The pupils were tiny chips of darkness, floating in furnace red.

"You should have *what*, Kuhal Moer? Lived an inconsequential life? Stayed in your dirtscrabble village, living out the same vile existence as your shit-stain of a father? At least now you'll be *remembered*. Those who the Gods choose to kill in awful ways often get their very own classical poetry."

I dropped Makara's head. I scrabbled backward, clawing a shard of glass into my hand to use as a crude knife.

"Zael! But I saw you..."

"You saw something you couldn't understand, and your primitive little brain made up a story to save your sanity," spat the God. **"So typical! So go on! Finish your fumbling little narrative. Send me back to the Unmanifest, where I can plot my vengeance,**

and reward you in a suitably saga-worthy fashion."

I hardly heard his words.

She was gone.

Truly gone – and to where, I could only assume.

That is, until I saw what was lying half-buried next to the broken husk of my poor, possessed demoness. It was a dented, broken ball of iron and gold, still fitfully sparking with witchfire lights.

I raised the knife over my head.

Zael smiled.

And I brought it down hard, stabbing into the earth beside his head.

"No. I think not. Not this time."

A look of confusion spread across Zael's stolen face.

"But you... you can't let me live! I'll *heal*, Khytein! I'll come after you!"

There was quite a lot of still-warm, twisted metal strewn about. It didn't take me long to find three good, serviceable nails. Any lump of stone would serve as a hammer.

"Has anyone ever told you," I asked the crippled Aziphem, "About the Good News?"

He shook his head. I jingled the nails in my hand, hefting their weight.

"Once, there was a God named Esau, and he was martyred for the sins of man..."

Zael started screaming then.

He didn't stop until long, long after I drove the last nail home.

Epilogue

AND SO THE end is the beginning. Which is, in it's own way, another end.

Clanbrother Zuris O will take my place, balancing the power of Esau and Zael, one martyred by his fellow Shards of the Divine to keep the other from poisoning the world.

I like to think that the Iron-bearer still squats upon his throne before the gates of the Outer Dark. But that the Estarene's sacrifice means that now *he* is the door himself – the very thing which keeps the Dwellers out.

It pleases me even more to muse that his only company, these last three centuries, will have been the ruined shade of one Jerrold Sinder, lately known as Dirge.

As for the Archaeon, the Coldblood, and any other machinations of the higher powers – I have come to care little for what they scheme. For three hundred years I have been a fable with which to frighten fractious children, a tale to chill the blood of drunkards, and the very reason that all of Sarem has enjoyed a golden age of peace.

Well – golden for some, perhaps. But less bloody, plague- ridden and brutal for nearly everybody else.

Empires dare not rise when a deathless tyrant stands ready to strike them down. Kings are less venal, and far less cruel, when they see what happens to their cruel and venal neighbours.

But the world turns, and even the pursuit of radical evil grows rather dull in time. I want to see what Sarem has made of the prosperity my reign has brought it. I want to walk among the nations I freed from the White Empire, anonymous, and enjoy some semblance of a normal life.

There is more, as well.

There are books and scrolls from Akhaz which have come to my attention – and others, too, from far Orisen and the ice-lands of Quornis. Techniques of resurrection and re-incarnation, which require only an imprint of the living soul...

I will take my Cerebrex with me – for I have discovered ways to compact the entire vast sphere of it down to the size of a ring or amulet. And I will walk.

So, the moral, then. Mother Aeveris says that all good stories should have one.

We will go with this -

"If you meet, in your wanderings, an old man, hunched over a staff, with a pack on his back, and wearing robes of sack-cloth, throw him a copper or two. Be kind, and offer him no false directions. Set him a place beside your fire, and share a bowl of broth, should you be fortunate enough to have one of your own.

Because he may *not* be Kuhal da'Hurik Moer, Grandfather Despair, The Lamenter, slayer of demons and summoner of more.

But if he *is*, and you refuse him, what do you think will happen next?"

That, I'm sure, would be an entirely new and different story.
And not one, like this, which should be told to all your children.

Dramatis Personae -

Kuhal Moer – Minor son of a Khytein warlord; necromancer neophyte and narrator of our tale

Zuris O – Zengaji assassin; last of his clan

Esau – the Martyred God. One of the Shards of the Divine, enslaved in mortal form by the Anganesse Empire

Zael – war-god of the Old Republic; an idol in Hurik Moer's collection of war-trophies; deposed by Esau in his homeland

Hurik the Scalptaker – Kuhal's father, a savage northern chieftain

Ulkar – Jarl of the Horned Boar; Hurik's eldest warrior

Colm – Chosen of Ciermakh; the Moer tribe's greatest fighter

Aerik Stormsong – Moer tribe warbard; a warrior-preist

Sei – a dead cat, made entirely of polished bone; familiar of Kuhal

Gernish Maudrin – Vhaur tribe warbard – ritual enemy of Aerik

Makara Vhaur – Young apprentice of Gernish Maudrin

Conn – Makara's brother; a skilled skirmisher and archer

Ulan Veth – a priest of Esau; castspaw of Jerrold Sinder

Jerrold Sinder – Pontifex of Anganesse; warrior-priest of Esau, servant of the Thearch and conqueror of Khytein

Elion Morekh – One-time Admiral of the Free Reavers; conspirator in the Archaeon's Cabal; Captain of the

Shadow of Blades

Soap – A giant crewman, protector and friend of Elion Morekh

Sothara Roege – Ancient necromancer, defeated and imprisoned in the Barrowlands nine hundred years ago

The Silence – One of the Nine Now Nameless; a monster created by sorcery from the servant of a dead God

Jenan – Zengaji outcast; highly skilled killer

Imkhantu – Jenan's brother, with similar credentials

The Archaeon – Father of Draken; an enormous, ancient monster trapped beneath the mountains of the Hiledoran

Corvo of Ontokh – Sorcerer-priest; conspirator in the Archaeon's cabal; exiled leader of the cult of the Stormlord

Tishande – Hallucinomancer, one of the Seeresses of Erys

Ricketts – Elion morekh's navigator

Rain – a gaint magpie; familiar of Corvo

Orduvis – Master gunner, Angan deserter, Elion Morekh's commander of the ordnance

Urzen the Mad – Last Forgemaster of the dead kingdom of Korisal; creator of the Nine Now Nameless; mercenary ally of Anganesse

Dirge – A mysterious figure, with a fixation on Kuhal Moer's demise and no small amount of sorcery

The Devouring Wind – One of the Nine Now Nameless; a powerful man-made 'demon'

The Eyeless – Another of the Nameless Ones; sometimes

known as the Doom of Sorenvale after his utter eradication of that town

The Shining One – Yet another demon of the Nameless, this time fashioned, horribly, from the body of a dead child

The Coldblood – Serpentine, horrific Demigod and ruler of the Akhazi people, an empire far to the south of Sarem

Vyrim Chaar – Regent of Ontohk; leader of this vassal-state of Anganesse, at least in name; a cunning and ruthless warrior

Balthus Schresse – Chaar's master; legate of anganesse

Sister Pain – One of the Nine Now Nameless; a terrifying living weapon

The Black Shepherd – Another of the Nameless Ones; the so-called torturemaster

That Which Walks – Most powerful of the Nine; a thing of living shadow and suffering

The Hanged Man – Most sly and cunning of the Nine Now Nameless. Tends to avoid open battle.

The Burning Dark – Last of the Nine to be created; the assassin among them, and almost impossible to destroy

Ulriq Trasse – past Thearch of Anganesse; a necromancer, who bound the God Esau and overthrew the worship of Zael, ushering in a golden age for the Empire

Osiryan Trasse – Ulriq's degenerate, octogenerian descendant, Emperor and Thearch of the White Empire

Also by Drew Bryenton
from sci-fi-cafe.com

The Alter Inferno Complex Trilogy

**Available as eBooks from Amazon, Apple, Google Play
and other good online bookstores.**

The human race tore itself apart during the Age of Judgment… that's what we call the Trillion Dollar War now, in our ignorance. We unleashed enough firepower to vaporize whole nations, poisoning the Earth and grinding civilization down to the politics of muscle and steel. Dark days came. War-dog days, like some ethanol-fueled b-movie.

Then came word of the Last City. A new Elysium welded together from the carcass of our old technology. A place ruled by a god-machine named Kronos, Guardian Engine of Humanity.

"Bryenton seizes the cyberpunk genre by the throat in this awe-inspiring trilogy with a scope so vast it staggers the mind. He gives the likes of William Gibson and Ian M Banks a run for their money with the kind of writing that you just want to devour. A book so hot, you'll need to keep your Kindle in the freezer!"

5/5 STAR REVIEW: *"I must admit that I was very impressed with this book, there are some fantastic ideas and the prose has a real eloquence that is both rare and rewarding. The vision of this post-human universe is lucid and vividly presented; all projected in a talented and confident voice."* SF Book Review http://sfbook.com/elysium-burning.htm

9 781910 779002